For What We Once Had

First, freedom.

1

A symbol traced in the dirt, a flash of magic, a drop of blood: these were the beginnings of the end, and the end of the beginning for Dryn ten Rayth as he made his way ignorantly along the narrow road from the ten Brae's farmstead into the village of Lesser Kryden. It was a cool night, made so by the sharp breeze that frosted his breath as the fated apothecary's apprentice marched briskly for the flickering lights of his home. The crunching dirt and leaves reminded the village youth that his sandals were far too worn, and his father still had not paid him.

Dryn could have worked for an apothecary in Greater Kryden or perhaps even in one of the cities in the south, but he wasn't so selfish. Some young men his age had left with dreams of glory and wealth, but Dryn couldn't leave his family or his friends.

He palmed the pouch of coins he clutched in one hand, wondering if his father could spare any of the copper Master ten Brae had paid. The apothecary had been visited earlier that day by Abrath ten Brae who declared his mother, the Mistress ten Brae, was suffering a terrible headache. Dryn's father had spent the better part of the afternoon concocting a blend of skullcap and several other herbs, and then had sent Dryn to deliver the remedy.

A bat passed overhead with a quiet spatter of flapping wings, tearing Dryn away from his thoughtful recollection of the day. He folded the neck of the pouch under his belt and pulled the thick woollen cloak tighter around his torso. There were rumours of cattle thieves targeting the region, and Dryn often worried about such bandits and rogues, especially on a moonless night such as it was.

There had been a council meeting two nights ago to appoint someone to investigate these rumours. Dryn had heard from his friend Keyth that Master Nalfar had been given the responsibility. Personally, Dryn refused to trust the foreigner. Nalfar was from one of the three Imperial Cities, and as far as Dryn and his father were concerned, Imperials should never be relied upon.

His friend Keyth was apprenticed to the village bowyer. Keyth's father had died a decade ago in the Leech's Plague, and more recently Keyth's mother had left for Greater Kryden. Dryn's friend had never been on good terms with his mother, and so Keyth had decided to remain in the village and board with the master bowyer.

A star shot across the sky, a blur that was gone almost as soon as he saw it. Shooting stars were common now; some called it an omen: that war was coming to the realm, or that a new plague would soon be upon them. Dryn didn't know what to think. He wasn't often swayed by omens or signs, but he did know that he hadn't seen a shooting star until his nineteenth name day, and had seen over a hundred since.

Just as the road had dipped out of sight of the village torches, Dryn's blood froze in his veins at the sudden sound of a voice. It called weakly out of the darkness, and he wouldn't have noticed it if he hadn't been focused on the eerie silence and the star so much.

"...over... here..." the voice croaked. "Come... to me..."

Dryn remained as still as the stars in the middle of the dirt road, the chill breeze no longer the cause of his shivers. The voice drifted from the thick foliage on the left.

Fumbling at his belt, Dryn hesitantly unsheathed the knife he carried with him at all times. Holding his breath, and scarcely believing his own actions, he began to creep off the road. The growing terror had become a hollow ache in his stomach and shoulders, and he couldn't help the chatter of his teeth clacking together.

"Hello?" he called into the shadows ahead of him, unsure if he should alert whatever lurked there to his presence or not.

"...I'm here..." the voice replied. "Please..."

The rest of it was lost to the sound of underbrush beneath Dryn's sandals. A cupped leaf spilled icy water onto his cloak as he forced his way around a thick bush. As he moved in the direction of the voice, his fear slowly started to ebb away. It was probably someone lost, or an injured traveller. Nothing to worry about.

That's when he noticed the first stain of blood. There was no moon, and in the forest even the stars didn't illuminate his footsteps. As he stumbled on a gnarled root, he grabbed a branch to balance himself and his hand came away sticky with a black smudge.

He quickly wiped it clean on his cloak and, standing still, surveyed the forest floor around him. His eyes still seemed to be adjusting to the night, but he could make out torn cloth and blood matted in the leafy foliage. He followed the gruesome trail until he at last found its source.

A man lay against the roots of an oak, as if he had been leaning on it and slid to the ground. Dryn had to correct himself. It was only part of a man. Amid all the blood and despite the darkness, he was horrified to see that the man's left forearm was missing in a bloody stump at the elbow, and his right leg severed at the knee. The man's clothes lay in tatters, and the weak body within bore a dozen gruesome gashes.

It was all Dryn could do to hold his supper down. "The Maker blind me," he whispered beneath his breath, and gripped the moss eaten trunk of a nearby tree to steady himself.

"Come closer," the voice said, and Dryn realized that the man was still alive.

He grabbed his stomach, gagging. How could someone speak from a state of such horrendous agony? The world seemed to be tilting on an angle, reeling around Dryn. *How can this be real?* he wondered. People didn't end up mutilated in the district of Kryden. *This just does not happen! It can't be!* he told himself.

"Please... I am almost... finished..."

Dryn could not believe his ears. Perhaps this dying stranger wished to impart some final wisdom or simply be companioned as he set off on the final journey, after the end. Shakily, Dryn stumbled through the rough brush and knelt in front of the man.

The stranger had a thick grey beard. Blood had matted in it, and dirt. As he spoke, blood bubbled at his lips, making it difficult for Dryn to understand him. "It is beginning," the man hissed.

"What is?" Dryn asked, confused.

"This world has... spited me," the dying voice growled. "No one understood my intentions."

"Your intentions?" Dryn returned, dumbly. Was the stranger reflecting on all of his mistakes, or the trials of his life? "What happened to you?"

The man moaned loudly, a terrible sound that garbled from his broken form. Then, as Dryn stared, the man's eyelids opened very slowly, revealing bright and sharp grey eyes. The moan turned into a sigh, and the stranger's right hand gestured at him. "You..." he said, nodding at his own remark. "You are the... one who will understand it all... everything..."

"Understand everything?" Dryn questioned. "I'm sorry, I don't understand anything right now. Who are you?"

"Me? I... am... Artemys Gothikar.... It was... never mind that... You will come to see it all..." the man whispered. The wrinkled and pained face peered intently into Dryn's. "It is beginning..."

"I'm sorry. Wait here, I'll get help," he told the man, intending to dash for town and bring a healer, his father and some guards to save this poor injured traveller.

"No!" Artemys snapped, roughly. His remaining hand clutched a fold of Dryn's cloak and pulled the young man to him. "Come close, and be silent!" he commanded.

At first Dryn struggled, but the man began muttering something under his breath, so Dryn leaned closer with one ear tilted to Artemys' face. He couldn't make out any words until he realized that the stranger was speaking another language. *"Hayen donbreth shoraz elkobo'ar ath draz!"*

With the last syllable, the man's right hand released Dryn's cloak, and smashed, palm open, against Dryn's chest. A searing pain lanced into his flesh, and every muscle in his body jolted; what felt like a volcano exploded within his head, and the burning on his chest grew into an inferno. He staggered away from Artemys whose head nodded forward into his last slumber. Teetering in agony, Dryn clutched his chest where fiery pain roared. The cloth of his tunic had been torn or blasted away, and as Dryn found his world rotating upside down, he glanced down to see a string of black symbols burnt into his skin.

Then another explosion tore through his mind, the shadows blurred over his eyes and he collapsed against a rotten log. Sleep slid into his head, and Dryn blacked out.

Keyth ten Arad was awoken in his loft in the middle of his sleep that night when the moon should have hit its zenith, if the Maker hadn't hidden it. He was shaken awake by the master bowyer, who handed him an unlit torch and a cloak and barked, "Get yer lazy behind to the town square, boy!"

Master ten Lenter was normally a fairly pleasant man, but Keyth knew that the bowyer despised early awakenings as much as his apprentice. Grumbling complaints under his breath, Keyth shrugged into the cloak as slowly as he could. Working his shoulder blades, he somehow found himself able to bend to his knees to put on his sandals. The door slammed beneath him; Ten Lenter left the hut, heading 'to the town square.'

His sandals laced, Keyth swung his feet over the small attic's edge, then grappled down the wooden ladder beneath his 'bedroom.' It wasn't anything fancy, but at least he had a place to sleep. Reaching the dirt floor at the bottom, he glanced around the bowyer's house. His eyes passed over the table, the chest with their tools and the bowyer's bed, and settled in the other corner. He scooped an apple from the shelf there, taking a noisy bite out of it before opening the hut door and stepping out into the night.

The streets seemed deserted as they should be on a dark night like this, but when Keyth left the maze of the village behind, he found the town square bustling with commotion.

As he was approaching, Magistrate Arbydn's voice boomed out over the crowd. "I've called you here tonight," he bellowed, "At Telper ten Rayth's request. His son Dryn has gone missing."

Keyth froze. *Dryn is missing?* "What?" he asked aloud, along with a dozen other men.

The Magistrate explained. "Late this afternoon Dryn delivered medicine to the ten Brae's farm, but he hasn't yet returned. I've called you all here so we can conduct a search between here and there."

Keyth was shaking his head. Dryn couldn't go missing. *Of anyone, he's the most cautious,* he told himself, but he knew he wasn't dreaming. He was too cold.

A man nearby shouted, "Someone should run ahead! Make sure he's not at the ten Brae's still..."

Another voice seconded it, so the Magistrate called, "Who here is the fastest?"

"A youth," Keyth heard one of the older villagers call.

At this, he heard one of the Bordus boys shout, "ten Arad's the fastest! He always won our races!"

The Magistrate cried, "Is the ten Arad boy here?"

Keyth found himself pushed forward until he stood at the well in the center of the square. Magistrate Arbydn looked him over and said, "Well, boy? Can you run to the ten Brae farm?"

"Certainly," Keyth muttered.

Arbydn combed his fingers in his thick black beard. "Alright... hurry to the farm, and find out if Dryn ten Rayth has been there, or left, or if he is still there. I expect you to be on your way back when you meet us on the road..."

"Of course, sir," Keyth nodded.

"And ten Arad? ...Take this," the Magistrate said. He handed him a long item that Keyth could scarcely make out in the shadows. As soon as he grabbed it though, he realized that the Magistrate had handed him a sword. In awe, he took hold of the hilt and stared at the weapon.

After a moment, Arbydn glanced down and demanded, "What are you still doing here? Get moving, boy!"

Keyth nodded, and wove his way out of the crowd. He got a few pats on the back, but ignored them. As he walked briskly down the cobbled main street he had a few moments to realize exactly what was going on. *By the Maker, Dryn's missing!* That meant he was lost, injured, or... Keyth could scarcely make himself consider it: dead. A search of the woods from the Magistrate's point of view meant a search for a body.

Or, Keyth realized, as he examined the sword he was carrying, perhaps it was a search for the thieves who had killed Dryn.

Wait! he told himself. *Dryn's not dead!* He couldn't let himself think like that. *Dryn can't be dead!* He simply could not imagine life without his friend.

He reached the north gate and took off at a sprint. He had lit the torch the bowyer had given him at one of the lanterns near the gate; it sputtered in the wind that rushed by him as he tore up the sloping road towards the ten Brae's farmland. Above him shooting stars cut across the heavens.

He fell once and felt the knee of his trousers tear. He cursed himself and forced himself to keep going; his knee throbbed and was probably bleeding, but he was more worried about how he could afford getting the hole repaired.

Above all though, he was concerned about Dryn.

He reached the trail to the farm fifteen minutes later. It wound jaggedly across their farmland until it reached the fenced off area of their house. Keyth swung himself over the gate. Landing on their property, he dashed up to the front door of the farmhouse and pounded on the door.

Waiting for them to wake up, he stepped back and looked around for any sign of Dryn. At last the door creaked open, and a crossbow came out, followed by Master ten Brae. "Who's there?" he questioned, peering at the torchlight.

"It's Keyth ten Arad," Keyth announced. "Pardons for disturbing you, sir..."

"I thought the thieves were upon us! This does nothing for my wife's health, youngster, so it had better be good," ten Brae growled, lowering the crossbow half a foot.

Keyth nodded and anxiously asked, "Is Dryn ten Rayth still here?"

"Still here?" ten Brae laughed incredulously. "Why, by the Great Glyph, would he still be here?"

Keyth paled, realizing that Dryn wasn't inside. "Because, sir, he hasn't yet arrived in the village..."

Now it was Master ten Brae who paled. "He's not back yet?" the farmer asked quietly. "Is there a search?"

"Yes, the Magistrate called the men together. They're searching as we speak. I must run now to inform them that Dryn isn't here," Keyth informed him, coughing from the cold after his run.

"Yes, yes, boy. Run like you never have..." ten Brae whispered. "I'll get my son, and we'll be along to help out..."

Without waiting for more, Keyth took off in the direction of town, this time jogging right across the farmland. He reached the road and dashed southwards until his vision started fading. He was forced into a walk; his lungs were heaving and his shoulders rose and fell with each breath. He prayed to the Maker and the Great Glyph that his friend was still alive somehow.

The grass was frosted by now. The night temperature was plummeting. He wrapped his cloak tighter around his body and kept going; the windblown flames of his torch could barely hold their heat, but cast enough of a glow for him to run. Eventually he saw flickering lights and clouds of dust ahead. He ran again, as much as he could, until he reached the group of villagers moving up the road.

Panting, Keyth wheezed, "Not there... He's not at the farm...."

Magistrate Arbydn bellowed, "Spread out, scour the woods! No one goes back to town until we find Dryn or..." he hesitated. "Move out!"

Everyone scattered into the woods, shining lanterns into gullies and holding torches over clearings. Anyone with a stick or pole poked it into the shadowy lumps of logs and stumps to make sure it wasn't human. Keyth stuck to the Magistrate's side after handing the sword back. "You did good, son," Arbydn told him. "What did Master ten Brae say?"

Keyth explained, "He hasn't seen Dryn since just after sundown. He's rousing his farm and will start searching as well..." He was slowly regaining his breath, but not his calm.

They followed the road for a while, and eventually there were only four men with them. Everyone else was searching the woods to the south. Arbydn gestured to the east and told a villager, "Check that way..."

Two men split off. A few minutes later Arbydn came to a standstill and looked around him, turning in a circle in the middle of the trampled dirt road. He wore a thick fur coat, a gift from Greater Kryden. He pulled it around his torso and cursed the glyph of coldness. "We'll never find him at this rate. He could be anywhere out here. Everyone's afraid to go on their own because of the damn thieves!"

Keyth nodded. "I don't care about thieves," he told the Magistrate. "I'll start searching the woods as well..." Without waiting for a response, he set off to the west, leaving the road with a little leap into the foliage. The torch he held in his right hand flickered, and the shadows of the forest shifted away from the light. He strode towards a particularly large pine and turned north from there, scouting for any tracks, signs of passage, or a body.

He had lost track of time and still hadn't found anything, or even crossed paths with other villagers. He found himself standing on a huge boulder overlooking a little river vale. Beside him a brook bubbled over the edge of a four foot drop and splashed into a pool at the bottom. The wind was blowing and the torch's light was scattered across the forest floor.

Swearing beneath his breath, Keyth turned away to the east. The road lay in that direction. He took a step away from the rocky surface on which he had stood, and began to make his way between trees when he heard a weak moan behind him. He froze. He thought perhaps it was nothing but the wind in the trees, but then, sure enough, he heard a voice groaning a few dozen feet away.

Retracing his steps, Keyth leapt over the edge of the little cliff and landed at the bottom. His foot caught a root and he stumbled, then fell to the forest floor. As he sprawled into the dirt, the torch plummeted right into the edge of the brook and, with a sputtering *sizzle,* the light vanished.

Now in the pitch blackness, Keyth pulled himself to his feet very slowly and brushed the dirt from his cloak. "Curse the Great Glyph," he muttered as he pulled the soaking torch from the water and shook droplets into the frosted leaves underfoot.

"Keyth?" a voice asked quietly, and he glanced up.

Dryn was five feet away, leaning against the thin trunk of an elm sapling. Keyth was at his side in a moment, "Dryn!" he gasped in shock. *He's alive!* Keyth rejoiced. Even in the darkness, Keyth could tell Dryn was not in good shape. "Are you alright?"

"I think so..." Dryn whispered, wrapping the thin cloak he wore around his chest. "So cold..."

"Yes," Keyth muttered, "Let's get you home."

Twenty minutes later, he emerged onto the road with Dryn leaning weakly on his shoulder, one arm wound behind his neck. "Found him!" Keyth yelled, "I've got him!"

Dryn's father was the first to reach them, panting, "Dryn, Dryn... what happened?"

Dryn was almost unconscious again by this point, and said nothing, simply hanging off of Keyth. Arbydn arrived and they began the slow trek back to the town. Keyth said, "He just needs some sleep in a warm bed now..."

Master ten Rayth was fearful for his son's health, continually checking Dryn's pulse and feeling Dryn's head. Keyth could understand his worry, but right now they just needed to get him home. They couldn't do anything for him out in the freezing night.

Arbydn sent a villager north again to let Master ten Brae and his family know that Dryn had been found. By the time they reached the palisade gate of the village, Dryn had nodded off again and was carried between Keyth and his father. They reached the ten Rayth shop and hauled him to his bed. Dryn had a small closet to himself. His cot was set atop a stained blanket to keep it from the dirt.

They laid him down and wrapped him in a clean blanket while Arbydn waited in the doorway. Dryn's father didn't take off his son's cloak, saying he had to keep warm after the freezing night.

And then that was it. Keyth, the Magistrate, and Master ten Rayth stood in the open space of the ten Rayth apothecary. "So," Arbydn broke the silence through his burly beard, "He'll live?"

"Yes," Telper ten Rayth nodded. "He'll live... He gave us quite a scare though."

Arbydn looked at Keyth and said, "You did quite a job tonight..."

"Thank you, sir."

"No, you have my thanks," the Magistrate told him, and Keyth's chest swelled. *The village Magistrate thanks me!* he thought, proudly.

Master ten Rayth glanced up at the Magistrate with his calm blue eyes and gravely said, "And you have my thanks, sir. We wouldn't have found Dryn in time if it weren't for your quick action."

The Magistrate shook his head. "Think nothing of it. Can never be too careful in these times. There are strange things in the woods."

Muted light awoke him, a groggy illumine beyond the view of his eyes as they rested beneath weighty lids. Heavy boots sounded on a worn dirt floor, and to his still-ringing ears it was a peal like thunder. There was a fiery pain in his chest, the irritating kind of agony. It was a sharp biting pain, and yet also an annoyance, an itch, a driving and bothersome ache.

Dryn lifted one hand from where it lay at his side and scratched his chest. The moment his fingers touched the skin, he became ice from head to toe as he felt the blistered marks burned into his flesh.

Jumping to his feet, he found himself standing in his room next to the apothecary. He yanked the cloak aside, surprised he was still wearing it, and grabbed a flat piece of polished metal nearby. Peering into the smudgy reflection, he saw a series of black symbols written in a column on his chest; an arrangement of dots, lines, and circles scrawled in a vertical line, surrounded by burn blisters from whatever heat had etched them there.

It wasn't a dream, was his first thought. *By the Maker and his Great Glyph, it really happened.*

He sat down solidly on his bed with a loud thump as his backside sank into the thatch within the cot. His breathing was heavy, rustling through his lungs in a harsh pant. He ran his hand over his skin again, tracing the symbols, and recalling the dead man who had done this to him.

'It is beginning,' the man had said. *What is beginning?* Dryn questioned fearfully, and, feeling the broken surface of his flesh, demanded *What do I have to do with it?*

The boots outside his room approached and Dryn hurriedly pulled the cloak across his chest, covering the symbols. His father opened the door a crack and peered in. Shoving the door open quickly, his father knelt by his side and whispered, "Glyphs, Dryn! You're awake!"

"I'm feeling tired still, but no longer asleep..." Dryn said. He couldn't quite focus on the present situation. His mind kept replaying the death of that man... *what was his name?* It was like fumbling for straws. At last he grasped it: *Artemys. Artemys... Gothikar.* The name was meaningless to him.

"What happened? You should've come straight home! Why did you veer so far off the road?" his father questioned, confused.

Dryn remembered seeing one of his friends beaten for not obeying his father, and Dryn realized that the Maker had blessed him with someone so gentle. "I thought I saw someone," he lied quickly.

"A thief? Why would you follow then? Those thieves are dangerous... by the Maker, Arbydn should've hunted them down by now!" Dryn's father snarled, standing slowly and stroking the short beard he kept.

"No, I didn't go off the trail after thieves!" Dryn said, "It looked like... a woman..."

"A woman?" his father questioned, incredulous.

Dryn thought quickly of where he would take this. "I tried to think of what she would be doing alone on the road at night, so I followed her to offer help..."

Telper ten Rayth ran a hand through his smooth black hair and tried to come to terms with what his son was saying. "You followed her, and then what? She knocked you right out and left you for dead?"

Dryn cursed himself for his foolishness. He racked his mind trying to find some reason he had been knocked out. "There was a cliff," he blurted. "Some sort of ridge... I stumbled off it and fell. Probably knocked myself out cold right there!"

At this his father glanced up. "A cliff? Right.... Your ten Arad friend mentioned something about that. A little vale..."

"Yes, exactly," Dryn said, and his memories of the night's encounter solidified. Blood everywhere, tattered cloth, wheezing moan.... All hidden behind the veil of darkness. He could have walked right past if he had been paying any less attention.

"What's wrong?"

Dryn snapped back to the present once more. "What? Oh, I'm just tired, like I said... Who knows how much of that is true... with the woman and all. It was freezing out, I might have dreamt it all up."

"That's alright, Dryn" his father said. "You can rest some more now if you wish. I put some bread on the table for you, if you're hungry."

"I'm thirsty... how long was I asleep?" Dryn wondered.

"We found you night before last You slept all of yesterday," his father said, "and now it's late morning. I'll grab you a cup."

His father disappeared through the door, leaving Dryn alone with his own thoughts again. In his mind's eye, he watched the eerie conversation once more, still trying to discover what it meant. 'You will understand,' Artemys Gothikar had told him. 'You will come to see it all.' Dryn couldn't fathom what in the Maker's Glyph it was supposed to mean. There were too many questions, and no answers. And the characters burnt into his torso... that was a question for which Dryn wasn't sure he wanted to know the answer.

When his father returned and offered him a cup of water, Dryn took a sip and decided, "I think I'm feeling up for a walk."

"A walk?" his father wondered. "Is that wise? If you can't sleep, I could give you some blindwort nectar to ease you off..."

"No, I'm alright..." Dryn glanced out the window at the sky. "Looks like a nice day out... warm. Just what I need."

"If you insist," his father muttered, worried. "I've got a mixture to prepare for Master ten Lenter's sister. Her baby should be coming along within a fortnight."

"You might have to bring it to her yourself," Dryn laughed dryly, as he stood shakily to his feet again.

"Of course!" his father boomed, chuckling. "I wouldn't think of making you deliver anything. Unless it was a letter to this mysterious woman of yours!"

Dryn rolled his eyes. His father sometimes acted like one of his friends, but Dryn didn't mind. Far from it, he actually enjoyed his father's antics. "I'll return shortly. I can't imagine I'll be up for long," he muttered, following his father out of his room and into the shop.

"Don't push yourself," his father warned him, as Dryn stepped out of the apothecary into the roadway.

Lesser Kryden was a small dirty sprawl atop a rocky plateau. It made the farming impossible on top, while the land around the village was greatly fertile. The town square was truly the center of the town, built directly in the middle of the rock when settlers had first set to work. The well wasn't a deep one. Some muttered that it had been a magician who had first dug it; who else could dig into solid rock? Because of the shallow dirt surface, none of their buildings could be raised above one layer, so to the well-traveled sightseer, the village seemed a flat maze of one storey huts. The palisade wall was constructed around the exterior of the stony plateau, leaving a good wide space between the edge of their houses and their defences. Travelling merchants sometimes set up their stalls in this clearing, and that was Dryn's destination as he followed the winding streets.

Someone was banging on an anvil, and the ringing din made Dryn dizzy. He took it slowly, as his father had cautioned him. He occasionally nodded to villagers he knew, but even ones he didn't know glanced at him and whispered, or waved, or murmured to their friends. *He* was the one who had gotten lost, who had awakened them from the warmth of their homes.

"Dryn!" someone called behind him, but he kept walking slowly. He felt so tired. He thought he would have snapped out of it by now.

"Dryn, wait up!" the voice persisted, and he recognized it this time. Turning, Dryn saw Keyth running down the street towards him.

"Where are you headed? Last time I checked in, your father said you were still asleep," Keyth explained, catching his breath almost immediately. His grey eyes seemed alight with curiosity.

He knew where he was going, but he didn't want Keyth along. "I'm just going for a walk," he said. "I –"

"What happened?" Keyth said before Dryn could continue.

Dryn shrugged. "I got lost. It was dark. I had no torch. Where are you headed?"

Keyth grinned. "The Grey Horse," he laughed. "You coming?"

Dryn shook his head. "I can't stomach it right now. Maybe tomorrow. After another night's rest."

"Sounds alright, as long as you're recovering," Keyth said, patting Dryn's back through the cloak. After another moment of walking side-by-side, Keyth turned away. "Well, I'll catch you later... gotta get some of ten Desser's brew in me."

"Have a great time," Dryn wished him, and kept walking. His head was ringing like one of the volcanoes of which his father spoke. After what felt like the longest walk of his life, Dryn found himself standing at the end of a shuffled line of wagons and stalls.

Books, he thought to himself. He walked idly along past the merchants until he came to a cart full of books. A board had been set across the corners of the wagon facing into town and several featured tomes were set title-out on top of the wood. His father often wondered at the inexpensive books they sold now; when Master ten Rayth was young, books were bound animal hide and cost a fortune.

When Dryn stepped up to the wagon take a look, a man swung his feet off the bench at the front of the cart and planted them in the near frozen mud.

"Lookin' for something, young one?" the man questioned with a thick accent. Not smooth like the Imperials, nor rough in the way Nalfar described the villagers. "Anythin' particular, that is?"

"Just looking around," Dryn told the merchant.

"You read much?"

Dryn nodded. "Anything I can get my hands on."

"Well, take yer time, lad. You'll find plenty o' them chronicles from the West. They've installed printing presses in most of the larger cities." The merchant smiled at him, nodding towards the cart. With the tightly braided beard and cropped hair, Dryn was reminded of Master Bordus.

Dryn put one foot on a spoke of the wooden wheel and pulled himself up until his knee straightened. Looking down into the crates of books, he began poring through them. One crate contained only such chronicles as the trader had mentioned; Dryn recognized the Journeys of Oban Hokar. Dryn skipped that box and scanned over the titles of the next. This box contained atlases and travel books, and Dryn felt a twinge of hope here, but it was to no avail.

He stepped back off the wheel he had been standing on and went to the next wheel, this one between the wall and the next stall. The merchant had ceased paying attention and was now rearranging a stack of books on his display board. Dryn peered into the next crate and interest sparked once more.

This crate contained scholarly treatises and, to Dryn's relief, there was a tome entitled, 'Brother Elkwen's Record of Foreign Dialect.' Dryn stepped back into the dirt and opened the cover of the book. Flipping through the first few pages, he found an overview of the book's contents. It was arranged by area; the first chapter was on the 'Southern Tongues' and the second 'Sea Language.'

With deepening disappointment, Dryn closed the cover of the book and leaned back up against the wagon-side. Gazing back into the box, he noticed that several books were taller than the rest. Upon further investigation, he found that there was another thick tome underneath these. He moved the other books aside and withdrew the book from where it lay below.

Leaning back off the cart, Dryn read the title and his heart stopped. The words 'A starter's treatise on the basic glyphs of magic,' were etched with gold leaf into the leather cover. *Is that what happened?* he wondered in horror. Although magic was a tale from the Imperial Cities and almost everyone in the village believed it truly existed, none had ever seen it.

Eagerly, Dryn peeled open the tattered cover of the book and examined the first moth-eaten page. The title was written again on the first page and under it was a string of symbols that were all too familiar. Similar characters were burned into his skin.

Glyphs... That's what happened in the forest. That wizard burned glyphs into me and died. Dryn was standing in the dirt again, the book open in his hands but unseen by his eyes. He was staring distantly, recalling what had transpired a night and a day earlier. *But why?*

"What you got there, young man?" the peddler asked, standing at the corner of the cart. "You decided on somethin'?"

Confused, Dryn snapped back to the present and shut the volume quickly. He still held the record of languages, so he put that one on top of the magic book, and spoke quickly, "Yes, sir, these. I'd like to get these two."

"Two books?" the merchant questioned. Thankfully, he didn't examine them. "I'll be kind to you, lad. Twenty copper pieces each."

Dryn had nearly forgotten he had to pay for them. He didn't have any money, as his father hadn't paid him in a fortnight. He needed new sandals, he remembered, and cursed himself for forgetfulness. *I'm going to have to go the whole way back home and beg Father for some coins.*

That's when it hit him. Almost without thinking, he scooped the bag of coins off his belt, the very pouch with which Master ten Brae had paid for the potion. Dryn was supposed to have given the money to his father upon return from the delivery, but after all the commotion, the coins had never changed hands.

Setting the books on the side of the cart, Dryn counted forty coins out of the bag and into the palm of the peddler. It was almost all of them, but he grabbed his books and nodded to the merchant.

He stumbled down the street out of view before he doubled over, hand on his knees, gasping for breath. *By the Maker, what were you thinking, Dryn?* he asked himself. He had just spent his father's money to buy two books when he only wanted one. Dryn intended to translate and perhaps understand the glyphs on his chest, but he didn't need the other book. It had been a decoy, a cover for an awkward moment. *Now what?* he asked himself.

By the time he got back to his yard, he was trembling from overexertion, fatigue, and fear of his father's reaction. There was a little signpost at the road that read 'ten Rayth Apothecary.' Most of the prefix was obliterated, Dryn noticed, as he leaned on the rotting wooden post.

Finally, he reached the door which creaked loudly as he walked inside. His father was sitting at the workbench on the other side of the room, his back to the door. "Ah, you're back, Dryn." Turning to face him, his father noticed the books, and smiled. "Some good reading material, I hope."

"Of course," Dryn said, quietly, innocently. "I think I'm going to lie down again though. I'm so tired..."

"Sounds wise."

Dryn walked past his father to his room. "Wake me if you need me," he said.

"Oh, I doubt I'll have need of you today. What about food?" his father asked.

"If I need it, I'll come out."

"Alright. Have a good sleep," his father muttered. "Oh, and I got the ten Brae's money you left."

"The ten Brae's money?" Dryn repeated, turning to stare at his father.

"Uh-huh," his father grunted, turning back to the half-filled pottery at his bench. "Keep prodding and I might give you some of it." His father laughed.

"Wait... the money for the delivery?" Dryn asked again, confused. Blaring in his senses was the weight of the pouch and its few remaining coins on his belt.

"Yes, Dryn... I found it on the table. Tomorrow, I'll work out an amount for you. Now, get some rest," his father murmured.

Behind the closed door of his room, with trembling Dryn pulled the pouch from his belt and emptied a count of twelve remaining copper coins onto his bed. Shuddering, he opened the cover of the book of magic.

By the time the pale sun rose through the mists of Agwar Marsh, Theos of Galinor had used up nearly all of his tokens. The teleports weren't working, and Theos had to assume that whoever hunted him had placed wards against them. Even Theos couldn't sense out *that* magic; though deemed one of the stronger mages in the Order, Theos found himself trapped by a power he couldn't understand.

Something howled behind and to the left of him, and he froze, peering back in that direction. One boot was on a slippery moss-ridden rock, while the other stood ankle deep in mud. He could see nothing through the greenish murk that filled the air. Even the tree by which he had just rested had now vanished into the fog behind him.

Cursing his weariness, Theos forced himself to continue on. He plunged through bush, thorn and swamp alike, running when he could and stumbling more. He sensed a whining flare before his ears had picked it up, and dropped instantly onto the muddy bank in front of him. A searing heat scorched the air over his head and burnt into a rotten sycamore to his right. The resulting explosion of dirt, beetles and fire pattered over Theos' pine-green cloak, singeing the rough skin on the back of his hand.

He rolled over and came up on one knee, blasting one of his last lightning tokens in the direction of the fireball. The stone tablet dissolved in his palm as blue and white energy shocked through the Marsh's reeking air. He heard a blood-curdling scream and immediately started running again. The unseen magician who had ambushed him was not alone; there were half a dozen more, as well as some moor dogs.

Theos knew of one way out of this wretched death trap: somewhere within the Marsh was a glyph-gate. He doubted those who pursued him knew of its existence and, even if they did, no ward could guard such a portal. He dashed up a small embankment and crouched at the base of a gnarled tree; the cloak he wore was tattered and a small gash on his left arm was dripping blood. From this outlook he could see miles of Agwar Marsh, a cursed blemish on the face of the world which he prayed he could soon escape.

He had heard about the massacre at the Olympus Guild, but had disregarded it. Even when rumours of Artemys' disappearance reached Agwar Watch, Theos had ignored them. But then the town went up in flames, and Theos found himself fleeing for his life in this forsaken hellhole, hunted like a wild animal.

"Mordus ogar terrynce dei," he whispered, lifting a twig. Throwing it in the air, he muttered, *"Dolper kin!"*

A golden pulse outlined the twig in mid air and it spun in front of Theos, then with a quiet *crack* it landed at his feet. Following the line of the stick, he lifted his gaze from it until he was staring northeast into the swamplands. Without blinking, Theos set off, trekking determinedly along this line.

Reaching the bottom of a hill, Theos found himself facing a deep black brook, which he jumped with a burst of air magic and a few words to control it. An abrupt growl was the only warning he had when his feet touched down, and he threw himself sideways.

He almost lost his footing and fell into the dark water, but with carefully directed muscles he rolled the other way. Coming up to one foot, he found a moor dog upon him, the gaping jaw snapping as fangs closed over his arm. Rolling again, Theos forced the dog to let go, else it be trapped beneath him, and in the moment it let go, his hand yanked a knife from his waist.

The dog barked and charged him again, a crazed blur of brown and black fur accompanying the sharp claws that slashed at him. Theos saw an opening and jammed his knife forward. The dog's paw connected with Theos' shoulder as he moved forward, just as the steel blade buried itself to the hilt in the dog's chest.

Swearing under his breath, Theos let go of the handle as the wild dog died, and pulled his arm back to examine the fresh wound. Three thick gouges were seeping red into the shirt he wore beneath the cloak. He tore the sleeve out of the way and tied the cloth tightly around the injury. The scent of blood in the air was enough to call a handful more moor dogs to where he stood, but he didn't want his blood dripping a physical trail for them to follow.

He reclaimed his knife, wiping the blade on the animal's fur. That is when he noticed a small glowing symbol on the dog's forehead. Further examination put a solid chunk of horror in Theos' stomach as he recognized the glyphs for 'animal' and 'control.' That's how his predators were using these dogs; the cursed sorcerers were breaking one of Artemys' most important rules.

Without waiting for more enemies to descend on him, Theos checked his directions again and set off on a north-eastern course. His earlier spell had pointed him right towards the glyph-gate he searched for.

For the next dozen minutes, he played a hiding game with his hunters, weaving around them, but always holding to his northeast route. He had no idea how far it was. His earlier spell had only directed him the right way. His legs' aching had passed the normal muted pain of overexertion and now plagued him with sharp twangs every time he stepped. He could barely run anymore; instead he plodded his way through the marshland.

He heard a twig crack behind him and he froze, crouching against a nearby cypress tree. As he watched silently, praying to the Maker, a robed figure stumbled by and stopped ten feet from Theos. Assuming he was caught, Theos readied his only remaining lightning token and raised one hand.

A distant voice echoed through the mist. He couldn't make out any words, but the man standing in view of Theos turned his back and walked away.

Breathing deeply, Theos lowered the lightning token and thanked the Great Glyph. Why he hadn't been discovered he couldn't fathom, but he knew he had been given a chance. He stood to his feet and set off again, dodging under branches and leaping over logs.

Within thirty paces he found the glyph-gate he'd been looking for. There was a small fog-shrouded hill, and as he climbed the slope, he saw before him two stone pillars marking the opening to a shrine of some sort. His mud coated boots made a squelch as they walked onto cobblestone. He passed more marked pillars until at last he stood before a stone archway. The moss was eating away at the once solid masonry, and vines were hanging over the threshold.

Within the arch, Theos could see a muted blue light hovering. Flickering within the blue energy was a complex glyph, a detailed description of where the gate led. All Theos needed to do was step across the threshold and he would be standing on the other side. His eyes deciphered the character by instinct and he smiled. *The Delfie School. This gate leads straight to Delfie!* Again, he had been blessed.

He took one step towards the archway and was met by an arm which extended through the portal, followed by its' robed and hooded body. The dagger held in the hand met Theos' oncoming torso and Theos found himself laying on his side on the grimy cobblestones.

It took his shocked mind a moment to snap from the daze and try to work out what had just happened. Someone else had come through the gate just as he was walking toward it. Someone had attacked him, stabbed him. His hand groped blankly for the hilt that protruded from his skin.

A pair of hands grabbed the neck of his cloak and hauled him to his feet. He felt cold stone against his back, a pillar, and warm slick blood pulsing down his skin.

"Do you understand now?" an icy voice asked him.

He forced his eyes to focus again, and the face within the hood swam into his vision. It took him a moment to recognize the vivid green eyes, arched nose, and sneering mouth. He managed to voice, "Pyrsius?"

"That's right, Theos. It's my turn."

He tried to understand what was going on. As black shadows wrapped around him, Theos hissed, "Pyrsius, you're the one behind all this? You forsaken earth-spawn... The Maker burn you forever!"

With that last exclamation, Theos tasted blood in his mouth and his sight lost all focus again. He heard Pyrsius laughing and then the last words he would ever hear:

"Yes, I'm the one behind it all... It's my turn to play with the world."

5

"Glyphs are the ancient language by which the Maker has spoken the world into reality," Dryn whispered to himself, reading from the introduction of the book he had purchased. Beside him on the dirt floor the record of foreign languages lay forgotten. "For everything around you there is a glyph that explains it, controls it, releases it," he read.

He sat back and pondered what the book was teaching. He could see the connection between the village fables and this outline. Everyone knew that the Maker had written the Great Glyph and with it the world was forged. The tale went that if one learned the name of a lesser glyph, he could control that element.

Dryn cautiously lifted his polished metal mirror and saw the unclear reflection of his chest in it. *Is that what these are?* he wondered, touching the broken surface of his skin where the symbols were scrawled; the blisters had already healed. *Glyphs?* That had been his goal in buying the guide to glyphs: he wanted to determine if the man who died in the forest had been a wizard and had put a spell on him.

Curious, Dryn flipped through the pages of the book, looking ahead. After the introduction was a title page called, "Elemental Glyphs" and an entire section charting such characters. The next chapter was called "Classification of Spells" and the third "Length and Amount." He could see foreign symbols on the pages, explained by a small description in Common Tongue. Each entry was also accompanied by a series of letters he recognized but understood as no Common word.

His heart pounded as he noticed the similarities. The spell branded on him was definitely written in these glyphs.

Starting to flip back towards the introduction, Dryn was surprised when a white paper fell out of the pages. At first he thought the ancient tome had lost a page, but when he picked the parchment off his cot's blanket, he realized that it was a sealed letter.

Turning the letter over, he froze and almost choked. Printed in plain letters was his own name. The letter was addressed to him! His first thought was both a question and a realization: *Someone knew I was going to buy the book?!* In trembling terror, he tore the letter open and slid the parchment out from inside.

He looked first at the end, searching for a signature, but there was none. He looked to the beginning and saw again that it was addressed to him. Then, holding the paper in shivering hands, he read:

"Dryn,
You have bought this book to investigate the symbols scrawled in your chest by the late magician Artemys Gothikar. Artemys was the greatest wizard of our time, and therefore there are no answers in that simple book as to the translation of the ward he laid upon you or the magic you now possess..."

Dryn dropped the letter and kicked himself back along his cot until his back was to the wall. Panting in fear, he shook his head and assured himself, "This isn't real... This can't be real." His hand unconsciously went to the black glyphs in his skin and his eyes squeezed shut. *It is real,* he knew.

He opened his eyes. The dropped books and the letter were still there. The glyphs were still written in his chest. The world was still the foreign danger it had become. Shaking his head to clear it, he forced himself to crawl back across his cot. He picked up the letter and kept reading.

"You will find that the book explains glyphs, magic, and the acquisition of magic. You need only this basic understanding: Magic is bestowed by a spell. Therefore only a wizard can grant someone else magic. In this regard, it is the decision of every magician to grant the next generation magic.

"Artemys Gothikar gave you magic. His motives are still not understood, but I am investigating. I urge you to read the book and memorize as much as you can. I will be in contact again to guide you. I will give you instructions for your first spell. It is imperative that you DO NOT use any glyphs until you receive my next letter.

"You must also come to terms with the fact that you are now important. Artemys Gothikar made you important. Simply being the one in whose presence Artemys died makes you a value to every wizard in the realm. Stay safe."

Dryn turned the letter over, but that was it. No signature, as he had noticed earlier. Some watchful wizard, perhaps? He folded the letter and replaced it in its encasement, and placed that between the pages of the book once again.

He moved back, put his head against the wall again, and closed his eyes once more. *What am I supposed to do now?* he wondered. *Read the book as the letter instructs? Can I trust this letter? Can I trust the book?* He remembered the magician in the forest, the blood, the mutilation, the death in his eyes. Dryn shuddered. *If that was the greatest wizard of my time... what could have done that to him?*

He glanced down at the words on the cover of the book: 'A starter's treatise on the basic glyphs of magic,' and he slowly cracked open the introduction again. "With practice and caution, a magician can learn to use any of the elements with simple words and a written glyph."

By the time his window showed the night, Dryn was halfway through the book and his mind was alive with ambition. Wizardry. Magic. Glyphs. The world may have become a dangerous puzzle, but it was also a book as open to him as the pages of the treatise he was reading.

He ate a quick meal, and his father barely noticed him. Later, as he lay in the dark of his room, he found himself unable to sleep. When at last his eyes fell closed, he was haunted by nightmares of a wizard named Artemys Gothikar and by dreams of letters sent to him from a mysterious magician.

6

Eight done, ten to go. Keyth's knife scratched aside the still damp wood leaving a notch at the end of the bow's limb. He flipped the arm over and carved away a mark at the other end. Next he drew a string of sinew through a chunk of beeswax and tied the loop of each string to the notches he had just made. When the damp wood dried, the string would be pulled even more taunt. The beeswax made it impervious to moisture. He set the bow aside and cupped his face in his hands.

Nine done, nine to go. Halfway. He stood up, and Master ten Lenter stopped winding string and raised an eyebrow. "Where do you think you're off to?"

Defensively, Keyth explained, "Just stretching my legs," and strode across the room. The bowyer's shack was small compared to Keyth's old house. His mother had told him that his father had once fought side-by-side with Royal Templers. Their house had been one of the larger ones of Lesser Kryden.

"I am not paying you to stretch your legs. Sit your behind down on that chair," the bowyer said as he slid the next bow across the table, "and string that bow."

Groaning, Keyth plummeted down onto the hard wooden seat and grabbed the unstrung bow. His knife whittled away the wood and the beeswax slowly disappeared until at last, over an hour and a half later, all eighteen bows were complete.

When he had strung the last one, and set it aside, he tentatively asked, "I suppose I need to deliver these somewhere?"

"You suppose right, boy," his master grunted. "Those are going to ten Eldar and his hunters."

"Eldar!" Keyth exclaimed, pressing the dirt under his sandal. "He could be anywhere!"

"He's east of the Syroh Water."

"East of Syroh Water," Keyth repeated, scoffing. "There's *miles* of forest east of the Water."

"That's your problem," Master ten Lenter muttered. "If you're still out there when dark falls, you can light a fire. They'll find you."

"They?" Keyth questioned. "Eldar's hunters? or the brigands?"

"You've got eighteen longbows."

"I can't fight bandits!"

Master ten Lenter rolled his eyes. "I didn't say fight them. They're thieves. What do they want with bows?"

"To steal them!" Keyth yelped.

"Alright, that's enough!" his Master snapped. Sternly, he continued, "You can bring your ten Rayth friend along if you like. He seems to know a bit about forests."

Ignoring the loud chuckling, Keyth proceeded to load the eighteen bows into two packs, nine in each. He slung each bundle over a shoulder and, groaning under the weight, swung the door open. He was tired by the time he reached the ten Rayth apothecary.

He pounded solidly on the door, and then swung the delivery into the grass between the road and the building. A moment later Telper ten Rayth opened the door and said, "Ah, Keyth. Dryn's in his room."

Keyth walked through the apothecary and tapped on Dryn's door. He heard a paper crinkle, a thud, and then the door creaked open. "Hello, Keyth," Dryn said, a smile on his face. "What are you doing?"

Dryn looked pale and there were big bags under his eyes. Keyth answered, "ten Lenter has me delivering bows to Eldar and the hunters."

"Now? It'll be dark before you can get back!" Dryn exclaimed.

"I know. I tried explaining that as well. But I'm going and there's nothing either of us can do about it," Keyth murmured. "Want to come?"

Dryn glanced over one shoulder, back into his room. "Uh... I guess, I could use some fresh forest air." He disappeared and, after a long moment, re-emerged wearing a double-layered cloak. "Father, I'm going with Keyth on a delivery... I'll be back tonight."

Telper ten Rayth looked up from his herbs and frowned. Then he glanced at Keyth and smiled. "I'll trust Keyth's sense of directions. Don't get lost again!"

Dryn nodded. "I won't."

Outside, Keyth shouldered a bundle of nine bows and grinned. "You can carry that one," he laughed.

Dryn shook his head. "So *that's* why you want me along." Reluctantly, he swung the other pack onto his back and walked to the road beside Keyth. "So, where are the hunters now?"

Keyth smiled. " 'East of Syroh Water'," he quoted. "Which means they could be anywhere in the forest!"

"Ah, well. Let's go."

They set off along the south road at a brisk pace. He didn't want to be outside all night. Dryn kept up, but Keyth could tell he was exhausted. "What's happening with you?" he asked quietly. "You look tired."

Dryn nodded, walking with his head turned toward Keyth. "I haven't been sleeping well..."

"No fooling," Keyth smirked. "Has it just been since the forest thing?" He remembered Dryn's scattered appearance when he had first found him.

"Yes."

"Your father can probably make something for sleep, right?" Keyth asked.

Dryn nodded. "He gave me a brew."

"And?"

"And it tastes terrible," Dryn grinned.

Now that's the Dryn I know, Keyth thought. He scratched his shoulder beneath the strap of his bundle. "So what happened that night?"

"Huh?"

Keyth snorted. "The night I found you?!"

"Oh," Dryn muttered. He blinked and looked off the roadway. They were now about a mile out of town. They weren't even halfway. Dryn looked torn, as if he wanted to tell something but wouldn't.

"Well?"

Dryn shook his head and muttered to himself. Then, glancing at Keyth he said, "I found something in the woods. At least I thought I did. But it's nothing."

"Nothing?" Keyth questioned. He shivered against a cold draft of wind moving along the road. Winter was coming. "Dryn, you were about ten minutes off the road! How did you find something that far away? And what was important enough to stay out there past midnight?"

Dryn winced. The next few steps were tread in silence, and then at last Dryn said, "I heard a voice call to me. Someone needed help. There was an old man, dying. I couldn't help him."

"An old man?" Keyth questioned, his mind whirling. "You found someone dying? Was he a traveller? What happened to him?"

"I don't know. I stumbled back from him and tripped through a bush. I hit my head or something, and must have blacked out," Dryn explained. His hand was touching his chest like he was in pain, but Keyth was caught on what he had said.

"Hold on. I didn't see anyone dead!"

Dryn nodded. "It must have been the foliage. It was night, right?"

Keyth blinked. "Right..." If Dryn did fall through a bush, that might explain it... but a dying man? Really?

"Hey, should we turn here?" It had been at least half an hour. Dryn was pointing at a little path winding off the dirt road.

Keyth shook his head. "No, the next one."

They walked in relative silence for a spell. They had been friends since childhood and just about every topic had been exhausted it seemed. They usually stuck by each other's side.

Keyth remembered that night vividly. "The Magistrate gave me a sword! When we were out looking..."

"Really?" Dryn questioned, equally excited.

"Yep! In case I was attacked by the thieves." That's when Keyth put things together. "Hey! Maybe that old traveller was killed by the bandits!"

Dryn's mouth slanted as his head moved side to side. "No, I don't think so."

"Really? Why not?" Keyth questioned. "Makes sense to me."

Dryn appeared deep in thought, but eventually he answered, "I don't know about these rumours of thieves."

"What?" Keyth questioned.

"I just doubt that we really have to worry that much about bandits on the roads!" Dryn murmured. He shifted his bundle of bows to the other shoulder.

Keyth walked a number of paces, pondering it. "I suppose you're right. No one has seen them..." Several minutes later they reached another path that branched off westward. It was a two hour walk from here to Syroh Water, which meant by Master ten Lenter's directions, the hunters could be anywhere along this stretch.

They went single file now, stumbling through the rough terrain of the woodland. After twenty minutes of the rigorous hike, Dryn called for a break and they planted the wooden bows in the autumn underbrush.

"Got an eye on anyone?" Keyth asked. "I hear Ernes is going to ask Tressa for betrothal..."

"Really?" Dryn asked, and Keyth nodded. Dryn shook his head and said, "Nah... I don't think much about that. I feel that I should at least work on my own and earn my living before... you know..."

"Before supporting someone else?" Keyth finished. "I know what you mean. But the other day the Corin family let me join them for their evening meal. They've always been friends with my... family."

Dryn laughed. "And?"

"And Yara is definitely interesting..." Keyth smiled. He picked up a twig and rolled it between his fingers.

Dryn chuckled. "Interesting, huh?"

Keyth looked south into the dimming sky. "Strange thought. Getting married."

Dryn sucked in his breath and then jokingly said, "Keyth and Yara... has a bit of a ring to it, doesn't it?"

Keyth rolled his eyes and punched Dryn playfully in the side. "That's enough then! Pick up your pack!"

"Yes, master," Dryn mocked. He slung the strap of his nine bows over one shoulder and waited as Keyth did the same. They set off again, continuing westward along the trail.

An hour passed and twilight shrouded them in a damp shadow. They would get back after dark, not something Keyth was pleased about. He hoped ten Lenter paid him well for this job. Keyth's callused toes were grimy with dirt... he was saving up for a pair of actual boots, rather than cheap sandals. He had long ago outgrown his childhood pair. Grumbling to himself, he jumped half out of his skin when Dryn said, "Stop."

"What?" he asked his friend.

"Smell. Wood fire," Dryn pointed out.

Keyth inhaled deeply and the familiar warm aroma of burning leaves and wood entered his lungs. "That must be them. Which way is it coming from?"

"I'd say farther along the trail," Dryn decided.

They set off again, eager to meet these hunters and be done with it.

Soon the blue tint of the air was illuminated by a flickering light. Keyth had walked the woodlands enough to recognize a campfire, even from this far away. Suddenly, a voice hissed out of the darkness, "By the Maker, get your empty heads down!"

A man with a wild beard and narrow eyes charged out of the forest to their right, knocking them both off the trail. "SHHH!" He had one finger raised against his lips. "Do not make a sound," he told them, his hair a mess around his shoulders. He was holding a short blade in one hand and had a quiver of arrows at his shoulder.

"What? Glyph guard me! Who are you?" Keyth questioned, drawing a knife from his belt. He doubted it'd be of any use to him though.

"Eldar! Gah! You don't recognize me?" the man questioned. "You're Kryden boys, right? Got bows, right?"

Keyth nodded, mutely. Dryn had already removed the bundle of bows from his shoulder, and as they watched, Eldar slashed the strap in half, spilling the clutter of bow limbs into the brush. He gripped one of them and lifted it to waist level. An arrow appeared as if from nowhere and the man had it notched, without the bowstring pulled.

"By the Maker! What's going on?" Dryn asked, pulling the words right out of Keyth's mouth.

"Bandits!" Eldar growled. "My band is dead or scattered. We've got to get back to the village!"

"Bandits?" Keyth asked. He rose up from the crouch they were in and peered back towards the firelight. After the afternoon's hike his eyes were accustomed to the dark, so he could only make out shapes in the light, bodies in the dirt, blood gleaming with each spark. He flinched and ducked low again. "Maker shield me... What are we going to do?"

"Run," Eldar grunted.

"Where?"

"No," Eldar snapped. "RUN!" He shoved Keyth ahead of him and Keyth found himself moving through the woods. He heard a thudding sound, and then another on his other side. "Don't stop to look, go!"

A third thump sounded, and Keyth saw an arrow materialize in the trunk of a tree two feet from his head. *Arrows!* he realized, and started to run like he never had. *Great Glyph protect me, someone is shooting arrows at us!* Keyth leapt over a log and tore through a thorn bush. He heard Eldar yell, "Go!" He glanced once over his shoulder to see Dryn right behind him and Eldar loosing a shaft towards the path.

Someone in that direction started shouting curses and cries. Eldar let fly again and this time someone began screaming until his fellow put him out of his agony. Then Dryn shoved Keyth, and Eldar disappeared in the forest behind them, swallowed by the shadows.

Dryn and Keyth dashed until they couldn't anymore, and then they jogged even longer. Eventually they reached the main road again. North of them was Lesser Kryden, a two-hour trek, and south of them was the log bridge, crossing the Syroh River. Hours further the road came to the gates of Greater Kryden.

They stood on the dirt roadway gasping for breath and trying to think straight. *Where is Eldar?* Keyth wondered, peering back behind them. Dryn answered that he didn't know, and Keyth realized he had spoken the thought aloud. "Should we wait for him?" was his next question.

Dryn shook his head. "I think we should get help. Tell the Magistrate or my father or someone."

Keyth nodded, seeing Dryn's logic. "Alright..." He bent over with his hands on his knees and sucked in the cool night air. It felt good, filling his lungs again. Then the cold got to him and he started coughing from exertion and the temperature. "Alright, let's go. Maker burn those earth-spawn."

Dryn only nodded. Together they set off again, walking along the road. Keyth was sore from all the running, first to find Dryn the other night, and now to escape the bandits. "They're real, huh?" Keyth gasped, looking behind them. "There really are thieves in the forest."

"I thought it was a rumour."

Keyth nodded. "Me too. But no more..."

"Off the road!" a voice hissed, startling the life out of them again. Eldar was standing in the woodland, glaring at them. There was blood matted in his wild beard. He gestured and they jumped off the road into the foliage. "All it takes is one brigand running his way along, and you're dead!"

"Sorry," Dryn whispered.

"It's not sorry! It's your own damn skin!" Eldar muttered.

Keyth and Dryn were quiet after that. Eldar snapped, "Let's get moving," and then led them north. The night was the coldest yet; Keyth could *taste* winter in the air, a dryness in his mouth and shiver in his shoulders. By the time they came into sight of the village's torches, Keyth took back what he had said earlier about Dryn. Dryn didn't look bad then. He looked bad now. The bags were still under his eyes, perhaps worse, and his lips had a pale blue tinge to them. Keyth hoped that Master ten Rayth had a potion to help.

They had been fleeing for two hours, and hadn't run into the bandits again. Eldar expressed that he knew his men were dead. He was likely the only survivor of the hunting expedition, which meant two things: a number of villagers were dead; and the village was now short a band of hunters. The former was a big enough blow to the village, but the latter became deadly when a harsh winter was quickly approaching.

When they reached the village, the gates were closed. They knocked and a small hatch opened, their short gatekeeper peeking through until convinced to open the gate. The hunter went straight to the magistrate's house while Keyth and Dryn walked home. They reached the apothecary first, and split up with only a few words.

Keyth walked into his own house as quietly as he could, and then jumped out of his skin when Master ten Lenter, lying in the dark, asked, "Took you long enough. Did you get them bows delivered?"

Keyth blinked and whispered, "Something like that."

Fire - *tal'oken*; air - *bor*; water - *arnar*; earth – *a'bor*; each with a corresponding symbol. Crossing lines, etched dots, waving curls, alive within Dryn's head. He turned page after page, absorbing the information and committing it to memory. Metal - *tal'azor*; light - *oken*; dark – *a'oken*. He could count in the language of magic and knew increments of time, the purposes of which he did not understand. Yet.

He spent the entire morning delving through the pages of the book, until at last hunger drove him from his room. He peeked out of his door and, as always, his father somehow knew he was there.

"Dryn, I was wondering when you'd get your nose out of those books," Master ten Rayth commented. "I was also wondering when you'd resume your work... After all, your 'lost in the woods' ordeal is now three days past."

"Well, I assumed with all that's going on..." Dryn muttered.

His father actually turned from the workbench and stared at his face where it peeked from the door. "I suppose you mean your flight from the bandits last night?"

"Yes, and..."

"The Magistrate and Nalfar have spoken to ten Eldar about that. I'm sure they will decide on the right course of action." His father glanced back at the table of his herbs and vials. "In the meantime, I need an assistant."

"Very well," Dryn groaned, realizing there was no way out of it, short of confessing to his father that he was involved with 'witchcraft.' "Let me get something in my stomach, and I'll be at your disposal."

"My disposal?" his father laughed. "I shouldn't want that. On the contrary, another delivery..."

Dryn groaned. He opened a cupboard in the corner and withdrew a tough loaf of bread. After slicing from it with a knife, he took a bite and chewed. His mouth complained while his stomach praised him for the decision.

"Don't worry. This one's in town." His father set a small pouch on the table between them. Dryn could hear the clink of glass bottles inside. "Take these to the Corin house."

Groaning, Dryn finished off the bread and took a wrinkled apple from a bowl. He grabbed the bag of concoctions and stepped out of the apothecary. He finished the sweet fruit after several steps and tossed aside the core. Five minutes later he knocked on the door of the Corin house.

Master ten Corin was a cobbler whose shop was a few buildings down the street from Dryn's house. Dryn wondered if the potions were for him or for someone else in the household. He had hoped he could finish the delivery at the house and not have to walk to the shop too.

The door opened and Mistress Corin smiled as she greeted him. "Why, Dryn ten Rayth... do come in."

He stepped inside and awkwardly held the pouch up. "My father asked me to deliver these to you." She took the pouch, at which point the door opened behind Dryn, and he shuffled out of the way.

Yara Corin walked inside and her face lit up when she saw Dryn. "Oh, hello Dryn! What are you doing here?"

Dryn nodded back. "Uh, just a delivery for my father."

She put a pair of boots down in one corner of the room. The Corin house had three rooms: a main room in which they stood, a bedroom, and a small storage closet. Mistress Corin took the pouch, then opened the nearby closet and stepped inside.

Yara glanced at the boots she had been holding and then at Dryn. "Don't tell Keyth yet. I had my father make him some boots as a gift. His name day is coming up in a fortnight."

"That's nice of you," Dryn told her. "Your secret's safe with me." *But I need new shoes...* he thought to himself. He realized all of a sudden that he still had a handful of coins from the fateful ten Brae delivery, plus a full week's pay from his father. *And that double pouch... Somehow we got twice the pay from the ten Braes. I should pay that back somehow.* Dryn thought that perhaps Master ten Brae had forgotten he had paid Dryn. "Is your father at the shop?" he asked, glancing around the room.

Yara nodded. "Yes, but he's not busy, if you need to speak with him."

"Alright, I think I'll head over there. I'll drop by and say hello again sometime," Dryn said, politely.

"I'd like that," she told him, and he opened the door.

"Here, Dryn," Mistress Corin said, entering the room again. "For the potions." She dropped a number of coins into the palm of his hand and Dryn pocketed them. He nodded farewell and stepped out into the street.

It was noticeably busier than when he had gone inside. He saw the book merchant walking the other way; the man would probably be leaving the village soon. Most merchants could only afford to stay a couple of days in a small village like Lesser Kryden.

He made his way up the street until he reached the cobbler's shop. Stepping inside, he received an amiable 'hullo' from Master Corin. "What can I do for you?" the thin cobber asked.

"I just made a delivery to your house and it reminded me that I need new sandals," Dryn said. He glanced around the cramped shop. There was a blanket laid on the ground beneath the furniture, instead of the traditional dirt floor. "Have you got anything already made?"

"You happen to be in luck," Master Corin told him. He itched the short stubble on his chin. "I recently finished a pair of laced boots. They're a bit more expensive than sandals. You know what, though? Business has been excellent with winter on the way. I suppose I could sell them to you cheap."

"Boots?" Dryn asked. He had once owned a pair, and he could remember the comfortable warmth of them. *But it'll cost you...* "How much are they?" he asked, wincing.

Master Corin went over to a shelf on the other side of the small, dimly lit shop. He grabbed the pair of boots down and set them by the lamp on one of the tables. "Looks like they'll fit you too. How about forty-five copper."

Dryn examined them quietly for a moment. He had enough money; he could afford it with the twelve copper from the first ten Brae payment and the pay his father had given him. He tried one on. It was a little large, but so comfortable. They were warm, and they would be far easier to walk in than sandals. Especially during the winter. He ran a hand through his hair.

"Alright," Dryn decided. "I'll get them. I'll have to grab some more copper though. I'll be back. Thanks, Master Corin."

"Please, no problem at all. Say hullo to your father for me."

"Of course," Dryn smiled. He walked back out into the street. He couldn't wait to have his own boots again. As he got back home and excitedly stepped inside, about to pass on Master ten Corin's greeting, his father spoke up first..

"Why haven't you finished yet?"

"What?" Dryn asked, confused.

"You came in here and gave me the pay from the Corins, and then I sent you out to split some wood. That was ten minutes ago. And last time I looked out the window, it still isn't done," his father reprimanded. "So get out there and chop some firewood!"

Dryn remained frozen. "I just got back though. I haven't paid you yet."

"By the Maker, Dryn! What's got into you?" Telper ten Rayth snapped, turning around from his apothecary bench. "Right here! Here's the money!" He was pointing to a number of coins spilled on the table.

Dryn stuck his hand in his pocket and felt the money Mistress Corin had given him. *Great Glyph! What is going on?*

"Now move your lazy behind and split some wood!" his father ordered.

Dryn stumbled outside and stood facing the road for a moment, trying to comprehend how extra money had appeared twice now. His father apparently recalled giving him the command to cut wood, and yet, by Dryn's recollection, it had never happened!

He stumbled around the corner of the building toward the uncut logs. He glanced first at the logs and then at the clean pile of cut firewood sitting beside their axe, and then back at the logs. *Hang on...* he stared back at the pile of split wood and his jaw dropped open. The firewood was already split and stacked.

Dryn picked up the axe and looked around. No sign of anyone else. He glared down at the pile again, trying to figure out who had done his job in less than ten minutes.

There was something white fluttering beneath the first chunk of firewood. Bending to examine it, Dryn went cold to the core and it wasn't from the breeze. Beneath the first log was a letter. On the front of it was his name. He tore the letter open and hurriedly scoured the words written there.

> "Dryn,
> I have finished the wood for you to give you some time. It is important that you begin your practice of magic today, so please do exactly as is written here. Your father will not check on you for some time. Go now to the Arbydn Green and you will find more instructions near the old burrow where you and Keyth once played. Please, do this immediately, and I will explain as much as I can."

Once again there was no signature. Dryn glanced around the yard again, and back towards the road, but there was no sign of anyone he didn't recognize. He stared at the wood and shuddered. *What is going on? Glyphs guard me... what is happening here?*

He folded the letter and walked into the street. The Arbydn Green was a grassland northwest of the village, named after the Magistrate's family line. Dryn looked back at his house. There was no indication of a change inside. His father probably wouldn't check for a while, and Dryn could be out of the village by then. He'd come back once he read this next letter, and it wouldn't be a problem to his father if he ran off for an hour or two. He had already done enough work, considering the delivery *and* the mysterious cut firewood.

Master Corin had his boots ready. Dryn strapped his old sandals to his belt. He would keep them in his room as an extra pair, but he didn't intend to return to his room for a while. He laced up the boots and paid the cobbler.

The gate of the village was open during the day, even with the thieves plaguing the countryside. Dryn hiked briskly along the west road, and tried to ignore the fleeting sensation of eyes watching him. He wondered if the brigands roamed this far north. He hoped not.

The icy wind carried light flakes of snow, and his frosted breath trailed behind him as he walked through it. Winter was coming, harsh as it had ever been. With it came a threatening blizzard, a mystery unfolding faster and crueller than any storm; Dryn's life seemed like a puzzle to him now. Since the night of Artemys Gothikar's death, nothing made sense. There was doubling money, glyphs scrawled in his skin, and now a chore that had been completed as if by the same mysterious author of the letters.

The person who wrote the letters would have answers. Dryn knew that much. If only he knew who it was, or had some way to communicate with him. It was a sorcerer of some kind. There was little doubt of that; the wizard knew of the symbols in his chest, something he had told and shown no one. The magician also had a precursory knowledge of Dryn's life. He knew the childhood burrow in which Keyth and Dryn had played as children.

It took Dryn just over ten minutes to get there. He strode up the first rise of Arbydn Green and found the fields empty as he had suspected they would be. Not many villagers left the town because of the rumoured and real danger. The burrow was located on the northern side, where the forests finally bested the fields. It had been made by a bear, they had figured; it was a massive dug-out hole in the earth at the edge of the woods.

Dryn leapt smoothly down into the pit, his boots absorbing the force of landing in the soil. He turned around, and found a third letter pressed into the dirt. He pulled it out and wiped it clean. Yanking himself up, he stepped out of the burrow and walked away from the forest. It was almost warm in the muted sunlight gleaming through the clouds, and he sat down on the grass.

The letter was the longest yet. Again, there was no signature.

"Dryn,
"War has begun!
"It is not yet open combat, yet there is no doubt it is a war. A dozen magicians have died; some were powerful, others were simply in the wrong place at the wrong time. It is unclear who is behind the struggle, but they are deadly and efficient.
"War has begun, Dryn, and you must learn to fight."

Dryn lowered the letter from his sight and looked around. *A war?* There had not been a war in decades. Long before Dryn's life began. *Maker protect us all… a war?*

He glanced back down and kept reading.

"You are probably wondering why. There are others, you would say. More adept for this than you. But that would be incorrect. There are others, but none quite like you. The words in your chest are a kind of a blessing, an enchantment. You have been unable to translate it because it is far more advanced than the glyphs of your book.

"The spell that Artemys put on you makes you nearly invincible, Dryn. It is literally a ward – or protection – against death by mortal injury. You cannot be slain by any blade or arrow. Your weakness is other magic. In other words, it will not guard you against magical attacks. The glyphs written upon you are not the gift of magic, which leaves no physical markings. This is a separate spell Artemys devised.

"And this is where we begin to understand Artemys Gothikar's motives. Someone has decided to end the era of magic. If you think it through, it is entirely possible to destroy the ability to use magic. If no one is left to pass it on, magic will cease.

"Magicians are being hunted and killed, and so begins the war between magic and might."

Dryn took a deep breath and absorbed this. *Immortality?* he wondered. *I am invincible to harm? I cannot die except by magic?* He was breathing deeply. First, a war. Second, this 'ward' that guarded him. If not for that haunting night, he would rip up this preposterous letter and throw it away in the wind.

But what of Artemys' motives? He kept reading, scanning over the words.

"Artemys was scorned in the end, betrayed, abandoned and killed. He was probably furious at everyone else, and so he gave you magic as a curse. If the war continues, you will be hunted to the ends of the world. He gave you protection from injury so you can watch every last magician suffer; no one can kill you except a magician.

"You might first assume that it is indeed a great protection, because if all other wizards die, you would become invincible. But this is not the case. Even those who cannot use glyphs can use tokens – magical items that are charged with spells. Our enemies have even swindled the assistance of one order of magicians to aid them in fighting magic. Pure deceit. I assure you, they plan to slay these magicians when no others are left.

"Therefore, you must be careful. Tensions will only escalate in the land, and battles will soon break out as the initial conflicts boil over into war."

He could recall Artemys' words that night: "The world has spited me. No one understood my intentions." The letter was truthful once more, and Dryn found himself in awe of whomever it was sending them. He flipped the page of the letter, revealing more written on the other side.

"Your training begins now. The last time I was in Kryden District, I warded the field in which you now stand. You can practice magic as long as you are in this field. I warn you not to use it outside of the ward, for each time you do so you risk attracting the attention of our enemy.

"Written below is the glyph for an air blast. You will notice the single glyph combines numerous other ones you have read about. Every spell must have basic components: an element or effect, a type, an amount, and a length of time. The more complex the spell, the more dangerous it is, so I impress upon you the importance of starting simply.

"Practice the spell below until you understand its power and purpose thoroughly. Eventually you can try adding in a different element, but do not remove the air glyph. Any attack spell without air will not move through the air.

"Train until the time is right. I will be in contact with you to give you more spells. If you need to contact me, leave a note in the burrow and I will read it at my next opportunity."

Dryn stared at the letter for a while, thinking. *I can contact him?* He was relieved that at last he had a way of replying. He could ask questions, and in that he found security of a kind. But then he returned to the other contents of the letter. *There is a war? I am...* immortal?

He knew that wasn't what the letter said. *Immune to death by mortal injury,* he reminded himself. *Magic can kill me. Magic!*

"Maker burn me," he cursed out loud. "Magic?" he asked the air. "What am I doing here?"

He stood up and started walking across the field, heading for the village. *Fool,* he told himself. *You see someone die in the forest and you start going insane.*

"I've gotta get a hold of myself," he decided. "Enough of this children's tale."

He was more than halfway across the field when he paused. *What if...* he thought to himself. *What if it does work... the spell?* He reached into the fold of his cloak and opened the letter once more. At the bottom of the second page was a combined glyph, as the letter explained. Beneath that was written the words of the spell, to activate the glyph, and a note on how to use it.

I can't give up without even trying... he told himself.

He followed the instructions, and traced the glyph in a patch of dirt where winter had eaten the grass back. It took him a few seconds; he had to get it right. He stood up, glanced at the glyph and at the one on the page. "You must give the spell direction, unless you want a whirlwind around you," he read out loud. He felt like laughing at himself. "Am I really going through with this?" he questioned under his breath.

He raised his hand and pointed across the field. Lifting the page, he read aloud, *"bor'sab irkono shokin ob."*

Instantly, a fierce wind tore through the field, parting the grass in front of him and scattering lazily falling snowflakes. The torrent lasted only a few seconds, and was finished. A clear trail of dirt and weeds was strewn in a straight line from his hand. The wind had ruffled his hair a bit as though it might have come from behind him. Or perhaps it couldn't all focus in one direction.

"Did... did that... did that just happen?" he stuttered, out loud. He burst out laughing in disbelief. Anyone walking by would probably think him a crazy man. But thankfully no one was anywhere near the Green.

It must have been coincidence... "It must have..." He ran a few steps east until he found a clear patch of earth again. This time he traced the symbol faster, and he knew the words to say without reading them. The 'starter's treatise on glyphs' had taught him that much.

He raised his hands and incanted the spell. Once again a sudden blast of air cut through the tall grass and the dirt was picked up and scattered throughout the air. "By the Maker," he whispered. "Glyphs really work. I have magic. The letters are real!"

He performed the wind strike a few more times, wondering what it would be like to blast someone back with it. He couldn't picture the spell killing someone, but it would be useful in keeping someone away from him. He became faster as he practiced. The glyph would be drawn in seconds and the words would roll off his tongue incomprehensibly. Blast after blast tore across the field. He tried it at different angles, and a series of attacks at once. At the end of a set of spells he knelt with both arms held sideways and the blast divided, tearing away in two directions.

He stood up, looking around him. "It's real!" *What about the other glyphs?* His hand felt Artemys' ward through the fabric of his shirt. *Is it real as well? How do I test that?*

He drew the knife he had always worn and at first intended to inflict some injury on himself, to see if he really was invincible to it, but he couldn't bring himself to do it. Eventually he sheathed the blade again, and thought through all of his knowledge of glyphs from that book. He knew how to perform a spell now, and the letter had said he could modify it.

Fire. He smiled. Let's try fire.

8

Steel was not uncommon in the packed streets of Avernus. The smallest of the three Imperial Cities, the metropolis sprawled through the rocky terrain west of the coast. Almost all of the citizens carried weapons or tools of some sort, but not many could compare to the sight of the Prince Periander Gothikar. He rode through the cobbled streets at this time in a robe only one of the Three Princes could afford; on his back was *Korbios*, perhaps one of the finest swords ever forged. Gleaming on the flat of the blade was a series of glyphs that granted the wielder an advantage. Very few wizards knew such an enchantment; Prince Gothikar's older son had made his father proud with the gift.

Rising above the dense streets of the city was the Palace of Avernus, three towers piercing the skies of Midgard. The crowds parted for the Prince with hushed voices pointing at their hero and ruler. Impatient, Periander urged his mount forward, a clatter of hoofs on the damp cobblestones. A dank breeze trailed its way down the street, carrying on it the odour of bread, blood, and smoke.

A stable boy took the bridle and led the horse away, after Periander had climbed from his saddle and strode towards the castle's massive oaken doorways. A porter had opened it before he reached it; a servant took his gloves and removed his boots once he stepped out of them. An attendant strode through the dank palace hall and announced to the Prince, "He has arrived. He is in your waiting room, my liege."

"It's about time," Periander snapped. He glanced in a mirror as he passed, and composed his wrinkled face. He kept his chin clean shaven, but whiskers had shadowed his skin with grey stubble. "My red robe, please," he ordered. A servant draped it around his shoulders as he made his way briskly through a winding corridor.

He knew his palace like the words scrawled on his emblem. "Korbios decadus abyron." Conquest stands alone. He passed the portraits of his ancestors and nodded to the sculpture of his father beside the door of his sprawling chambers.

"Wine, sir?"

"Not now," he hissed, and waved a meek attendant away. He stormed into his living chamber and roared, "Pyrsius, you have gone too far! I should have you thrown in the stockade!"

"Ah, my lord Prince Gothikar..." a robed man murmured from where he lounged in a cushioned chair. "I – "

"On your feet when you address me!" Periander growled. He walked past the chair to his desk in one corner, and pulled the scabbard of *Korbios* from his shoulder.

"Of course, *sir*," Pyrsius replied, standing up and turning to face the Prince. "I received your summons."

"I have heard rumours. The Delfie school massacred? Magicians hunted and slaughtered? Olympus reports the entire guild has vanished!" Periander breathed. "And perhaps you know where Artemys has gone? Tell me this isn't your doing, Pyrsius!"

Pyrsius casually lowered the hood from around his face. There was a small curve to his lips, a quaint smile of sorts. "I am only getting started."

Periander slammed the sword down onto the wooden surface of the desk, knocking other tools out of the way. A pewter cup rolled off the table and clattered onto the floor. An incoherent curse left Periander's lips. As a servant knelt to scoop up the mug, he bellowed, "Get out!"

Breathing harshly, he waited until the iron hinged doors thudded shut and he was alone with Pyrsius. His voice came out rugged as he growled, "Give me one reason not to have you hanged, you treacherous leech!"

Pyrsius cleared his throat and a shadowy figure walked out from the corner of the room. He was wearing a dark robe, a hood and brandishing a sword. "I was hoping it wouldn't come to this."

"You!" Periander sputtered, "You would capture your own father?"

"Please don't make this personal..."

Periander was speechless. He walked back towards his desk and the sword. "I don't understand why, Pyrsius?"

"You don't?" There was laughter. Periander drew the sword. Pyrsius lifted a small grey stone and smiled.

"Korbios decadus abyron... I stand alone."

"You bastard!" Periander shouted, "You – "

Then the token broke between Pyrsius fingers, crumbled dust piling on the floor like hourglass sand. A gleaming glyph spread across the front of Periander's torso and he found himself paralyzed.

"You would know," Pyrsius replied to the outburst, "wouldn't you, Father?"

9

Breaking the rough horizon, the sun gained its hold on the sky and fought to rise above the world. The clouds tried to block it; fog rose from the sea only to be burned away in the onslaught of its might. Only one opponent claimed the world back from it, only one enemy could block out the heat of the sun: winter.

It was snowing in Kryden. Dryn was in the field again, even as the sun climbed its early morning journey. As he walked towards the burrow to check for letters, he gave the snow a blast of wind, tearing a trail through the snow-filled air. He had left the moment he awoke, telling his father he was going for a walk in the snow. Smiling to himself, he drew a different glyph in the snow, including the symbol for fire; this time he included, *"Bor tal'oken...",* instead of just '*bor*.' A burst of fire tore into the air and Dryn felt himself warmed momentarily. Droplets of water spattered into the snow, sizzling with a burst of steam between the hot and cold.

He was eager to read the next letter. He had left correspondence of his own in the burrow, as he had been told he could. He wondered how the wizard knew to check, or even how the checking happened? Dryn hadn't seen any strangers in town. That implied the letter's author wasn't anywhere in Kryden District, so how then did he receive messages? Perhaps a spell of some kind.

He jumped into the pit and slid his hand into the dirt hole in one side. Sure enough, he felt a piece of parchment within. Excited, he tore the letter open and climbed out of the burrow as he read it quickly, ignoring the damp smudges.

"Dryn,

"In answer to your previous letter: I apologize, but I cannot reveal my identity. It is of grave importance to the survival of our kind, to the resistance of this war, and to perhaps the Great Glyph itself, that I remain an anonymous assistant to you.

"You also asked about tokens, and how to make them. In theory, a token is simply a more portable way of using glyphs. You could carry a dozen pieces of paper with spells already written on them; that way you'd only need to say the words to activate the spell, without tracing the glyphs on a surface.

"Self-activating tokens are those you can activate simply by breaking the token itself. This greatly improves the speed of performing the spell, and is useful in combat. These tokens can be made from any object, but are greatly time-consuming to create. A series of other spells must be written and used on the token in order to prepare it, and then you may draw the glyph you wish the token to perform. I will include the details and the afore-mentioned spells in my next letter.

"Today, I have included a modification for the spells you already know. The numbers and glyphs below will allow you to cast strike spells that launch numerous attacks in successive order. I caution you in the use of this method: if you are fighting three opponents and use a spell that launches five strikes one-after-the-next, you must realize that, should you kill your enemies with the first three, you will still have two strikes to put somewhere. This can be dangerous for allies or even yourself if you are not careful with where you direct your magic.

"At the same time, using multiple-strike spells is extremely useful when fighting multiple enemies as you won't need to trace the same glyph again and again during the battle.

"I will send you another letter in the next few days with the spells to create tokens and instructions on their making. Practice the above multiple-strikes and get a feel for their timing."

Dryn folded the letter away into his cloak pocket. He would put it with the growing pile of letters under his cot. He read over the glyphs and the pronunciations for numbers, and tried out an air strike with the symbol for three. As before, a blast of air tore through field; Dryn left his hand pointed forward and a blink later another strike parted the snowfall. Then a third, and Dryn lowered his arm.

That is helpful, he decided. He tried three again, and moved his arm to different directions this time, as though he were attacking multiple targets. He tried his fire strike with it as well. *Very helpful.*

. . .

Keyth awoke with the groaning certainty that today would be a bad day. He laced up the boots Yara had given to him, and smiled when her name entered his thoughts. He pulled on a tunic; not the cleanest of clothing, but he didn't mind. He descended the ladder aware of Master ten Lenter's eye upon his back.

"What today?" he asked, turning to look into the room. The bowyer was seated at the table, and Keyth was surprised to see Master Nalfar in the other chair.

"Oh, 'morning Keyth," Nalfar said.

"Nothing today," Master ten Lenter grunted. "You're staying here. Nalfar and some men are going to the old mine. I'm going along."

"The old mine?" Keyth questioned. "Why?"

"We found them. The thieves are camped out there. We're gonna get them off our land," Nalfar explained. "Now stay in the village, and we'll be back by nightfall."

Keyth could only watch in bewilderment as Master ten Lenter walked out the door with Nalfar. Keyth looked around the empty workshop for a moment; ten Lenter had taken his prized composite bow and his quiver of arrows. He broke his fast from a cupboard of food, and sat at the table for a while. A little ant was crawling across the worn wood. It reached the edge and stared off into space wondering where to go from there.

I should tell Dryn! He shrugged into a cloak and, after peeking out the door, he put a second robe over it. It was a short walk up the nearly deserted streets to the ten Rayth apothecary. He walked past the old sign, now sprinkled white, and pounded on the door.

There was no answer. He knocked again, and still no one came. Disappointed, he tried to think of where Dryn might have gone. He walked back towards the road and noticed fresh footprints in the snow. There was a deep set of worn boot-prints, obviously Master ten Rayth's. *Likely on his way to join this thief chase.*

The other set was a perfect boot print, obviously new footwear. They weren't deep at all, someone light of foot. Dryn. Keyth followed the footprints slowly, but couldn't keep track of them once they reached the road.

He glanced around. *Where in the world would Dryn go on a day like this?* The snow was building up a white surface on his shoulders and in his hair, so he knocked it away and peered through the snow towards the town square. He set off in the direction of Yara's house, but before he got to the first corner, a voice called him, and he turned to see Dryn coming toward him.

"What are you doing out here?" Keyth questioned.

"Just went for a walk in the snow. And you? Shouldn't Master ten Lenter be enslaving you with some cruel work?" Dryn laughed, sounding more lively than he had in a week.

Keyth had to chuckle as well. "No, not today. When I woke up, Nalfar was talking to him. They went out to chase away the thieves... apparently the brigands are camped out by the old mine."

"They went after them?" Dryn questioned, immediately concerned.

"Yes, and I think your father went as well."

Dryn hurried down the street to the apothecary, and Keyth went right behind him. The inside was still warm despite the moss covering the fireplace. Dryn disappeared into his room and re-emerged a moment later. He went to the chest beside his father's work bench; Keyth knew it contained his father's belongings.

From within, Dryn took a foot-long dagger. Keyth's jaw dropped. "What are you doing?" he questioned.

"Going after them," Dryn said, determined. He glanced around the room, checking for anything else to bring.

"Going after them?" Keyth questioned. *Great Glyph, this is insane!* "Are you out of your mind?"

Dryn glanced up at him and laughed, "Maybe. Come on." Without waiting for a reply, he opened the old door, letting a gust of snowy cold air in. Keyth followed mutely, as they made their way out to the road. Shivering after the warmth of the house, he grumbled under his breath.

As they reached the south gate of the village, he asked, "What do you think you're going to be able to do? I mean, aren't we just walking into danger?"

Dryn rounded on him, and said, "If the thieves are dead and our men are okay, we've got nothing to worry about. But if the thieves hold out and our men aren't okay, I'd rather not sit around in the village waiting for bandits to show up and kill us!"

Setting off determinedly onto the road, Dryn didn't wait for his friend. Keyth watched for a moment, thinking through the logic and realizing the truth. Dryn was right. They had to do something. He dashed to catch up to his friend.

10

At first, Dryn struggled with his own logic. He didn't quite know why he was trekking through a blizzard toward the old mine where either thieves or villagers waited. Part of him pleaded to turn back, explaining that the village men could handle it all. The other part of him argued, with a blunt and obvious truth, that he had been gifted with magic.

And if the letters could be trusted, he had also been gifted with near-immortality.

He pressed through the snow, Keyth tagging along beside him. He wondered if he should tell his trustworthy friend to return to the village, but his gut twisted with a sickening realization. If he did so, Keyth would question why Dryn thought he could go on alone. Keyth knew nothing of his powers, and Dryn wanted to keep it that way. He didn't know why exactly, but nagging parts of his mind told him that none of this was actually happening. He didn't entirely believe it himself, so why would Keyth?

Protected from the snow by the new boots, he felt entirely able to walk miles, even in this weather. Half an hour later he was still alright, however Keyth was tiring. His friend was normally tough and durable no matter the weather, but today Keyth was panting and struggling to keep up. It eventually got bad enough that Dryn stopped to let his companion rest.

"What's got into you?" he asked, "You don't get tired out so easily..."

"No, Dryn... by the Maker... what's got into you?" Keyth demanded, his face confused. "You're fast... and you're tougher or something... You should have worn out long ago."

Dryn was taken aback. He turned to look south into the snow. The river would be close, which meant the mine would be a mile east. *I am quick...* he realized, bewildered. They had made excellent time getting from the village this far.

"I can't go on much further," Keyth told him. "You go ahead... and find the men. I'll come as soon as I can."

"You sure?" Dryn questioned, concerned. "It's dangerous out here," he said, voicing the thoughts that worried both their minds.

"I'm fine," Keyth assured him. "Go on..."

Dryn took a few steps away and paused. "I don't like this," he muttered. A torrent of air whistled through a cranny somewhere in the surrounding woodland, raising a hellish screech.

"What, me?" Keyth questioned. "I'll be alright, I told you! If you're scared... on your own... then wait... 'til I catch my breath."

Dryn nodded. He was more worried about Keyth than the bandits. The power of magic blowing through the meadow earlier was enough to assure him he would be fine on his own. Besides, the letter had said he was invincible. His mysterious trainer had been right about everything so far... he felt he could trust the letters.

"Alright," he told Keyth. "I'll see you shortly..."

"Right!" Keyth called after him, as Dryn set off into the forest.

After trekking so far in the blizzard, Dryn's eyes were beginning to play tricks on him. The thousand flakes of white became a blur, a pattern flickering around him. He traced glyphs in the air with his eyes, connecting snowflakes with invisible lines. Blinking and rubbing his eyes, he tried to clear his head. His boots scraped in the dirt and gravel of a riverbank and he fumbled for a branch near his head. A moment later he found himself lying on his back in the snow above the bank. He had just about walked into the icy river.

Cursing his foolishness, he pulled himself to his feet again. *People die that way,* he reminded himself. He remembered his terror two years earlier when Master ten Lenter's brother had fallen into the river. He had lain on a cot in the apothecary as Dryn's father worked away trying to save him, slowly losing his life as the cold ate away into his limbs. Dryn's father had said that even removing the frostbitten leg would not save him.

Dryn set off again, this time cautious of the snow's hypnosis. He was travelling east now, and was sure he must be getting close to the old stone quarry. Maybe fifteen minutes away.

"Hurry," someone said. "They might be following..."

Dryn froze and looked around him. In this white setting there would be hiding from anyone paying attention. Someone was coming his way and he would have to face them. He lifted the frosty metal blade he carried, so as to look as though he knew how to wield it.

Another voice muttered, "No, they know they hit us hard enough... they'll let us go... damn brigands..."

That last part reached Dryn's ears and he lowered his sword. These weren't the thieves coming, but someone else. Presumably the villagers. *'They hit us hard enough?'* Dryn worried.

"Glyphs, is that you, ten Rayth?" the first voice questioned, and several villagers appeared through the snow. At first Dryn could just make out grey and brown shapes of cloaks, and then their snow-coated despondent faces.

"It's Dryn," he told them.

"What are you doing out here?" the first voice asked, and he recognized the speaker as Nalfar himself. The man's clipped beard was weathered and his eyes wide with adrenalin, and perhaps shock.

He noticed a few of the men carried a makeshift stretcher between them. The blacksmith was lying unconscious on it. *Maker guard me... we lost...* he realized with sickening dread.

"Is my father here?" he asked, rather than answer them.

Nalfar looked at one of the others. Magistrate Arbydn was among them and he stepped forward to Dryn. The mayor was pale beneath his beard, and Dryn noticed he drew his breath in uneven gasps. "Listen, Dryn," the man murmured. "The attack didn't go quite as planned..."

"Where's my father?" Dryn insisted, desperate now. *Maker, please, no...*

"We lost a lot of good men back there, Dryn. We have to get back to the village..."

"Where is he?" Dryn hissed, panicked. "You left him back there?"

"We had to get out before we lost more..." Arbydn explained, as if trying to reason it out. "Your father – "

"No! You left him!" Dryn was terrified. And furious.

"Listen, Dryn," Arbydn snapped, sternly. "You must come with us, back to the village. Did you come alone out here?"

Dryn stepped back, breathing deeply. He was trying to figure out what to do. He needed to go. He needed to find his father and save him. If it involved fighting, so be it! *I've got magic, and by the Maker, I'm not giving up without using it!*

"Keyth ten Arad came as well..." he told them. He glanced around at the falling snow, the mesmerizing white flakes. *I need to get away from the villagers,* he decided. *That way I can return to the old mine without pulling them back into it...* "We split up. He's... right over there," Dryn pointed northeast as though he knew exactly where his friend was.

Arbydn glanced where he had gestured and then looked back. "Are you sure you're alright?"

Dryn nodded.

"Well then... You go fetch him and meet up with us. Go straight back to the village!"

"Y-yes sir..." Dryn stammered. "I'll get him right away..." Without looking back, he walked in the direction he had pointed and stumbled through knee deep snow. Forcing himself to keep going, he prayed the men behind him didn't suspect anything.

After five minutes, he glanced back at last and, thankfully, there was no sign of the villagers. "Alright, Dryn," he said out loud to himself, "Now what...?"

He set off eastward, still not thinking clearly. *My father... Telper ten Rayth never harmed them... what happened out there? Maker... please let him be okay... Please... I have to get there quickly...*

He stumbled back onto higher ground where the snow wasn't so deep. The leaves under the snow were slippery and he fell once as he lost his footing. Shortly after getting up, he found himself looking out over the ridge of the quarry. Below him snow-coated colors of grey and bronze outlined the rocky pit. The woodlands parted to north and south and, stretching for a half mile ahead of him, empty snow-filled air drifted above the small canyon. On the northern slant of the quarry was the old mine, a hollowed out tunnel carved into the earth like a cave.

Dryn let himself down the rock face slowly, scrabbling at the rough earth with bare fingers. Icy cold and now bruised, he found himself on the floor of the quarry. There was no sign of any bandits nor his father.

Making his way across the open would have been a foolish idea, so he set off towards the mine by following the rocky cliff he had just descended. It ran northward and then bent east, eventually reaching the mine. He kept low, scared he might be spotted. It was far slower travel than even trekking through the deep snow.

Dryn forced back his fear and kept going, stumbling across the rough terrain until he was nearly upon the mine. He could make out muted voices, but not what they said. The cliff he was following dipped at an awkward angle until it became vertical adjacent to the cave's opening. He was forced to descend onto the open floor of the quarry and, after ten paces, he heard a shout. "Oy! Someone's there!" He dashed back for the cliff wall, amdist the sounds of stones and commotion. There were multiple echoes of a loud snapping sound and then a deadly quiet.

Dryn felt something impact his right shoulder, and found himself tumbling through the dirt and snow. His vision faded and he nearly lost all sight. The icy cold snow filled his gaping mouth and he rolled to one side, trying to get back up.

Then the pain hit him.

It was like a waterfall, a thousand pounds of water crushing him, except it burned like fire. His muscles knit together, pulling his skin taut. His eyes clenched closed against his will, and his mouth snapped shut. He tasted blood and rolled in the snow, writhing in agony. It didn't stop. For what seemed like hours, he was ravaged by pain. He didn't black out; he knew from the pain he should have, or gone into shock. He longed for the relief that would bring. Instead his mind remained vividly aware of *everything*.

Fighting the pain, he forced himself to roll up onto his knees. All around him the snow was soaked with blood. It was like the old man in the forest; Dryn had never seen so much. It was splattered brightly across the battered surface of the snow, and had melted steaming trails into the ice.

He groped for the source of the agony and found a crossbow bolt buried in his shoulder.

11

During the first two fortnights of his raid, Kobias Hutl couldn't believe his luck. The Kryden District was undefended against any sort of assault. Cautiously, Kobias and his men had started robbed outlying farms and posts. Slowly he began more aggressively targeting any resources outside of the villages themselves. North of the river seemed safer; Greater Kryden had sent armed guards to search its countryside.

But north of the Syroh... there he discovered open lands for the taking. Now he found villagers at the doorstep of his mine headquarters. The nerve! His men had dealt with them easily. They had lured the fools into the mine itself, until, deep in the cave, an ambush had destroyed the villagers.

A few others had escaped, of course. Kobias didn't care about them. There were few enough of them now that Kobias was contemplating an assault on the village itself perhaps. There were no guards to speak of, and the remaining village men could put up little struggle. He should act now, before Greater Kryden interfered again. A few survivors remained after the day's assault; he could use them for ransom.

"Oy, someone's there!" echoed down the mine shaft, and Kobias stood up from his wooden bench. *Sounded like it came from the opening itself.*

He set off toward the surface and got a few paces when he heard someone screaming. It was a youth's voice... not one of his men. *Another villager?* he wondered. *Were any of them foolish enough to attack again?* He quickened his pace to find out and reached the quarry after a few moments. Several of his men were also heading that way to learn what the commotion was.

Sure enough, there was a villager flailing on the ground, blood tattooing the snow with a gruesome halo around the body. Another cry left the young man's mouth and Kobias was surprised he was still alive. "Just the one of them..." Argin, his most trusted man, told him. "Cursed fool."

The villager was groping for the bolt protruding from his shoulder, as though to pull it out. "Someone put him out of his misery," Kobias muttered, hands on his thighs. He turned towards the cave and walked back through his footsteps. *Cursed stuff, snow... There's so much of it this far north...*

He had just crossed the threshold of the mine when a huge mass flew past him and crashed across the rocky floor. It scraped along the ground until it hit the wall, and Kobias didn't realize it was a body until it came to a halt.

Gaping in shock, he stepped towards it; as he did so, shouting arose behind him and a chorus of crossbows twanged loudly. This resulted in more screams. The cries of his own men.

Whirling, he fumbled for his sword and charged towards the entrance of the mine. The first thing he saw was the boy standing sturdily on his feet, one hand held outward. The second thing he saw was Argin on fire, clawing in the snow and leaving a trail melted through the ice behind him.

"Maker blind me," he swore. The boy moved his arm and a fireball burned through the air, catching another man and scorching his life away. Kobias cursed his luck and ran back into the mine. Behind him his men burned and bled, their screams chilling him to his rattling bones.

He sprinted towards the prisoners. There were three; only two were conscious. He grabbed one of them and snapped, "You didn't tell me you had a damn earth-spawn spell-caster!!!"

He threw the man aside and kicked him in the gut. Drawing his knife, he grabbed one of the others. "Tell me his name or I kill your friend here!"

They both shook their heads. "There is no 'spell-caster'," one of them stammered, trembling in terror and pain.

Kobias plunged the knife into the man on the ground and turned back to the other. "Last chance, fool. Tell me his name or his true glyph."

"I don't understand..."

Kobias hefted the knife in one hand and stepped back. "Village magicians tell their true glyph! It's the only way to gain the village's trust! By the Maker, what is it?" he demanded in fury.

The man shook his head in confusion and Kobias backhanded him to the earth.

Abruptly a torrent of wind hit him like a soldier's shield, and he was thrown across the room; the villager was knocked away as well, but the blow had focused on Kobias. He landed on his feet, groaning from the impact with the wall, and dropped to his knees, fumbling for the knife on the ground.

12

Maker save me was his only thought, repeated again and again in Dryn's head as he blasted man after man with fire or wind. He fought his way into the cave and found a man with a sword almost upon him. He jumped aside, and scrawled the glyph for three fire blasts in the dirt beside his boots. The words left his mouth in a hiss and a bolt of fire smashed the man in the chest. His clothes afire, the brigand stumbled back and clawed in the dirt as his life thrashed away in a crackle.

Dryn had cast away the crossbow bolt in the snow and was only just realizing the truth. He was, in the words of the letter: 'impervious to death by mortal injury.' But he certainly wasn't impervious to pain. *Will I bleed to death?* he wondered, but knew he couldn't. *I cannot die from injury.*

His shoulder was still an open wound, and pain was still raking sharp claws across his flesh. It took focus and concentration just to walk, to fight through the agony and force one foot in front of the next.

It was tricky to get the numbers right. Two bandits had been in the entrance of the cave, so he had chosen to do three fire blasts. Better too many than too few, as they were his only weapon, since he had lost his father's knife in the snow somewhere outside. The first two fire blasts had destroyed his opponents, so he let the extra one sear a black circle into the dirt.

He eventually reached the back of the cave, where another brigand stood over the body of a dead the village baker, speaking to two others. Dryn traced glyphs in the cavern wall and raised his hand, giving the man a gust of air. As the man grunted and landed on his feet, Dryn used a fire strike, which not only set him on fire, but, because of the angle, crushed the bandit into the earth.

Kneeling only caused the skin of his shoulders to crease and another wave of pain hit him; he almost fell over again, but he balanced, and checked the pulse of the villagers. Two lived, both unconscious, and another was dead. Master Desser, the innkeeper, moaned quietly. Dryn's father was the other, *Thank the Maker!* but had a vicious gash along his right side.

Frantically, Dryn stood up and tried to clear his head, a difficult thing to do with such an injury in his flesh. The fires he had created crackled as a million thoughts passed through his mind. *How do I heal my father? Get him back to the village? How do I heal myself? Wait until it heals on its own? Can I endure that? How do I explain all of this to the village?*

There was no way he could carry two unconscious villagers back to town. He would need to get others to come help him. He stumbled through the tunnel, sometimes coughing on dust that fell from the weak beams supporting the ceiling. The pain in his shoulder had become a dull throbbing; his back was stiff with blood that had now frozen in the cold, weighing heavily on the cloth of his shirt.

Soon he reached the opening of the cave into the quarry. He almost walked past the fluttering white parchment held nearby beneath a rock. *Another letter! This is madness!*

He knelt, grunting against the agony, and yanked it from under the stone. Standing again to ease the tension on his shoulder, he tore it open and scanned the familiar writing.

"You fool! You have changed everything in your rash attempt of heroism! It is more than your own skin on the line, or the lives of your family and friends!

"You will find another letter upon your arrival home.

"For now, I will help you out of this crisis. Below is written two healing spells. The first will heal yourself: I warn you that using spells on oneself is extremely draining. When using an air strike, the spell harnesses the energy of the air. When using a spell on yourself, it will harness your energy.

"The second spell heals others. It is also draining, as it draws energy both from the caster and the person receiving the spell. I suggest you heal yourself first, and then attend to your father. Return with haste to the village."

Dryn carefully read the wording of the spell and scrawled the glyphs in the dirt at the mine entrance. Incanting the words, he pointed one hand towards the wound, not knowing what else to do. Abruptly, every muscle in his body clenched at once and pain lanced throughout his form. His shoulder felt as though someone were pinching it. When the pain faded, he felt exhausted. Sighing, he touched his fingers to his shoulder to find the skin unbroken. His shirt was still soaked with blood, but there wasn't a mark on him anymore.

Taking a breath, he stumbled back down the mine shaft, and realized that his feet no longer ached. The spell had healed all pain he had felt, even his bruised toes.

He kept going until he reached the unconscious villagers and the burning corpse of the bandit nearby. He knelt over his father and performed the other healing spell, quickly tucking the letter away once he had finished with it. His father awoke moments later and sat up dazed. "Maker guard me, what happened?"

"It's alright," Dryn murmured.

"Oh, Dryn! I thought we were going to die... Last thing I remember was fighting a bandit... what happened?"

"Uh.... Most of the villagers turned back, but the thieves were dealt with," Dryn explained. *I can't heal Master ten Desser now.... How would I explain that to my father?*

"I thought I was... wounded," his father muttered. "Didn't I get stabbed?"

Dryn helped his father to his feet and told him, "No, I just found you unconscious here, and waited until you woke up. I can't carry Master ten Desser on my own..."

"Right, of course," his father said. "We should get back to the village..."

"We should hurry," Dryn added. Together they lifted Master Desser up. When his father asked about the other villager, Dryn explained that the man was dead.

Dryn's father noticed the bodies of the brigands, and once Dryn feared he might ask how they were killed, but they left the quarry behind in silence. Hidden from his father in Dryn's pocket, the letter felt like a brand burning against his skin.

13

Torrents of snow prickled Keyth's skin as he watched Dryn disappear into the blizzard, heading south toward the river. His friend seemed unaffected by the cold, while Keyth was freezing. After waiting close to half an hour, Keyth followed in Dryn's footsteps, and almost immediately was met by a group of villagers.

"ten Arad?" a thick voice questioned, and Keyth noticed it was Magistrate Arbydn who stepped forward.

Feeling a familiar connection after the night they found Dryn, Keyth spoke quickly, "Yes sir, Keyth. Did you come across Dryn? He went on ahead of me..."

"Ahead of you?" This was Nalfar, separating himself from the crowd of frozen villagers with his apparently shocked outburst. "That fool said he was going to fetch you since you were nearby!"

"Nearby?" Keyth stuttered. "I'm sorry, I'm confused..."

Arbydn clarified, "We ran into Dryn east of here, along the riverside." He glanced back into the white blur of falling snow; vertical brown lines were all that could be seen of the dense forest around them. "He told us you were nearby and then went off to fetch you..."

Nalfar whispered in horror, "He went off alone? He was supposed to find you and head back to the village!"

"How many times can that boy lose himself in the forest?" Arbydn questioned, frustrated. "It's too dangerous out here for him to roam on his own. Nalfar, let's pair up the men and start a search. Meet up at the village..."

Nalfar proceeded to issue directions to villagers while Keyth asked the Magistrate, "The attack on the brigands, I assume it didn't go well?"

Arbydn's eyes narrowed grimly and he muttered, "Not well at all. We lost a few good fellows back there... Dryn's father among them."

Keyth froze. Dryn's father was gone? *Maker shield him,* Keyth thought about Dryn. *And guard us all... our village is without a healer... the bandits have beat us.* "What can I do?" was his first question, spoken in a rush before he had decided on any course of action.

The Magistrate quickly thought about it, instructing him, "Head back to the village and make sure Dryn didn't return. He could be grieving for his father and unable to get near the mine. He wouldn't know where to go with his father not at home."

"Of course, sir... And if he's not in the village?"

"Then you better stay put! I don't want to scour the woodlands for two foolhardy youths..." Arbydn grumbled. He lumbered through the snow towards Nalfar and a couple of villagers, and Keyth turned away north.

Once again the hike had him winded, fatigued and frozen by the time his recently spotless boots stumbled upon the threshold of the city's south gate. There was a merchant wheeling his cart out; they passed each other without a word and Keyth strode through the otherwise deserted streets. *Come on, Dryn...* he was thinking. *What are you thinking? Running off on your own?* This pondering was contrasted by the shocking reminder that Master ten Rayth had been lost during the attack against the bandits... *Great Glyph... is he really gone?*

Keyth soon found himself in front of the apothecary. There was at least an inch of snow on top of the worn sign, and the rotted wood was coated with frost. He stumbled through the snow towards their door and gave the bleak grey sky a baleful look as it continued covering him in white. The shop's door was unlocked and opened inward on well-oiled hinges. The shutters were closed over the windows, and would likely remain that way until winter had passed.

Keyth grabbed the lantern from beside the doorway and pulled a block of tinder from a pouch at his belt. The tiny flame lit up the small room and led Keyth across to the fireplace. He threw back the moss mat that kept the coals live, and set fire to the pit once more with the lantern.

As heat slowly rose between his spread fingers, he sighed and his limbs began to thaw. Keyth suspected Dryn would have come out to meet him if he was home, but decided to check anyway. Once he was satisfactorily warmed, Keyth crossed to Dryn's door, knocked, then opened it when there was no answer. The room was pitch black and cold. Shivering again, Keyth raised the lantern and stepped inside. There was no sign of Dryn in the small space, but Keyth did notice something unusual.

There was a piece of paper sealed in a folded envelope lying on Dryn's cot. It was addressed to his friend. Puzzled at who might leave a letter on Dryn's pillow, Keyth let out a grunt as his cold behind sunk into the straw mattress.

Recalling the time Dryn had shown him a love note from a village girl, Keyth was quite sure his friend wouldn't mind his curiosity. And in these pressing circumstances, since Dryn's father might not return, Keyth knew he had to look. He slowly unfolded the letter and began to read.

> "Dryn,
> I cannot understand or believe this rash thing you have done. Not only did you risk everything to save your father, but you have likely set in motion an extremely dangerous series of events."

To save your father? Keyth wondered, the hairs rising on his neck. He glanced at the bottom of the page for a signature, but the letter had no name. Riveted, Keyth read on:

> "Using your powers outside of my warded field has likely alerted our enemies of your presence. The northlands are currently being searched for the remains of Artemys Gothikar, as is most of the realm. If any of these enemies sense your use of magic, they will be at the doorstep of Kryden within days. They will stop at nothing to exterminate every last magician they can find."

Magician? Keyth reread. He stared at the printed letters and looked around the room in confusion. *Magicians? 'Artemys Gothikar'? 'Your use of magic'?* Keyth reread that sentence. The letter was addressed to Dryn and *had* been left in his room. *Dryn ... knows magic?* Keyth wondered.

He blinked, holding the letter aside to rub two fingers on the bridge of his nose. He froze. His weight on the cot had creased the side of the mattress, lifting the bottom slightly at one end. Beneath the pallet, he noticed a number of similar letters, spread in the dirt and obviously hidden by Dryn's own hand.

Keyth set aside the letter he had been reading without finishing it and opened the first of these hidden letters. It was addressed to Dryn in the same fashion as the others. Dryn was involved in something dangerous, Keyth knew it. He dropped the letter back beneath Dryn's cot and took a deep breath. *I should just ask him about it.* He stood up. *But what if Dryn believes that? Believes in magic?* It was a mad thought. Sure, they had included magic in their fantasies as children, when they fought fictional renegades in the woodlands. *But what if Dryn really believes in magic? What if he's going to fight the bandits!!!*

He grabbed the letters beneath the bed again. Within twenty minutes he was standing in the middle of the room staring at a pile of open papers on the bed. The lantern was set on the dirt floor, flickering candlelight around the dark room.

He didn't know what to think. He couldn't keep his mind in any straight direction, and his only definitive knowledge was that Dryn was involved in something far more serious than he had initially thought. Whether or not magic existed was an object of fable and speculation. Whether or not Dryn could use magic was a confusing argument within Keyth's mind. Whether or not this war truly was endangering the fate of glyph-users... Keyth had to pause and wonder what the Maker had thrown into their petty village.

In the end he picked up the newest letter and finished reading what he hadn't before.

> "You must leave Kryden. You must leave at once. If you love anyone who lives within the town walls, the enemy will find them. You must take only that which you need and depart without leaving any trace of where you might go. THEY MUST NOT FIND YOU. You must drill this deep into your mind, Dryn. If they catch you, they'll kill you. Take what you need and leave Kryden now.
> "I will leave another letter at the Iron Crossing Inn of Greater Kryden with instructions of where to go. If

you value your life, or those of your friends, heed this
letter and give it every ounce of trust you've given any
of those before it. Leave the village while you still
can, and don't stop running.
"My only fear is that you do not read this in time."

Keyth dropped the letter and absorbed the shocking
instructions Dryn was supposed to read. Could he allow Dryn to
read them, now that he had first? If he did, would Dryn truly
leave Kryden, following only a mysterious stranger's advice?
Surely, Dryn wasn't foolish enough to accept these ... fantasies...

A thud outside startled Keyth, and he hurriedly sheathed
each letter back into its envelope. It was only someone beating a
rug in the neighbour's yard.

All the letters still lay around him though, and Dryn would
see them when he walked in. Soon he had them all tucked away
beneath the bed once more, all except the newest letter. Keyth
clutched it in his hand, wavering with indecision. He knew he
couldn't believe a single thing he had read. Magic? Foolish. A
war? Preposterous. Dryn involved with it all? Downright
madness.

Finally, Keyth tucked the letter beneath his cloak and
closed the door to Dryn's room behind him. The fire had given
the room a cozy warm glow, but it seemed lonely and forsaken
without Dryn's father or Keyth's friend.

Keyth covered the fire with the thick moss mat and without
oxygen, the flames chocked and died. He blew out the lantern
and stepped outside into the freezing cold, shutting the door
behind him. He was relieved to find that the snow had ceased
falling; the cloud-streaked skies churned uncomfortably
overhead, but they had stopped the blizzard at last.

It seemed lately that he couldn't think straight unless he
was in one person's company; he knew the way to Yara ten
Corin's house like the back of his hand, and he set off away
from the apothecary in that direction. He reached the corner to
her street and froze at a loud knocking sound.

Almost against his own will, his head turned to the side
until his chin touched his left shoulder and he was staring back
down the street at Dryn's house. A tall figure stood at the
apothecary door, so dark that Keyth thought he had only seen a
shadow. He couldn't make out details from this distance, but he
knew one thing instantly: this was no commoner of the village.

The man's head nodded slightly, as he began to turn to look down the street, and Keyth dove back into the snow behind a nearby fence. Clawing at the snow he pulled himself back far enough to be positive his feet couldn't be seen. Gasping in terror, he scraped at the boards of the wooden fence until he found a hole.

He put one eye to the opening and stared at the apothecary. The stranger slowly glanced the other way down the street, and then seemed to disappear. Keyth's eyes barely caught the crack of the apothecary door as it shut; the man had glanced cautiously both ways and then stepped inside as fast as Keyth had ever seen someone move.

Maker's Glyph... Maker's Glyph... he prayed, his mind in panic. *Shield me...* was his next wish. *Some part of this is real... Dryn... what've you got us into?*

He crawled on all fours along the fence line until a building obscured the apothecary from view. He sprinted down the street as quietly as he could, now thankful for the muffling snow which he had cursed earlier. He found himself in front of Yara's door and tapped quietly on the wood. *Maker guard me...* he prayed, as he anxiously tapped again.

After a moment that seemed like years, the door opened and Yara's innocent smile greeted him. "Keyth!" she said loudly, "What are you doing here?"

"Shhh," he hissed, and shoved her in front of him as he stepped through her doorway. He closed the wood solidly behind him and stumbled over a bench as he collapsed in front of her window, overlooking the street.

"Well, do come in..." she muttered, sarcastically. "What has gotten into you?"

"QUIET!!" he mouthed, and then whispered, "Someone is in the village..."

"Someone's in the village?" she repeated in shock. Keyth was thankful she now kept her voice low.

"Where's your mother?" he asked, almost under his breath. His eyes were locked on the snowy deserted road.

"Keeping an eye on the shop. My father went on the bandit hunt this morning," she explained in hushed tones. Her wide green eyes regarded him in fear. "They should be back soon; the day is almost gone. What's going on, Keyth?"

"Letters... there were these letters.... magic," he rambled. "Dryn has magic... and there's a hunt... Someone's here for him... and 'his loved ones....' Yara, we have to get out of here, now!"

She held up her hand, questioning, "Magic? By the Three Princes! What are you talking about...?"

"We have to escape..." Keyth repeated. His eyes blinked once and he glanced up at Yara. She was standing beside him, out of sight from the window, wearing a plain green dress that fit perfectly. He turned, and glanced back out the window, jumping as he did so.

There was a man walking slowly down the middle of the street. He wore a pair of full length trousers, over which a tunic dropped almost to his knees. Over the tunic he wore a black jacket; the sleeves cuffed at his hands, but the back dropped, almost like a cloak, around his feet. Upon his feet, Keyth noticed, he wore tall riding boots, dull metal spurs piercing the surface of the snow. On his head, above the raised collar of his jacket, sat a black hat which only accented his trim black beard.

Keyth threw himself back and pulled Yara with him. Soon they were both lying on the wooden floor, Keyth praying like he never had before, and Yara trembling on his shoulder. For many moments they lay there, until at last Keyth risked a peek through the window again.

There was no sign of the stranger. The street appeared deserted once more. Keyth righted the bench he had tripped over on his entrance, and sighed deeply as he sat upon it. A shudder worked its way up his spine and he closed his eyes for a moment.

"Who is he?" Yara whispered.

"I don't know..."

She sat down beside him; her hands slipped into his and she asked, "What does he want?"

"I don't know that either. But I think we need to warn Dryn. Grab a coat."

14

Dobler Rewan had been the household chamberlain of the Gothikar family for twenty years and had never once feared his masters. Now he had become the Prince's *page* as well as chamberlain; he managed the palace affairs in Avernus and at the summer castle. He received and sent messages, he answered every bidding he was given, but he trembled in fear the day Periander Gothikar disappeared.

At first the Gothikar household was in disarray. Some servants left, others stole. Under Rewan's stern direction, calm was eventually restored to the Avernus Palace, although House Gothikar remained without a lord. Artemys, the older son and heir, had vanished months earlier, and now Periander followed in the mystery. A fortnight following Prince Gothikar's disappearance the Nobles of Avernus elected Pyrsius as his heir, to be raised to the status of Prince after a period of forty days, should the former heir not reappear.

With Pyrsius raised to the status of Gothikar heir apparent, Dobler Rewan found himself entering the service of Periander's younger son. Pyrsius was a strange master, giving Rewan some of the strangest jobs he had ever done. Once, he was told to deliver a chest to the city of Eldius, nearly four hundred miles south. He was not permitted to look within the box, but was instructed that should he fall under attack on the road, he must use the contents to defend himself.

Such a seemingly abnormal task soon became his ordinary service.

One day, he was called to his new master's chambers early in the morning, as the sun first peeked over the coastal mountains. Pyrsius sat at the old wooden desk in the study, which had been hand crafted by Periander's grandfather. He looked up at Dobler's arrival, raising his head from his hand and said, "How many commoners do you suppose use magic?"

"I don't quite follow," Dobler stammered. There was only a single candle lit on the desk, the only light source for the entire study; it cast a flickering pale light across Pyrsius' angled features and arched nose.

"Most nobles and lords are listed in Magician's Guild of Olympus. But there isn't a single document I can find that lists commoners who have been given magic," Pyrsius explained, his narrow mouth articulating every syllable. "How would one find such people?"

Dobler had a momentary flashback to the day Prince Periander had given his elder son the blessing of inheritance. Artemys had just finished his schooling, and Periander had told Dobler earlier what he intended. Even as the pronouncement left Periander's lips, Dobler could recall, Pyrsius' features had twisted with a hateful and jealous mask that shocked him. Pyrsius had never been granted magic, let alone inheritance, and resented his father and brother since that day.

"Dobler?" Pyrsius questioned, his eyebrows raised in annoyance.

"Ah, sorry sir..." Dobler murmured, snapping back from his memory. "I was thinking through your question..."

"I didn't ask you to think it through," Pyrsius sneered.

"Again, my apologies," Dobler whispered, bowing his head in submission. He immediately answered, "I suppose each town might have a listing of sorts. I know that here in Avernus resides a Wizard's Coven. They would likely keep in archive such a record of individuals..."

"The Wizard's Coven?"

Dobler nodded. "But a mere commoner's den, my lord. I could send someone to collect a list..."

"Very well. Dobler, you worry me occasionally...." Pyrsius had glanced back down at an open book in front of him.

"My Prince?"

Pyrsius' sharp green eyes flicked up and into Dobler's face for a moment. Dismissively, they fell back to their reading. A moment of silence passed, and Dobler understood Pyrsius would say no more. The heir was peculiar in such a fashion, although it was not Dobler's place to question.

He paced briskly out of the study and, sandals clattering on the stone walk, he made his way toward the courtyard. Through an archway, he descended the battlement stairs into the slowly awakening yard, nearly oblivious to the sun peeking over the horizon.

As he slowly crossed the cobblestone road, he heard a storm of hooves south at the gate. Very few of the palace's inhabitants were awake yet; Dobler wondered who might be on horseback. He was already headed in that direction in search of Aevo to carry out the heir's instructions. Deciding to investigate the rider he had heard, he took a left turn and passed into the bailey.

The man was dismounting as Dobler approached and glanced up with a blank expression. "To whom should I deliver a message... for Lord Gothikar?" he asked quickly, gripping the reins in a gloved hand.

Dobler smiled, "I am the steward. I can deliver your message to him."

The man glanced around for a moment, but the courtyard was nearly deserted. "Very well. It is a message from Commander Rychard of Tarroth who is currently residing at Athyns. He says that an agent operating five hundred miles north has found the remains of Artemys Gothikar and is requesting troops to investigate the locals. He wishes an immediate reply."

Dobler nodded blankly, but something wavered within him. *Troops?* he wondered. He would deliver the message. It was his duty. But he had to wonder in what game Pyrsius had engaged the Gothikar family. Certainly the locals were not involved in Artemys' disappearance, so why the need for troops? *There isn't a war,* he told himself, *and there hasn't been one since Periander's youth.*

But he already knew Pyrsius' reply. Send the troops.

15

It was close to a three hour trek for Dryn and his father to return to the village, bearing the still unconscious Master ten Desser between them. The innkeeper didn't have any visible injuries apart from scrapes and bruises, but Drýn's father pointed out what looked like a massive red rash and said he was probably bleeding internally. That was about all that Dryn's father said for the entire trip, remaining wrapped in ponderous thoughts.

Dryn was exhausted physically and emotionally. First, fighting with a hole in his shoulder had taken most of his energy. Following that, he had performed two healing spells; he was left fatigued and his body weary. Thirdly, besides his physical condition, his head had enough thoughts flying around to become opaque like the blizzard around them. The letters told the truth so far: he couldn't be killed by a mortal wound. That said nothing about feeling pain. *What does this mean?* he asked himself again and again. He had singlehandedly destroyed the thieves, he had been shot by a crossbow, and his advisor had left him another message at the scene of the crisis. Which meant that the mysterious correspondent had been present at the quarry during the battle.

Dryn set his jaw in frustration and helped his father lift Master ten Desser over a snow covered log. *Why is it so important that we don't meet?*

The question remained unanswered as voices called out to them from the forest. A trio of villagers approached, Nalfar among them. After a heated outburst from the latter, Dryn's father explained that he had awoken among the slain thieves when Dryn had shaken him. Nalfar found himself forced to accept the story, realizing there was no other way he could be speaking to Dryn's father. A few moments later, they decided to set off again, and eventually they reached the village, staggering through the smaller door; the larger gates remained barred. Immediately, a commotion of villagers surrounded them.

Master ten Desser was quickly taken by two helpful men, and Dryn's father told him, "I'll have to help him... I'll talk to you later at home."

Dryn nodded. "I'm glad you're alright," he said quietly, smiling as his father stumbled away with the injured innkeeper. Master Arbydn was arguing with Nalfar, and, among the gathering of villagers, Dryn didn't notice Keyth until his friend tugged on one sleeve.

"Dryn," Keyth was saying, his face pale and bewildered. "You have to come with us..."

"What's wrong?" Dryn questioned, glancing at Yara, who was standing at Keyth's side looking equally shaken. "What's going on?" The last time he had spoken with Keyth had been in the forest when they separated.

"We have to leave. *You* have to leave!" Keyth exclaimed. "He's probably seen us... He's probably here already..."

"Slow down!" Dryn commanded, frustrated.

Yara added, "A man is in the village looking for you..."

"A man?" Dryn questioned sharply. *Maybe it's him... The correspondent who's been helping me!* "We don't have to leave..." he told them calmly.

"Great Glyph, you don't understand!" Keyth muttered. "Come away from this crowd," he ordered.

Dryn had no choice but to follow Keyth and Yara away from crowd. Keyth eventually stopped under the eaves of the inn, the closest building to the gate. There were long icicles hanging from the shingles. The afternoon sun had started breaking the clouds apart and water droplets splattered on Dryn's shoulder as he stepped beneath it.

"That man isn't your friend," Keyth warned him, eyes wide.

Isn't my friend? Keyth doesn't know anything about the letters! Dryn thought. *He must mean 'isn't friendly'...* "Don't worry," he assured his friend. "I don't think he means me harm..."

"Damn it, Dryn!" Keyth snapped; Yara flinched at the word. Keyth's hand reached into his robe and reappeared with a crinkled white parchment. "Read it! It was on your bed!"

Dryn grimaced, taken aback by Keyth's words. *On my bed. This is the* next *letter.* He took the paper in shaking hands and wondered, *By the maker, what was Keyth doing in my room?* He opened it quickly and absorbed the words as fast as he could. As his eyes scanned the writing, his heart beat pounded until he thought Keyth surely could hear it. 'Leave the village while you still can, and don't stop running,' he finished, and his eyes blurred past the page. *Leave Kryden? They're coming for me?*

When charging rashly for the quarry to save his father, he had considered everything except this outcome. He had worried about his life at the hands of the thieves, he had worried about magic, he had worried, most of all, for his father. He had *never* thought this magnificent gift of magic would chase him from his home. He hadn't considered the letters when he fought the bandits; if he had, perhaps he would have realized the danger that enemies could sense his magic.

"Someone is *here*," Keyth whispered, desperately.

Dryn took a deep breath. His mind was still reeling. *They've found me? Keyth knows... Keyth knows??* "How much did you read?"

Keyth winced. "All of them," he admitted. "You've got yourself into some pretty mad stuff, Dryn... All of this foolishness... No wonder someone's after you..."

"Foolishness?" Dryn questioned.

Keyth's eyes widened in surprise. "Yes, foolishness!" Leaning closer to Dryn, he mocked, "You think you can actually use magic?"

Dryn stepped away. Did he? Keyth's question brought out all of Dryn's previous doubts. But then he recalled that his father was alive and the brigands lay in their own boiled blood. Keyth wouldn't believe it without seeing it, though. Dryn knew him well enough to realize that.

Yara spoke again, her lips tinted blue in the cold. She was freezing in only a dress, a coat and shoes. She exclaimed, "Forget arguments! Look around, Keyth! You came to warn Dryn!"

Keyth nodded to himself, but it was Dryn who spoke next. "It might be the person who writes the letters..."

His friend frowned and explained, "That letter tells you to leave without looking back, Dryn! Even if the man we saw was the one... he told us to leave! So let's get out of here!"

"Us?" Dryn questioned. "Wait one second... We can't just leave Kryden now!"

"Did you read that letter?" Keyth growled, incredulous. "You *have* to leave! Right now! I'm coming along... he might have seen me.... Either way, I'm returning as soon as you are safe in Greater Kryden."

"Safe? You think I'll be *safe* in Greater Kryden?" Dryn asked sarcastically. "If I start running, I have to expect to 'never stop running....' I'm not ready for that!"

"Maker burn it, Dryn!" Keyth cursed. "I saw that man! I am not *letting* you stay. You must leave and I am going along. Let's get out of here before he shows up!"

Dryn was quiet for a moment, wrapped in thought. The crowd of villagers near the gate had dissipated, and Keyth, Yara and he were the few left. *Leave Kryden?* he pondered. The idea was madness. He had never left the village's surrounding woodlands. *Great Glyph... if this threat is real, though...* The letters hadn't lied yet. Everything he was told was true. *Must I trust it now as well?* He had trusted it about his invincibility, but that hadn't been the full truth. It had said nothing of the pain. *What if I stay?* he found himself wondering. *Could this stranger hurt me?*

But hot on his fingers was the letter Keyth had given him. 'Leave the village while you still can...' *Leave the village...* Keyth said he would go as well. *I'll just leave for now, and return when it's safe...* Dryn told himself. *Just until things calm down.*

"Fine," he told Keyth. "I'll go to Greater Kryden and find safety. Promise me you'll return when I'm safe..."

Keyth nodded. "Fine, I swear it."

"I swear it too," Yara murmured, quiet and sweet.

Both Keyth and Dryn turned on her, stuttering. In that moment, a door thudded nearby and all three of them froze. Dryn put a finger over his lips and put his back against the wall beside them. Sidestepping towards the corner of the wooden wall, he peeked silently towards the front door of the inn.

A tall man was standing in front of it, a long black jacket obscuring his figure. His sharp cheekbones and slick black beard marked him a foreigner. Dryn stepped away from the corner and stopped breathing altogether. He glanced at Keyth and Yara, and mouthed, 'It's him.' His friends paled. Dryn next formed with his mouth the words, 'Run when I say...' and gestured to himself.

They nodded blankly, and Dryn waited for something, anything, to tell him to move. There wasn't a sound though, so Dryn held up three fingers. "Three... two..." he mouthed, but before he could breath 'one', the door of the inn slammed again and Dryn bolted for the gates.

Without closing them behind him, he dashed for the forest cover. Behind him, Keyth and Yara sprinted across the snow, the crunch of their feet breaking the surface after him. Somewhere miles south was the river, and south of that, eventually, the gates of Greater Kryden. Safety.

So far away.

16

Yara ten Corin stumbled through snow that reached above her ankles and clung icily to the skin of her legs. Ahead of her, Dryn raced along as if he knew no obstacle, and behind her Keyth took up the rear. The smooth surface of white blurred past her, every twig and leaf obscured by her stumbling jog; she fought to keep the pace Dryn was setting, as they flew south from Lesser Kryden.

She had never crossed the Syroh River before. She knew there was a bridge; her father made yearly trips to sell his footwear in Greater Kryden, but she had never been that far south. She glanced back over her shoulder to see the walls of her village vanish below a hilltop.

In the murky blue twilight, she and her two friends stood out as vivid black shapes on the white roadway; ahead of her, Dryn was a noticeable shadow lumbering across the cold surface. She glanced back at Keyth and panted, "We're too visible. If we're trying ... to get away... without being seen..."

Keyth glanced back over one shoulder and then he stared at Dryn's shifting back. "Dryn," he rasped. "Stick to the tree line!"

Dryn looked around and realized Yara was right. He slid down the side of the road embankment, clambering through the deep snow, and gestured for them to follow. Moments later they were all running along the edge of the winter woodland, blending in with the dark shapes of the trees; the stars and moon were lost in deep clouds, and the night was quickly blackening.

Several moments later, Yara gasped, "Stop..." and the other two froze to stare at her. "I can't run like this... I'm freezing and exhausted."

Dryn nodded. "I'm exhausted too... After today..." he trailed off, his gaze turning as he stared away from them.

Keyth blinked. "Today?" he asked. "What happened? The villagers said your father was dead, but you returned to the village with him.... We had better keep walking at least." He gestured and Yara set off again, following Dryn's lead.

Dryn remained quiet, until Keyth muttered, "Dryn, tell me you don't believe all the madness in those letters."

Yara could hear the bitter frustration in Keyth's words, and yet Dryn still said nothing. Keyth sighed, and Yara looked back over her shoulder. He scowled and shouldered past her, grabbing Dryn by the arm and turning him round to look him in the eye.

"If you're some earth-spawn magician... then show me!" Keyth snapped. "By the Maker, if you can control these 'glyphs,' you should be able to prove it easily enough!"

"Let go of me, Keyth," Dryn ordered, sternly shaking Keyth's hand from his cloak sleeve. With a pained look, he told his friend, "I'd show you if I could. Trust me. Now that you know, I *want* to show you... so that *I* know I'm not going mad."

"Then why don't you?" Keyth blurted. Yara shot a nervous glance over her shoulder at the road that bent behind them. If anyone was travelling along it, they would surely hear the argument.

"They can sense it. I don't understand how yet. But that's why that man is in the village. I used magic, and he found me," Dryn explained. "I simply cannot show you... I would risk all our lives."

"You already have," Keyth growled, and shoved past Dryn, taking up the lead and heading south along the tree line. Dryn looked at Yara, his brow creased. Frustrated, he set off again in Keyth's footsteps, giving Yara no choice but to follow.

A wind started picking up, whistling loudly through the highest branches and hissing against the needles of stiff evergreens. Yara was freezing, her teeth clattering and her knees threatening to buckle with every step. She didn't know where she stood in their debate. She wasn't sure if she believed the threat itself, or if she simply could not accept the contents of the letters as Keyth had explained them. *How did all this happen?* she wanted to know. *How did Dryn ten Rayth, a poor villager of the northlands, become threatened by some wizard-hunter?*

Finally, they reached the bridge over the Syroh River. Yara crouched beside her friends in the snow and brambled bushes nearby. "Once we try crossing," Dryn was saying, "we'll be in the open. Maybe we should go one at a time."

"Out in the open?" Yara asked. She couldn't help herself, and questioned, "Do we even know he's after us? Do we need to rush? Do we need to *fear* crossing our own district bridge?"

Both Keyth and Dryn stared at her with wide eyes. It was Dryn that spoke up first. "Yara, I know all of this is new and probably quite unreasonable for you... I'm surprised you came along at all..."

"That man was definitely not from around here," Keyth explained. "And the timing of the letter *and* his appearance cannot be coincidence."

"So far," Dryn carried on, "everything within the letters has come true." Keyth glared at him, but Dryn continued. "I've learned they are trustworthy. If they say I should run, then I should. If they say there is danger, then there is. I am going to Greater Kryden, with you... or alone if I must."

Yara blinked. She looked at Keyth who was nodding as though he was connecting with something Dryn had said. If Keyth was going through with it, she felt a little better. She would go with them to Greater Kryden, and then she and Keyth could return to their village. "Alright," she muttered. She felt like swearing as she'd heard them swear; *Great Glyph...* or *Maker burn it...* or even *earth-spawn...* but she couldn't bring herself to push them from her mouth. "I'll do as you say until we reach the city. One at a time over the bridge..."

"Yes," Dryn said. "I'll go first, then you, and then Keyth." At Keyth's agreement, Dryn stood up and scaled the bank of the road. Glancing north towards the village, he nodded that the coast was clear and then dashed across the narrow bridge. Yara could see from where she stooped that its sides were made of stone. She wondered how long ago it had been built, and by which wealthy individual.

Dryn disappeared against the dark shapes of trees on the other side and Keyth looked at Yara. "Your turn," he told her. "Don't worry. Just get across quickly, and don't look back. You'll be fine."

She nodded, drawing a shaky breath, and then she followed in Dryn's footprints. The slippery slope put her on her knees before she ascended the bank. Shivering and sore, she sprinted across the icy cobbles of the bridge and almost fell on her behind once. Finally, her feet sunk into snow on the other side and she dropped to safety off the road. Her breath caught and she glanced back to make sure Keyth was safely across. She saw the shadowed shape of him fly across the bridge and then he was right beside her.

"Alright, but we're not safe yet," Dryn hissed, appearing between them. The night was pitch black; she could only see them in the contrast against the white snow. "Let's keep moving."

He set off and Keyth followed. Forcing herself to keep going, she took up the rear, stumbling after them on swollen limbs. *Can't we rest? Can't we just take a breath before fleeing through the cold?*

A horse neighed behind them and Keyth's hand pulled her to the ground, snow scraping her legs; she clutched her dress around her and glanced in the direction of the sound. There was a momentary clatter of horseshoes on stone and then silence again. It took her a moment to realize it had been the sound of a horse crossing the bridge at a brisk trot. Then crunched steps in the snow passed them quickly and all was silent.

Dryn, who had squatted high enough to see the roadway, returned and knelt beside them. Yara could feel him trembling where his knee touched hers. A moment or two passed, and he whispered, "It was him... He was on a horse..."

"A horse?" Keyth hissed.

No one in Lesser Kryden rode a horse unless it was an emergency. There were probably only a few in the entire village. Certainly none of the villagers would be out on one tonight. The town wouldn't start worrying about their absence until later, because all three of them were gone. So who rode a horse? Yara realized with growing dread the truth of her friends' fears.

They were being hunted.

They kept moving, quickly at first, and then slowly as they realized that their pursuer was ahead of them. Yara wasn't sure how much more she could take of this rigorous adventure, but she decided she shouldn't allow herself doubts right now. She kept the pace Dryn set, and she clung close to Keyth's side.

It must have been well past midnight when a flickering torchlight appeared in the distance south of them. At first they feared it might be someone on the road, but soon noticed a second light. By the time they neared it, there were a dozen torches, flickering at the tops of buildings or above gates. They had arrived, at long last, at the city of Greater Kryden.

Doubling or tripling the population of Lesser Kryden, the sprawling settlement was built at the mouth of a huge valley. It was as though the land itself had opened up for the Lyrin River, eager for a taste of the Syroh's southern sister.

Yara had never been to the city; she knew Keyth had been once, but he rarely spoke of it. His visit had been during unsettling family times, when his mother moved away from their village. She wasn't sure if Dryn had been before, but she saw the look of awe in his face as he approached the walls.

Greater Kryden's gates were twice the size of those of which they were familiar. The wall was higher, and the gate grander. A sign had been nailed into the wood. Neat writing informed them, "Knock twice. No admittance in early morning." They had little choice though. Dryn grabbed the metal knocker and slammed it against the wood on which it was hinged.

The loud noise made Yara jump. She glanced behind them, but the firelight from the city made the snowy path behind them obscure. If the rider that hunted them lurked there, he would have heard their knock. She felt vulnerable here in the open roadway.

"Hullo?" a muffled voice questioned. A section of the gate folded inward, revealing a smaller door and the city inside. "Come in, then," the voice huffed, frustrated. "I'm not holding this open forever!" A face appeared in the opening, half illuminated by the torchlight. The thick beard and soft eyes reminded her of Magistrate Arbydn, but the man had a pot shaped helmet on his head and links of chainmail covering his shoulders. In the flickering light, she could make out a weapon at his waist, but he made no move for it.

Dryn stepped tentatively through the doorway, and Keyth followed. He turned and gestured for her to follow.

"What, by the Maker's kind face, do we have here?" the sentry asked, amiably. "Adventurous lads, and a young mistress? My... you lot have been through quite a fitful evening, haven't you?"

Dryn nodded. The man closed the gate behind them and lowered a sturdy oak bar into place. "I was just about to shut my eyes in the guard house," he told them. "You're a lucky bunch.... It'll be cold tonight."

Keyth asked, "We're looking for the... Iron Crossing."

The guard nodded. "Ah, yes. A fine inn. Head straight down here and keep going through the town square. It should be on the south side of the square. Hope you've brought money. It's an expensive place."

"Expensive?" Dryn questioned, confused.

"Well, if you want a cheap bed and board, try the North Wind. It's by the West Gate," the guard told them. "Although, it looks like your young lady friend could use a clean bed at the Crossing..." He chuckled and disappeared through a door beside the gate.

Confused, Yara examined herself. Her dress was torn and tattered around her legs, and mud and snow were plastered over her skin and in the ruined fabric. Embarrassed, she asked, "Keyth... what about your mother? Can't we stay with her? It wouldn't cost anything."

He smirked and said dryly, "It would cost plenty. We're not going near her."

Dryn explained, "Besides, that most recent letter said we have to get the next at the Iron Crossing." He took a few steps away from the gate. "Come on, let's get inside."

Yara tried to ignore the fact that her finest dress was ruined and her feet were in terrible pain. She was freezing, but she put that aside as well, and followed them down the street.

The first thing she noticed about the city of Greater Kryden was that the buildings were very tall. She had never seen anything like it. Some reached three storeys, massive corner beams supporting three entire floors. She couldn't understand how such a thing was possible.

Dryn also gazed up at high windows, but he continued briskly down the street. It was a lengthy stretch to the city square. Unlike the small well at Lesser Kryden's centre, Greater Kryden sported an entire pond, detailed masonry curving around it. The water was frozen, but even so, the city centre was breathtaking.

The Iron Crossing was on the opposite corner, across the square from them. There was a simple wooden sign hanging from the eaves, and a lantern flickered beside the doorway. Through the front window warm firelight drew them in.

Keyth opened the door for Yara, and Dryn followed her. The common room was a well kept and tidy room; the chairs were pushed in and every table clean. A bald heavyset man was leaning back in a chair in the corner with his head against the wall. At the sound of the door closing, he started and looked their way. His face lit up and he rubbed the corners of his eyes.

"Ah, you've made it at last!" he said, standing up. "I had fallen asleep," he laughed.

Keyth glanced at Yara, confused as to who the man was, and somewhat bewildered at his comment.

"Sorry, I suppose a proper introduction is in order. I am the innkeeper here at the Iron Crossing, Arbo Jolyn. I'm assuming you are the travellers I have been waiting for," the man rambled. Seeing the befuddled expressions on their thawing faces, he exclaimed, "You *are* from Lesser Kryden, right?"

"Yes..." Dryn said. "You were expecting us?"

"Well, yes..." the man trailed. He untied an apron from around his waist, and began folding it.

"I only know I am supposed to get a letter here," Dryn began, cautiously.

"Well," the innkeeper muttered, "I don't know anything about a letter... But your room is the first up the stairs."

"A room?" Yara blurted, confused.

Arbo Jolyn rolled his eyes in annoyance. "Yes! My finest room was paid for in advance! That's why I was expecting you!"

17

Wearily, Keyth fumbled the key he had been given into the lock and the door to their room opened silently. Yara stumbled in ahead of him, barely able to stay on her feet any longer. Dryn, wavering on shaky knees, entered after her and glanced around the room. Keyth noticed as he entered that it was likely the fanciest room he had been in. There was one bed, wider than any he had seen. There was a dresser made of some imported wood, a chest that matched it and a desk varnished with some deep green potion. The room itself had a scent like lavender, and two gold-gilded lanterns illuminated it even at this hour of night. Yara inhaled deeply and then turned around to marvel at the tapestries and paintings on the walls.

"Look," Dryn gasped, pointing towards the bed. There was a white folded envelope on the pillow. Just as the last letter had promised, Keyth realized, the next would be at the Iron Crossing Inn.

Keyth set the key onto the low table beside the bed and sighed. "What does it say?" he asked as Dryn opened it.

Yara shivered, and glanced at them. "I'm still freezing," she told them. She held a fold of her dress in one hand, and muttered, "The snow is still melting."

Keyth decided she would need to change out of the icy clothes. And she needed rest. "Dryn, let's see if there's another room..."

"No," Yara said. "It's alright. Just step outside for a bit and I'll change out of this dress. I'll climb in bed and then you two can sleep on the floor. We don't have any money. How do you expect to rent another room?"

Dryn was absorbed in the letter, so Keyth said, "You sure?"

Yara nodded. Her eyes closed dazedly. "Just give me a few minutes."

"Alright," Keyth muttered. "Dryn, come on. You can finish that in the hall." Closing the door behind Dryn, Keyth's first thought was Yara's comfort. But his second thought was a reaction to Dryn.

"I can't go home."

Keyth spun away from the closed door to face his friend, whose laden eyes regarded him calmly. "What?" Keyth questioned.

Dryn answered quietly, "They've set up a watch on the village. They'll catch me." Before Keyth could respond, Dryn went on. "The war is real, Keyth. You've got to believe it."

"Shut your mouth, Dryn," Keyth growled. *I've had enough of his foolishness. I've had enough of this forsaken escapade.* "I don't believe a word of it. None of this magic insanity, none of those letters. It's crazy, Dryn."

"The room was paid for," Dryn pointed out.

"Damn it, Dryn! That doesn't mean there's a war!" Keyth hissed. "Get these mad ideas from your head!"

"Mad ideas?" a slight voice asked. They both turned from their argument and gaped at the speaker. Standing at the top of the nearby stairs was a girl taller than either of them. She wore a skirt that only hung to her knees, and her bare legs disappeared into a pair of unbuckled riding boots. She wore a boy's tunic and long sleeves beneath it. Keyth had never seen a young woman quite like her before. Her hair was half the length of any villagers' from Lesser Kryden, only slightly longer than a boy's.

When they said nothing, she pranced forward, crossing the distance towards them. "There's plenty of wars. The mountain tribes against the Borderlands. The Buccaneer's Navy against the Imperials. The Brotherhood of Andrakaz. The question is... why are you boys looking for one?"

Dryn stuttered, "We're not..." He slid the letter into the back of his pants.

Keyth was still partially stunned by her abrupt appearance; he quickly decided to use this foreigner's knowledge against Dryn's foolishness. "Do you know of a war against magicians?"

The girl's brow wrinkled dramatically and she stuck out her bottom lip a bit. "Such rumours aren't spoken of even at the dirtiest dock tavern of Olympus... Why would you boys want to know about that? Besides, you're either looking for a war or you're running from one. Unless you've got no clue and get pulled along without realizing it. But neither of you seem *that*... commonplace..."

She had an accent Keyth hadn't heard before and spoke quickly enough to confuse him. Dryn started to raise a hand towards his face, likely to run it through his ruggedly messed hair, but the young woman stepped forward as quick as a flash, grabbed his hand and shook it. "I'm Iris Lanteera, by the way."

She released Dryn's hand and stepped toward Keyth with the same hand held out, the other behind her back. But instead of shaking Keyth's, she spun away and opened a paper in front of her face. It took both Dryn and Keyth a moment to realize she had snatched the letter from Dryn and used the shaking of hands to obtain it. Dryn stepped forward, but Iris only backed up more. "I'm assuming *you* are this 'Dryn'?"

"Give it back," Dryn ordered, anxiously. "It's private. Not for you to read!"

She refused, her eyes aglow with a lively light. It was almost as though she enjoyed their distress.

Keyth knew how much Dryn believed in the importance of the letters, and so for his friend's sake, Keyth stepped forward, intending to grab it back. Besides, he didn't want her thinking he bought into this foolery.

The girl taunted Dryn, saying, "If this is so important... get it back." She held out the paper towards him, then clutched it back when he tried to grab it. Her flitting laughter echoed down the hall; Keyth hoped no one was awakened by it.

"Give it back, now." Dryn was staring at her darkly. "I'm serious."

"What are you going to do?" Iris teased. She raised her hand and suddenly there was a knife in it. The blade vanished instantly again. "I'd like to see you get – "

A fierce torrent of wind abruptly shrieked through the hallway. It caught Iris full on and she tumbled backward with a tapestry that was torn from the wall. Smashing into a desk, she plummeted with a flutter of papers, pens and wood onto the now cluttered carpet.

Dryn lowered his hands and sighed. He walked briskly in her direction and snatched the crumpled letter from the floor.

Keyth's mind froze. *By the Maker and his Great Glyph... Dryn was telling the truth. Dryn is telling the truth. There is a war.*

Keyth expected the girl to be furious, perhaps enough to attack them, but a smile lit up her shocked face, and the gleeful light returned to her eyes. "Ah... a magician... I get it now." She burst out laughing. "If you really are being watched like that letter says... you had better get out of here."

Keyth spun to Dryn who was watching him cautiously. "You *were* telling the truth?"

Dryn nodded quietly. "Sorry about that... I just ruined this night even more, Keyth. We have to keep going. Greater Kryden isn't safe now either. That man we saw at the village might be here any second."

"Keep going?" Keyth questioned. "I can't imagine going any farther. I'm exhausted, Dryn."

"I am too. I healed twice today..." Dryn muttered, as though that meant something. Keyth caught himself wondering where his childhood friend had disappeared to.

The door to their room opened, and Yara peeked out, a look of confusion on her face. Seeing the girl getting up from the floor and Dryn standing over her, she asked, "What is going on out there? It was loud; are you fighting?"

Keyth shook his head. "Dryn, we can't leave. All of us are too exhausted. We need sleep."

"Leave?" Yara questioned.

Iris was standing, smoothing her tunic and skirt back into place. "Ha, I knew it couldn't be two boys on their own..."

Yara glanced her over, and asked, "Who is this?"

"Someone who's going to help you, that's who."

Dryn and Keyth regarded the stranger in surprise. Downstairs, a door slammed, likely the innkeeper coming to investigate all the commotion. Iris gestured towards their room. "You three stay in there. Dryn, give me your cloak. I'm going to make it look like you're leaving town."

Keyth couldn't understand why she would want to help them. "Why?" he asked.

"I've got my reasons."

"I don't understand..." Keyth muttered. He stepped towards the door of their room.

Iris snapped, "Great Glyph... do you boys need to 'understand' everything?" She laughingly grabbed the cloak that Dryn held out and slid into it. "Get some sleep. I'll be downstairs in the morning."

While they stood watching, Iris pulled the hood up and headed down the stairs.

18

Rychard of Tarroth was not impressed by the latest report. "The targets have escaped their village and pressed on, out of the district, during the night..." he read, trailing off and tossing the letter down on the table in front of him. He walked to the fireplace at the end of the room and sat with his feet propped towards it. His posting in Athyns had been barely tolerable. He found the warmth of the flames calming. He had done another execution earlier, but now this report was damaging the good day.

He opened the pages of the chronicle he had been reading. It was the history of the Trionus War. He had just reached the election of the High Prince, when the Imperial forces started acting like real armies. It was amazing what stern leadership could do to morale. It was even more remarkable what morale could do to soldiers. Like a miracle enchantment. He had never seen such efficient bloodshed until he served with Periander Gothikar during the first campaign in the Cerden Range of the West. Now there was a man who could inspire killers. Such a pity that he had to be replaced.

Not that Rychard had become regretful. The entire plot hinged on Pyrsius Gothikar; it was fortunate things had gone so smoothly in Avernus. Rychard was one of the handful who knew about the plans. And even he didn't have all the pieces of the puzzle. He could think of only two men who did.

There was a tap at his door and he shouted, "Come!", folding a cloth between the pages of the book he read. He stood up as the door of his chambers opened.

A man in Imperial armour marched in, chainmail jingling loudly. "Captain Findius, sir. Reporting as ordered. My men are assembled outside."

"Shall we?" Rychard asked, gesturing to the door again. He led Findius into the corridor and towards the stairs at the end of the building. Rychard's Athynian barracks wasn't nearly as grand as the Imperial one at Olympus, though it was faintly reminiscent of his estate in Tarroth.

Fortunately, this barracks wasn't without its charms.

Tied in the middle of the courtyard, a man leaned against a pole, shivering in the northerly wind. He would likely be dead by tomorrow. *About time*, Rychard thought. The prisoner had attempted to aid a magician. Rychard was sure the fool had never regretted something so much.

On the other side of the yard, three dozen men stood in full armour, sweating beneath the open sky. As he approached, Findius barked "Attention!", and the troop flinched as one to a salute position. Every soldier stared ahead blankly, awaiting instruction or examination.

Now, here are fine fighters... Rychard decided, and began his inspection.

He paused only once, eyeing the youthful face of one soldier. "How old are you?" he asked, curious.

The young man answered calmly, "My twentieth name day has just passed, sir."

"Go kill that man," Rychard ordered, pointing in the general direction of the prisoner. He watched as, without a word, the soldier crossed the dirt yard and ended the prisoner's life. Quickly. Efficiently. "Findius, I commend you. Avernus gifts me with quality Athyns can never provide."

He began to stride back towards the main building and Findius matched his footsteps. As they walked, Rychard explained, "The northlands are massive and unoccupied. Sources send continuous reports of magicians hiding there. In addition, these unsettling rumours of Artemys Gothikar's body. But there is no solid evidence. I intend to send out your troop in groups of three."

"Separate them, sir?" the Captain questioned.

"Yes. That isn't a problem, is it?"

Findius shook his head. "Of course not, sir."

Rychard continued. "The groups will remain close enough to one another to give assistance... and we will scour the northlands.   If the soldiers reach their destinations and everything goes as I have planned, we will rid the whole region of every last glyph user by Spring."

19

Rubbing the soles of his feet, Dryn sat up from the hard floor and looked around. For one disconcerted moment he wondered where he was; the adorned walls were not those of his room, and the smooth hardwood floor was not his normal sleeping area. The moment passed and memories of the previous night came crashing down on him.

"It's confusing, isn't it?" a familiar voice asked quietly.

He shifted and glanced at Keyth. His friend sat in an armchair with his head tilted against its back. "The first thought is 'where am I?' and the second is 'why?' I still can't answer that second."

Dryn nodded. "I'm still just starting to grasp it." He glanced once more around the inn room. He could see Yara, still sleeping in the bed.

"By the Maker, Dryn. You were telling the truth. You really can use magic," Keyth said, tipping his head forward to stare at Dryn. "You saved your father, right? That's why you left me in the snow? Oh, and in the forest! What really happened that night?"

Once more, Dryn told the story of the old man; he could recall Artemys Gothikar's last words, but that was the only thing he did not tell Keyth. "That's how I first got magic. That's why I never really explained what happened to anyone."

Keyth remained silent for a minute, then asked "Why didn't you tell me before it came to all this?"

Dryn grimaced. "I couldn't believe it myself, Keyth. Even when I started using spells, there was always a wall of doubt I couldn't get past."

"Except when you decided to turn 'hero' and save your father."

Dryn nodded. "I wasn't planning that. It just sort of happened."

They were quiet for a few more moments. The quiet was broken finally by a tap at the door. Keyth glanced at it and froze. Yara's eyes opened and she sat up with the bed covers pulled tightly around her. "Is it Iris?" Keyth asked.

Dryn stood up very slowly and walked to the door. One of his hands poised by the wall, should he need to trace a glyph. *Please let it be her,* he prayed, and asked through the wood, "Who's there?"

"Me, you fool village boy!" a girl's voice hissed. "Open the door!"

He opened the door a crack and glanced out, then opened it enough for Iris to enter. She was wearing a pair of breeches and the same tunic she had yesterday. In one arm she carried his cloak, which she pressed against him as she passed. He took it from her and set it aside, as she glanced around the room.

"How did you afford this room?" she questioned. "If you're just villagers from Lesser Kryden...."

"Did you lure that man away?" Dryn returned, setting his jaw sternly. She was so obnoxious. Last night, it had taken a fair amount of self control not to use the fire spell.

She grinned and shifted her weight to one leg. "For now," she said. "But he'll be back..." Seeing Yara still under the covers, Iris muttered, "You people rise late around here."

Keyth said, "We had a rough night..."

Iris barked a laugh and tossed her hair. "So I heard."

There was a stretch of silence. Dryn folded up the blanket he had slept on and returned it to the shelf where he had found it. As he was closing it, Yara asked meekly, "Do you have a dress I could wear? My other is ruined."

"A dress?" Iris scoffed. "What do you take me for? A lady?"

Keyth laughed, but Yara remained staring at her blankly. Dryn found himself annoyed at Iris once again.

"But I'm sure I've got something you can wear. Boys, why don't you head down to the common room for a bit." Iris was grinning widely, apparently finding something humorous in this.

As they stepped out, Dryn told them, "I'm heading down to the market..."

"It had better be important. Keep your head down," Iris warned him as he followed Keyth out of the room.

Downstairs in the common room Keyth grabbed his arm and said, "Don't go yet. We have to talk more." He pulled Dryn to a nearby table and asked quietly, "You aren't returning to Lesser Kryden, are you?"

Dryn flinched. He hadn't thought it through yet. He wasn't sure what he was doing. "I don't know, Keyth. Right now I'm wishing I could wake up from this nightmare. That's why I'm following the letters. Perhaps I will make it through this terrible dream."

"And what do the letters tell you now?" Keyth asked. "The one you found last night?"

"The one from last night told me that the Maker must favour me. Whoever is writing them knows how close we were to getting caught. They also told me that further instructions await me, if I speak to a merchant near the south gate," Dryn explained. "I know you'll return home, Keyth. I get it. All of this has happened too quickly. I'll go on alo – "

"I don't know yet, Dryn," Keyth said. "Seeing you use magic last night changed a lot. I still haven't sorted out everything in my head. It feels... Great Glyph, it feels like the adventure we always wanted. But what about Yara?"

"That's why you have to go back. She's got a life. She's got a family that loves her." Dryn shook his head and started to stand up. "I'm going to get that next letter. I'll talk to you when I'm back."

"What about this Iris girl?" Keyth asked, grabbing Dryn's sleeve again before he could leave. "Can we trust her?"

"No," Dryn said sternly, and he walked away. His head started to clear a bit once he got out into the street. He almost felt normal, except the buildings towered around him, and the people looked different, and he had symbols burnt into his chest.

The store he was looking for was relatively easy to find. Most of the buildings near the south gate were houses, but one first floor sported a wide window, and the sign 'Ulysan Books' hung from its sill. Inside he found an assortment of books. Lesser Kryden had no book shop, so it was a new experience for him to walk between stacks of leather bound tomes.

"Hello," a voice greeted him. A short man waddled out from behind a shelf and said, "I'm Ulysan. Can I help you find something?"

He quickly recalled the response the letter had provided. "I'm looking for the fourth volume of the Journeys of Oban Hokar." Anyone who had read those tales knew there were only three books.

The man's smile faded and he said, "This way." Behind the shelf was a doorway and through that a crammed chamber; the man walked behind a desk and Dryn waited as the shopkeeper bent beneath the surface. "Here," he said, setting a weighty pack on the wooden top.

Dryn stared at the dusty sack blankly. He glanced back up at Ulysan. The storekeeper ran a hand over the scruff on his chin and gazed at him with blue eyes. "You're supposed to take it. I don't know what's inside. I'm not allowed to."

"Alright," Dryn muttered, quietly. He picked up the pack and was surprised by its weight as he swung it over one shoulder. Awkwardly, he looked back at the short man.

Ulysan gestured toward the door they had entered and muttered, "Good luck..."

Dryn found himself standing in the street with the pack on one shoulder and the door closed behind him. Curious of what was inside, he walked a few steps towards the gate and rounded the corner of the building. Setting his back against the plaster wall, he undid the knot and loosened the tie that held the pack closed. Inside he found two books. One was the 'Starter's Treatise on the Basic Glyphs of Magic' which he had left in his room in Lesser Kryden. The other had gold lettering set in the leather cover; it read: 'Delfie School's Record of Advanced Magic.'

Held between the two volumes was another folded note. He slid out the paper and opened it to reveal the familiar printed words. Eagerly absorbing the latest correspondence, he scanned the page.

"Dryn,
Once again I must marvel at the turn of events. The appearance of this Iris character is something I could not predict. She is both useful and dangerous. If she remains with you and your friends, you must find out her true intentions and her past. Your use of magic has shortened your stay in Greater Kryden; the hunter that Iris distracted will return shortly.

"You must set off for Ithyka at once. The road will be long and likely dangerous. Iris could prove an effective guide as she is from the southlands. I have placed a map in the pages of your basic magic book, along with the letters I retrieved from your room."

Dryn glanced around with trembling fingers. The correspondent had been inside his room! *Who is this?* he wondered for the hundredth time. *Ithyka? I have to go to Ithyka?* He had heard of the city; a city south of the Kryden District, beyond the Lyrin River. *When will this end? This hopeless flight from my home?* A momentary thought of paranoia boiled up past the others. *What if the letters aren't good? What if I'm being lured somewhere?* But he dismissed it when he recalled how much they had already helped him.

He continued reading:

"Keyth and Yara must travel with you now. The way that the enemies track you is to center on your use of magic. It is called scrying. Using a complicated spell, they can focus on one distant target and view everything around it.

"It is likely that, in using your spell last night, you have given them the faces of Keyth, Yara, and Iris. If Keyth and Yara return to Lesser Kryden, they will be found and interrogated. From the point of view of the trackers, even a single magic-user slipping through their fingers could undo their entire plan. Added to this, they have found the remains of Artemys Gothikar, and have made it a priority to find anyone who has seen him.

"Included in this pack is another book which will develop your vocabulary of glyphs. I wrote a note in the cover to teach you how to further and diversify your own spells. There are a number of rules you must follow for safety's sake. Also included is a number of spell tokens. As reminder: to use them you need only break the stone and direct the spell. Written on the back of this letter is the spell needed to turn an object into a token. Practice these skills and learn the glyphs in the spell books.

"But now, you must return to your friends quickly. Take Keyth and Yara with you; Iris may accompany you as well, if that's what you decide. Head for Ithyka."

He folded the letter quickly and tucked it away into the pack. Sliding his fingers past the books, he drew out a small rectangular stone. The corners were rounded slightly and the grey surface was covered in glyphs. He read the spell for a single fire strike within the characters.

He dropped the token into the pack again and shouldered it. Turning back towards the street, he found himself suddenly face to face with Iris.

20

A few moments after Iris left Yara's room, Keyth returned, his soft brown hair still ruffled from the chaotic night. Yara caught him staring at her legs, now covered by a pair of breeches. They were so restricting compared to her dress; Iris had laughed after Yara tried them on.

Yara was beginning to like Iris. The 'dirty-mouthed, unashamed adventurer' was an idea that had caught Yara in its path like a storm. Iris said what she thought, how she felt, and didn't cover it up under the propriety of being a 'lady.'

"Dryn went down to the market. Said something about another letter," Keyth told her, and Yara nodded, then stood up from the bed upon which she had sat. "They're real, you know..."

"I do..." Yara said.

Keyth plunged on with what he was saying, "You've gotta believe. Everything he told us was true. He's not just involved with the wrong people, he's way over his head in something big. Really, really big."

"I know, Keyth."

"But it's not his fault either," Keyth continued. "All of this just happened and he didn't do anything to cause it! Maker protect us, this kind of thing can't just happen to normal people!"

At last his agitation abated while staring at her quietly, and she at him. After a moment, she returned to what had been on her mind from the start, and asked, "What about Iris?"

"What about her?" Keyth returned. "She's snobby, rude... What gives her permission to poke into our affairs?"

"Kind of like you, huh?" Yara asked, grinning widely.

His jaw dropped and he burst out laughing. "You!" he snapped, jokingly. "Yes, just like me. I don't know what we're going to do with her, though. Probably find out where she came from... that would be a good start."

"Wait, you don't like her, do you..." she trailed. It wasn't a question.

"Not particularly. Although Dryn... you should see the way Dryn looks at her," Keyth told her.

"He certainly despises her too..."

"Huh?" Keyth responded, slightly confused. "I meant... he likes her."

Yara tipped her head out of confusion. *Now that's a big mixed message...* "He *likes* her?" she asked. "Seems to me the opposite."

"We'll see..." Keyth whispered slyly. Almost with his words came a knock at the door. Yara's gut twisted up in a way that reminded her of a village cleaning lady winding a damp cloth.

Alarmed, Keyth strode towards the door, then opened it very slowly, peeking out. "Oh, Master..."

"Jolyn, sir," the innkeeper murmured politely. "Arbo Jolyn. I just wanted to let you and your companions know that our noon meal will be on the table shortly, if you're interested."

"Thank you," Yara told him, smiling towards the crack in the door from behind Keyth.

"We might be down, then," Keyth told the friendly man.

"No need to hurry at all," Master Jolyn told them. "Sir." He bobbed his head and added, "Milady."

Once he had gone, Keyth shut the door quietly and turned back to her. With a mock gesture of one arm, he asked, "Milady, shall we to break our fast?"

Smiling at his game, she glanced around her and returned, "Maker burn me, I'm no lady. Where's my dress? Where's my finery?"

He raised an eyebrow at her language and his smile grew. "So be it, road fellow. To lunch?" This time his voice had a thick West Mydarius accent to it. She burst out laughing and accepted his arm. Together they strode out into the hall and headed for the common room.

As they set their feet upon the wooden floorboards at the bottom of the stairs, the door of the common room opened. Iris strode purposely through, came to Keyth's side and took his other arm. "Without looking into the room, walk with me outside," Iris told them sternly.

With neck muscles yearning to glance, Yara forced herself to glare forward and soon was standing in the snowy road. The sun was contrary to the icy earth, and beamed on them hot from its zenith. Iris released Keyth's arm and ordered, "Follow me..."

They moved swiftly down the road. Yara was surprised at how much warmer the pants were in comparison to the dress she'd worn previously. Iris led them tight against the buildings, until they had circled the square and began walking down one of the streets.

"Glyphs, what is going on?" Keyth questioned. "Where is Dryn?"

"The tracker was in the common room. When he lost me in the night, he must have retraced his steps to the inn. Dryn got another letter, directing him to Ithyka, and he's gone now," Iris hissed, not even slowing her pace. "I came back to find you two. Now we're following him. We're going to meet him at the Lyrin."

"What?" Keyth snapped. "He left?"

"The tracker found us."

"We don't even know that *is* the tracker," Keyth rumbled. "It could just be another traveller!"

"Feel free to head back there and find out!" Iris told him, turning to walk backwards, facing them for several steps.

"Keyth..." Yara muttered.

"Maybe I'll just head back to Lesser Kryden!" he exclaimed.

"Keyth!" Yara shook her head, and squeezed his arm.

"You could do that too." Sneering, Iris said, "But you'd lead the tracker back there."

"What?" Keyth questioned. "What does he want with me?"

"He scried you, thanks to Dryn's little stunt last night. Scried both of you," Iris told them, winking at Yara.

"What, by the Maker, is that supposed to mean?" Keyth growled.

"It means he sensed Dryn's magic, and then *saw* all three of us as well," came the explanation. She turned again with her back to them.

Yara looked at Keyth, as confused as he was. Keyth whispered to Yara, "Can we even trust her? I mean, maybe she never even spoke to Dryn. Maybe *she's* the hunter!"

"I'm right here," Iris laughed, but seemed to ignore them.

Yara shrugged, "I don't know. Where do we go from here? Ithyka? And then? What about home? My parents?"

"Are you listening?" Iris interrupted again. "You're coming with me whether you want to or not. Dryn told me to bring you either way. For your own safety." She winked and a little dagger flashed across her knuckles again, appearing from nowhere and disappearing up her sleeve again.

Yara's jaw dropped. Was Iris willing to harm them? Maybe Keyth was right, that they couldn't trust her. Although Keyth stared at Yara with concern, she could also see that he wanted to go along. He wanted adventure. He wanted to follow Iris and find Dryn.

That's why Yara liked him so much.

"It's alright," she told him. "We'll go along. We'll find Dryn."

"What?" Keyth asked, confused again. There was hope in his eyes now. He might not even know how much he wanted to go, but Yara understood. And Yara wanted to go as well.

"We'll go to Ithyka. And from there, wherever Dryn goes. We'll return home," she told him, "but not if we're going to be a danger to our families."

Keyth nodded mutely. A moment passed. "Are you sure?"

"Yes," Yara said. "Don't worry. I want this too."

"Touching," Iris snapped, laughing as though it was funny. "Now, a little silence please?"

21

Scurrying along the road out of Greater Kryden, Dryn felt like he was leaving everything he knew, leaving a part of himself in the familiar snowy streets north of the Syroh River. Slung over one shoulder was the pack he had been given at the store in Greater Kryden. He had pocketed the spell tokens for easy access. *Just in case...* he told himself.

The road curved southward out of the Kryden district, opening into a huge dale. Following the valley south, the road eventually intersected with the Lyrin River. Beyond that lay the city of Ithyka.

It was close to a two day trek. Having left Kryden just before noon, Dryn was still descending into the valley when darkness fell. His feet ached terribly; even after years of deliveries for his father, he was ill prepared for such a journey. The snow hadn't been so bad at first, but by the time it was night, Dryn was freezing despite the two cloaks he had put on the previous day.

He was surprised to realize that yesterday he had fought the bandits. It seemed like a month had passed. He slipped one hand under his shirt and felt the smooth skin of his shoulder. Thirty hours earlier it had been split by the solid head of a crossbow bolt.

Two days had changed his life. But he knew the changes had begun sooner. Artemys Gothikar had started them more than a week ago.

The moon was out tonight, lighting the way for his feet. He was thankful for that as he pressed on for several hours into the night. At last he decided to set up a camp. He journeyed off the road for a few minutes, until he was sure no passing traveller could spot a fire.

It was hard to find dry wood, but he eventually found a burrow where an ancient elm had forced its roots into an umbrella. Beneath it he found enough kindling and dry wood to get a small fire started. He cleared snow away with his feet and lay one cloak flat for himself to sit on. He had slept in the woods several times before, but never on his own.

Curling up close to the warmth of the flames, he stared up at the stars and hoped Keyth was alright. He knew his friend wouldn't trust Iris, but Dryn hoped he had made the right decision. She had spotted their pursuer on his way into the inn, and had found Dryn quickly where he waited outside of the book shop. Warning him of the danger, she had helped him formulate a desperate plan.

As the hunter could track only Dryn, he would travel on ahead of his companions. Perhaps separation would provide enough distraction that Keyth and Yara could escape with Iris' help.

That is... if Iris could be trusted.

The fire began dwindling, and Dryn put another scrap of wood on it, before shutting his eyes. Attempting to fall asleep proved a fruitless effort; after an hour of restless worry, Dryn gave up and began reading the glyphs on the tokens he had been given by his correspondent.

Several were just fire attack spells and variations of them. He found one interesting stone with the glyph for air inked on it and a series of other glyphs he didn't recognize. He instinctively started to grab for his original spell book, but on an impulse, reached for the new one instead. The introduction was brief, yet interesting. It even mentioned the Great Glyph, which had always been a folktale to Dryn.

'The Great Glyph,' the book told him, 'is an ethereal glyph made up of every other glyph in existence. In this way, all aspects of the world fit together as one all-encompassing Glyph. It is, in nature, the very essence of the Maker's creation.'

Beyond that there was no further explanation, but Dryn found his curiosity peaked and he reread the sentence a few times, deep in thought. He flipped through the volume, reading chapter headings and section names. It contained a record of the elements, as well as general glyphs beside the elements. One of them was marked as Life, another as Death. There was even one glyph with the written word 'Time.'

Eventually, Dryn found the glyphs he couldn't read from the token. It was marked as 'self protection ward.' He hadn't a clue what that meant, except that the correspondent had 'warded' the field for Dryn's use of magic. Perhaps it was simply a defence spell.

Intrigued by the new book, Dryn leaned closer to the fireside and continued to read through the new information. His vocabulary of magic was growing. He knew how to create tokens because of the spell written on the last letter. He knew several elemental attacks. He hadn't tried using water in place of fire, but he was sure he could use a water blast.

Turning the page to the end of the chapter, a glyph jumped off the page at him. It was the last one in the section with no further spells mentioned. The glyph caught his attention, firstly, because it was far more complicated than the others, and more importantly, because he had seen it before. He pulled the collar of his shirt down enough to reveal the symbols burnt into his skin.

Sure enough, second last in the string of glyphs was the one he had just read in the book. He stared at the spot on his skin, and then, shaking himself from the daze, glanced at the words in the book that explained it.

"Great Glyph reference," he read aloud. That was it. "What's that supposed to mean?" he questioned, annoyed with the lack of information. A complicated glyph explained by only three words of Common.

Frustrated, he read on into the next section. The title was 'True Glyphs' and on the next line, 'also known as Name Glyphs.' Intrigued, he read the introduction of the chapter.

'Every sentient being, or human, is represented in the Great Glyph by their own unique symbol. These glyphs are known as True Glyphs by most magicians. True Glyphs are used as guideline or reference points when using a spell to involve a particular individual. Scrying is normally based on the target's True Glyph (for more information on scrying, see the seventh chapter).'

Dryn stopped reading. Scrying is how the enemy was tracking him. *Do they know my True Glyph?* he wondered, alarmed. The fact that there was a glyph representing him seemed dangerous knowledge if in his enemies' hands. He flipped through the book until he found the chapter on scrying.

'Scrying is the ability to view another person or place from afar using only the power of glyphs. It is considered the beginning of intermediate level by most magic schools. The following spells are the main components of a scrying spell. The blank is substituted by a person's true glyph in most cases, but can, in fact, be filled by nearly any glyph. For example, using the simple element of fire is possible. The user would be able to siphon through every spark of fire in existence. For most magicians, that many images being forced into their thoughts is overwhelming and can even prove fatal. Beyond scrying an individual, the second most commonly used scry is for the use of magic itself, allowing the user to see anywhere magic is currently being used.'

Following this introduction there was a set of long spells with blanks in the middle. It was some relief to know that his enemy could scry him without knowledge of his True Name. Sometime he would read that chapter fully, and perhaps learn a way to find his own True Glyph or block scrying.

He closed the cover of the book for a moment and thought about all he had just learned. How useful it would be to scry someone. That's when the thought hit him. If he could scry their tracker, it would balance the biggest advantage the hunter had over them.

But how could Dryn scry him without the man's True Glyph?

It was hopeless. He spent a few dozen moments flipping through the pages of the books, but couldn't find any way around the problem. Defeated, he lay his head down on his cloak and slowly felt sleep come, slowly pulling him into his dreams.

He awoke with a start several moments later, sitting up beside the dying fire as though a chapel bell had rung through his head. It must have been something he was dreaming about that had given him the idea. 'Great Glyph reference' the book had said.

Madly flipping through the pages of the new book he scanned for the glyph of that spell in the final page in the chapter. It was one of the glyphs written on him, yet the book gave no explanation of what it did. *Why not try?* Dryn wondered. The letters had warned that experimentation with magic was dangerous, but the way Dryn saw it, he had little choice.

In the dying light he could hardly make out some of the letters, so he bent close to his fire. He traced the glyph into the ashes at its edge and he read aloud, *"Elkobo den triios al'dei."*

Nothing happened.

The glyph in the ground stared at him blankly and he compared it to the one in the book. That wasn't the problem. He reread the pronunciation and sank back onto his cloak. *Why isn't it working?* he wondered. He ran a hand through his hair, trying to think of what was wrong. *Should I wait and ask the letter writer?*

It hit him again as abruptly as he had awoken from his sleep. Words of magic always activated the written glyphs. "The spell's already been written down!" he whispered. He quickly scratched over the glyph traced in the earth. His words hadn't activated it, because the spell didn't know which one to activate: the one in the ashes or the one in his skin.

He whispered again, *"Elkobo den triios al'dei..."* and this time a pain lanced through his chest as though the glyph itself had been lit with fire. He clawed at his shirt, and as his vision flickered, he fell back, pressing his head into the snow, instinctively bracing his muscles against the agony.

And then, like an explosion within his skull, he saw *everything.* He couldn't comprehend the chaos. It was as though a trillion glyphs appeared before his eyes, dominating his thoughts and threatening to drive him mad. True agony began, as he tried to shut it out, tried to fight back hundreds of libraries in which he was drowning.

He tried whispering the spell again, tried shaking his head, tried hitting his head, but the agony of such chaos was still pressing upon him. *Go away, go away!* he was shouting inside, gasping for breath. *What does it want?* he wondered, trying to understand why this glyph felt like it was hunting down his every thought.

I just wanted to find him, I just wanted to find that cursed tracker! he thought, and then, like a lightning bolt ripping asunder the heavens, a single glyph tore through the pattern he was seeing, and banished all the others.

The pain receded, and then, slowly, this final solo glyph faded like the great one had.

Dryn opened his eyes in relief to find himself staring up at the clear starry night. Still lying on his cloak beside the flickering fire, he pressed one hand against his chest as the last of the agony fled his senses. Trying to find reason in what had just happened proved futile at first. "Was that the... Great Glyph?" he whispered to himself.

The spell was a 'Great Glyph reference.' Perhaps it allowed people to perceive the Great Glyph. *Then what happened with that last glyph?* he pondered. He ran one hand through his hair again and rolled onto his side to stare at the dying embers beside him.

The True Name... he realized in a daze. That massive pattern of glyphs had just sat there, waiting and ... *probing* him, until he had consciously remembered that he had been searching for the hunter's identity.

Did that spell just give me his True Glyph? he wondered. He quickly traced the symbol in the dirt, so that he wouldn't forget it. Flipping back through the book to the chapter about Names, he read, 'True Glyphs can be recognized by the signature dot above them; a characteristic shared by every human's glyph, yet not found in any others.'

He glanced at his drawing in the earth, and saw the dot above the character. *Dryn, you lucky little earth-spawn...* he told himself. Reading from the book again, he reminded himself of the scrying spell, and set to work creating a spell to locate his enemy.

When he had finished, he stared at the ground, memorizing the string of glyphs so he could use them again. Then, whispering a long string of syllables that slurred together, he activated the spell, entering the True Glyph he had learned as the target.

His vision flickered white, and he put one hand to his eyes in surprise. Abruptly color surged into his sight and he lowered his hand, focusing instead on the scrying.

The first thing he recognized was the road, a winding hairline across a smooth sea of snow. A black dot was trotting along the road... a horse, he realized. The vision dropped like a falcon making the kill and he found himself following behind the rider's shoulder. A black hat, and long jacket. Dark hair, a hilt at his side. The reins went taut and the horse stood still in the road.

The rider tilted his head back around, and his eyes flickered along the road, meeting Dryn's. Dryn wasn't even there, just his sight, just the scrying. The man whispered, "I see you..." and then kicked his spurs into the horse's sides.

The black steed whirled off the road, and, churning up a river of snow, galloped east from the dark road of frosted dirt, towards a thin, barely visible trail of smoke in the starry night sky.

Towards the makeshift camp.

Towards Dryn.

22

Orion of Edessa spurred his black horse across the snow, undoing the fastenings of his scabbard should he need the blade within. Digging his spurs into the heaving sides of his mount, he tore through the tree line and plunged through the foliage towards the blaring beacon of magic. *Background scrying is so useful,* he thought, reflecting on his training and clutching his dark hat so it didn't blow off.

The only thing that had him on edge, as he neared the camp, was figuring out how the villager he was hunting had made it from using no magic to scrying in two weeks. *That can't be possible!* Orion had spent ten years in the Edessa Arena before Rychard's recruitment had found him. After that, he had been trained for a year in the use of magic before being put into the field.

Was it something about Artemys? The Crown Magician himself had given this villager magic; perhaps that is why the fool was learning so quickly. With no actual training, learning magic from a book was extremely time consuming, and also dangerous. The late Artemys must have had his hand in this.

It is of no matter... he decided. Even at the pace he was learning, the villager couldn't surpass Orion's knowledge in less than three months. And considering that Orion now rode upon the fool's camp, he assumed that very unlikely.

The camp was empty of course; Orion reined in his horse and scoured his surroundings with his eyes. No movement. Not a sound. *Well, the fool had some mite of intelligence.* He glanced at the dying embers and an abandoned cloak laying flat across the surface of the snow where the villager had slept.

Orion whispered, *"Eldrin,"* and a glow of light lit up the small clearing. There was no source, the light seemed simply to appear from nowhere, illuminating the ground and night air around him. A clear set of tracks led him out of the clearing. His horse neighed as he forced it past a thorn bush. The mystical light followed him, illuminating the trail his target had left in the snow.

It was slow going. The villager had weaved back and forth so Orion couldn't follow him in a straight line. Stopping every now and again, Orion listened for any sound that might give the fool away; the night remained silent apart from his own rugged breath and that of his mount.

"Find them, and kill them all," had been his orders. It didn't bother him. He knew what was going on. He knew the reason for his mission and the end result. Destroy magic. Level the playing field. Kill off most of the magicians and magic could take decades to recover. Kill off all and, without a magician to imbue new users, magic would, be gone forever. "Kill them all."

Now some ignorant villager was eluding him. Cursing the deep snow that slowed his horse, he plodded in a straight line across the weaving pattern of tracks. "Ah-ha!" he shouted, "I see you!" He saw nothing, but such an outburst could draw a reckless flight from his prey; this time, the forest remained quiet.

Maker blind me, he ranted inside. *How does this fool get away?* He eventually found the tracks again, this time veering west. Following them determinedly, he soon found himself back on the road. "Great Glyph..." he hissed in frustration. The villager had made it back to the road and was nowhere to be seen ahead on the highway's flat surface.

Orion kicked his horse's sides and trudged along the road for as long as the animal could take it. Whenever he stopped, the tracks were still there, headed south towards Ithyka.

When the sun rose over the Lyrin River Valley, it found Orion of Edessa walking beside his fatigued horse. Ahead of him was the bridge into Ithyka. No sign of the villager.

Maybe he wasn't a fool after all.

23

Like fireflies blinking out, the lights of Greater Kryden eventually vanished behind them as Iris led Keyth and Yara down into the vale. Above them, a giant white eye followed their progress; it was nearly a full moon, and Keyth had never been so thankful for its light. This night was so much more peaceful than the last, than the desperate flight from his home.

"Should we be on the open road?" he asked Iris, who walked briskly ahead of him. The road reminded him of a snake, winding back and forth, wider in some places than in others, and openly dangerous.

Iris didn't answer, didn't even turn her head to glance at Keyth.

Great, he thought, *she's ignoring me now.* He glanced back at Yara, who shrugged and smiled at his concern. She seemed content to walk for hours without explanation, while Keyth was frustrated by every boot track he left on the snowy trail.

Trying to get on Iris' good side, he asked, "So, you are obviously not from around here... what brings you to Kryden, Iris?"

This time she responded with an exclamation: "Maker burn me, you can't even stay quiet for a single minute!"

He flinched, and decided to shut his mouth. She obviously didn't care what he thought, and did not want to share anything about herself with him. But he was alright with that. He didn't like her a bit either.

A few minutes passed in silence as they strode down the gradual slope. From where they walked at the mouth of the valley, Keyth could see westwards across the lowlands. Against the horizon was a cluster of dark shapes, storm clouds maybe. Or mountains. Keyth had never seen mountains.

"I wanted a normal life," Iris said abruptly, and Keyth glanced at her. She was staring at him, as if confused why she was telling him this. "I was tired of being waited upon, fed by a silver spoon. I wanted to travel." She paused. "I wanted to be alone for once. And work until my hands blistered. Until I sweat."

She was quiet for the next few steps and Keyth managed, "Oh." She was staring at her feet now, as she strode determinedly ahead of him. Something about her posture struck him as pained.

She went on. "All my life there has been an eye watching, a serving woman to dress me and clean my clothes, a guard to protect me, a tutor to teach me. But I have always wanted to live a normal life. Like you."

Again a long pause as the earth levelled and they began the slow trek across the bottom of the vale. "You were a lady?" Yara asked confused. Keyth blinked. That was entirely the opposite of the Iris that led them along the snowy road.

"I was." Iris glanced over one shoulder at them. "But I never knew my parents. Someone paid for my care... someone made sure I had the realm's finest. But I never met this guardian. And I left." She laughed abruptly, a sudden sound like the song of a bird. "And the road is safe to travel on. We can see as much as anyone else. We'd see them coming too."

Keyth chuckled to himself that she had, with that, answered both his questions. Yara nudged him in the back. He hadn't realized she was walking so close behind him.

"One of the reasons I've decided to help you..." Iris muttered. "Well, Dryn is fighting to survive. And he's had the life I've always wanted. I've decided to fight with him. No one should be forced into a fight they didn't ask for."

Keyth was starting to understand her, he thought. *If such a thing is possible....* He laughed to himself. *She's fighting to be normal ...* Yet, in comparison to the villagers of Lesser Kryden, she was unique and strange.

"So, you've been to cities bigger than Greater Kryden?" he asked, curious.

That loud laughter came again. "Just about anywhere is bigger than Greater Kryden, farm boy..."

121

"I'm not a farm boy," he snapped, testily. "I am a bowyer's apprentice."

"Really?" Iris asked, seeming genuinely interested. "You good with a bow then?"

"I am," he said, half-heartedly.

"I reckon I could hit a target throwing this knife, better than you could with a bow," she taunted, a glint of steel catching his eye as she held out that knife again, tip between her fingers.

"Well, I don't have a bow with me," Keyth explained, grinning, "but when I do... I'll take that bet."

"I'll match my gold against your copper," Iris teased.

"Gold?" Yara questioned, intrigued.

Iris' high-pitched amusement filled the air again. She grabbed something from her waist and it flew over Keyth's head. He turned to see Yara scoop a pouch from the snowy earth. Opening it filled her face with dimly reflected sunlight. Keyth leaned closer to see that the small pouch was full of gold coins.

They both gaped at Iris, who grinned and told Yara, "Keep it."

Yara's jaw dropped. "What...?" It was a small fortune by most standards in Lesser Kryden.

"There's plenty more where it came from," Iris winked. "I left two full chests in Ithyka when I passed through... I wasn't sure how far north I'd continue before settling down as a commoner."

"A commoner? With two chests of gold coins?" Keyth asked, stunned. Yara passed him half a handful of coins, which he tried giving back to Iris, but pocketed at her adamant insistence. He kept one out to examine. It had a face imprinted on it. "Who's face?"

"Odyn, Prince of Olympus," she muttered. "That's where I started off."

"Olympus is real?" Yara inquired.

Iris spun in confusion. "I didn't realize I was *that* far north," she snorted. "Yes, Olympus is real. The realm has three great cities. The Three Imperial Cities."

"We've heard of the Three Imperial Cities," Keyth said. "Olympus is one of them?"

"Athyns, Olympus and Avernus," Iris explained. "Each is ruled by a Prince. The Three Princes are elected, each by their respective city's Three Nobles. Together, the Princes comprise the Triumvirate government which has ruled the realm for more than two hundred years."

Keyth glanced back at Yara. They knew none of this. "And you've been to Olympus?" Keyth questioned.

Iris pulled her faded blue cloak tighter. "Been there? I lived in Olympus until my fifteenth name day!"

"You left home when you were fifteen?" Yara asked in awe.

"No older," Iris said. "Of course, I had visited other cities before then. I knew where to go. Who to talk to. I knew how to escape from Olympus."

"Escape? You were a prisoner?" Keyth wondered, feeling like he was missing something.

"Not a prisoner of the law. Just a prisoner of life. A prisoner of *that* life," Iris muttered. "It is no small matter to change places in this culture. It is hard to change. It was hard to leave all that... land and wealth. Just so the world isn't all watching you."

Glancing back over one shoulder, Keyth had to agree. Even Greater Kryden had disappeared behind him. He was leaving behind everything he had known or recognized. It *was* hard to leave. He knew it was for different reasons than Iris'. *But, by the Maker, it* is *hard.*

24

Hours melted away like the icy snow pressed against Dryn's cheek. His skin felt gouged by the snow, even though the pure white surface on which his face was pressed was as soft as a blanket. Shivering, he didn't pull the cloak away until he was sure the hunter was long gone.

Beside him the dead embers from the night before lay undisturbed in their makeshift pit. The trees around him had parted their branches where the horse and rider had forced their way through, and a series of deep tracks passed within three feet of Dryn. He wasn't sure he would still be breathing if not for that space of three feet.

The night before he had scried the hunter, who apparently had been scrying him at the same time. The result was the enemy's immediate recognition of Dryn's location. With only moments to find a way out of the life or death situation, he had decided that to flee on foot would result in a hopeless chase.

The plan he had decided upon had seemed nearly as desperate, and yet he rose safely that morning, when he pulled back the cloak and looked up into the now-cloudy dawn sky. Upon returning to his own vision after the scrying, he had hurriedly lain in his melted imprint in the snow. Pulling the cloak over the snow hid him completely, and made it appear as if he had run.

It was hard to breathe beneath the cloak, but Dryn could survive on a few short breaths more easily than he could with the hunter's horse right behind him. *The Maker himself must be smiling down on me,* he decided. The plan had worked perfectly in two ways.

Firstly, morning had come and Dryn was alive; he had avoided a catastrophic night. Secondly, he now had two advantages he did not have the day before. He could scry his enemy, and that enemy was now ahead of him instead of behind him.

Likely, Dryn decided, the hunter had ridden the entire way to Ithyka during the night, giving Dryn a clear road the whole way there. He pulled the second cloak off the surface of the snow and wrapped it around him. Damp and cold as it was, it trapped more of his body's warmth inside than one cloak alone. He shouldered the pack containing both books and his letters, and he set off southwest.

Within a half-dozen steps he crossed two sets of tracks. One was obviously the hunter's; deep and thin holes in the smooth snow meant horse hooves. The other set of tracks made Dryn stop in mid-step. They were boot tracks.

Who was out here? Had Dryn's hiding inadvertently set the hunter's pursuit onto another unsuspecting traveller? *Or Keyth? Maker shield them... if the tracker stumbled onto Iris, it could mean disaster.*

After a moment of panic, Dryn realized that there was only the single line of boot-prints in the area. So it could not be his friends. There would have been three sets of foot tracks.

Maybe this is why the hunter left my camp so quickly, instead of investigating.... He couldn't recall if there had been tracks near his camp before he lit his fire, but for all he knew, there might have been. He quickly realized, *This set of tracks might've saved my life last night....*

He set off again, trying to subdue the confusion that kept bubbling up within him. It was very strange finding another boot tread so close to his camp. He had certainly not made them himself. Eventually, he told himself to stop wondering because there was no way to resolve this on his own. Perhaps his pursuer had saved him from a robbery.

Breaking the tree line, he found the road open and abandoned in front of him. It took him a few minutes to climb through the deeper snow at its edge and ascend the embankment onto the highway. He glanced back north. The road bent with the valley, and even the hill up to Greater Kryden was hidden from his view. He hoped Iris, Keyth and Yara had made it out of the city without any trouble.

He turned and set off southward. With growing anger and frustration, he wondered why this was happening to him. Fate had somehow picked him to be the target of a quickly changing world. He recalled Artemys Gothikar's words about being spited by the world, and he felt like yelling at the old man, *You didn't have to destroy my life to deal with it!*

In some spots the snow had completely covered the roadway, in others the ruts were open to the sky. Because of the width between tree lines on both sides of the way, a wind had picked up and was carrying snow in curtains against Dryn. Frustrated because of the treacherous footing, he made slow progress. He nearly fell off the side of the embankment when his cloak caught an errant blast of wind, and he cursed, forcing the wild cloth back against his body.

It was a lengthy and tiresome trek past the repetitive scenery. Snow dressed evergreens and naked oaks, an erratic pattern of similar shades all blanketed in a sheet of snow. After a while, the sun poked through the cloud cover, and Dryn had to squint his eyes against the brightness with which it shone off the white ground.

He pulled the newer spell book from the pack and tried reading; he kept an eye on the road, glancing up occasionally to be sure the hunter did not come riding back his way. The opened covers of the volume kept the reflecting snow-light from his eyes, and the downward angle of his head shielded his vision from the sun itself.

Of course, having his nose caught amongst the pages did nothing for his balance. He found the wind tearing at him more than once, and there was nothing calm about the way the pages loved to fly with the strong breeze.

He also glanced at the map again; the pack he had received from the Greater Kryden book shop had contained a map, another gift from the ever-mysterious correspondent. Written beside the dot of Ithyka was a simple instruction: 'Next letter at First Hearth Inn.' At least he knew exactly where in Ithyka he was supposed to go.

He wondered where this dangerous flight would go from there. Still southward? Or west? Or east? He knew basic landmarks only. South was the Mydarius Sea and the Imperial Cities; west, the Sinai Mountains; east, eventually, the Valharyn Sea.

He folded away the map in frustration. It was only a regional map, containing the regions local to Ithyka. *This wild hunt could end anywhere!* he realized. *I cannot continue these encounters! Three feet away from my hunter is far too close!*

It scared him to think about it. He had never asked for this struggle, and yet he had no choice in complying with the advice and directions he was given. It was the only thing keeping him alive. On his own, he was sure he would be far worse off. *Why me?* he wondered once more.

Come on, Dryn, he told himself. *Get over it. This is where you are, you just have to come to terms with it.*

And yet his feet stopped in their tracks. He found himself staring northward again. Back home. Back to Kryden. He stood in this way for a long drawn out moment, the fierce wind tearing at his cloak as he gazed longingly homeward.

After what seemed an eternity of indecision, he turned once more, and with a determined glare, continued southward.

Again, the hours melded together as he followed the road to Ithyka. Eventually it bent southeast. He was surprised when he started pressing onward with almost an eager pace. He was nearly there. He heard the sound of water before the hour was past and knew that the bridge would be around the next bend. That is where he and Iris had decided to meet.

He again questioned her trustworthiness. Would she come through? Had she been honest in wanting to help? If she had executed the desperate plan, such a responsibility to guide his friends to safety would earn his trust. If she had not kept her word and not brought Keyth and Yara.... He wasn't sure what he would do. Scry them perhaps? Using the Great Glyph spell he had discovered. He would have to find them. He couldn't just leave them lost somewhere.

It took an annoying length of time to reach the bridge, but when he had followed the curve of road and finally saw it, he found a welcome sight awaiting him.

Iris stood by the river's edge, staring north along the road. Her face lit up when she spotted him, and she gestured to someone hidden at the forest edge. Keyth and Yara appeared, stumbling from the foliage where they had been hiding.

Relieved that they were alright, Dryn hurried along the roadway and called, "Good afternoon!"

They embraced briefly, relieved that they had all survived. Yara seemed to be in her usual satisfied mood; Dryn had been worried about her reluctance to leave their home district. "Iris managed to gain your trust enough that you came," he said, curious as to how it had happened.

Iris' face lit up with a bright grin, while Keyth's broke into a frown. "She flicked that knife around, that's all! Call it 'trust' if you like!"

Dryn spun to Iris who laughed at the accusation. "It was hardly a threat... just persuasion."

"Just persuasion?" Dryn questioned, angrily. This information had dampened his gratefulness. "Iris! You weren't supposed to scare them! Just tell them that we had to leave!"

"Dryn!" Yara snapped, "It's alright!"

"What?" Dryn asked, turning on her. "What do you mean it's alright? Great Glyph, Yara! She drew a weapon on you!"

"No, Dryn, calm down!" Yara said, glancing at Keyth for help.

"Yara and I wouldn't have gone somewhere without a fight, if we refused to go," Keyth told him. "We decided on our own to accompany her."

"But still..." Dryn muttered, sullenly.

"Magic boy, please," Iris murmured. "Please don't ruin your nice little reunion over it."

"She's not so bad, Dryn," Keyth told him. "Once you get to know her..."

Get to know her? Dryn wondered. *I suppose that is the result of ten hours on the road with someone.*

"Why did you get here so late, magician?" Iris asked. "You left Greater Kryden ahead of us..."

"Please, my name is Dryn," he said. "I call you Iris. If you're going to continue to 'help out,' you will have to use my name..."

She laughed. "Alright, *Dryn*... How was your journey?"

"I camped last night," he told her. "I'm assuming you three didn't. That might be how you passed me."

"We had a few rests along the way, but never set up camp," Keyth said.

"Your tracker got ahead of us during the night," Iris explained. "Obviously, he didn't catch you."

"It was close," Dryn muttered. "Really close. But I'm still alive, and he's been tricked into Ithyka, I think."

Iris smiled, and with one hand played with her hair. "I won't ask how you managed that.... You seem capable enough on your own."

Now that he had confirmed a basic ground rule of respect with her, she almost seemed friendly. She was wearing the same pair of pants he had seen her in when they left Greater Kryden, and he was surprised to notice Yara was wearing a pair of breeches instead of her dress. She had a pack slung across one shoulder; the plain woollen garment was likely within it. Iris had a pack as well, containing her belongings; it was a fairly large pack, but she carried it easily enough.

"Where to now?" she asked. "You seem to know enough to have destinations set out. That part I still don't quite understand, because it seems like the three of you left without planning."

"The First Hearth, I believe," Dryn said. Then, he added awkwardly, "I... uh, I believe has good rooms...."

Keyth blinked at him; the bowyer's apprentice knew him well enough to recognize when he was covering something. Thankfully, Keyth knew about the letters, *and* understood to keep them a secret for now.

Although, Dryn thought, *Iris proved trustworthy in guiding them... perhaps I can let her know about this correspondent...* It would take some convincing to satisfy her that the source was safe enough, especially as they still didn't know who was sending the letters.

"Right..." Iris muttered. "I suppose the First Hearth will have to do. Isn't quite as rich as your last choice of bedding.... But who am I to argue?" As she stumbled away towards the bridge, he heard her murmur under her breath, "Only the daughter of some fool lord..."

Dryn followed behind Keyth and Yara as they set foot on the cleared cobbles of the bridge. It was twice as wide as the bridge of the Syroh River, twice as long as well. The Lyrin River was a torrent fifteen feet below them. Dryn glanced down into the small canyon. He could see rocks jutting from the white-crested waves. Against the far side, which they approached, he could see a large pipe protruding from the stony cliff wall. It was covered by a rusted and dirty grate. A sewer. He glanced up from it, giving the city above it a closer look.

Across the Lyrin, rising like some mountain of Imperial majesty, was the seemingly immeasurable bulk of Ithyka. The wall couldn't contain the city, it appeared. Some buildings were built against the wall, huts crouching for cover under the battlements. Huge stone buildings rose above the ramparts, windows and icy balconies keeping watch against the skies themselves. Directly ahead of them was a gate, guarded by two massive sentry towers. Faded thatch covered the tops of these; Dryn could spot guards pacing those pinnacles.

Having crossed the bridge, he found himself only a dozen feet from the huge walls. Chivalric carvings decorated the framework of the gate. Huge words were carved there. He could barely recognize the letters spelling out: "The last guard against the north."

Guarding against what? he wondered.

25

Naught but a single sentry stood at the foot of the gate; Iris recalled the night she had left Ithyka for the northlands and thought she recognized the thick moustached face that had eagerly watched her from behind as she crossed the bridge. *Creep,* she had decided.

He nodded to her as she neared with her present companions, and droned in a deep voice, "Welcome to Ithyka, travelers. Don't cause trouble or you'll find out how nice the jails are."

She walked past him in annoyance, not waiting for the others to reply. She didn't need the fool guard filling their heads with fear. They had enough to worry about.

"The First Hearth is on the south side of town," she told them, without really looking at them. "It actually means the first hearth you come across, although it is aimed to appeal to southerners." When they didn't reply, she glanced at Dryn, who was gaping upwards. "Yes, the buildings are bigger than your Kryden towns..."

Ithyka was actually an impressive town, even by her standards. It wasn't very big, but neither was it small. It was relatively clean for a city its size, and there were a number of houses worth seeing. Many rich southerners purchased mansions in Ithyka; it was one of the many delicacies and traditions that shaped the arrogant culture she wished to leave behind.

"How do they build them so tall?" Keyth asked.

"They build them deep," she explained. Most of the buildings on which they gazed at were two or three storeys tall.

"Most have a basement, and maybe a second level under that. Just to anchor it in the earth, you know?"

"Sure..."

After a moment, her new friends snapped out of their daze, and looked to her for guidance. They were likely bewildered by the new sights and smells, although Iris had seen it all. They were approached by a spice salesman almost immediately after heading south. The narrow streets were completely full of poor and rich merchants. In some locations, wagons were sitting against crowded storefronts. Occasionally a long table of merchandise was set up so it reached into the street, forcing the townspeople and travellers to look at it as they tried to cram around it.

Overwhelmed as they were, Dryn and his friends set a slow pace as they crossed town. Iris didn't even bother to tell them that she was making a detour. If Dryn was right and their tracker had entered the city, the center square could be very dangerous.

It took them an entire hour to eventually reach the First Hearth Inn. The skies were beginning to darken overhead. *Earlier than normal,* Iris noticed. *Hopefully not a storm...*

"It just goes on and on..." Yara murmured as they rounded another corner, revealing yet another crowded street. The packed townspeople and merchants raised quite a din, and Iris couldn't hear the rest of what she said, but Keyth answered clearly, "I know." Dryn remained quiet.

"Alright," Iris told them, "there's the First Hearth Inn. We'll get rooms, and then I will go get my possessions. I left some items at a warehouse." She glanced at Keyth and said, "You know... all the gold..."

She led them across the street towards a middle-class inn. The first level tavern was crowded and stunk thickly of ale, sweat, and smoke. Built into the front, beneath the second-storey windows, was a makeshift stable, crammed with a half dozen horses. Some of the shingles were missing, but a steady cloud of smoke was rising from the chimney, and right inside the innkeeper greeted them cordially.

"I am Argus Galain, son of Aiden Galain. Call me Argus," he instructed, earnestly shaking hands with Dryn, and then Keyth. He bowed politely to Iris and Yara. "Are you travellers? Or simply here for the common room? Or perhaps a meal?"

Iris glanced around the overcrowded tavern room; the bar was lined with the curved backs of men focusing on their drinks, while most tables sported gambling, whether by cards or dice. A particularly loud group of men burst out in cheers and groans as someone made a winning play. The loud clatter of coins was impossible to miss. Grinning with anticipation, Iris told the innkeeper, "We'll get two rooms, but by the Maker, the common room sounds like a plan!"

Argus smiled. He was surprised, Iris knew. A woman playing the tables was a sight to be seen. But Argus Galain turned out to be professional enough not to let his surprise show. "That's a sure thing, friends!" he boomed, happily. "Two rooms for a night will come to twenty silver coins."

Iris reached into one of the pockets on her belt and handed him two gold coins. He nodded to her, and, producing a huge keychain with one hand, he gestured across the busting common room. "If you'll just follow me," he said loudly, trying to speak over the laughter and shouting that filled the room.

"By the Maker, the First Hearth was a fine choice, Dryn!" Iris told him as they followed Argus across the room. He eyed her uncertainly.

Their rooms had no style compared to the Iron Crossing in Greater Kryden, but there was a roof over their heads and two beds in each room, which suited their needs perfectly. Iris and Yara took one room, while Dryn and Keyth disappeared into the other. Iris dropped her bag onto one bed and turned to Yara, who had pulled off her shoes and was massaging her feet.

"I'm going to get the chests I left in the city. The warehouse is across town, so I will likely be gone for some time," Iris told her. "I'll ask the boys if one of them wants to help carry."

Yara nodded mutely.

Iris strode for the door and laughed at the sound of Yara's stomach growling quite audibly. "You can eat in the common room. Maker knows you could afford it with the gold I gave you."

The hallway was narrow and a drunken man stumbled by, forcing Iris to almost press against the wall. She knocked on the rough wood of the boys' door and Dryn opened it a moment later.

"Either of you want to come along?" Iris asked. "I'm grabbing my gold."

Dryn glanced at Keyth, who was lounging on a bed in the background. "The stranger got ahead of me, remember?" Dryn told her. "Shouldn't we be careful about going outside in the city?"

Iris smiled. "Not really. Think about it... in the countryside, how many crowds are there to blend into?"

Dryn appeared subdued by the response and nodded. "Lead the way then..."

He grabbed his cloak which was hanging over the bottom board of the second bed, and stepped out of the door beside Iris. As it closed, Iris called to Keyth, "Yara is going to grab supper soon, if you want to join her."

Outside the air had taken on the bluish hue of twilight. The air was colder than the previous night, and the cloud cover wasn't going anywhere. Again Iris prayed that a storm wasn't brewing overhead.

Iris followed the packed street north again, retracing their steps. "Besides," she continued her earlier response as she turned and led him eastward. "By example, he is likely investigating wealthier inns. You stayed in such style in Greater Kryden, he likely thinks you'll choose an establishment of similar quality. Just don't use any glyphs, please..."

"I don't intend to."

"You know..." she said, "something's been puzzling me." He glanced at her and she asked, "Who taught you magic? To me, there doesn't seem to be many magicians out here in the northlands."

"Oh, you know them on sight? What about back at the inn in Greater Kryden... you knew I was one?" he asked, but laughed before she could answer. "I don't know magic, Iris. I'm still learning it."

She ground her teeth. "Fine. Then, who is *teaching* you magic?"

Dryn shook his head, and remained silent, looking away.

"Are you learning from a book or something?"

"Sort of."

Iris groaned. "Sometimes you're as simple as a street urchin. Other times, you're as cryptic as a Noble!"

"That's a good generalization," Dryn muttered, "Since you've known me for *so* long..."

"This way," she said, ending the conversation and walking faster, ahead of him. *It must have something to do with that letter...* she realized. He had attacked her to get it back. She hadn't even read it all, but now she wished she had.

The warehouse was similar to one of the banks Olympus provided, although, instead of managing the money of lords and ladies, it was a storage place for travelers or those who had more belongings than they could house. The proprietor recognized Iris when she entered the small corner office. The room was cramped with boxes and shelves, bulging under the weight of their loads. He rummaged through his desk for a few moments when she requested to pick up her two chests. Eventually, he found the key ring he was searching for and flipped through a number of keys.

The interior of the warehouse was divided into several different rooms on several different layers, to protect people's belongings. Items of most value were kept closest to the center of the maze, so the owner led them around several corners and up a flight of stairs before stopping in front of a door numbered '14'.

Inside was a number of chests, barrels and crates. The man glanced over some, tore off two notes tied to them, and told them these were the two chests. Dryn lifted one and grimaced. He asked, "You say there's just gold in these? How much is that?"

Iris lifted the other and they began a very weary trek back to the First Hearth Inn. The tavern was just as packed as it had been when they had left, so manoeuvring through the patrons was quite a feat with two heavy cases. They put both in Yara's room, and found the girl herself in the boys' room with Keyth. They stuttered in their conversation and greeted Iris and Dryn awkwardly.

They were either discussing something private, or me... Iris thought to herself, amused. Expecting the offer to be turned down, she asked all three of them, "Anyone want to join me for the evening in the common room?"

Keyth and Yara passed, but Iris was surprised when Dryn decided, "Sure."

Tantalized and curious as to how much experience he had in tavern life, she grinned at him and followed him out of the room. Despite his polite resistance, they each filled a pouch with gold from one of the chests in her room, and Iris led the way towards the common room. "Do you know King's Gambit?"

"Uh... no."

"What do they call it this far north...?" she muttered. "Magician's Expense?"

"Heard of it..."

"How about Herymus?" she asked, naming another popular game.

"Nope..."

She rolled her eyes. "Do you at least know how to play dice?" When he didn't answer, she glanced at him and growled. "Great Glyph!"

He cringed. "Sorry. I thought you meant 'eat in the common room'."

"Maker burn me!" she barked.

They took seats at the bar and Iris ordered a mug of Keeper's Finest. The ale was bitter in comparison to that of Olympus, but that was years ago and she had tasted far worse than First Hearth's. Dryn had awkwardly requested the same, and his eyes widened as he drank it. "This is far different than Kryden ale!" he exclaimed, lowering the mug from his mouth.

A nearby table boomed with the end of a hand, some men cursing their luck, others thanking the Maker for their petty winnings. She recognized King's Gambit, even from where they sat, just from the set up of the cards.

"Come on," she said, and walked away without waiting for him. "Hullo, boys!" she called, "Got room for another player?"

A man with a wild black mane glanced up from the opposite side of the table and laughed, "Wo-ho! Look at what we got here!"

Another gave the first a hit in the shoulder and said to her, "Don't mind Sylus. He's had far too much of Master Galain's ale. Call me Irden. And feel free to join us." Irden had a close trimmed square of straw hair and a thick moustache. The three other players shifted their chairs as Iris pulled one over from another table. Dryn sat on an angle behind her, staring at the cards curiously.

"Magician's Expense," Irden said as he shuffled the cards. "Standard 10 card count, plus the Wizard's face card."

She nodded. Different names in Olympus. But the same game.

Irden started dealing. "You have to bet with each play, and you have to match the equivalent of your play in copper. We add that last rule around here to keep things interesting."

She smiled. "Very well.... In that case, though, does anyone have extra copper? I'll trade in some gold so I have smaller coins."

Irden raised an eyebrow and grabbed a pouch of coins from a pack hanging at his chair. He tossed it to her and she caught it smoothly. She flipped one gold coin back across at him and he pocketed it. The other players stared at her, not bothering to hide their disbelief.

Iris glanced at her hand and grimaced. It wasn't the best, but it wasn't terrible either. A two, a five, a six, and a ten. She emptied Irden's pouch on the table in front of her. Two silver coins, which meant eighty copper.

The man between her and Irden played first, revealing a two as he slid it towards the middle of the table and flipped it face up. He tossed two coppers with it.

Iris matched his play with her two, and tossed in two copper's for the card, to keep the bet. Because she was playing an equal number, she paid an additional half bet; she tossed a third coin, and Irden nodded.

The game went fast and Iris lost the first round. Dryn muttered something under his breath as he watched the man between Iris and Sylus pocket a full handful of copper coins. She grinned and asked if he wanted to try. He shook his head sullenly. She played a few more rounds, won some copper and called it quits. She hadn't won back all she had bet, but she was bored with the game. She had always preferred dice. She got another mug from the bar and led Dryn around the common room in search of a different game.

Close to the window a group of men were standing around two players. There was a familiar rattle, and then an explosion of released breath and comments after the results were absorbed. She watched for a few moments until one of the players muttered, "I've had enough."

Disappointed that their entertainment had come to an end, the audience sighed and started to scatter, until Iris chirped at the winner, "I'm in!" It was similar to a game called Glyckhawn, a game she had learned in the east. The mountaineers had many strange games, and yet a similar form of dice gambling could be seen on any side of the Mydarius Sea.

There was a piece of cloth lain flat with a grid traced over it. The numbers in each grid square corresponded with faces of the dice. If the number was rolled, the player must gamble a coin onto that square. If coins were already there, the player won them with the roll.

Her opponent set the dice down, offering her first roll. She dropped a copper on the Wedding square, labelled with the number seven. Her first roll came up with a four and a five. She dropped a silver onto the nine square.

The man grinned. "I like to know who I'm betting against..." He bought into the Wedding, dropping a matching copper there.

"So do I," she told him curtly with a grin.

He laughed, meeting her smile. "Dobler. Dobler Orae."

"Iris Lanteera," she said. Lanteera was the name used by the steward of her castle in Olympus. Iris was a name she had chosen for herself when she had left.

"Nice to meet you," he muttered. He rolled the dice and set two copper coins on the three square. She rolled and matched his bet on the ten square. His next roll came up a ten and he removed the copper.

The game continued in such a way until there were more than fifty copper coins on the board. Not a huge winning in comparison to some games Iris had played, but it was enough to hold the attention of the audience. At the top of the grid was the twelve, or Prince. If either of them rolled a twelve, they took everything. At the bottom was the Rebel, who took everything except the Wedding square. The game ended when someone eventually rolled a twelve and removed all the coins, or if someone rolled the seven, removing the coins from the Wedding.

It was a simple game once played; Dryn nodded as he watched them, already grasping the premise without any explanation.

Dobler rolled a six, and hissed between his teeth with the sigh of the crowd. One number away from ending the game. Iris rolled, watching the two dice collide and clatter across the table. The first settled showing a six, and holding her breath, she glanced at the other. It landed with the five face up. One number off as well.

Dobler shook his head and rolled again. Receiving a three, he removed a silver and two copper coins from the square. Iris rolled, and this time the second die came up with another six. The crowd seemed to explode; some among them had been betting on who would win. Dobler sat back as Iris lifted one end of the cloth board, pouring the coins in front of her. A fair winning, she decided.

"Again," Dobler snapped. The previous player handed Iris his dice, thus cutting back the time of sharing one set. Iris lost the second game, less than she had won, but a sore loss just the same.

"The game *can* be played with a group..." she murmured. Glancing around at the audience, she exclaimed, "I need some help beating this fellow."

Two others joined the game, as well as Dryn. She smiled, hoping he didn't lose too much money. She slid some of her winnings across the table and he tossed her one of her own gold coins in return. One of the two that joined was Sylus, the card player from the other table. Humoured, Iris asked, "You just love losing money to me, huh?"

He smiled and commented obscenely, "No, that's not what I love about you..."

Iris rolled her eyes and then the dice, starting the game. Dryn didn't do badly, but at the end of the game Dobler had won all thirty coins.

As the evening blurred into the night, and the moon peaked between clouds, their games blurred together in Iris' mind. She won a fair bit, accumulating quite a pile of various coins in front of her. Soon Dobler stumbled away from the table, but the remaining four continued playing. The crowd remained intently watching the game, eagerly gambling against one another on the players' chances.

Sylus was still slurping away at ale, his movements sloppy and his rolls wild. He won occasionally, since the game was all luck, not skill or wit. But he lost a lot of money, placing his bets foolishly. Eventually he grimaced, glancing at the table in front of him when it reached his turn.

"Well... I am out of coins..." he said. "How's about I... I bet... this instead of... the other stuff..." He withdrew a white parchment from beneath the table and held it for them to see.

Iris' jaw dropped. Clutched in Sylus' hand was a letter bearing the name 'Dryn'.

"What in the Maker's...." Dryn trailed off. "Give that to me!"

"Dryn..." Iris said cautiously. She didn't want another disaster on her hands. A bar fight. Or worse... if Dryn used magic....

Sylus smiled, and explained. "If you win, you can have it! If you don't win... I burn it...." He held the letter back over the nearby fireplace.

"NO!" Dryn burst out. "You're supposed to give me the letter, not destroy it!"

"Dryn, careful..." Iris repeated.

Sylus, ignoring Iris completely, said, "I'll give it... if you win..."

"Glyphs... you Maker-forsake–" Dryn exploded

Iris grabbed his arm tightly, saying, "Dryn, get a hold of yourself! Play along! Don't ruin it again!"

Dryn glared at her, his eyes snapping away from the letter to lock onto hers. "I need that letter, Iris," he hissed. *"We* need it."

She blinked. "I don't care," she snapped fiercely. "Play along, or we walk right now. And don't you dare try to *take* it..."

His face flushed in fury and his jaw clenched visibly. He grabbed the dice from between him and Iris, and rolled them roughly onto the wooden surface. He glanced down at his roll and took the coins from the ten square accordingly. He stared at the table in front of him, refusing to look at Iris or the drunken earth-spawn beside her. Iris rolled and put a few coins on the eleven box.

Sylus rolled and got the Rebel. He pulled all the coins away, except the Wedding square. Iris flinched, but thankfully Sylus didn't burn the letter yet. As he had said, Dryn had to win. The letter didn't count as part of the grid-based winnings, but was a bonus prize.

Dryn picked up the dice and took a deep breath. He was still red with rage, but he rolled the dice gentler this time. One of them disappeared off the table, and Iris scooped it up from the floor. "Roll it again."

The die on the table showed only one pip. Dryn sighed again and took a drink from the mug nearby. He let the remaining die go, and it danced across the table. Iris nearly yelped in surprise when it landed with a six. Dryn had rolled seven, which meant he won the seventh square, effectively removing the last coins from the grid, and winning the game.

Dryn held out his hand and said, "Give me the letter, earth-spawn.

Sylus was still staring at the dice. His eyes flickered at Iris. "You switched them. You made sure he would win. It's a weighted die!" He stood up, Dryn and Iris rising with him. The crowd stirred, warily watching the events unfold. Sylus pointed his finger at Dryn. "Or you! You did something!" he sneered.

Dryn trembled visibly. "Give me the letter." His voice was strained and forced.

Iris was ready for anything. The dagger hidden in her sleeve cuff itched against her wrist and her ankle shivered where another was stuffed between the stocking and her skin.

"You cheated, you little bastard!" Sylus hissed, and threw a blow which took Dryn in the side of the head.

Taken off guard, Dryn tumbled backwards over the table, which tilted, depositing him on top of a chair and then on the floor with the chair. The crowd erupted with laughter. Iris grabbed Sylus' outstretched arm and rammed her elbow into her gut, taking him three steps away until he slammed into a chair and collided with the floorboards. As she made this tackle she shouted, "Someone hold Dryn's arms!"

Dryn had jumped to his feet, but found himself held back by two burly men from the crowd; one of them forced his arms behind his back, as Iris had ordered. She didn't want him to be able to write a glyph.

She scooped the letter from the floor and held it out so Dryn could see she had it. He settled down at that point, and Iris spun to where Sylus was climbing to his feet. She tried to grab him, but he swung a punch at her as well. It was a slow and drunken move, and Iris easily ducked beneath it. She grabbed Sylus' arm and forced it around behind him, jamming the forearm up his back in a most painful way.

"Outside," she growled, and forced him across the room in front of her. The patrons watched her, and someone even opened the door for her to manoeuvre him out.

It was black outside, except for the light from the common room and some lights she could see from down the street. "How'd you get that letter?" she asked him, walking away from the inn.

Pained by her grip on him, he spat, "I got it. That's all you're gonna know."

"Maker burn me if I accept that for an answer, you filthy spawn!" she snapped. She spun him around, releasing his arm, and smashed him with a solid punch to the face. He toppled backwards, tripped on his own drunken feet and hit the back of his head on a wooden fence in front of the building across from the inn.

Groaning in the dirt and cradling his head, he glared up at her and whimpered, "Some guy paid me, alright? He told me to give the letter to that villager. I was just trying to have some fun..." he coughed, gagging on the blood that ran from his nose and the alcohol churning in his stomach. "... burn you, you crazy..."

She had turned to walk away, but spun back and kicked him in the gut, snapping a curse at him as she left him clawing at the cobblestones.

Inside, Dryn waited for her by the door. "Thank you," he said.

"Shut your mouth."

"I'm just glad you did something before I wrecked our stay in Ithyka..."

"What don't you understand about what I said?" she asked, spinning on him. She could see the surprise bubbling out of his eyes. "I didn't mean.... Just be quiet or tell me what, by the Maker, is so damn important about this letter!" She held it up.

He remained silent, snatched it from her and proceeded to open it as they walked down the hall away from the common room. "Wait here." She set her behind against the wall as he disappeared into his room. It was dark inside; she assumed Keyth was asleep already.

She tipped her head back against the wall as she waited for Dryn. Her short hair hung back away from her face and the cool breeze running along the hallway began to calm her after the ordeal.

"I bought this book," Dryn murmured, coming out of his room, "and began to read it out of interest. A letter fell out, addressed to me, as though someone already knew I would buy the book. I read the letter and have received many since. They teach me about magic. Things going on in the world. Spells. Directions. At first I was very sceptical, but the letters haven't once lied, and have earned my trust over the last few weeks."

"Letters?" she questioned. "That's why they're important? That's how you're learning magic... from letters?"

"Yes."

"Who are they from?" she asked, eyeing him curiously.

He shook his head and his brown hair shook around his face. "I don't know. They haven't said. They also have told me that it's important it stay that way."

"Right." Iris stood away from the wall and glanced at the pack he held open. "And the books?"

"Spell books."

"May I?" she asked, grabbing one of the volumes from him. She paged through it briefly. The symbols meant nothing to her, but there were explanations written in common. Occasionally there were also printed notes. *By Dryn, likely...* she realized. She read a few of them, as Dryn seemed absorbed in the latest letter she had rescued for him. One of the side notes mentioned, 'as in the field in Lesser Kryden...'

She closed the book and handed it back to him as he finished up the letter. "Well?" she asked.

"Read it for yourself," he said. "We should leave in the morning."

She accepted the letter from him and he vanished into the room, instructing her to give it back to him in the morning.

"Dryn,

"I hope you receive this letter alright. As your scrying trick caused the hunter to reach Ithyka before you, I had to leave the city prematurely.

"Your ability to scry already astounds me. You have likely discovered an extremely rare ability to view portions of the Great Glyph itself. I can think of no other way in which you could have found your hunter with no knowledge of his identity.

"However, the crisis is not over. The hunter scours Ithyka as you read this. Thankfully the city is larger than your previous locations. Don't worry, the means to a true safe haven lies ahead of you.

"Beneath Ithyka there sprawls a large sewer and dungeon system. The city was originally the capitol of a smaller realm long before the founding of the Imperial Triumvirate. Within this sewer, and also scattered across the face of the realm, are portals known as Glyph Gates. These doorways allow you to step across their threshold and, yet in that step, cross hundreds of miles. The magic uses a similar system to True Names or True Glyphs. Every location contains its own unique pattern of glyphs. These Gates were constructed by our forefathers to allow faster travel. You needn't perform any spell or use any magic to activate the gate, simply step through the portal itself and you will find yourself on the other side.

"The reason I refer to this as a possible final escape is because this particular Glyph Gate will send you south, almost to the city of Athyns. If you arrive there safely, you will likely be outside of the hunter's current radius of searching and scrying. While there are many more hunters near Athyns, none of them will be looking for you specifically. Simply head through the Gate and do not use magic again. Seek out the magician Kronos Accalia, who is in sanctuary with Prince Theseus.

"I wish you the best of luck in this final leg of your journey. I will likely be unable to send you further letters, once you have travelled through the Glyph Gate, so I wish to tell you I am glad to have aided you.

"Also within this envelope is a spell token that will teleport you and anyone you are in contact with to a safe location near Athyns. Use this only as a last resort to escape an emergency. I repeat that this token should only be used if all else fails.

"Once more I wish you luck in your travels and hope to correspond with you once more someday in the future."

It seemed odd to have such a final statement with no signature. It left Iris hanging in mid-thought. Dryn had taken the envelope with him when he went to bed, and he likely carried the token in his pocket already. Iris knew their destination. She had been to Athyns. She had never passed through a Glyph Gate, let alone seen one.

She folded the letter and entered her room. It was pitch black, and Yara was fast asleep on one of the two cots. Iris dropped the letter by her pack and shrugged out of her tunic. Curling up in the blankets, she mulled over the events of the evening in her mind.

But when she finally dozed off into a restless sleep, there was only one thing left unresolved in her mind. Why was the printing in the letter so similar to that in the margin of Dryn's spell book?

26

Prince Theseus of Athyns knelt before each of the three statues in the corridor, each of a founder of the Triumvirate system. At the end of the hallway a ceremonial guard called to him as he rose from the silk cushion in front of the third icon.

"Who approaches the Throne of Midgard?" the sentry asked.

"Theseus, Prince of Athyns," he answered, holding his ground five feet from the guard and the carved everwood doors.

"Welcome Prince of Athyns. The Throne bids you proceed," came the expected response.

Theseus walked forward, his soft-soled shoes scuffing the stone floor. The porter who stood beside the ceremonial sentinel moved forward and, with the soft whine of the ancient latch, opened the thick doors before Theseus. The Prince passed beneath the gilded doorframe, reading the words engraved there once more. *'Antigion in'trios attikus.'* "Forget not the cost of peace." The maxim of the Dominion's forefathers, the precept upon which the Triumvirate had been built.

Beyond the everwood doors was the familiar yet breathtaking Council Chamber of Midgard. At the head of the room, directly opposite the Mydarius window, was the small wooden throne, adorned only with a silk drape and a vein of gold in each of the armrests. No one had sat in the Imperial Throne for thirty years, since Periander Gothikar stepped down following the Trionus War. The window across the room faced eastward and revealed a grand view of the Mydarius Sea stretching away until it faded into the horizon.

Between the Imperial Throne and the window was an everwood table, carved perfectly into an equilateral triangle. Seated already, with his back to the window and face towards the throne, was Prince Odyn of Olympus. His chair was set slightly back from the east side of the table and he nodded to Theseus as the Prince of Athyns seated himself on the north-western side, on Odyn's right.

Behind Theseus, finishing the processional, Pyrsius Gothikar greeted the guard with the traditional words. Theseus had known before leaving his palace in Athyns that Pyrsius would be taking the Avernus seat, yet he still found it surprising that the Three Nobles had elected a replacement for Periander so quickly.

The loss of Periander Gothikar was a mysterious tragedy in itself. In Theseus' opinion, the man had been the noblest and greatest hero in the history of the Triumvirate. During the Trionus War, he had been elected unanimously by the Council to High Prince, the first in a hundred years. Many had taunted him and pressured him to retain this higher office after the conflict was resolved. Many more had expected him to. But Periander had stepped down to the rank of Prince and the government continued to function as usual.

Now Pyrsius entered the Council Chamber and seated himself on the side of the table for the Prince of Avernus. Theseus was unsure what to expect; he wondered what Odyn thought of the thirty year old, a boy to either of them.

Following Pyrsius' entrance, three aides strode through the everwood portal. They took positions behind each of the Princes.

"You are both aware of the situation," Prince Odyn said, throwing etiquette into the Mydarius and cutting straight to the issue at hand.

"Is it such a problem already?" Pyrsius asked, ignorantly. "The Nobles of Avernus have only just granted me the rank of Prince... I am unaware of the magnitude of this situation."

Theseus stared at him and, in the corner of his eye, saw Odyn gape as well. "Your father's disappearance is a casualty, Gothikar," Theseus murmured. "And you ask if it is a problem?"

"My father is a casualty in the same way any man is a casualty," Pyrsius returned. "I know he would not want any of us shedding more grief for him than we would for our own soldiers. Looking at it in such a way... he is only one of the few losses I know of. So I ask once more, 'Is it such a problem?'"

Odyn held out a hand to his aide, who handed him a paper from a bundle of parchments. The Prince of Olympus slid the paper across the table towards Pyrsius. "We estimate that seven of every ten magicians have been slain. We have lost the Delfie School, Athyns' Academy, and even the Olympus Guild was massacred within the very walls of my palace!"

Theseus paled. He knew it was bad, but he hadn't expected this. Whoever was behind this crisis had orchestrated the genocide with ruthless and brilliant prowess. Surely, it had been underway for no more than a month. Yet such a death toll. And such a harsh long term consequence. "Has anyone claimed responsibility?"

"Not a word about it. We've tried tracking, tried scrying..." Odyn said. "The attackers rarely use magic, and after every attack, they seem to vanish."

"My father could have found out..." Pyrsius muttered. "If only he were here instead of me."

"No, I'm sure the Nobles of Avernus elected you to replace him, having judged you were worthy of this honour," Theseus said.

"But I am not a magician," Pyrsius said. "My father was the only magician on this council. And my brother Artemys, the Crown Magician... he has vanished as well!"

Something about his mannerisms reminded Theseus of the boy's noble father. But Pyrsius' words stirred suspicion in Theseus as well. It was like a puzzle piece suddenly finding its place in a complex web of details. Artemys' disappearance. Pyrsius' speedy placement. The intercepted communication between Olympus and Athyns, recently brought to Theseus' attention. And the way Odyn sat in his window-side chair, staring at the throne across the room.

"How is the search for a new Crown Magician coming?" Theseus asked, probing.

Odyn glanced at Pyrsius, and replied, "Magicians are scarce now. None of the survivors we have found would be able to pass the trials. How is the search in the north?"

"The north has never prided itself in magicians," Theseus replied. "My court wizard, Kronos Accalia, has attempted the trials and failed. He continues to search for magicians, but a wizard travelling the countryside now is in danger."

Pyrsius spoke up abruptly, shifting the subject. The new Prince of Avernus questioned, "What now? What course of action shall we follow?"

Odyn replied as if on cue, his palms flat on the surface of the table and his angular beard greased to the solidity of stone. "Conducting our own searches and our own defence of magicians is a foolish endeavour... Dividing the realm into three has never been the answer to such a crisis."

"What do you suggest?" Theseus asked, well aware of the dangerous route this was taking. His mind was racing, searching for a way out of the political disaster on his hands. The triangular table suddenly felt more isosceles, and he was seated on the short side.

Odyn took a deep breath. "I call for the election of a High Prince."

Pyrsius' jaw dropped, but Theseus saw it was an act. Pyrsius knew exactly where this was headed. The man had a gleam in his eye, almost one of pride. Theseus let out his breath slowly, and turned his glare on Odyn. "A High Prince?"

"The Triumvirate system is designed to agree under the rule of a single wartime commander," Odyn said. "I would consider this a state of civil unrest and past time for a –"

"Don't quote law to me," Theseus snapped. "What of the Crown Magician? We cannot call for the election of a High Prince without his approval!" He could not allow this to happen.

"But there is no Crown Magician," Pyrsius reminded them. "I must agree with Odyn. We must give command of our armies to a single Prince."

"Without a Crown Magician, we must delay such a decision," Theseus argued. "We must follow the statutes of this government!"

Odyn grimaced. "The laws say nothing of delaying the election during the incident. If I didn't know better, Theseus, I might suspect you of wishing more magicians to die. That is the only thing that would occur should we delay this..."

"Odyn! Don't you point fingers at me! You were the one nearly expelled by Periander Gothikar at the end of the Trionus War. Your request to elect a High Prince should be denied!"

"Who will deny it though?" Odyn returned.

Pyrsius sat back in his chair. "Princes... let's take this issue under consideration. Theseus, please think upon the issue. This crisis is a disaster already. You must see that action must be taken."

"I know action must be taken," Theseus replied. The glint in Gothikar's eyes seemed to burn into Theseus. Theseus had seen similar behaviour in both madness and genius. And both could spell catastrophe.

He glanced at Odyn, and back at Pyrsius. Something rotten was growing here in the very throne room of their realm. Theseus knew that if it came to a vote for a High Prince, his vote would mean nothing. Odyn would nominate himself, and Pyrsius would agree.

Theseus closed his eyes for a moment and took a deep breath. An errant thought crossed his mind and he caught himself wondering if they were the ones behind the genocide. It made sense. The slaughter of magicians would provide the civil crisis needed to call for an election, and it would also get rid of the Crown Magician, the only person capable of stopping an election. But surely the Princes of the Imperial Triumvirate were not so corrupt. Such a plot could tear the Dominion to shreds.

"Let us reconvene in two weeks time," Theseus declared. "We may vote for a High Prince at such time. This will give us a chance to consider all the options. This incident has begun so quickly, I am not sure we all understand its ramifications."

Something close to rage passed across Pyrsius' face and was replaced instantly by the mask he had worn the entire time. The mask that looked like Periander.

Odyn agreed within a moment. "Very well, Theseus. We will prolong the solution. Return to Athyns and *consider* all you wish. Meanwhile, casualties will continue to rise."

Theseus nearly lost self control of his growing fury. *Don't blame the casualties on me!* he nearly shouted. *And don't try to change my mind by imposing guilt!*

Pyrsius also conceded to Theseus' proposal, and the session of the Imperial Council was adjourned. They left in the order they had arrived. Ahead of him, Theseus watched Odyn bow respectfully to the three statues in the hallway. This made Theseus grow even angrier and his own bow was poor and stiff.

In the courtyard below the Tower of the Imperial Throne Theseus was immediately approached by Kronos Accalia. "How did it go?"

"Write your teleportation spell," Theseus ordered, without answering the question.

"That bad?" his magician asked.

"Within the month we may have a full war on our hands," Theseus said. He glared across the courtyard to where Odyn talked quietly with Pyrsius, and then glanced back at Kronos. "Let's return to Athyns."

27

When Yara awoke that morning, she certainly wasn't expecting a journey into the sewers of Ithyka. Even less was she expecting the events that would unfold there.

When she awoke, she rolled groggily in the blankets to see Iris sitting in the stream of sunlight from the window. The girl held a parchment in her hands, poring over the words. Yara blinked in the bright light and sat up. "How long have I slept?"

"Past breakfast," Iris murmured, not looking up. "The boys grabbed food already, but we have to leave soon. If you want to eat first, you'd better move yourself..."

"Where are we going?" Yara asked. "Further south?"

"South, but we're not walking. Dryn knows about a portal of some kind. It will help us travel faster..."

Yara blinked. "A portal? How does Dryn know about this? He's rarely heard of Ithyka before this trip...." She stepped out of bed and quickly changed into the shirt and pants Iris had given her in Greater Kryden. "Where is this portal?"

Iris glanced up from the paper and folded it as she said, "Below the city. There's a complex network of sewers, and apparently a dungeon of some sort. The portal is within the ruins of this sub-terrain."

"We're going into the city sewers?"

Iris rolled her eyes and stood up. "I can't imagine them being much worse than those of Olympus. Now, when those sewers get backed up..."

Yara reflexively gagged. "Alright, I'm sure today's journey will be fine!"

She ate a rushed meal in the nearly deserted common room, served by the innkeeper himself. Argus Galain was as respectful and kind as he had been the previous night.

While Yara ate, Iris organized their packing. The two chests of coins were divided into pouches and then placed in four packs, so that all four of them would share the load. Dryn and Keyth bought some food from one of the street markets nearby and came upon Yara as she finished her meal.

Together they wandered down the hall towards their room. "I was smart enough to buy a couple of torches," Keyth told her, excitedly. In one hand he was carrying a bundle of the smooth wooden handles.

She could tell he was excited for their adventure. Instead of crushing his enjoyment, she instead turned to Dryn. "What portal is this...?"

Dryn nodded. "I don't really know. The latest letter included a sketched map of the way. It will still be a difficult search.... These 'Glyph Gates', as they are called... they aren't exactly in common use."

"The letter?" Yara knew that both Dryn and Keyth believed the letters, and she had no reason not to, but she found herself irritated that she was going to explore a sewer on the order of some unknown correspondent. *Probably some manipulative Maker-forsaken sorcerer....* Was Dryn right though? Were they still alive only because of that manipulative wizard?

In her room Iris had laid out four packs made of tanned hide. She took the supplies given to her by the boys and divided them into the packs. She sent Yara to Master Galain to have four canteens filled with water; the innkeeper happily obliged and Yara returned to the room to find the packing completed.

They set off from the First Hearth and Iris took the lead. Dryn's map only showed the way through the sewer; he had no clue how to get there. Iris eventually turned off the main street and, at the back of an alley, led them into a small garden. In the middle was a vine-covered well. Yara had a momentary vision of trying to climb down a well, but Iris led them past it into the back of the garden.

A pair of wooden cellar doors were built on an angle against the rear of a building there.

"Here we are," Iris muttered. "Brace yourselves," she warned, gripping the handle of each door. Throwing them open released a wave of stench that hit Yara like a thunderstorm. She had to take a step back until her nose started blocking out the foul smell.

Iris seemed un-phased by the stink. She fumbled in her pack and withdrew a torch. After playing with a flint for several moments, she struck sparks that eventually lit the torch ablaze. The light illuminated a dank set of stairs, fading into the shadows out of the firelight.

"What a stench!" Dryn coughed, one hand cupped over his nose.

Iris laughed. "You'll get accustomed to it. I suppose if there truly are remains of some ancient dungeon, the sewer smell might not have reached it. For that matter... we might not either."

"We will," Dryn decided determinedly.

Iris and Dryn led the way down the stairs. The rotten wood drooped under Yara's feet as she and Keyth followed. They found themselves in some sort of cellar. The walls were lined with empty shelves, and a half shattered crate lay on its side in one corner. Another flight of stairs descended in the same direction as the one from which they had entered.

These steps were stone instead of wood. At the bottom was the source of the smell. A long tunnel stretched perpendicular to the stairwell. Murky water flowed along a trench in the middle of the room, and vapour rose from the fetid river. A grate in the arched ceiling above them let grid-like beams of sunlight into the space, but they seemed to fade long before the floor. Iris' torch illuminated a circle around them, flickering light into the beady eyes of rats which scurried for cover.

Trying to keep her breakfast down, Yara approached Dryn's side. He was reading the map and declared, "There's a door on the other side, at that end."

Iris found a narrow bridge several feet away, a catwalk connecting their side of the floor to the one divided by the sewage. The stone bridge had barely enough room for two feet side-by-side, and no railing or handhold to speak of. Iris was across without wavering her balance, Dryn close behind her. Yara nearly fell, but after much shuffling of sandaled feet, she reached the other side. She somehow found herself thankful for the repulsive brick floor on the other side.

As Keyth crossed, one of the stone tiles on top gave way, sliding across loose shale. The rock plopped into the waterway beneath, and Yara thought Keyth might fall in with it. He somehow landed on hands and knees on the next tile of the catwalk and arrived, panting for breath, on their side.

No one said a word. Dryn was poring over the directions and drawings on his parchment, and Iris was examining an old crate against the wall. Yara broke the silence now that Keyth was closer, checking to see if he was alright.

He nodded, his face pale, and followed Dryn's lead. At the end of the long room was a door with spaced iron bars that divided it into eighths. The latch was covered in rust and wouldn't move under Dryn's hand, but a solid kick shattered the weak metal and the door creaked open when he forced it.

Yara followed them down a narrow corridor which wound right and left. Eventually, they reached another grated door. Again, Dryn forced his way past it and his friends followed. For well over an hour they proceeded to follow the map through hallway after hallway, room after room, gate after gate.

Out of breath and sore, Yara was about to call for a break when Keyth asked for one. The next room on the map was a storage cellar of some kind and they rested on the old boxes and barrels set against the walls. Yara set her head back against a box, and ran a hand over her greasy forehead. *Could we even find our way back to Ithyka if we needed to?* she wondered.

"Do you know the way back?" she asked of no one individually.

Dryn answered. "I suppose we would just follow the map in reverse. Strange, it says there's a room behind that wall."

Iris walked to the other side of the room and peered at a hole smashed in the wall. Bricks were laying across the floor, and her torchlight barely seemed to pierce the dark beyond. "Look at this," she called.

Yara groaned when she stood on her feet again. Her heels were slabs of stone. Stumbling to Iris' side along with Dryn and Keyth, she peered at Iris' find. There was a four or five foot drop before a smooth stone floor stretched away from the wall. On either side of this next passage were stone walls, composed of black panels hewn from some dark rock she did not recognize. Patterns were carved into the sections, complex weaves and decorations, like a tapestry had been sewn in the stone.

"This is definitely not part of the sewer," Iris murmured, slinging one leg then the other over the remaining section of wall. She dropped down into the new hall, landing lightly on her feet and inhaling deeply. "Smells better, Yara!"

That was a short break... Yara thought to herself. Soon the four of them stood in the glow of Iris' torchlight. Yara glanced back and asked, "How do we get back up there?" The rock wall was smooth apart from the scrawling artwork.

Iris noticed it as well. "Should have left a rope..."

"We're not going back that way," Dryn said.

Yara turned to him. "What if we can't find this magical gate of yours?" she questioned.

"We will." Dryn's words were solid and stern. "I trust the letters. The Glyph Gate will be there. So far this map has been correct as well."

Yara felt like snapping a curse as Iris might have done. Iris remained silent, and so Yara did as well. She glared at Dryn. She wanted to trust him, to lean on the strength in his voice. But she couldn't.

The passageway was wider than the halls in the sewer behind them. The black stones absorbed the light, so Yara could only see a dozen feet ahead of them. Once she thought she heard a thud behind them, but she glanced back and saw nothing.

After a few minutes, Dryn muttered, "That's odd.... We're supposed to turn right soon..."

"Turn?" Iris asked, confused. The hallway appeared to continue straight with no joining passages.

Then abruptly their steps brought them into the crossroads of four corridors. It was as though the walls had suddenly opened up to allow more hallways. Iris took a few steps backward and burst out laughing. "That's brilliant..." she chuckled. "The walls have a slight angle to them. Just enough that you can't see the hallways..."

They followed the passageway to the right, and within several steps the previous corridor had eerily vanished. This hallway seemed to stretch infinitely as well. Dryn directed them to the left, and another mysterious intersection appeared.

This time, the passage opened into a circular room. Rocks had fallen from the domed ceiling and the floor was littered with debris. Iris blatantly stepped over something that glinted under the flickering light of her torch. Yara knelt and picked it up.

"A coin!" she gasped in surprise. It looked like gold, but was dusty and wouldn't clean when rubbed.

"Let's see," Keyth said. He gazed at it in awe. "Who's face is that?" he asked.

Yara squinted at it. "I don't know..."

"Here," Iris said. She picked it out of Yara's hand and beheld the bust on one side. She responded with a tone of surprise. "That's Tiberon Odyn. One of the founders of the Triumvirate..." She flicked it back through the air. "See the date?"

Yara read the other side of the coin as she followed Iris across the room. "214?" she asked. "What does that mean?"

"That's the year..." Iris answered, turning back.

"Who numbers years?" Yara asked, confused. "Don't people name the years?"

Iris laughed loudly. "Some people do. But most of the world numbers them as well. Year One is when Olympus was first founded."

"What year is it now?" Dryn asked, curious.

"588."

Yara's eyes widened and she stared at the coin in her hand. "It's more than three hundred years old?"

"Old, isn't it," Iris asked. "I knew this dungeon was old, but I didn't know Ithyka was around that long ago."

"It wasn't called Ithyka back then," Dryn said. He pointed across the room. "There's another hall over there."

Yara stashed the treasure in her pouch and followed her friends across the room. The passage they entered was identical to the previous ones yet opened almost immediately into a second domed room. In the center two rough columns of dark stone rose several feet into the air and met in a slanted arch. Between them a black hole had seemingly been torn in the air itself, an abyss which absorbed their torchlight even as they neared it. In the middle, barely visible against the bizarre spectre, was a winding symbol, a single character composed of a dozen angular lines, circles, and dots. It seemed to float in the air itself, directly in front of the abyssal backdrop.

"Is that the gate?" Yara asked as they approached. She looked at Dryn, who was bending down, replacing the map into his pouch.

A crack of noise tore the silence of the room, a deafening screech that ended almost as soon as it had begun. A bolt of lightning slashed horizontally across the room and seemed to explode directly in front of Dryn. Sparks of white light zapped through the air and Yara jumped back.

Dryn jumped to his feet and the air seemed to surge in front of him. "Get through the gate now!" he shouted.

Another bolt of energy cracked across the room and nearly struck Dryn who leapt headlong towards the wall. A man stood near the door of the chamber, his hand raised in their direction and crackling with light.

Yara found arms around her waist and Keyth hauled her towards the black portal. She glanced at the abyssal doorway through which Iris vanished. As Keyth pulled her through, she saw a burst of fire scorch away from Dryn towards the attacker.

28

Dryn had led the way into the room and was instantly drawn towards the gate in its middle. He stopped and opened his pack to replace the map. Since entering the dungeon area, he had been carrying the map and a water defence token. The spell would create a pool of water in midair, blocking most types of magical attacks.

There was no need for it now, so he was replacing it at the bottom of the pouch with the map, when Yara said something and he glanced up. His eye caught movement in the corner and then a loud bang blared against his ears. Instinctively, his muscles braced themselves to be hit by something, coincidentally causing his fingers to clench.

The instant the stone token broke between his fingers a water shield shimmered in front of him at the exact moment to catch the first bolt of lightning. Dryn grabbed a handful of tokens from his bag and cast an air blast at the attacker, shouting "Get through the gate now!" to his friends.

Another explosion of lightning nearly struck him, but Dryn threw himself to his left. As he came up on one knee, his finger traced in the dirt the glyph for four fire attacks as his lips hissed the ancient words. He lifted his hand and the first shot through the darkness at his enemy.

Short of killing the hunter, there was no safe way out of this. *Not this time...* he realized. There was only one exit and he doubted safety lay beyond it if he could be followed. He would have to find a way to defeat his enemy *before* escaping.

By the time the fourth fire blast scorched across the stone, Dryn found himself staring at the open doorway from which they had entered. He jumped up from his crouch and planted his back against the wall. In each hand he held a token: one for fire, the other a shield.

"You really don't stand a chance, boy," a thick voice called. The sound echoed, and Dryn assumed the hunter was standing at the end of the hall, having backed away. "Your little scrying trick might have been unexpected, but you really have no chance."

Dryn remained silent, creeping towards the dark hallway with the fire token clutched between his thumb and first finger. Without Iris' torch, it was impossible to see anything in the black room. The Glyph Gate gave off a flickering light, but it was dim and didn't reflect on the dark stone walls.

Abruptly a blast of light appeared as a flurry of fireballs shot through the doorway. Dryn was so close that he could feel the heat sear his skin as it passed. As he watched, the small pricks of fire soared around the room and then arched back toward him.

"Great Glyph!" he cursed, and leapt across the opening of the door. Two fireballs impacted the walls on either side, showering Dryn with sparks and gravel, but the remainder flew past and exploded inside the hallway. The eruption of heat caused Dryn to cringe. Hoping his opponent was down or dazed, he rolled into the open doorway and sent his own fire blast down the hall.

It seemed weak in comparison, a single fist-sized ball of flame, but amidst the settling rock, dust and smoke from his enemy's attack, his blast made it the entire way down the hall before exploding prematurely against an invisible barrier. *A ward...* Dryn realized, remembering their description in the letters and books. *Was it destroyed by my fireball? Or is it still there?*

He rose and took a tentative step down the hall, pieces of shattered rock grinding under his boots. He withdrew another spell from his pocket.

"Aborder tal'oken – koevenos!" the man's voice incanted, and the earth suddenly seemed to quiver beneath Dryn's feet. Before whatever spell his enemy had used took full effect, Dryn dashed forward into the hallway. He heard stone rumble behind him and felt a wave of heat catch him in the back. As he was thrown forward, he broke the fire token and cast the spell

directly through the doorway. He heard the man shout and then Dryn hit the ground.

Rolling, he came up on all fours, his hand already tracing air attacks into the dusty floor. A blast of air caught him before he finished and he found himself dragged across the rough floor. He grabbed a random token from his pocket and slammed it against the stones under him.

A blinding light filled the room and his enemy shouted in pain. Dryn planted his feet firmly and stood up. The fading light illuminated the man standing near the doorway. His jacket was hanging tattered around his shoulders and his hat was missing. Beneath the dishevelled black hair, his eyes glared at Dryn.

"How did you learn that spell, fool?" the hunter asked. "You are a beginner trying to grasp mastery spells."

"Why are you hunting me? I never did anything to you!" Dryn snapped. "Leave me alone!"

The man burst out into loud laughter. "I'm not hunting *you*," he told Dryn. "I'm just following orders. You're in way over your head, boy. Killing you... well, that's doing you a favour."

"Try... just try to kill me," Dryn threatened, attempting to sound dangerous. In one hand, he clutched the teleportation token. *Just break the token,* he told himself. But he had to buy more time. *Let Iris get them away from the Glyph Gate... get them to safety....* He wasn't sure where he would end up when he activated the spell, but he knew he would be far away from this hunter.

"Try?" the man hissed, furiously. "TRY? Let me show you a bit of what I can do!" He raised one arm and, before Dryn could move, a token shattered into a dozen pieces in his opponent's fist, dust falling through the air.

Immediately, Dryn couldn't move. He couldn't even close his fingers around the teleport token. Panic tore into his every thought. His body rose to float several feet in the air. He couldn't break the token even though he could feel its brittle surface in his fist.

"Do you see it yet? Oh, what's that? You can't see spells yet?" the hunter questioned. "Well, if you knew up from down, you would know what I have done. I used a control spell. I bound air under my control. Don't worry, it's only temporary.

The Great Glyph has rules..." The man moved one arm outward, and Dryn's body followed.

This can't be happening.... He could feel the smooth material of the token in one hand, but couldn't muster a twitch to use it. *Let me go!* he wanted to shout, but he couldn't speak.

The man's stoic face broke into a smile, and he thrust his arm out in front of him. Blinding pain slammed into Dryn, and it took him a moment to realize he was lying on the floor. Stone shards tumbled across him, slabs from the wall he had impacted. He lifted his head and glared dizzily through the agony. His eyes eventually focused enough to see the token lying several feet away.

"No!" he gasped, and tried to lift himself to his feet. As his arm clawed forward, the paralysis returned, and he found himself lifted until he was face to face with the hunter.

"Who taught you?" the man questioned. "The amount you have learnt so quickly.... Speak, boy! Is there another magician in your hometown?"

"Maker burn you!" Dryn spat. The air tightened against his chest, quickly squeezing the air out of him. He coughed, and felt something crack inside. Pain burned against his skin, and his vision almost failed. He could barely feel the safety token in his fingers.

"It is of no consequence. I don't feel like torturing you... I will simply burn the village itself..." the man decided.

NO! Dryn shouted, but no sound left his mouth. He tried desperately to fight against the air that held him in place. *LET ME GO!!!*

"I'll get this over with," the hunter decided. He lifted a handful of tokens and appeared to ponder the glyphs. "Which.... How shall I kill you...?"

Dryn belatedly realized that he could die. The man was fighting him with magic, not metal. He thrashed against the invisible force holding him, and still it was of no use. The man chose a token from his hand and lifted it up. "See that?" he asked Dryn. "Light. I'm going to kill you with light."

He broke it in a grandiose gesture and cast his hand towards Dryn, fingers splayed. A blade of glorious white parted the shadows of the room and smashed across Dryn's undefended body. Shattered shards of stone and light seemed to dance before his eyes and then shifted to reveal the stone floor slanted away from his eyes like a wall. There was thick red blood splashed across the stones, and Dryn realized in a gut-twisting gag that it was his own.

The pain hit like a clap of thunder and he found himself writhing against the dank dirty floor. That only made things worse: he felt a tearing sensation in his chest, and something warm spread through his shirt. Then, one thrashing hand found the token lying in the blood and broke it.

Orion of Edessa followed the villager and his friends through the eerie underground until they reached their destination. He could sense it in the first domed room, a tugging at his magical senses. A Glyph Gate. *By the Maker, how did that fool find out about a Gate down here?* he wondered in surprise.

The ambush went perfectly, although the villager's friends got through the portal safely. They were relatively insignificant, so Orion focused his assault on the target itself. The villager blocked the first attack, but moved as expected – away from the Gate.

The ensuing skirmish was rather annoying, Orion decided. The fool managed to survive his fire-earth attack, a spell which normally destroyed his opponents. It must have been the layout of these ruins. The walls themselves seemed to choose sides.

After that immature taunt, 'Try to kill me,' Orion chose to quit the game with the villager. He bound his True Glyph to the air and took control of the situation. He threw the boy across the room to demonstrate his ability, and then hauled him upright again.

He chose a light-spear to finish the villager off. It was such a gorgeous spell. The glyphs' translation meant something like, 'blade of the sun.' Orion broke the token and slashed the spell across the fool's torso and face. The boy tumbled back through the air and smashed bodily into the wall. Amidst a shower of shale and black masonry, his body crumpled to the floor and twisted in agony.

"Well..." Orion muttered. "That's done with. Took damn long enough!" He pocketed his remaining glyphs and smiled down on the boy. Blood was splattered all over the floors and walls, and Orion could only imagine what devastating pain was ravaging the dying body.

Then the boy's fingers seemed to close over one shard of stone and Orion jumped back. It was a spell token! The air around the villager flickered briefly, as though a section of Orion's vision had shifted to the right several inches and then back again. When it settled, the boy was gone.

Orion shouted incoherently in rage, a bellow echoing through the halls. "MAKER BURN YOU!!!" he added. He rammed one fist against the nearby wall and took a few deep breaths, trying to calm himself.

A faded blue symbol shimmered over the debris where the teleport had been activated and Orion bent to read it. "Where have you gone?" he wondered aloud. Every teleport left its destination in the aftermath. He could see the ancient letters spelling the fool's village. "Why would you go back there?" Orion asked. "You could have gone through the gate to Athyns with your friends..."

But there was something else written there. An odd character he had never seen in actual use before. "What's this...?"

"The end of the road for you, I'm afraid," a voice murmured. Pinpricks of energy seared into Orion's back, and he spun, as a full storm of lightning surged through him. He found himself buried a foot into the stone wall, earth rolling down around him.

One last image swam into his vision, something that could not be. Held for one instant in his fading sight was the face of the villager he had just fought. A thick scar ran down the boy's cheek, meeting his cheekbone where Orion's light-blade had cut him. But it was a fully sealed wound.

That face seared into his memory and, was then lost, as his mind faded and death wrapped around him.

30

An errant leaf fluttered against Dryn's ear. A cold breeze tried to carry it past the obstacle of his head. The tail of his woollen cloak flapped against his legs. The air held the aroma of pine and the stench of his own sweat and blood. He gasped as his mind floated into consciousness, like a pocket of air trapped underwater. An elaborate symbol bubbled to the front of his memories and his finger traced it numbly in the cold moss beside his face. *How do I say it?* he wondered and, of their own accord, the words rattled across his tongue like the dice Iris threw.

Dryn gasped again as the healing spell surged through his body. It sealed the deep gashes in his face and chest, and drained what little energy still dripped through his muscles.

He woke again when another leaf brushed his cheek, and he rolled on the moss until his back settled onto a bed of fallen needles. He was in a forest. He stared at the sky, where trees framed a circle of night directly over his head. As he gazed at those lofty heavens, a line of light shot across the window the treetops had made. Shooting stars were common now; some called it an omen: that war was coming to the realm, or that a new plague would soon be upon them.

How did I get to a forest? he asked himself slowly. He remembered a dungeon. Ruins. A dark portal.

He sat up. *I know this forest....* In the direction he faced, he could see lights flickering between the trees. A village. He put one hand on the moss beside him to lift himself to his feet, but immediately pulled it away and wiped blood onto the thick wool of his cloak.

His stomach would have emptied itself, if it wasn't already. He had lost a lot of blood. It was smeared across the earth all around him and his clothes were soaked with it.

Trying again, he climbed to his feet and looked around. Teleport. He remembered the fight now, and landing close enough to the token to escape when his attacker released the air-grip on him. *I'm supposed to be near Athyns...* he realized. *That's what the letter said.*

He turned around, examining the foliage and peering through the trees at the village. It struck him without warning. He *knew* where he was. *This is Kryden...* For one disconcerted moment he stood dumbfounded, staring towards the village, his home.

Glyphs... what am I doing here? he asked. He glanced down at the debris and blood where he had been. No snow. *By the Maker... what is going on??* There was no snow on the ground, only a cold wind whining through the trees.

Something else fluttered on the ground. He knelt to the moss on which he had lain. A letter. *Great Glyph... another one?!*

It was held beneath a fist-sized rock, the wind whipping the parchment back and forth. He set the rock aside and stood up again. The envelope had his name written on one side as usual. He opened the top and pulled out the letter. *There had better be a fabulous explanation for all this...* he declared, as he began to read.

> "Dryn,
> "You have reached a turning point in your journey. Likely you have likely not realized yet that the token you used sent you back in time, instead of to Athyns. That is not an error... The token you were given in your last letter not only sent you to safety, but also teleported you into the past."

The past?! What does this... What is going on?! Dryn held the letter in both hands, staring at the words. There was a lot more written. The familiar printing covered both sides of the parchment. Confused, he continued.

> "You must follow the instructions I have written on the other side of this paper. At the end of it you will

find yourself back in the present, two and a half weeks from now. The truth, you will begin to realize, is that you are teaching yourself magic, Dryn."

Dryn's eyes continued to move, but he stopped reading. Moments passed as he stared blankly at the letter, trying to understand what it meant. *I have taught myself magic?* He tried thinking it through, but it baffled him. He found his mind running loops, trying to comprehend how he could be 'back in time' as the letter was explaining.

"I know very little more than you do, only what I have learned from these letters. Somehow, by some spell written by the Maker himself, perhaps... somehow, I – or we – have created a loop in which we learn magic and leave Kryden.
"You will find your pack by the nearest tree. Follow the instructions carefully. You must be sure to word every letter exactly."

Dryn glanced away from the letter and saw the shadowy shape of his pack lying nearby. A thought was growing in his mind, piecing together the logic of it. If he *had* gone back in time, he could go to each place and leave a letter for ... himself.

It played tricks on his mind though. *How did it start?* he wanted to know. *Was it my idea? Or was it his?* He had to correct himself though. He was the only one involved...

There was one last paragraph at the bottom of the page.

"I wish you luck. As I write this, I do not know what the future holds, anymore than you do. I urge you to study from the books as much as you can over the next two weeks, as you carry out the following instructions. This is a chance to double your skill in basically no time. After completing the instructions, you will kill the hunter and join your friends beyond the Glyph Gate of Ithyka. I do not know what awaits you there."

Following this last line was his own name, as the signature.

Dryn dropped the letter. *Maker help me...* he prayed. *How does this make sense? How did this happen?* He was trembling, partly from confusion, partly from terror. The letters... all along, they had been from himself? How did he learn the information though, in order to write it in the letters? He had learned the information from the letters in order to later write it there again?

The events of the past hour had created an earthquake at the base of his reality. Everything that he knew was shuddering and groaning under the weight of this revelation. Magic... was it only something he had made up in his head and taught himself? That question was easily answered. The hunter used glyphs as well.

But this war? How did he find out about it? From the letters?

He started taking deep breaths, trying to force down the panic and bewilderment. *I need to get through this,* he told himself. *I need to follow the instructions and try to figure this out.*

He picked up the letter from where the breeze had carried it through the pine needles. He read the back, and then carried out the instructions step by step.

1. You have just enough time to get to Greater Kryden and back. The first magic book from which you learned is still owned by the bookkeeper there. Buy the book from him and bring it to Lesser Kryden. Find the first letter you put in your pack and copy it onto a new piece of paper. Place this in the book and leave it for yourself to find. (someone has to write the letters, somewhere, sometime; leaving your copy of the letter, instead of creating a new one, could have dire consequences. Be sure that you still have all the letters at the end of these instructions).

He set off at once and, the following morning, retrieved the book from the merchant's wagon. He did as he was directed, copying the first letter onto a new piece of paper and placing it among the folds of the spell book.

2. After the younger version of yourself, Dryn, leaves home in the morning, place a pouch with forty copper coins on the apothecary table. Your father must find the money, so that Dryn can buy the spell book without being caught.

3. After Dryn leaves for the Corin's house, wait ten minutes. Then walk into your house. Your father will ask you to cut the wood. Take three logs and cut them elsewhere. After Dryn returns home and your father scolds him for not cutting the firewood, replace the uncut logs with your cut wood. Also, place the second letter there.

Dryn spent the next week placing letters around for his younger self to find. Some were straightforward, such as leaving one on his own bed, or in the burrow where he could remember playing with Keyth as children. Others required some stealth, such as leaving a letter outside the thieves den while his younger self fought the bandits.

He was required to make several tokens. He knew the spells to create tokens, which had been written on the letter describing their function. One of the steps included the spell for time travel, thus allowing him to create the token that would send himself back in time.

He organized a second pack, including tokens and the second magic book, and paid the shopkeeper in Greater Kryden to give it to his younger self later. Looking back on the day he had retrieved that very pack, he now understood the man's peculiar looks. From the shopkeeper's point of view, Dryn had paid him to hang on to a pouch and give it back to him the next day.

He then followed Dryn out of Greater Kryden and waited for his younger self to begin using the Great Glyph. Careful not to bother this process, he walked past the camp and created a maze of footprints leading to Ithyka. *So that's where the prints came from...* he realized. *The hunter really did pursue me the whole way to Ithyka.* Standing alone in the middle of the forest, he burst out laughing. It was confusing and yet ironically humorous.

Then came the night in Ithyka. Iris and his younger version left the First Hearth in order to reclaim her treasure trove. Wrapped in a hood and cloak, Dryn gave a man named Sylus a letter, and said, "Go, have some drinks on me. Give this to the boy sometime during a game..."

The man had looked at him quizzically, but complied. Not many men were offered a gold coin for such a trivial task.

The next morning, following the last step of his instructions, Dryn waited for his friends to leave the inn and descend into the Ithykan sub-terrain. He waited nearby until their hunter entered as well. Keeping a dozen feet behind the hunter, Dryn proceeded after him throughout the entire dungeon.

Careful not to be seen, he watched Iris lead Keyth and Yara through the Glyph Gate, watched the catastrophic fight between himself and the agent, and watched the time-teleport pull his younger version through the fabric of time and into the past. *It really warps the mind...* he thought. He could remember everything vividly: the pain, the light, and awaking on the other side. And yet now he watched it, waiting calmly.

He saw himself lose to the hunter, and then waited to see what the hunter would do. Before following his friends through the Glyph Gate, the fool bent to examine the teleport that had been used.

Dryn walked through the dark, broke a powerful lightning token in one hand, and killed the damn earth-spawn.

31

Gentle as the morning fog, a breeze rose from the sea and wafted through the short bushes until it whistled through the fallen architecture of the ruins. A shore gull floated through the sky and landed lightly upon a moss-covered stone. Beneath the weather-worn masonry, a rune flickered in mid-air, as though a figment of sunlight reflected off a plane of metal. Behind it an impassable wall of darkness seemed to bore a hole through the stone and earth itself.

From beyond this opaque pane, a booted foot appeared, striding onto the soft soil and leading a leg behind it. Attached to that came a body and face, and Iris Lanteera glanced around her new surroundings.

Behind her, stumbling in their hurried escape from Ithyka, Keyth and Yara appeared, and followed her down the crumbling steps onto the moist earth. The sun blinded them after the dark chaos of the dungeon from which they had traveled; Keyth raised a hand to shield his eyes and asked, "Where are we?"

Iris raised a finger to her lips for silence. "I don't know yet. Be quiet and we will determine if we are alone or not..."

Keyth watched as she moved away, investigating their surroundings. He peered in the direction of the Gate and saw the grass stretching away from the stonework within which they stood. "We're obviously not *in* Athyns, not yet..."

Yara looked at him concerned. "What does that mean?" she wanted to know.

He grimaced and led her after Iris. "I don't think any of us expected to step through a Gate to be in front of the city itself..."

"Where's Dryn?" she asked.

"Fighting that hunter..."

Yara stopped him in his tracks and raised her eyes to meet his. "Can he win?" she asked.

Keyth grunted, and kept walking. *Can he?* After a moment he turned back to look at Yara. "Maybe. I don't really understand it myself. Let's just follow Iris. She'll know what to do."

"Shouldn't we help somehow?"

Keyth shrugged. "I don't have a weapon, and I don't know how to fight. We would likely get in Dryn's way more than aid him in the battle."

Yara turned back to the Gate. "So I'm just supposed to wait and hope he doesn't get seriously hurt?" She spun back again to Keyth. "How long do we wait here, before we have to assume he's...?"

"Yara," Keyth said, "we've only been here a few moments."

Suddenly croaking loudly, a bird rose from near the gate and flapped away. A cloaked shape strode through the portal and a man appeared, staring at them.

"Dryn?" Keyth asked, shocked. Yara whirled and together they rushed towards him.

Dryn embraced Keyth, surprising him with a new strength, firmer than Keyth remembered. Dryn turned to Yara and hugged her as well. He stepped back to stare at them both and breathed, "I missed you two so much!"

Missed us? Keyth wondered, stepping back. Dryn had been walking beside them no more than a dozen minutes earlier. Before he could reply to the odd comment, he noticed something on Dryn's cheek, and was horrified to see a scar running down his friend's cheek. Horror turned to confusion as he asked himself how he had missed noticing such a scar. He could recall Dryn telling him of the crossbow bolt... Dryn had healed himself and no trace remained, not even a scar.

"Dryn!" Iris exclaimed. She stood several feet away, having just returned from scouting beyond the ruined stone wall. "What happened? Where's the hunter?"

"He's gone..." Dryn declared, his voice trailing off numbly. Keyth saw an emotion in Dryn's eyes that he had never encountered there before. "We should continue to the Palace of Athyns as ... the last letter instructed."

Keyth blinked. *'He's gone?'* *Dryn was able to kill the hunter?* "By the Maker, Dryn!" Keyth muttered. Iris had approached and seemed fixated on their friend's scar as well. "What happened under there?"

Dryn's eyes became blank, like beads of ice in their sockets. "Nothing happened, Keyth." He walked past them several steps, and examined the remnants of masonry around them. Yara followed next, and Keyth glanced at Iris before they continued after their friends. "We should continue to Athyns," Dryn repeated, not even turning back to them. "Iris, do you know where we are?"

Iris gazed at Keyth again as she answered, "Somewhere along the coast. See." She stepped past them and past the obstacle of the wall. Keyth and Yara followed and froze in awe.

Across a soft slope, the land fell away, and water stretched beneath the sky until it was lost in the horizon. A haze of fog blurred the seascape, but Keyth couldn't look past the water.

Yara murmured, "So much water..." and Keyth whispered agreement. The unbelievable panorama astounded Keyth and made him marvel at its beauty. Another part of him shook in terror. The sea belittled him, but it was more than that. It reminded him of how big the world had become. It reminded him of how far he was from home. Without the gate nearby, he had no idea how to return, or how long it might take.

"I'm assuming that is Midgard Cove," Iris declared. "So, that way is east," she pointed towards the water. "Athyns must be a few days northeast."

Keyth and Yara remained gazing out to sea, while Dryn glanced in the direction she had indicated.

Iris laughed slightly and asked, "Really, Dryn.... You couldn't get us a bit closer to the city?"

Rattled, Dryn raised an eyebrow. "It wasn't me... the Gates..." he stuttered. He turned his vision east again. "Maybe I could have..." Then he laughed, but it was the harsh expression of uncertainty.

Soon they were marching northward. Keyth reflected that they had walked south for days, on the other side of the Gate. Now they were retracing their steps, so to speak. They would travel north a few days. He found himself walking beside Iris again; Dryn led the way and Yara took the rear.

"Is this type of thing normal...?" Iris asked him.

Keyth glanced at her. "What?"

Her voice was quiet enough that only he could hear. "You know... running for several days because *he* isn't strong enough to best the hunter... and then killing him in a few minutes? 'I missed you?' What is that supposed to mean? Since I've met Dryn, there's only mysteries.... Is this normal for him?"

Keyth stared at Dryn's back where he walked ahead of them. "I'm not sure anymore," Keyth said. "Seems to me a different Dryn has joined us."

Iris nodded. "Killing someone can do that... Dryn is likely still dealing with it."

"I don't think so..." Keyth responded. "Dryn has killed before. He got rid of an entire band of thieves in Kryden. Last week." He couldn't stop the dismay that it had been only a week ago. *We were still in Kryden. There was still snow on the ground.* Mud squelched under his boot as he stepped over a fallen log in the brush. "Why *isn't* there snow?" he asked abruptly.

"He killed a group of thieves?" Iris questioned, as though she hadn't heard his question.

"Apparently he thought his father had been killed by them," Keyth explained. "Left me in a blizzard and took on a troop of them. More than our village could handle."

Iris remained silent for the next few steps, her eyes staring at the tracks ahead of them. Dryn didn't appear to have heard them speaking. Several moments passed before Iris spoke again. "There's no snow because we're south."

"Why should that matter?" Keyth asked, curious. "Snow only goes north?"

Iris laughed. "The further south you go, the warmer it is. If you cross the World's Foundation, there's a desert. Too hot and dry for plants to grow."

"The World's Foundation?" Keyth questioned. *No plants can grow?* He hadn't considered that before. The only time plants couldn't grow was in the winter, when it was cold.

"One of the longest mountain ranges," Iris explained. "South of the Mydarius Sea."

"Oh." Keyth glanced through the branches of the trees around them and stated, "And that's the Mydarius Sea." Once again, he felt overwhelmed by the magnitude of the world outside of Kryden.

They had been on the move for the better part of an hour and Dryn was holding pace as fast as Iris had when she led Yara and Keyth out of Kryden. Keyth was still thinking about the words they had spoken near the Glyph Gate. It struck him that Dryn seemed older. Perhaps Iris was right and killing the hunter had changed Dryn somehow.

It was past noon by the sun's course. They rested near a small brook to drink, and all ate a bit from their packs. Keyth rubbed his shoulders through the rough wool of his cloak. Even divided four ways, Iris' fortune was a heavy burden.

An hour after their lunch, Iris declared loud enough for all of them to hear, "There's a village ahead."

"How do you know?" Dryn asked.

"The gulls," Iris explained, pointing. Keyth glanced to the sky and saw several groups of shore gulls floating in the wind above them. Dryn looked too, and then set off again.

Keyth remained staring upwards. "How do you know, because of the gulls?"

Iris smiled. "The waste. The birds clean most of what the villagers discard."

"The villagers waste a lot?" Keyth asked.

"Every village has a certain amount of resources or supplies that aren't used. Spoiled meat, broken things..."

"Well, Kryden doesn't..." Keyth argued. "We don't waste. If something breaks... you fix it. I never throw away anything."

Iris smiled. "You don't? What about the bows you and Dryn brought to the hunters?" When Keyth stared at her in bewilderment, she explained, "Dryn has told me the story.... What about those bows though? The hunters didn't use them."

"Someone will use them. I'm sure Master ten Lenter has already found them and brought the bundle back to the village," Keyth muttered.

"Are you sure?" Iris asked, smiling at him.

"Well, the bows wouldn't attract shore gulls..." Keyth returned.

Iris burst out laughing, followed by Yara, who must have overheard them from where she walked behind them. Iris chuckled, "You're right... they certainly wouldn't attract shore gulls..."

They came to a thick hedge of thorns, and Dryn led them the long way around the brambles, until they broke through the foliage and emerged onto a grassy slope. At the bottom a road ran from the rocky edge of the sea until it twisted past a hill.

Several trails of smoke were rising from behind the hill, fading into the hazy sky.

Iris gestured and took the lead. Dryn fell in step behind her and Yara approached Keyth's side in the rear. They took to the roadway; Keyth noticed the cobblestones instead of dirt. As they walked, with Kcyth staring at Dryn's stiff shoulders, he decided to find out what *had* happened under Ithyka. He was determined to find what secret now plagued his friend.

32

Held between two hills, the village immediately caught Iris' attention as both an ordinary and a strange place. The buildings were wood and thatch, with occasional brickwork foundations and the fenced yards. Smoke was rising from chimneys and fire holes. But Iris noticed that very few villagers walked the streets. One man stood in the middle of the road watching them, a gnarled walking staff supporting his weight.

The second peculiarity was the absence of sentries. Apart from the man staring at their approach, no guards patrolled the circumference of the village. For such a place without walls she would expect several villagers to be given sentry duty.

Dryn walked beside her, and he too seemed to glance around the village in confusion. As they approached the centre of town, the man who watched them spoke up loudly. "This is the village of Scion." Iris had opened her mouth to greet him, but closed it once he voiced the words after "Scion." She heard him continue, "We have expected you. You are not welcome here. You will be allowed to sleep tonight at our inn, but must leave in the morning."

By the Maker... not quite the reception I expected... Beside her Dryn blurted, "You knew we would come?"

"Not I," the man said. He slid the staff a short distance away from him and limped a step, thereby turning away from them. "The Prophet of Scion has seen your arrival. Follow our instructions or you will perish."

Iris watched as the stranger moved away. Even with the limp, the man seemed to glide across the rough stone road. *The Prophet of Scion?* she wondered. Abruptly, she recalled a peddler rasping a story to an eager and drunken common room, somewhere in Athyns. Hadn't he spoken of Scion? "The Prophet of Scion?" she asked, walking after him. Behind her Keyth called her name, but she ignored him.

"You would do well not to question the Prophet's existence, Lanteera," the man called over one shoulder, continuing his retreat.

"How do you know my name?" she snapped, coming closer to him. "Glyphs... what devilry is this?"

"Shall I call upon the soldiers?" the man returned.

She regarded him sceptically. "I doubt this village sports any soldiers."

"Why would a village with a Prophet train guards?" the man agreed. "Not our soldiers.... No... they seek him." The man extended a finger towards Dryn, his hand as twisted as the staff he leaned upon.

"There are soldiers here?" Dryn questioned, concerned.

"So many questions..." the man hissed. "Go now to the inn. You will be safe there until the morning." He continued his graceful exit, passing through an open gate into the yard of a small house.

"Is the Prophet in there?" Dryn asked Iris, quiet enough that the stranger didn't hear.

Iris regarded him cautiously. It seemed as though Dryn might barge into the hut after the man, if she answered yes. "I don't know," she muttered. "Many villages and cities sport petty sorcerers and soothsayers. I haven't encountered anything like this though. There are some who believe viewing the future can be achieved with the magic you use..."

Dryn nodded. "I can believe it. I want to speak with this Prophet..."

She grabbed his arm and was surprised by its strength. Keyth was right. Dryn was different now. "Don't," she told him. "I believe the man when he says it would be dangerous. It is probable that the Prophet is hidden outside of the village or protected somewhere within it."

"But..."

"Dryn!" she snapped, sternly. "He promised we would be safe until we leave in the morning... I suggest we take the offer."

Dryn took a deep breath; the look of resignation returned to his eyes, the same numbness she had sensed when he followed them from Ithyka. "You're right..." he decided. "Let's find the inn. And, Iris," he said as he turned toward Keyth and Yara, "no gambling this time."

She rolled her eyes and considered a witty remark in return. On second thought, she decided to let it go. "Fine," she replied to his rule. This Dryn was more forceful, more stern and sure of himself than the boy who had come along to fetch her gold. She wasn't sure if she liked the change or not, but she still found herself impressed with him.

Keyth seemed deep in conversation, saying to Yara, "The soldiers are still hunting us, even though Dryn killed that hunter, so we still have to be careful..."

A cloud had seeped its way across the face of the sun and a shadow fell on the village. They had trouble finding the inn, until Iris took the lead and pointed out a long building on the east side of the town.

The door's latch was slightly rusted. It emitted a loud metallic screech as Dryn opened it for her. The tavern interior was poorly lit by a single window on each side of the lengthy room. The innkeeper introduced himself as "Good ol' Flaydian" and seemed to have the same precursory knowledge of their arrival. "I've got one room for the young lads and another for the young mistresses. If you'll follow me."

As the innkeeper unlocked the doors for them, Iris overheard Dryn muttering beneath his breath, something about 'Prophet' and 'so confusing now....'

The rooms were cramped and filthy, but Iris didn't mention it. She had enjoyed more than her fill of pristine floors during her time in Olympus.

Yara sat down on the bed in their room and sighed. "Do you think he'll be alright?" she asked Iris.

"Who?"

"Dryn." Yara gestured towards the wall, beyond which Dryn and Keyth were unpacking. "He seems different. Well, he's mostly the same, but there's something troubling him."

Iris grimaced. "He's being hunted for no reason. He probably just wants a normal life, and somehow he's been given a curse – he's been given magic and will never be able to return to that life he had." *Maker...* Iris thought. Standing in Dryn boots was tragic. All Iris wanted was to have a commoner's life, and Dryn's had been lost in time. "And he killed that hunter," Iris said, "which was likely very different than killing bandits.

He killed them to save someone else. He killed the hunter for survival. Possibly out of anger as well."

"Maker knows I would be angry..." Yara murmured, nodding at Iris' explanation.

Someone knocked at the door and Yara jumped up. She opened it a fraction, and then Dryn stuck his head in. He glanced around and focused on Iris. "Would you like to *eat* in the common room?" he asked.

33

Dawn was like an everyday miracle in the village of Scion. Thick fog crawled up the shore and wrapped the cozy huts in muted light and damp dew. Dryn jumped out of his sleep and blinked at Keyth who was shaking him. He sat up in surprise and then gaped out the window. In the general direction of the horizon, a glorious painting rose into the sky, colors stretching from blue, through grey, violet, salmon, orange and back into blue.

"We have to leave!" Keyth said, releasing his grip on Dryn's shoulders.

"What?" Dryn asked, dazed from his sleep and the view. "When is it?"

"Time to leave...."

Dryn shook his head to clear it, and swung his feet off the bed. "Why?"

Keyth kicked his feet into his boots. "Good ol' Flaydian says the soldiers are looking for us."

"What?" Dryn questioned again, jumping up. He hurriedly shrugged into a tunic and threw his cloak around him. "The girls?"

"They know, too. Flaydian knocked on both doors. Hurry!" Keyth hissed. He grabbed his pack and swung it around his shoulders. Dryn followed suit, still trying to worm his feet into his boots.

"How'd they find out?" he asked, following Keyth towards the door.

"I don't know. Someone must have told," Keyth muttered, and opened the door. They moved a few steps down the hall and Keyth stepped into Yara and Iris' room.

"KEYTH!" Yara's voice screeched, and Keyth slammed the door closed again. He glanced at Dryn, face flushed, and muttered, "They're not ready yet..."

"I saddled horses!" someone declared. Dryn glanced down the hall to watch Flaydian stride towards them. "The Prophet said to give you four. The village doesn't have many, but the Prophet said it was important."

"The Prophet again," Dryn muttered. Thinking about such a person only reminded him of Ithyka, the time spell, the hunter and the letters. Ithyka itself now signified the shadowy spells that Dryn could not understand. And the Prophet was included in that incomprehensible group.

"Let's go," Iris declared, leading Yara out of their room. Yara and Keyth eyed each other, embarrassed. Dryn followed Flaydian down the hallway.

Outside the color scheme had shifted so that only a small aura of grey was caught between the two misty blues. The sea had nearly met the sky, and the sun was rising over them both to burn away the fog. The innkeeper led them to a nearby stable and held the door for Dryn's companions to enter.

The damp building was dim in the early morning light, but of course Flaydian knew the surroundings well. He opened stall after stall, and quickly ushered each of them onto a horse. Dryn had ridden a horse once before, and he found himself able to mount with ease. Keyth was also able; however the innkeeper took several moments trying to get Yara on horseback. Iris had already turned her mount and had ridden out of her stall.

It took longer than it should have to get everything in order, and by the time Iris led them cantering down the road outside, the two blue brush strokes had met in the middle of the horizon and the sun had pierced the clouds.

As dawn broke around them, they left the village of Scion and its Prophet in the fading fog. Dryn swore to return at a time when the Prophet couldn't turn him away.

"Hear that?" Iris asked. Dryn didn't know how she could hear a thing above the sound of their horses' hooves. "They're coming." She kicked her horse into a gallop and the others had no choice but to follow.

Dryn gasped for breath even though he depended on his horse's exertion. The road rushed past on either side of him, as blurred as the colors in the heavens. Trees held their arms above him, damp leaves occasionally brushing across him. Now he could hear the sound of shouting in the distance, and he knew they were being chased.

Why won't they leave me in peace? he wondered. "I can beat them," he said aloud. "Iris, let's stand our ground. I've had enough of running."

Iris turned her head so her voice carried back over one shoulder. "Are you out of your mind?!" she called. "You take them on, and you'll probably win. You'll probably also call all our enemies down on us!"

Dryn bit his lip before he shouted, *Let them come!* He remained silent and followed Iris' speedy flight. Behind him, Yara struggled to stay in control of her horse; Keyth rode beside her to help when he could.

Dryn had almost died fighting the hunter beneath Ithyka. He hadn't healed his wounds soon enough and had the scars to pay for it. As invincible as he now felt, he didn't want to try to face 'all the enemies' Iris knew could come.

'There is a war...' the letters had told him. And he was stuck in the middle of it.

Dryn nearly fell off his horse, and was immediately jarred back to the present. The voices behind them had died away. An occasional shout echoed through the dense forests, but the horses had clearly given them a clean escape. Iris eventually slowed to a walk again, her horse visibly heaving from the long gallop.

We're running again. How will it end this time?

There was so much that Dryn's mind incessantly pondered. First, time had folded so he could train himself. Immediately afterwards they had found a Prophet, someone who predicted their arrival and the events surrounding it as though he had read time itself. *Is it coincidence? Or has the Maker himself grabbed hold of my life?* A sceptical voice whispered doubts also, *If it's fate that controls me, why did it chase me away from the Prophet so quickly?*

"Dryn!" Iris snapped.

His mind wrenched back to the present again. Ever since Ithyka, he was having trouble staying focused. He realized she had called his name several times.

"Yes?" he replied, riding up beside her.

"Look at this!" Annoyed, she pushed a patch of chainmail into his outreached hand. Next, she pulled a sheathed knife from her saddlebag. He examined the two items, keeping one hand holding the reins.

"Where'd you get these?" he asked. There was a small triangle etched into the rough leather surface of the sheath. Inside the figure was etched the letter 'A.'

"These saddlebags. That is an emblem of Avernus, one of the Imperial Cities. I wonder how it ended up in Scion..." Iris said, puzzled. "Unless..."

Dryn tossed the chainmail and blade back to her, and tore the strap open on his own saddlebags. Within was a similar dagger, a loaf of tough bread, and a folded parchment. "Look here," he called, dropping the first two items back into their place. Holding only the paper, he read the thin inked letters out loud. "To Captain Findius, stationed at Cuross. You and your troop are to report to Commander Rychard in Athyns. Follow his orders until told otherwise. Pyrsius Gothikar, Prince of Avernus. Year of Olympus 588, Seventh of the Fourth Cycle."

"A fortnight past..." Iris muttered. "Those are orders straight from the Prince of Avernus... Which means... Maker save us, he's the one hunting you."

Held in his hands was the source of it all. Dryn had a name. The letters before Ithyka had told him of the war, the hunt for magicians and the results of such a genocide. If all magicians were slain, magic would be lost in time forever.

Pyrsius Gothikar, Prince of Avernus. "An Imperial Prince is trying to destroy magic?" Dryn asked.

"What?" Iris returned. "What are you talking about?"

"The letters! The plan is to destroy anyone who can use glyphs, then magic can never be revived," Dryn hurriedly explained. "This Prince... this Pyrsius... he wants to even the battlefield forever. He wants to... separate us from the Great Glyph..."

Iris stared at him blankly for a moment and then questioned, "Are you accusing the Prince of Avernus... of trying to murder his own people?"

Dryn laughed dryly. "Don't you understand? This is much more than murder. He could end the era of magic." He held up the letter and in the corner of his eye caught Keyth gaping at him. "This is the proof. Pyrsius is behind it."

Keyth asked, "Just an order to move troops to a garrison in Athyns? How is that proof?"

"The fact that we found it in the saddlebags of the men who hunt us," Dryn muttered. On second thought, he added, "I suppose this Commander Rychard could be behind it..."

"No. A Commander wouldn't have nearly enough influence to orchestrate such a... massacre." Iris was still staring at Dryn. "The more I think about it, the more I begin to realize that only a Prince *could* do this."

Yara asked, "Then what does this mean?"

Iris turned in her saddle. "It means that we're on the verge of war."

It was as though a rip of lightning had torn the painted skies. All of them tried to absorb this revelation. Dryn knew only a handful of men from their village who had lived during the last war. Keyth and Yara were staring at Iris, similar thoughts racing through their heads.

"War?" Keyth managed.

Dryn grimaced. 'The war has begun already,' the letters had said. *And I'll fight in it,* he knew. Ahead of them lay Athyns. Still pounding on Dryn's senses were the memories of Ithyka and the two weeks he had lived as four.

The solid blue remnants of the horizon had faded into grey.

34

Slums, smoke, stench – this was Olympus. A vulgar waterfront, a weedy market district, a hundred teetering towers, the constant stink rising from sewer grates and sewage that flowed in the streets themselves. Then there was the golden walls and gilded gates of the Imperial Sector, the sprawling courts of the wealthy, the three palaces of the Nobles. By far the largest city in the Dominion, Olympus was a city of contrast and complexity. Without caution, a traveller could lose himself in the squalor.

Seated within the golden walls and behind the gilded gates, Odyn XI lived with intended ignorance of the poverty beyond his prosperous court. His father had died in the war, dropping the city into Odyn's hands fifty years earlier, before Periander Gothikar had become High Prince. Until the recent addition of Pyrsius in the Triumvirate, Odyn had been its youngest member. Periander and Theseus were equal in their seniority, both having lived as young Princes during the Trionus War.

"Pyrsius continues to move his troops," one of his Commanders was reporting. "His searching continues to find new pockets of magicians. A recent report from the People's Council credits Imperial soldiers with the slaughter of a wizard's coven in Avernus. The citizens are troubled, unrest is growing."

Odyn wasn't listening. Frankly, his Commanders were all fools. *Pyrsius now...he shows promise.* The Gothikar heir had designed the plot jointly with Odyn himself. Odyn had set his terms, and Pyrsius didn't block them. Pyrsius wasn't in it for power. Odyn couldn't quite comprehend why Pyrsius was involved at all. Odyn had all the benefits, the way he saw it.

The Commander still prattled on, "... The Isolation Camp at Calydon is overflowing. Our political captives and the magicians continue to taunt the troops, and morale is low. It seems Periander Gothikar is a leader. Even the control tokens seem to have their restrictions and he knows the way around them..."

Odyn lifted a finger from each hand to rub white circles into his flushed temples. It was a hot day in Olympus. Out in the infested streets, flies rose in clouds and festered in the fleece of livestock. Inside the Imperial Sector the heat was reflected in a simmering feeling at the back of the neck where sweat collected. *Pyrsius is a good young fellow. It's a shame how this has to end.* The young Prince was brilliant. Very likely mad, but genius as well. Odyn often found himself pondering the magicians' proverb, *'Hammer metal hard enough and the sparks will paint the sky. There's only one way to sharpen a sword.'*

Odyn raised his chin and finally gazed at his rambling subordinate. "Construct a new Isolation Camp at Paxos."

"Sir?"

"That's far enough from major settlements. It should clear up any overpopulation at Calydon," Odyn decided. He stood up and his Commander stiffened. "Have Periander Gothikar taken there."

"Yes sir," the Commander barked.

"And deliver this message to Pyrsius: We cannot fight all our enemies at once. Try to avoid angering the people. We can deal with that later. We must choose our battles carefully." Odyn grabbed the hilt protruding from a wooden chest beside his throne. The bastard sword felt natural in his hand, an extension of his limb. "There will be war, but if it begins too soon, we will fall." For several moments after the declaration, the only noise was the clip of his boots on the smooth stone panels of the floor.

"Is that the entire message, sir?"

"For now," Odyn said, smiling grimly. "That's all for now..." His slow path across the floor took him to the window where he stared north into the Mydarius Sea. The door shut without a sound apart from the slight squeal of its latch. Alone in the palace throne room, he glanced down at the gold-trimmed scabbard held in his hands. The master-crafted sheath could have bankrupted the majority of merchants in the city.

He pulled the blade a few inches from its scabbard and watched a beam of sunlight reflect into the shadows of the chamber. Staring at the brilliant light of sun and steel made something swell inside of him, some pride or anticipation. The Throne would be his. The world would be his.

Sparks will paint the sky...

35

Two days of bouncing in a saddle was a sore thing for someone who had never ridden horseback before. Yara had spent the evening of the first day standing stiffly by their campfire, unable to sit comfortably. The insides of her legs were aflame with blisters and an intense ache coiled up her back and around her shoulders.

That first night after leaving Scion had been spent on the roadside. They huddled beneath their cloaks as the temperature plummeted around them, and Yara fell asleep with her head on Keyth's shoulder. They had set off again early in the morning, in case the soldiers had pressed on during the night.

Dryn had held the lead as much as Iris did. The two of them had become almost interchangeable. Iris and her dreams of a normal life, and Dryn... who's normal life had somehow been denied him. Yara asked Keyth about it once as they continued on their way. She wanted to know what was changing their friend so much more than them. Dryn was entirely different than the boy who had left Kryden. A different man, she had to correct herself, examining his stoic face as he watched Iris ride beside him.

The second night, as twilight hid the sea from view, they arrived at Athyns. All they could make out were the lights of the city. Yara couldn't tell the size of the city apart from the field of stars stretching away from her. The flickering dots of firelight illuminated streets, buildings and towers, but no details about them.

Their arrival at the gate brought her in front of the largest structure she had ever seen. The walls of Athyns were stained from erosion and rain, ancient stone battlements that disappeared into the shadows above her and ended in a few winking torches.

The gates themselves were taller than the walls of Ithyka. Keyth's head looked as if it might fall off, hanging as it was against his shoulders so he could stare at the heights of wall and gate. Yara couldn't help but laugh, and he grinned at her sheepishly.

"Welcome to Athyns," a guard muttered as though he meant anything but welcome. His comrades leaned against the stones beside the entrance, eyeing the four horses as Dryn led them through the open gates.

The streets stretched in three directions, divided by a variety of new and old buildings. The heights were familiar, and she remarked, "Almost the same as Ithyka..."

Iris laughed. "By the Maker... almost the same! Here? Ride in any direction for more than an hour, then tell me it's the same."

Yara blinked. Everything that left Iris' mouth snatched her attention and admiration. Even insults or reprimands had Iris' own personality emblazoned on them, the casual curses and the smooth rhythm of words. Yara hoped she didn't visibly appear in awe. Keyth glanced at her, and smiled. "Glad you'll sleep in a bed again?" he asked.

She smiled. *Why do we divide the rooms by gender?* she wondered, an errant and unexpected thought. She immediately erased it and scolded herself. She would never have thought such a thing a month earlier. But now that the thought had crossed her mind, she found herself considering it more closely. Iris and Dryn did seem interested in each other.

Yara had always dreamed of settling down. Keyth seemed to fit most of her ideas for such a life. *What would he think of that?* she wondered, watching Keyth as he dismounted.

"Yara?" Iris asked. "Glyphs... did no one hear me but Keyth?" Dryn glanced at Yara and, dually reprimanded, they dropped from their mounts onto the cobblestone road. Dryn seemed so ponderous lately. She couldn't blame him.

They chose an inn at Iris' recommendation. Their well-travelled companion had spent more than a month in Athyns, working and gambling as she saw fit. The tavern was named the Blind Packhorse, though Yara couldn't comprehend why.

They paid for rooms and a dinner. The innkeeper prepared a fine stew that banished any night chill from Yara's limbs as it bubbled down her throat. Iris and Dryn played a dice game that both she and Keyth watched in amazement. Several of the men in the room tried to win some gold, but between the two of them Iris and Dryn won far more than they lost.

They met in one room, though they had paid for two. After unpacking necessities, they discussed their plan for the next few days. Dryn thought it would be smart to investigate the area near the palace first, before seeking out this Kronos Accalia. She wasn't sure why he had become so cautious all of a sudden; he had trusted the letters unwaveringly, but now he wanted to check this one.

"So we'll get a full rest, and then in the morning a full breakfast, scout around the palace a bit, and then meet here again," Dryn decided. "That way, we can meet this magician in the evening or the next day. As I see it... as long as I don't use magic we're safe. In a city of this size, they can't find us. And escape would simply be a matter of blending in again."

"The streets are packed during the day," Iris muttered in agreement. "Let's get some sleep, friends. The morning will come quicker than you expect."

Keyth stood up first, and opened the door for Dryn to leave. Yara glanced at Iris and then back to the door which was still open. Keyth gave her one last look, and then closed it behind him.

Iris laughed to herself and said, "He's wrapped around your little finger..."

"What?" Yara asked, confused.

"I mean," Iris explained, "he won't notice anyone else in the streets, but you."

36

"By the Maker, I thought I was the only one who didn't sleep in," Iris commented, quickly slumping into the chair opposite Dryn. Her short hair was ruffled from sleeping, and she ran her long fingers through it as she tilted the chair back.

"I'm restless," Dryn admitted. *I could tell her about the time spell....* He realized abruptly that he trusted her enough to tell her. *But even I can't understand it. Why would she?*

"I know what you mean," Iris muttered, winding a strand of hair around her finger. The common room was completely deserted apart from the innkeeper working behind the bar, scrubbing noisily. "All night I was tossing and dreaming..."

"What do you dream about?" Dryn asked. He could vividly recall nightmarish images of the man he had killed beneath Ithyka. He wondered if he had been dreaming about it or if the face had just stuck in his memory.

Iris blinked in surprise, then answered, "Olympus. The mansion I was raised in. It was in a wealthy corner of the city, but occasionally the rioters would march past the door."

"Rioters?" Dryn asked. Outside, the streets of Athyns seemed quiet and peaceful under the rising sun. With this impression of an Imperial City, he couldn't imagine a mob storming past.

"I have images of broken glass and torches flickering in the street below. I was very young," Iris mused, her fingers no longer playing with her hair but held along one cheekbone. "The people of Olympus have never been happy. And with good reason.... But enough of that! I don't imagine there's ever been a riot in Kryden."

"Of course not," Dryn laughed. "We're peaceful people."

"Peaceful?" Iris asked. Her voice took a mocking tone as she questioned, "What of the first time we met? Within five minutes you had struck me down with a blast of air!"

Dryn saw the innkeeper pause in his work, and then resume cleaning.

Iris saw the look in Dryn's eye and muttered, "Don't worry. I chose this inn with good reason."

He sighed in relief. "I hope you're right. I'm sure those soldiers have reached the gates by now." Folded within his pocket was Pyrsius' letter they had found. He knew how important it was.

"If we get that letter to the palace and this Kronos Accalia you are searching for... we should be safe. I imagine the Prince himself would like to know what is going on within his own government," Iris murmured.

Dryn raised an eyebrow. "Can we trust him? The Prince, I mean? Wouldn't I have – " he cut himself off and began again. "Wouldn't the letters have told us to go straight to him, instead of the magician?"

"You don't think that the entire Triumvirate is trying to get rid of magic, do you?" Iris questioned.

"I'm from Kryden, remember?" he chuckled. "I haven't been around the world enough to know."

Iris smiled. "I, for one, doubt that all three Princes are corrupt. They normally plot on their own, and I would assume that Pyrsius Gothikar does so as well."

"I hope so. Otherwise, the Palace of Athyns may not be as much a haven as we imagine it," Dryn muttered.

Iris spread her hands on the table top, and Dryn caught himself staring at the elegant fingers. Pondering intently, she didn't notice his interest and murmured, "Last I heard, Periander Gothikar was still Prince of Avernus."

Dryn blinked, and forced himself to look up into her face. She smiled, and he realized with a twist that she knew what he had been thinking about after all. "Periander Gothikar?"

That's when things fell into place. He had known something was familiar about the name. He hadn't remembered where he had heard the name Gothikar and couldn't believe he had missed the connection. Artemys Gothikar was the magician who had given him magic; Artemys, who had died shortly after, and remained lying in the woods.

Still grinning smugly, Iris explained, "Periander is Pyrsius' father. There were two brothers."

"Artemys Gothikar..." Dryn whispered, dazed. He was no longer thinking about Iris.

"Yes!" Iris exclaimed. "You aren't such a village boy after all..."

"So..." Dryn muttered. "Artemys is ... Periander's father?" He could only recall the aged face and the distant light within those eyes. Familiar eyes, somehow.

Iris laughed. "Stop paying attention to my hands," she mocked. "Why, by the Maker, would you think that?" He was staring at her eyes now, but he started at her comment. She explained, "Artemys is Pyrsius' brother. He was the Crown Magician. Who is... basically the conscience of the Princes."

"Pyrsius' brother?" Dryn hissed, sitting up straight. "He was an old man!"

"What are you talking about?" Iris questioned, concerned. "Periander is the old man. He was High Prince during the Trionus War. I had one of the finest scholars of Olympus tutor me."

Dryn remained staring at her in shock. *Pyrsius and Artemys were brothers.* Even without the age discrepancy, it made Pyrsius and Dryn connected somehow. *Artemys gave me magic, and Pyrsius is trying to kill me. Maker blind me... there must be a connection!*

"How do you know Artemys?" Iris inquired, her eyes aglow.

"I must have heard the name somewhere," Dryn lied. *Glyphs, you already decided to trust her!* He glanced down at her hands again, hoping it might distract her.

"Maker," she laughed. "That was blatant."

He flushed, sheepishly raising his vision. He held his tongue though.

"Fine," Iris said, the laughter cut short. She smiled slightly and tilted her head. "I can live with secrets. We all have them." She lifted her hand and started playing with a strand of hair again, as though taunting him. "You know of Artemys somehow. Perhaps the letters. But I won't pry. You and the Gothikar family have secrets."

"Something like that," Dryn winced, bothered by the turn the conversation had taken. He yawned, tried to stifle it, and asked, "Who are the other Princes?"

Iris grinned and lifted a hand. Counting on her fingers, she said, "Gothikar, Theseus and Odyn."

He bit his lip. Her hand lowered from counting, and slid across the table top as she leaned towards him. All of a sudden she was kissing him, her lips pressing at his until he lost his breath, and then she sat down again, breathing heavily and staring at him.

He gasped and shut his eyes for a moment. When he opened them, he was still blinded by surprise. "What was that?"

"I-I'm sorry," she muttered. "I'm not normally..." she trailed off. Now she was the one flushed, her cheeks as rosy as her lips. "Ever since Ithyka, I've found you irresistible," she admitted. "I hope I didn't make you uncomfortable, but this conversation has made you even more mysterious, and I couldn't hold back."

Mysterious? he wondered. He blinked again, ran one hand over the rough whiskers around his mouth. "Uh... I ... I don't mind," he stammered, and then chuckled awkwardly. The innkeeper was still minding his own business. "I'm glad we have some privacy."

She smiled, but for the next few moments they just eyed each other silently, at a loss for words. "I guess what I'm trying to say is that I'm starting to love you," she whispered, her eyes alight.

"I'm feeling the same way," he agreed. He felt like he was going to burst. He had been so frustrated by Iris when they met, but he had no hindrances now. He still couldn't believe he was sitting in a tavern in Athyns across from a wealthy orphan who had just kissed him. It seemed like yesterday that his first air spell tore the grasses of the Kryden Green. But a part of him wouldn't change a thing. Recalling the time spell, he realized, *I likely could change things if I wanted...* but he didn't know for sure how any of it worked.

"See," Iris said. "That look, right there. You know something, or you think you might. And the entire world is at your fingertips. I just... ah!" Iris laughed. She was across the table again, her lips meeting his, and his heart seemed to implode all over again.

"Um... Good morning," a familiar voice stuttered. Iris jumped back from Dryn and tilted her head so her hair partially covered her face. Flushed, Dryn glanced across the room at Keyth who had just entered from the hallway.

By the Maker, this is awkward!

"Morning, Keyth..." Iris muttered.

"How did you sleep?" Dryn asked, concerned. "I didn't wake you when I left, did I?"

"Nope. I slept well." Keyth was staring at Dryn, and some unspoken word of congratulations seemed to pass between them. Keyth glanced at Iris and nodded, then walked towards the open bar and kitchen. A man and woman entered, also looking for breakfast.

"I should go see if Yara is awake," Iris told him, excusing herself. She stood up and commented, "We ought to begin this tour of the Palace..."

Dryn watched her prance towards the hallway and disappear from view. He rubbed a hand over his eyes to clear them. *She's liked me since Ithyka? I must have really changed in those two weeks I spent trying to catch up.* The two weeks that never happened. He still carried all of the original letters in his pack, but he couldn't truly say they were original.

"So... you finally got somewhere with her, huh?" Keyth asked, sitting down. He held a small loaf in one hand and eagerly tore into it.

Dryn laughed. "No, she made the first move."

Three more men entered, making their way toward the inn's rooms along the hallway.

"Did she?" Keyth asked. "If I didn't know better, this new you might have gained some confidence."

"New me?"

Keyth snorted. "You've been different ever since you killed the hunter under Ithyka."

My thoughts exactly. Dryn leaned back in his chair. "I suppose you're right."

"What happened?"

Dryn shook his head. "Nothing really. We fought, and in the end I killed him. It was the only way we could get away safely."

Keyth cocked his head in disbelief. "I don't believe that for a moment. The scar itself is enough to disprove that story. Your healing spells erase scars. The way I figure it, you must have been hurting for a while in order to end up with a scar."

Dryn ran a finger along it, a similar motion to wiping a tear away. "I got this right away, when he used that fire burst, before you escaped... Maybe that's why – "

He was cut off by a scream. It was a familiar voice, too. "The girls!" Keyth gasped, dropping his loaf of bread onto the dirty tabletop. Dryn was three steps ahead of him, dashing through the wooden frame of the doorway and down the corridor.

The door to their room was ajar, and Dryn glimpsed a man throwing one of their bags into a larger sack. The girls' room was open as well, and Dryn led Keyth to it.

One man held Iris against a wall. She was writhing against him and trying to escape. A third man stood between Dryn and the pool of blood spreading around Yara. "Damn, didn't even see her..." the man hissed.

Dryn struck him in the back of the head with both hands clasped together. The man tumbled onto Yara, and Keyth shouted, "Maker burn you!" as he hauled the man off her.

The man who was holding Iris hesitated, shifting one hand momentarily, as Dryn rushed towards him. Iris' hand flashed out with a dagger, and the man coughed blood onto the floor before falling facedown.

Keyth knelt over the first man, blood oozing from his knuckles. Dryn heard commotion from his room. The third man stumbled into the hallway and dashed towards the street. None of them gave pursuit.

"That's enough," Iris snapped, and Dryn pulled Keyth away from the unconscious man.

Yara had been stabbed in the side, below her ribcage. Even the dark color of her tunic couldn't hide the flood of blood that had gushed from the wound and into the rug. She had lost consciousness already, and her lips trembled from some feverish dream.

Iris knelt and pressed two fingers under the wounded girl's chin. "Her heart beat is uneven, and her breathing as well. She needs help now!"

Keyth grabbed Dryn. "Heal her!"

Dryn was breathing quickly, trying to think of what could be done. Keyth shook him by the collar of his shirt and shouted, "Heal her, Dryn!"

"I can't!" Dryn pleaded. "We have to find a healer."

"Damn you, Dryn! HEAL HER!" Keyth shrieked, his voice breaking. He slammed Dryn back against a wall, a chair trapped behind him.

"She won't last until we find a real healer," Iris explained, still kneeling by Yara's side.

This can't be happening... Maker save me, I have to help... Please, please protect us... Dryn prayed. He lifted Keyth's trembling hands from his shirt and dropped by Iris' side. Taking a shuddered breath, he placed a hand over Yara's wound and felt warm blood under his palm. His other hand traced the glyphs into the floor rug, and he whispered, *"Telvyn al'ross. Azur neeros dei."*

The skin beneath his hand rippled and formed into a solid layer over the wound. The flow of blood ceased and every trace of the injury started to recede. Dryn felt energy pour out of him and into Yara. Her eyes fluttered open as the injury was undone.

He stood up as she began to recover, and turned to Keyth. "Come with me. We need to see what supplies we have left. Iris, pack Yara's things. We have to keep on the move now. The guards will be here soon."

37

Athyns was a large city. Some travellers said the greatest. Not the biggest, but the greatest. There were, however, three things such a traveller might warn of. Firstly, despite the honour of its Prince, the city was continuously hounded by bandits and thieves. Gangs hid in the shadows of alleys, and an occasional criminal stalked well-off merchants for loot.

With such an alert in mind, the citizens parted for the armoured soldiers that stormed the streets. They only blinked once at the crossbow bolt released toward the front of the Blind Packhorse Inn, cutting down a cutpurse with a sack thrown over one shoulder. The man stumbled, planted his face into the cobblestones with a sickening crunch, and died moments later.

Secondly, an experienced wayfarer might glance across a mug of mead and tell the story of the skill of Athyns' sentinels. With calculated efficiency and ruthless decisiveness, the veteran soldiers invaded the tavern, ravaged the interior and re-entered the street in pursuit of a young man of northern complexion. The suspect bolted down the street, weaving a speedy course around pedestrians.

One of the men engaged in the chase stopped in his tracks and, with nimble fingers, rummaged in a pouch at his belt. He withdrew a small rectangle of brittle stone and snapped it between his fingers. Energy flared in a circle around him and arched out from his raised hand to slam back into the earth, forming a dome the width of the street and containing them all. The lightning bright energy drew shouts and screams from the citizens, who fell or ran in fear.

The young man in flight found himself caught within the dome, and helplessly spun to face the group of soldiers. In a matter of moments he was face down on the stone cobbles, his arms roughly forced behind his back. A burst of fire encompassed him and his attackers, and instantly this brilliant blaze sent them reeling away from him with agonized shouts.

Another token was broken, and the target gaped as the fires winked out. The young man traced a glyph across the street's surface, but nothing happened. Again he was knocked to the earth and, after a brief struggle, bound.

Outside the shield of energy, a girl with short hair pounded against the barrier until it seared her elegant fingers, and her friends dragged her back. Nothing could be done, they realized. Perhaps the Maker had turned his fortune away, turned his back on them.

The road-weary adventurer would shrug and tell of the third noteworthy characteristic of Athyns. There were the Imperial dungeons, maintained by the Prince's own rules. And there were the other dungeons. The hidden ones. The darker ones.

The fair-haired young prisoner was marched to a barracks and then into this latter sort. His friends followed as far as they could, shoved against the guards, were pressed back by jabs from the blunt ends of spears, and were shut beyond the gates. The young man was borne past a thick door, still struggling against his captors, and through cold shadows.

A soldier fumbled with flint and a shuttered lamp coughed light into the hallway. At the end of the passage a narrow set of stairs spiralled downward. Down and down into the darkness the prisoner was dragged, until his thrashing weakened and his resolve began gasping for breath.

His cell was narrower than the length of one arm. It wasn't tall enough for him to sit up straight, and it wasn't long enough for him to lie. A shallow slot carved into the stone, the dark tomb gaping at him like the maw of some demonic creature. Screaming profanities, the young man kicked and flailed helplessly as the ruthless soldiers lifted his legs. They tilted him until the hole vanished from his sight, and he was thrust head first into its jaw. Swallowed, consumed, devoured.

Gone.

The creature had closed its mouth and he was trapped within. He cried and shouted and screamed and moaned until his throat lost its voice. He pounded on the stone wall until the skin of his bruised fist broke and blood mingled with the stains in the   coarse rock.   He turned and rolled and kicked at the rusted metal shutter covering the entrance until his mind lost sense of direction, until he wasn't sure how long he had lain within the tomb. His tears were the only moisture, his breathing the only sound, his thoughts the only life.

He lifted his hand once more, clenched the raw bruise into a fist and pounded once, twice more on the stone.   With a coughing moan, he struck it a third time, and then let his muscles go slack. Panting, he cradled a bleeding hand.

But still, a accomplished traveller would say, Athyns is a great place.

38

Commander Rychard of Tarroth hated the smell of ink. It seemed invasive in his nostrils, seemed filthy on his skin. He rubbed his index finger against his thumb and then both on a dirty rag nearby. His other hand dropped the quill into its inkwell, and he folded the letter he had written precisely. He didn't even bother to reread what he had written. He knew it by heart. He had been waiting to write it for quite some time. *'The prodigy of the Northlands has been caged.'* Those words had kept him awake for close to a fortnight. How despicable that a youth's journey should trouble him so.

As he stood, he ran a finger up the cover of the latest chronicle he had been reading, *History of the Maker's Kinship*, but decided it was past time to meet the captive. He paced away from the desk, lifted a cask of Trident spirits from a nearby table and poured the powerful alcohol into one of the pewter mugs that were scattered around. Made from the lush vineyards near the Trident Rivers of Sinai, the potent drink cost a fortune and tasted like a fortune as well.

Taking a sip, he strode to the door, and then into the corridor. "I'll see our newest guest now," he said aloud. "The Main Hall would be fitting." Without looking at the guard, he shuffled down the passage toward the stairs at the far end.

He had let the young man sit, well partially sit, for two days without hearing a word or seeing a blink of light. He had the youth fed daily; that is, yanked from his cell without warning and forced to devour the scraps from the soldiers' meals. Back into his coffin the young magician was shoved.

Two days should be enough to soften him, Rychard decided, meandering out of the stairwell and sipping another mouthful of spirits. The Main Hall was poorly lit and smelled of ale. Littered with the soldiers' mess, bones, dogs, and the occasional grizzled veteran, the room always seemed dirty to Rychard.

He seated himself in the armchair at the head of the Hall. He set his boots up on the tabletop, slouching back in the chair. Letting the bottom of the mug rest on one wooden arm, he placed his elbow on the other.

Commotion at the far end of the hall announced the return of the guard and the arrival of his guest. Rychard took the opportunity to examine the prisoner as the young man was marched down the length of the Hall. The magician seemed frail after only two days of imprisonment. His dirty blonde hair was ruffled and bloodstained, one half of his face coated in dirt, and a massive bruise coiled around one fist, visible even from where Rychard sat. The young man's eyes stared out of his face as if from a mask, but apart from the light within them, the Commander could recognize nothing to separate this young wizard from the many others he had put to death.

"Welcome to my fortress," Rychard greeted him, lifting his cup as a form of salutation. "I apologize for your accommodations, but I find they loosen the tongue." He let out a small chuckle and let it die slowly. He expected the youth to ask what Rychard wanted of him, but no words left the tight lips.

The guard forced the prisoner onto a bench across the table. Rychard glanced past the two of them at Mordyn. The robed man was the only member of Findius' troop able to use glyphs.

Rychard dropped his feet from the table and leaned forward in his throne. "Open your eyes, man," he told the prisoner, who was squinting at him. "Perhaps the courtyard was bright after the shadows of your... room."

The young man continued to squint across at him, saying not a word. Rychard grabbed a lantern from its hook nearby and set it on the table in front of the boy. "That should help you adjust to the light again," he told the captive. "Now... we haven't been properly introduced. What is your name?"

The magician winced from the light of the lantern, but his parched lips held tight. The guard raised a curled whip in one hand, looking to Rychard for confirmation.

"No, not yet," Rychard said, waving him aside. Rychard returned to his throne and drank more of the Trident spirits. "You may have noticed Mordyn there," he told the prisoner. "He is one of our soldiers. You have likely noticed your inability to use glyphs... this is his doing."

The fool didn't even blink. Rychard wondered if anyone resided inside, or if the short stay in the dungeon below had leeched him away already. Rychard continued, "Maintaining such a ward is another matter. Mordyn must focus on the spell day and night so that you will never be able to activate a glyph. Ever."

The magician glanced up at him finally, but the words were not what Rychard had expected. "So you keep your own soldiers imprisoned as well?"

Rychard's jaw closed and he tensed for a moment.

"Seems to be a very... lonely position you hold..." the young man whispered.

Rychard jumped from his chair and struck the lantern off the table. It clattered against the prisoner, spilling hot wax across the boy's skin. The metal rim seared a curve into his flesh. The lamp clattered onto the floor stones, the flame extinguished.

The prisoner yelped, then bared his teeth as the heat burnt its course. As Rychard watched the youth adjust to the agony, he tipped the remaining contents of his mug into his mouth. Sighing loudly afterward, he set the pewter onto the table and walked toward its end. His eyes remained focused on the prisoner, analyzing him anew. *I've underestimated you, magician,* he had to admit.

He could recognize pain and confusion in the young man's eyes; they followed Rychard's every move, reading him in return. The shirt was rough wool, marking the magician as a commoner, and the occasional hole and tear let Rychard know that the captive wasn't concerned with appearance. *Noble sentiments. Comes with a respect for life. Which builds concern for familiars.* Rychard's mind calculated the most effective method to follow.

"Your friends," he muttered. "They put up a greater fight than you have." Rychard leaned against the table near the prisoner's stool. "Your sharp words got you nowhere. They were much smarter than you've been."

"My friends?" the boy asked. Rychard caught the prisoner mumble beneath his breath about his eyes. *Perhaps he is already breaking...*

"I've had all three of them here," Rychard lied. He knew there were three from the guards' reports. "Giving me your name is one step towards freeing them. As I've said earlier, I wish only for information." *Then I can kill you and be done with it...*

The young man fell silent again, and now his eyes were locked straight ahead. "My name doesn't matter," he said. "Dryn."

"Dryn," Rychard muttered. "Dryn ten..."

"Dryn ten Rayth." This time the voice was stern. "I've given you my name. Now release my friends."

Rychard laughed. "Release them? Not yet, Dryn..." he chuckled. "No, first I need to know who taught you magic. Do you know the whereabouts of Artemys Gothikar?"

The prisoner blinked. "He's dead. Died in the forest. When this all began."

"So who taught you magic?" Rychard questioned. "Firstly, I disbelieve he is dead. Artemys is one of the most powerful men alive. We found only the remains of an old man in the forest. Who taught you magic, Dryn? Tell me that and I will release one of your friends."

The young man flinched and glanced up at Rychard, full of confusion. He opened his mouth to speak and then shut it. Lowering his head, Dryn muttered something about his iris again. Perhaps he had been squinting for a reason other than the lighting.

Rychard sighed. He turned around and grabbed a pitcher sitting on the table. Sniffing its contents, he barked, "Give him five lashes." He refilled his mug while the guard carried out his order, and drank some of the stale ale as Dryn grunted against the fiery pain.

"Who taught you magic, Dryn?" he asked the captive.

The boy's head didn't budge. "Alright, enough of this," Rychard snapped. He gestured for the guard to grab Dryn, and then he marched toward the end of the hall. The courtyard was nearly deserted. Most of the soldiers had already served duty during the day.

The guard strung the prisoner up at a stake in the middle of the yard, as instructed. "Another five lashes," Rychard ordered.

The soldier put his strength into it this time, and the magician shouted for mercy by the end. Rychard grabbed his gaunt cheeks roughly and demanded, "Who taught you?"

"Maker burn you," the captive hissed, spitting at Rychard.

"Five more!" Rychard growled. The whip cracked across the prisoner's back, the wool tunic torn to shreds. Soon Rychard could see bright red streams seeping from the raw gashes on the captive's arched back. "We can do this all day, Dryn. Who trained you?"

Dryn moaned something about an iris again and pressed his head against the stake.

"Great Glyph, what is wrong with your eye?" Rychard relented, unable to resist it anymore.

The trembling head fell back and laughter echoed off the ramparts of the barracks. "You don't have my friends! You don't have them! I won't tell you a thing! You've got me tied up and stuffed in that cell, but you can't cage my mind!"

Rychard snatched the flail out of the soldier's hands and tore it across Dryn's skin as hard as he could. Dryn let out a gargled scream, and started coughing. Rychard gave him another. "How'd you learn?" he shouted. Again and again the whip drew blood until Rychard was sweating. He dropped the whip and grabbed Dryn's hair.

Yanking the boy's head back, he barked, "Who trained you?"

Dryn started smiling, his teeth blotted with blood and his eyes drowsy from pain, shock and fatigue. "I did!" he admitted, quietly. "I trained myself!" He burst out laughing again, as if it was a joke.

Rychard stepped back, his head dipping down to stare at the bloodstained dirt. "You killed one of my finest hunters with self training!? And you haven't even had magic for a full cycle. You lie to me. You fool... I've had enough of whipping you. We'll see how your back heals, crammed in your cell."

The guard stepped forward to untie Dryn, and Rychard froze again, one hand held out to stop the soldier. *What by the Maker...?* he wondered. He stepped forward, and with one finger parted the woollen tatters that hung around his prisoner's shoulders. "Glyphs... I'll be damned..." He glanced up at Dryn's dazed eyes. "You have a spell *on you...*"

At last he saw the look of terror in Dryn's eyes. *I've got him at last...* Rychard spun and shouted, "Mordyn! Get over here!"

The robed man approached quickly as ordered. Rychard instructed him to copy the glyphs from Dryn's chest. It was a most extraordinary spell, using symbols that even Rychard couldn't read, for although he had not been given magic by the Order, he had studied the language at length. Despite this, the spell that was burnt into Dryn's flesh seemed nearly meaningless.

"You'll never understand..." Dryn whispered, his eyes peering at Rychard's.

"Get out of my head, fool. You're going to die here." Rychard spun on one heel and marched back towards his rooms. He would drink the Trident Rivers dry tonight.

39

"How long has it been? A fortnight?" Iris snapped. "Burn you, Keyth! He's not going to get out on his own!"

"Shut your mouth, Iris!" Keyth returned, certain his face was as livid as hers. He glanced across the room of the inn where Yara sat. She was staring out of the third storey window, her face blank apart from a single tear. "We don't need this!"

Iris stepped towards the door, but froze. "Damn it, fool villager! *You* don't need this?! Can you imagine what he's going through? I don't think you can. I *know* what they're doing to him."

"You think I'm not hurting as well?" Keyth questioned. "Burn *you,* Iris! By the Maker, what could we possibly hope to achieve on our own?" He stood up and stepped after her. *I've known Dryn for my entire twenty years, and she's known him for less than a cycle!*

"There are other options! By acting, I don't mean fighting the enemies ourselves! There's got to be some way to persuade law keepers to help us! This can't be legal!" Iris blurted, turning to face Keyth again.

"Both of you be quiet!" Yara ordered. She spoke quietly, but stern enough that Iris and Keyth both spun to stare at her. "Iris, take a walk," Keyth's friend said. "Keyth, calm down. And each of you start thinking about other perspectives. I agree with both of you. Action seems futile, but we can't sit around and let them kill him!"

Iris threw one hand in the air and stomped out the door, furious, though reprimanded. She was probably going to look for the next inn at which to stay. The door closed behind her, leaving Keyth alone with Yara in the small room. It was their second inn since the capture – supposedly keeping on the move was better for them.

Yara rubbed her hands across her eyes and sighed. "Maker, I still can't believe this is happening..."

Keyth shook his head. Of them all, he felt he knew Dryn the best. They had spoken of the past fortnight, and Dryn had thanked Keyth for invading his room and reading the letters. Without that, Dryn had said, he might've been caught by the hunter in Lesser Kryden itself.

But Keyth knew there was nothing he could do now. He had considered every option, and he was forced to come to terms with it. Iris and Yara thought him heartless, or cowardly, but that was as false as it could be. It had nearly destroyed him to accept that Dryn was beyond his reach.

It had been ten days since the capture. They had heard not a word from the barracks, and seen no sign of Dryn. The city, even the neighbourhood, seemed completely unaffected by the quick assault at the Blind Packhorse. The inn had opened its doors hours later, after only a brief assessment of damage.

"I wish Iris was right and there was something we could do..." Yara murmured.

Helpless and frustrated, Keyth shook his head again and opened the door. "I'm going for a walk as well. I'll be back later." He ducked out of the room and shut the latch behind him.

Athyns seemed to quell his fear of the world. The feeling that it was too large for him still persisted, but somehow the massive city of Athyns felt comfortable. Despite the agony of Dryn's capture.

He wasn't sure how he could accommodate these, but they were two separate feelings. The city of Athyns held him in its palm and almost cradled him, feeling as secure as Lesser Kryden. And at the same time, he was terrified for Dryn. Would his friend manage to survive again? To escape against all odds?

Keyth's footsteps took him into the street and then north. It was just after noon, and the streets were still packed with daily pedestrians, merchants and citizens of all kinds. He didn't mind the constant buzz of bartering and conversation, or the looks he received from some of the wealthier traders. A lowly villager. A commoner. *Let them look,* he conceded.

He soon found himself in front of the Blind Packhorse tavern. *Glyphs, what are you doing here?!* he asked himself. He let his breath out slowly and looked around. Several feet away was a dark ring tattooed in the street where the soldiers had used their barrier spell. *That's where they took him.* It seemed distant in the past. They had left their homes only two fortnights ago, and for the past one, Dryn had been imprisoned.

The bar inside was almost deserted, although many of the tables were occupied. The stool Keyth chose seemed to tilt back, so he found himself leaning forward. He slumped with his elbows on the bar and his hands on his cheeks.

"Can I get you something?" a feminine voice asked. He glanced up to see a small barmaid across the counter. She was comely, attractive in both form and face, and when he lifted his head from his hands, she stuck out her bottom lip. "Aw... why so down?"

"I'll have a drink..." he muttered, ignoring her concern. "I don't know what kind. Anything."

She spent several moments mixing a drink for him. "This is a tonic which a friend from Cuross taught me to make. It should cheer you up..."

He didn't press her to know that he didn't want to be cheered up. He drank it, slowly, savouring it. He set the glass down and ran a hand through his hair.

The barmaid returned and grinned. "This might help as well... The innkeeper recognized you and gave me this. Apparently, it was dropped in all the commotion last week."

He didn't look up, so she slid the object across the counter to him. A white parchment appeared in his vision, folded in half. He stared at it blankly for a moment and then examined it further, unfolding the paper.

There was writing inside which began, "To Captain Findius...." *This is the letter from that Prince... the commands to the soldiers...* Keyth realized. He glanced across the page blankly, his mind travelling beyond it. He was reliving the conversation between Iris and Dryn upon discovery of the letter.

"This is proof... Pyrsius is behind it..." Dryn had said.

Like a star streaking through his mind, an unexpected realization crashed into his plans. *Iris was right...* he realized. *We can help Dryn... We can try...*

He raced back to their inn, and up the stairs, even as such thoughts continued their course in his head. Iris was speaking to Yara when he barged in and interrupted. "I've got it!"

They both started at his abrupt entrance. Keyth held it up. "I found the orders to the soldiers at the Blind Packhorse! We can save him, I know it!"

"Great Glyph, what are you talking about?" Iris hissed, frustrated with his sudden change.

"Follow me!" Keyth said, but didn't wait for their compliance. He set off down the hall, through the common room and into the afternoon streets. He didn't know the way exactly, but it wasn't hard to get near the massive palace grounds in the centre of the city.

The Imperial District of Athyns was a huge arrangement of buildings. It included the Prince's palace and mansion, his spotless barracks, a stable, and a dozen buildings, the purpose of which Keyth could not guess. Guards stopped them at the gates to the District, one of them holding a hand out towards Keyth's chest.

"Uh..." he trailed off, staring at the letter in his hand.

"Courier?" the other guard questioned.

"Official business," Iris snapped, nodding to him. The guards accepted this and granted them entrance. As Keyth resumed his quick pace towards the palace, Iris grabbed his arm and yanked him to face her.

"Where are we going, Keyth? Have you gone mad? We can't command guards and, as you said earlier, a direct assault on the dungeon would be insanity," Iris admitted. "What is this plan you have?"

"The Prince! He isn't possibly aware of Pyrsius' actions, if orders are being given by letters such as this. Dryn said it himself. This is proof!" Keyth breathed. When they stared at him blankly still, he shook his head and said, "Trust me, just this once. You won't be disappointed."

Yara nodded slowly, and that was all Keyth needed. He resumed his fast pace and reached the main palace moments later. The guards at the fortress gate crossed spears and one demanded, "Proof of business."

"Official courier," Keyth said, prepared this time.

"May I see the letter?" the guard asked.

Keyth awkwardly eyed the letter. "Its contents are private," he explained. *Maker, please let us pass!* "For the eyes of its intended reader only."

"For my eyes as well, or you ain't passing this door." The man's gaunt face set grimly and his eyes turned to stone. When Keyth didn't reply, the guard asked, "It's standard protocol. Is there a problem?"

Racking his mind for some excuse or escape from the situation, Keyth stepped back a pace.

At that moment, the door behind the guards opened and a robed man strode out, an indigo cloak draped from his shoulders. The man appeared to be about his own business, and strode forward, until he was stopped by the spears. "Is there a problem here?" he asked, sternly, his sharp features peering from the cowl he wore.

The guard immediately paled and the spears withdrew. The spokesman begged, "Pardons, Master Accalia. Of course you may pass. This is simply a mishap with these messengers."

The man shook his head and muttered under his breath, striding between the guards and past Keyth and his friends. The spears crossed again, and the guard opened his mouth. Before he could speak, though, the name fell into place and Keyth turned away.

"Master Accalia!" he called, running to catch him. The girls murmured fearful objections. One of the girls tried to hold his arm to stop him from making a fool of himself.

Master Accalia turned. "Yes, lad? I'm afraid I will be of no more help than those tin caps back there..." The man's small face seemed to draw Keyth closer.

"You are Kronos Accalia, yes?" Keyth asked. The man nodded sharply, and Keyth breathed, "We must speak with the Prince of Athyns." *I don't even know his name...* Abruptly unsteady, he wondered, *What am I doing here?*

"Why is that?" Accalia questioned. "May I see the letter you intend to deliver?"

Keyth froze. If Kronos Accalia was trustworthy, as Dryn's letters had told them, doing so could save Dryn. If Accalia wasn't, it could mean arrest for Keyth and his friends, or worse. *For all I know, he could himself be the correspondent of Dryn's letters! Or he could be one of those tricked into loyalty to Pyrsius!*

"Very well, if you won't speak on it, I wish you luck with the guards," Kronos spun away, his robe swishing behind him, and continued on his way.

"Magic," Keyth called. "That is why we must speak to the Prince!"

Kronos paused and laughed. "What of it? You, villager, seem not the type to be a spell caster. I've spoken with both Noble magicians and common ones. Even a Prince magician."

"I am not a spell caster," Keyth said. "But I know one and must save him. I can also promise you that the contents of this letter will intrigue your Prince."

"How can I believe that? My master, Prince Theseus, does not wish every adventuring villager to beg his audience," Kronos said. This time, the question went with the eyes, both testing Keyth.

Keyth blinked for a moment and turned to Iris. "You mentioned your disbelief," he whispered almost beneath his breath, "that the Princes are working together?"

She nodded.

Keyth turned back to Kronos. "The letter is signed by Pyrsius Gothikar. If that is not reason enough to see the Prince, I shall leave."

Kronos raised an eyebrow, slowly walking closer to Keyth. "Are you messengers from Avernus? I think not. *I* am now intrigued. The Prince will certainly be. Follow me, commoner. And mind yourself with His Highness."

They marched between the two guards who now anxiously avoided Keyth's eyes. The gateway opened into a small courtyard inside the front of the palace. Huge pillars rose around them, supporting the arched ceiling far above. Kronos led them along a hallway around the outside of the massive room and through a doorway on the west side. A flight of stairs spiralled up out of their sight and Keyth marvelled at the architecture. He had never seen a set of stairs that turned, and as he followed the robed man up them, he found himself disoriented and confused.

The next corridor opened onto what seemed a balcony, and abruptly Keyth realized they had returned to the first hall and were now several floors higher. He could see the midsections of the pillars, the ceiling much closer.

They followed along a dozen other hallways and doorways before Kronos stopped in front of a large double door. The masonry of the frame had been carved to resemble a flag or banner of some kind, and letters of an unrecognizable dialect were etched there.

Kronos noticed them staring at it, and read, " 'Korbion qiren seeros qi ordin.' It means 'Conquer thyself before thy enemy.' The words of House Theseus."

The door opened without a sound as Kronos led them inside. The room was dark, but the magician led them quickly across it to a curtained doorway. He disappeared onto the other side, gesturing for them to wait.

"A messenger of sorts has arrived. He carries a letter from Pyrsius, but does not carry it *for* Pyrsius. He wishes your assistance in rescuing a magician with whom he is familiar. May I bring him out?" Keyth could hear Kronos' voice through the curtain.

Before the other voice answered, the curtain opened again and Kronos nodded. "Just you," he said, gesturing to Keyth.

Keyth glanced at the other two and locked eyes with Yara. She wished him luck, but said not a word. He stepped through the curtain with Kronos and found himself on a balcony. He was standing in the air above the city, which stretched away from him almost as far as he could see.

"Belittling, isn't it?" someone asked. A man nearby was writing in a book, seated in a chair with its back against the wall. He folded the book shut and set it onto the stone railing that surrounded them. "I spend a lot of time out here, because one day it will be gone. Someone must give it its due."

Keyth blinked. *This is the Prince of Athyns?* he wondered. "I find an element of safety in it..." he murmured, unsure of how to reply to such a man.

"...milord!" Kronos finished for him.

Theseus glanced at the magician and nodded, his mouth twisted with mirth. "That will be all, Kronos," he declared, and the magician left reluctantly.

Keyth was reminded of Magistrate Arbydn by the Prince's voice and the respectful authority within it. "Milord, are you aware of the ... war?" Keyth questioned, cautiously.

Theseus' eyes had followed Kronos' exit, but now flicked back to lock on Keyth's. "Most of my subordinates refuse to acknowledge it will go so far, but you have accepted we are there already. Kronos said you brought a letter of Pyrsius?"

"My companions and I have been chased out of the northlands, and have barely survived. The letter we found belonged to soldiers that tracked us." Keyth held the letter in Theseus' direction and the Prince stood up.

"You have a magician among those companions?" Theseus asked, as he took the letter and opened it.

"Not now. He has been imprisoned in this very city."

Theseus froze. "By whom?"

Keyth shrugged. "There is a barracks in the city, not part of your district."

Theseus shook his head. "There are two dozen barracks in the city! You don't know the name of its Commander?"

"No," Keyth said, shaking his head. "I am certain the Commander serves Pyrsius Gothikar."

"Rychard..." Theseus muttered. "By the Maker, I had hoped we would have longer before the first battle in this war."

"A battle?" Keyth questioned, concerned. *Are we going to need to fight, to free Dryn?*

Theseus laughed humourlessly. "Not yet... but soon." He opened the parchment and read it quickly. Then he let out a long sigh and handed it back to Keyth. "It would seem things are about to change in Athyns. And with it, the Dominion will change."

"Sir?"

"My father, Verin Theseus, once told me that I would learn and despise the truth of this Dominion during my days. That was fifty years ago," Theseus explained, his eyes distant. "I am finally beginning to understand..."

40

A narrow slot in stone was Dryn's new home. Every moment seemed to hold the same terror, the same agony as the one before. Every minute seemed to creep past him like the drop of blood weaving a weary path down the stone before his face. His thoughts seemed distant and unrelated. His back was uneven, riddled with diagonal and straight slashes, the scabs of which tore whenever he shifted in his cell because of how it pressed against the stone.

It was as though he had been buried alive. A dark fear had settled in his gut, as if gravity was tugging at his very soul. The skin of his hands had broken from pounding and clawing at the walls and roof of the cell. The end of his index finger was a bloody ruin from repeatedly tracing patterns against the rough surface beneath him.

Glyphs. He traced one now, blood smearing from his finger. *Deserted. The Maker... has left me here.* It wasn't an emotion of anger, or betrayal even. Just a numb realization that the ability to use glyphs had been torn away from him.

The man. The magician. He grabbed onto it immediately, one thread of hope. Perhaps the wizard Mordyn would lose focus. If the ward faltered – even for an instant! – it could be enough for Dryn to use a spell. He began writing a spell that would transport him to Ithyka, far enough away to be safe.

Ithyka. The next realization gripped him in terror and defeat. Ithyka represented his travel through time. *If I get free in the end, I know I can go back in time and stop myself from being captured.* It was a simple concept, but with huge ramifications. He knew that if he survived the prison cell, he could save himself. But the fact that he remained in the prison meant that he would die before being freed. *Since I haven't saved myself, I must die. That's the only thing that would stop me from saving myself.* This was also a simple concept: survival. If he could save himself, he would. In the future, he hadn't returned to save himself; therefore, he knew with a growing certainty that he would die here.

So it really is a tomb... he decided. Attached to the thought was horror and a sharply painful panic. Wildly, he lashed out with a foot, pounding on the cage door at the end. It wouldn't budge of course, and he remained trapped within his grave.

The commander of the barracks had been anxious to meet Dryn in a battle of wills. Dryn had won the first round somehow, but he quickly learned no victory was possible. His life had taken a turn toward defeat.

Now his enemies had copied Artemys' ward. They would be able to find his weaknesses, and likely forge soldiers with his near immortality. But none of it mattered to him anymore. He spent every moment trying to ignore the prison that held him.

A squeal invaded the darkness and something grabbed his foot. He found himself torn from the cell, his limbs scraping on stone and jarred by the fall to the cold floor a few feet below. A crust of bread landed on the dank floor, followed by two peach pits. "Eat, dog," a voice snarled.

Dryn glanced up to be blinded by the magnificence of a torch, firelight scorching holes in his eyes. He used to puzzle at the heartlessness of the men who fed him; how could such men live with themselves, to treat someone in such a way?

Now he had learned thankfulness. He clawed the bread into his mouth, swallowing the dirt and ash with it. The peach pit held moisture! The wrinkled remnants of fruit soaked into his gums until he had sucked every last vein off the pit.

"Water," the voice allowed, and immediately water began falling from above Dryn. He cupped his hands to catch some, then opened his mouth beneath the stream. Gulping the liquid with relief, he couldn't help some excess running down his chin. It dripped into his hands or onto the dark floor. The rain stopped as the guard corked the canteen and Dryn slurped the last drops from his hands, licking between his fingers to find any he had missed.

"Back in your cell," the man grunted. Rough hands gripped Dryn's arms as he thrashed and fought back. He shook his head back and forth, blinded by the torchlight. He glimpsed the mouth of the tomb again, before the darkness swallowed him like the bread crumbs he had devoured.

The hands released him and the small door slammed shut across the window of torchlight near his feet. Instantly blinded in the cell, he slammed his head back against the stone wall in frustration.

Shortly, his limbs were groaning again, cramped against one another until the muscles screamed at him for freedom. His fingers resumed their constant drawing; they, at least, refused to give up. He kicked until his toes went numb, but the dull clanging of his cell door only built the ache that already ravaged his head.

At last he whispered, "Take me..." His voice startled him. He laughed quietly. "I'm not alone after all," he told himself, chuckling. "I taught myself magic... I can keep myself company!"

He asked, "Why are you even here?"

"I healed a friend. I knew what it would cost."

"Was it worth it?" came the next question.

He closed his eyes. In his mind's eye, Keyth was smiling alongside Yara. "Yes."

"So now you're here." He tapped the wall with one finger. "How long is it going to last?"

He shook his head. "I don't know."

"Are you going to give up?"

"I already have," he answered. "I would have saved myself already. I'm going to die here. I've already given up."

He didn't have any questions after that, and the cell fell silent once more. An abrupt spasm took him, and he slammed himself against the walls again and again, slapping the bricks with the palms of his hands and his heels. "LET ME OUT LET ME OUT LET ME OUT!!" he shrieked. His agony bellowed from his soul. He slammed his head sideways into the wall and a sharp ridge in the old bricks drew blood from his cheek. "Get this over with..." he moaned.

The walls slowly constricted around him until his knees were tucked into his chest and his arms folded across them. His eyes could see empty space between him and the door, but he couldn't move. He couldn't move at all. Frozen in terror, he slowly shut his eyes and waited.

His finger traced no more glyphs upon the stone.

41

Beneath the barracks, in a dungeon hallway, a slight wind brushed against the walls as a section of air seemed to shift, flickering to one side before resolving into its place once more. As it settled, a man appeared, lying upon the dank bricks and rising painfully to examine his surroundings.

Dryn loathed these surroundings. He shivered in his tattered sackcloth tunic and began walking down the hall. The hallway itself seemed as narrow as the confinement he had just escaped and his heart quickened. *Not the cell again...* he told himself. *I'm safe...* He brought images of Kryden Wood to mind. Slowly his muscles relaxed slightly.

He wasn't sure how this would happen. If he freed himself earlier, would he still retain the memories of his imprisonment? Hopefully not. *It will have never happened...*

There was a row of slots in the wall, numerous cells. He wasn't sure if any others were occupied, and he preferred not to know. Trying to ignore feelings of restriction, he continued towards the base of the stairwell. A few cells more, and he would reach his own.

Dryn thought he saw something beside him, and when he glanced at it, another form appeared, a square of reality seeming to wink and resolve into place again. When it settled, the shape of a man rose from one knee and glanced around.

Dryn jumped back, and his hand reached for the wall to write a spell to destroy this newcomer. Before he reached it though, a voice snapped, "Stop!"

Something in the voice struck him as peculiar, and glancing up again, he found he was face to face with... himself. He was staring at the visage of a sandy-haired young man. A narrow scar ran down his left cheekbone.

Speechless, he remained frozen, staring at an alternate version of himself and trying to comprehend what was happening. His mind slowly put the puzzle together and he let his breath out slowly. "By the Maker... is this even possible?"

"It would seem so..." the other said. "I'm from further ahead than you are."

"The future?" Dryn asked.

"Yes," his counterpart affirmed. "I have returned to tell you several things. Firstly, you mustn't free yourself."

"Glyphs, why not?" Dryn demanded, stepping back a pace. "That was... the worst thing that has... worse than I could imagine. I need to erase it... stop it from ever happening!"

"You can't," the other said. "It is imperative that you meet Prince Theseus. When you used the time spell just now, you came from the cell itself, correct?"

"Yes..."

His older self nodded. "Prince Theseus and his soldiers are the ones that broke the ward holding you... You must remain in your cell so that you can meet him. The future depends on it..."

"Depends on it?" Dryn asked. "How? If I ignore you and free myself, then the future will be different. And you will never have to come back here to stop me."

"That train of thought proves that you won't free yourself," the counterpart murmured.

Dryn grimaced. It was so confusing and somehow ... exhilarating. "So I have to endure the cell."

"Yes."

Maker burn me... Why?! Only the future would tell. He stepped back and leaned against the wall, still tired and sore from the cell he had left only moments ago. He could recall being curled in the corner and noticing a strong change in the atmosphere. He had reached out a hand and scrawled the teleport to Ithyka. He was shocked when he found himself standing near the Glyph Gate there. After a moment, he had used the time spell to return to the dungeon hallway to free himself. He sighed, trying to think everything through. *Glyphs, I'm speaking to myself!!!* He asked, "You said there were two things?"

"The second is the hardest. You are unable to travel forward in time. You have never tried it, and if you do, you will find the spell does nothing," his alternate warned.

"What?" Dryn gasped, horrified. "I'm stuck in the past now?"

"In the Ithyka incident, you lived until you caught up to the present because you had to send the letters and teach yourself magic. However, if you had tried simply to travel forward in time, you would have been unable to."

Dryn tipped his head back against the cool stones, his hair ruffling on the worn bricks. "Now what?" he asked. "I leave here and train for two weeks until Theseus and his men break the ward?" After all, there was yet another version of him still trapped in the prison cell.

In the plan he had described, he would return to the dungeon the moment that he had travelled into the past, thus seeming to his rescuers that he had been there all along.

"Yes, but you must teleport from here directly to the Arbydn Green. That remains the only safe place you know in which to use magic. Teleporting straight there will avoid giving your enemies suspicions. Keep track of the days. You were in your cell for two and a half weeks, and you must return at the end of that time," his counterpart explained. "Now that I have delivered this message..."

"Wait," Dryn exclaimed. "How will I know when to return and deliver the message you just have given me?"

"Once you get to your rooms in Theseus' palace," his alternate self laughed.

"What?! How do you know I'm supposed to meet Theseus then? It sounds like you just met him too!" Dryn accused.

"I did. I only know you must, because I was once in your shoes and received the same message." With that, his older self broke a spell token and vanished in a flicker of air.

"Great Glyph..." Dryn hissed, standing up straight again. *I'm going on his word that I must, and yet he is only going on our words as well!* It was confusing to think about. He doubted he could ever fully comprehend it. Kneeling, he wrote a spell and adjusted the teleport spell to take him to the Green.

The wind suddenly tore at his cloak and he breathed deeply, spreading his arms in the cold gale that raked across the Arbydn Green. He could see trails of cook-fire smoke rising from the village several miles away. He was free from the cell and free from the pain. For several moments he simply absorbed the size of the space around him.

He was free.

42

Three dozen soldiers accompanied the Prince, in full arms, through the streets of Athyns. Theseus was certain that his target would be entirely aware of his approach long before the crowds allowed his troops to reach it. One of his royal steeds had been saddled even as he awoke that morning. He had prepared entirely for the short journey in the days before, and now as he neared the barracks, he prepared himself for the likely conflict within.

Behind him, also riding animals of Athyns' stables, rode the villager Keyth ten Arad and his companions. Theseus thought he had seen one of the girls before, but he couldn't place the bizarre familiarity, and dismissed the puzzle for a later date.

In less than a fortnight the Triumvirate would meet again in the royal city of Galinor at the Throne of Midgard. Theseus dreaded the outcome, because he knew what it would be. Odyn and his ally would not wait any longer. They would call for the election of a High Prince, knowing Theseus would be unable to prevent it any longer. Even so, Theseus doubted Odyn would be satisfied with the simple wooden throne of the High Prince.

As the ramparts of Rychard's barracks loomed over the rooftops, Theseus sent one of his soldiers to run ahead to warn of their arrival, to keep the gate open and to ensure their foolish enemies did not attempt to create a siege within the city itself.

"Arad," Theseus called, and the villager answered. "I must warn you to remain silent, even if the life of your friend is threatened. We will try to save him. However, my actions today will have implications far beyond a rescue mission."

"Yes, sir," Keyth answered.

Theseus caught Kronos eyeing him. They had been Prince and advisor long enough that now they considered each other friends. Kronos knew how worried he was and knew the ramifications of this journey.

"Welcome to Lord Rychard's barracks, Sire" a guardsman called, as Theseus and a select few separated from the troops within the courtyard of the fortress. "Milord will be down shortly to meet you, sir."

Theseus took a chance and ordered, "While I wait, you may release your prisoners."

The guard flinched and looked up at Theseus cautiously. "I'm afraid milord would object, sir. We should wait until his arrival."

Theseus grimaced. *It's going to be the hard way, then...* He slowly dismounted and those with him did so as well. Some of Theseus' soldiers took their reins and led their mounts closer to the street.

The courtyard wasn't the tidiest of locations, especially in comparison to the strongholds in Theseus' Imperial District. A stockade was built to one side, but was empty. Similarly, a large wooden stake was deserted where it had been thrust into the trodden dirt of the courtyard floor. Several buildings joined the walls, and the larger Keep stood on its own in the middle of the yard.

He caught a glimpse of Keyth ten Arad's paled face before a voice called, "Ah, my Prince!"

Commander Rychard was nearly as tall as Theseus, and wore a similar fine blue cloak. Beneath, the man wore a tanned leather cuirass. Embroidered into the chest were three towers rising behind the letter 'A', the emblem of Avernus.

"What brings you to my humble fortress?" the Commander asked.

"You hold a magician within your walls. The first thing you shall do today is release him," Theseus ordered sternly.

"A magician?" Rychard asked. A small smile curved his lips and he suggested, "Perhaps milord means Mordyn, one of my soldiers. I assure you he is in no danger in my service..."

Theseus regarded the Commander grimly. "Kronos, see to the release of their prisoners." Theseus stepped forward and breathed, "Rychard, you are under direct orders from a Prince: you will not hinder my advisor, nor his men."

Kronos commandeered four soldiers by name and the small group marched across the courtyard. Rychard winced and glanced over his shoulder. A robed man had gathered with the small crowd of Rychard's men. *Likely this soldier Mordyn...*

Theseus backed up several steps and instructed one of his captains, "See that none of them return inside."

"Sir, I warn you that our prisoners are dangerous," Rychard declared. "We only hold them here to ensure they are taken care of appropriately."

"Hold your tongue before a gull holds it for you," Theseus breathed. "You have lied to me twice today, Commander. Take your men and leave Athyns, while I still allow you to go peacefully."

Rychard flushed and crossed his arms. "The tenets of our government, milord! The Triumvirate's laws permit each Prince to set a barracks or embassy in the other Imperial Cities. The laws do not permit you to banish me."

Theseus nearly struck him. He stepped toward the man and growled, "Don't quote laws to me, Commander, when your superior is the one breaking them. This... *war* is going in one direction, and if you want to still have eyes to see how it ends, I advise you to take your troops and leave."

The Commander gasped in shock. "Very well, milord," Rychard conceded. "Allow me to pack my belongings and I – "

"Your possessions will be sent to Avernus after you. You will walk directly to the waterfront, board one of your ships and depart. You will never return to Athyns. Any soldiers who remain will be executed for treason," Theseus announced. The other Princes had foretold long ago that it would come to war. Theseus was tired of hoping otherwise.

Rychard and his men began to move toward the gate, and Theseus' troops stepped aside to allow them passage. One man, however, bolted back towards the Keep. Theseus' captain released a single arrow and dropped the man to the cobblestones. Rychard called out, and Theseus realized it had been the magician Mordyn who had been struck down.

Two of the soldiers held Rychard back until the Commander gave up trying to reach his fallen companion. Theseus led his company forward and the captain knelt over Mordyn. "He's still alive," came the verdict.

"Give him attention. We'll bring him back to the Palace. I should like an interview with a magician who has sided with them," Theseus decided. "I want everything inside analyzed. Anything that could shed light on the motives of our enemies should be included in a report. Burn everything else."

Several moments later Kronos and his soldiers returned to find the courtyard empty of its original inhabitants. Along with them a young man emerged, spreading his arms in the open air of the courtyard and stretching.

Theseus strode across the yard, and those with him followed, except Keyth ten Arad who had run ahead to embrace his friend in relief; the two girls were close behind. By the time Theseus met up with Kronos, the villagers were deep in conversation. Intending to allow them to finish, Theseus stepped aside with his advisor.

"Prince Theseus," a voice greeted, and Theseus turned to see that the prisoner had separated from his companions and now bowed slightly. "I am certain the reasons for our meeting will soon become clear."

Theseus raised an eyebrow. He was rarely addressed first, much less by a commoner. Surely the young magician was aware of the context of his rescue. "I am glad to have been of assistance..." He left his sentence unfinished, prompting for an introduction.

"Dryn ten Rayth." The villager's voice made him seem aware of something which Theseus was not.

"Your friend convinced me to rescue you. He also brought proof of Pyrsius' involvement in this," Theseus explained. "You likely wish to rest and eat. You are welcome to my palace and will be given chambers, both you and your companions."

"My thanks, lord," the young magician said. "I wish to ask if you have begun an offense against our enemies?"

Theseus raised an eyebrow. The villager was concerned with such things, so soon after his rescue? Theseus sighed. "Not yet, but after this I suspect things will intensify."

Dryn ten Rayth was given a horse, and half of Theseus' troops set off. The other soldiers remained at the barracks to carry out Theseus' orders. As they left the gates, Kronos rode up to Theseus' side and murmured quietly, "The villager is powerful."

"I suspected as much. After speaking with Rychard, I realized he wouldn't keep a magician around unless there was an intended use for him."

"No, Dryn ten Rayth is more powerful than I, sir. He may not know it yet, but I can sense it," Kronos said.

"What do you mean?" Theseus asked. "I understand that magic is all a matter of knowledge."

"It is. But there are different ways to acquire that knowledge. And everyone has their own... potential, if you will, for understanding it," Kronos explained. "I don't quite understand it yet, but the moment Mordyn was shot, I sensed a sort of teleport within the prisons. The more I think about it, the more I suspect it was two spells used simultaneously."

43

War was the focus of her dream. Swords and arrows darkened the air with a spray of blood. Death trimmed the dream as though it were the satin on a lord's robe. The walls of a city were repainted the color red and a fire blazed in the city's palace. There was the loud sound of an axe splitting wood, and Iris came awake with a start.

She was alone in her room, in the quiet dead of night, wrapped in sweat-dampened blankets. She waited until her breathing calmed and still could not find sleep, so she sat up and looked around the strangely familiar quarters. They reminded her of the manor in which she had been raised; every decoration in the room was worth far more than it need be.

After a dozen minutes had crept past her, she swung her feet out of bed, shrugged into a robe and stepped out of her room. The quarters had a small living chamber, a bed chamber, and a short hall that served as an anteroom. The hall beyond stretched away into the palace, lit only by an occasional lamp.

Iris wandered along, past adorned tapestries, and tried to recall the dream that had awakened her. She believed in the significance of dreams. They revealed something about herself or the future. Was there to be a war, as so many of them had become convinced?

At the end of the passageway was a doorway onto a balcony. The rampart surrounded the entire floor, and could be accessed from most of the corridors. She opened the door and stepped out of the hall onto the terrace.

The dark mass of Athyns stretched almost as far as she could see, defined only by the few lights still lit at this hour.

The city of Olympus was the only one in the land larger than Athyns.

Olympus. She could recall the stench rising from the waterfront, and the sewage in the streets, and it was a bittersweet memory. Parts of her missed her childhood, but she wouldn't go back even if she could.

"What are you doing up?"

She spun to see the shadowy form of Dryn sitting with his back against the wall. "I couldn't sleep," she explained. "You too?"

"No, I might have been able to sleep," he said. "I didn't want to."

"Oh." She stared at him blankly for a moment and then sat beside him. "What happened in there?"

"I had to go back in," he whispered. "It was the worst... thing that could ever..."

"What?"

Dryn glanced at her as though he had just realized he was talking to her. For a few moments, a war of its own kind was waged across his face, but at last he set his head back against the cold stone bricks. "I need to tell someone, Iris. You can't repeat this ever again, to anyone.... I need to tell you how it all happened."

"Sure, Dryn. You can tell me. What's wrong?"

"I taught myself magic. The letters... they were from me." Iris blinked, and stared at Dryn in confusion. Before she could speak, he continued. "One of the letters taught me a spell I was to use 'in an emergency', if I needed to escape. It was a teleport spell that would send me to safety."

"How did you arrange to pick up the letters in all those strange places?" she questioned. Now, suddenly, she could recall the writing in the margin of Dryn's spell book and how it matched the writing of the letters.

"The teleport spell sent me back in time. I used it when I was nearly killed beneath Ithyka. It sent me back two weeks to the time when I found the first letter. I found another one nearby where I appeared. It explained that somehow I was the one sending the letters. I still can't wrap my head around it entirely. It's like a loop. For that period of two weeks there were two of me in the world, until I caught up to the present and watched the past-me teleport to escape the hunter. Then I killed him."

Iris stared at him. For the next few minutes they remained as quiet as the palace night, while Iris puzzled through what he had said. Somehow, it began to make sense. Who knew which 'Dryn' started it, but one of them taught, and the other learned, until they escaped Ithyka. *That's why he was so different after... he said he missed us...* she remembered. *For him, two and half weeks had passed since he last saw us. For us, it was half an hour.*

"I know... it's impossible. I'll understand if you don't believe me."

Iris shook her head. "No, it makes sense. It all fits together...."

"No it doesn't. How did I learn that spell?" he asked. "From myself? How did 'myself' learn it?"

"That doesn't matter as much. The fact remains that you learned magic from yourself. What happened next?" she asked. "We went to Scion." She laughed and muttered, "That's why you wanted to see the Prophet so badly. Two days after your time traveling we ran into someone who can see the future..."

"I know. I still intend to return there sometime," he said. "Next we made it to Athyns, and I was captured."

His voice broke on the last word, and Iris glanced away from the stars to look at him. "What happened?" she asked softly.

"My cell was intentionally too small for me, like a form of torture itself," he explained. "I still don't know how long I was in there, Iris... How long?" he stuttered. His face was twisted as though he were in pain.

"Two weeks," she answered. "We tried..." she said. "We didn't know what to do..."

"Two weeks," he repeated. "It was... horrible," he whispered, his voice slipping away brokenly. He had pulled his knees up and wrapped his arms around them.

She pulled him against her. "I'm so sorry, Dryn... I'm so sorry... You'll be okay... It'll just take time to get past. You're free now."

He began speaking again, his voice muted against her shoulder. "When Theseus came to rescue me, the ward vanished and I could use magic again. I teleported to nearby with the intent of freeing myself, but was stopped when another teleport appeared. Another version of me appeared, from the future, and told me I couldn't rescue myself earlier, because it was imperative that we meet Theseus."

"You were free?" she asked, confused.

"I went to Lesser Kryden. To the field. And I was free." He sat up. "For the first while I simply sat and laid in the wide open space. And ran around.... Then I trained for most of the remaining time. I kept track of days and then had to scry to make sure I teleported at the right moment. As soon as the imprisoned version of me left for freedom, I returned to the prison."

"Why?"

"I had to. They had to find me as a prisoner and rescue me. It was the only way.... If something gets messed up in the past... who knows what would happen. And for some reason I need Theseus..."

"So you returned to the prison and we rescued you moments later?"

"Yes..." Dryn whispered. He shut his eyes to block the tears that Iris could see forming within them. "I had to crawl back into my prison cell. I had to go back in. It was worse than I could ever imagine. I had spent two weeks in there, buried alive in a cell that was too small.... and then I was free. But I had to force myself to go back in. *I had to imprison myself....*" he hissed.

They sat in silence again as Iris tried to comprehend how he could do such a thing.

"Now I know it," he continued, breaking the quiet. "Now I have to go back again and tell myself all of this. To complete the events in order I have completed them."

"What?" Iris questioned. "Can't you wait, at least to understand why Theseus is so important?"

"No... the person that stopped me... he didn't understand yet either. He was simply carrying out instructions as I have to now..." Dryn shook his head. "But I don't want to. I don't want to remember the prison cell."

Iris took a deep breath. She knew what he needed. He needed someone to tell him to do it. To make him go back. She hated to do it, but she knew she had to. "You must," she said, sternly.

"What?"

"Go back now," she repeated. "Get this over with. Then I'll help you forget the cell. Theseus is important in his role as

Prince, and if this is important to the timeline somehow... you have to trust in ... the Maker. It's the only explanation. You have to go back."

"I don't want to... please..." he begged, more of himself than of her.

"Go back and do what you have to," she whispered. "And then we'll figure things out."

Trembling, Dryn stood to his feet, and opened one hand. Clutched within was a small stone token, riddled with runes Iris could not read. Without another word, Dryn broke it and was gone.

ЧЧ

By the time the sun reached its zenith the next day, Keyth and Yara were still looking for their friends. Eventually they ran into the captain of the troop that had supported the rescue. He told them that Dryn had been summoned to a meeting with Prince Theseus and Kronos. Keyth told Yara that he was sure they should be at such a discussion as well, and when she found it hard to agree, he pointed out that he had been the one to involve Theseus in their lives in the first place.

Soon they were speaking with a porter outside of Theseus' council chambers, who allowed them entrance without argument.

The room to which they were admitted was longer than it was wide and centered around a long oaken table. At the head of it sat Prince Theseus. On his right side sat Kronos Accalia and three men Yara had never seen before, all garbed in silken robes and wealthy jewellery. On the other side was Dryn and Iris. Yara followed Keyth across the room, where he then sat beside Iris.

Kronos was in the middle of speaking. "... Pyrsius Gothikar has been busy hunting magicians."

"How is he getting away with it?" one of the three men asked. "I know he's only been Prince for a cycle, but surely his efforts were initiated long before that... Periander Gothikar would not allow such treason!"

Theseus nodded. "Then obviously, Periander did not know."

"But the Nobles of Avernus... now that Pyrsius is Prince, what of the Nobles?" the man questioned.

"It doesn't matter," Dryn said. "Pyrsius *is* doing this, and we need to do something about it."

Theseus sighed. "At the last Triumvirate session, I witnessed a connection between Pyrsius and Odyn. I suspect they have sided together. Also, Odyn was the one who called for the election of a High Prince."

"A High Prince?" Dryn asked.

"It is similar to the government here in Athyns," Kronos explained. "These three Nobles elected Theseus to his position after his father passed. They could have chosen to elect someone else, but they didn't. The Triumvirate Government is made up of three Princes – Avernus, Athyns, and Olympus. In times of war, a High Prince is elected by the three, giving him complete powers over the entire realm until the crisis is resolved."

"So Odyn wants to be High Prince?"

"Apparently. If Pyrsius supports Odyn, there is little we can do to stop them. The Crown Magician is gone," Kronos continued.

"The Crown Magician?" Keyth asked.

"Artemys Gothikar," Theseus answered. "The role of the Crown Magician is firstly to decide the protocol for the use of magic in the realm, and also to decide if the election of a High Prince is necessary."

"Artemys Gothikar is the man who gave me magic," Dryn muttered. "I still cannot explain it entirely, as some people have given me contrary information. But the man who gave me magic, three and a half weeks ago... he called himself Artemys Gothikar."

They all stared at him, even Keyth. Yara remembered them mentioning the name on the road out of Kryden. Kronos muttered, "So he's dead then?"

Dryn nodded.

Theseus exhaled roughly. "We had assumed so already."

"So, without a Crown Magician..." Dryn prompted.

"There is no one to stop the South from uniting against us. It would mean war, unless we surrender," one of the three Nobles added.

"And we mustn't surrender," Theseus muttered. "It would mean the loss of a way of life. It might mean more, but none of us knows what would happen should the Great Glyph be lost to us."

The remaining Noble, who hadn't yet spoken, snapped, "I don't believe this Great Glyph legend... It has never done anything for me..."

"I have seen it," Dryn said. "I used it to find the name of the hunter, in order to scry him."

Kronos blinked. "You did what?!"

"I found a glyph that allowed me to see the Great Glyph. All I had to do was focus on a target," Dryn said. "Next I found the hunter and then knew his True Glyph in order to scry him."

"By the Maker..." the other magician breathed.

Theseus stared at them both. "What does this mean?"

"I have no idea!" Kronos exclaimed. "I have *never* heard of this before..."

"So it's an advantage?" the first Noble questioned, his hand playing with his greasy beard.

"It's a huge advantage, I'd assume," Kronos answered. "I'm not sure of the ramifications and will have to learn more..."

Theseus glanced at Kronos. "Do you think he could pass the trials?"

Kronos hesitated and slowly began to nod his head. "It's possible... He continually surprises me."

"What trials?" Dryn asked.

"The Trials of the Crown Magician."

Everyone froze, some of them staring at Kronos, others at Dryn. Yara was shocked. *Crown Magician?* she wondered. It was a strange term to her, but a comparison of her friend Dryn to the mysterious Artemys Gothikar... was a bizarre idea.

Dryn laughed. "No, no... you've got it all mixed up," he said. "I've been lucky so far. I'm a long, long way from being anything of a master of magic."

"You beat a veteran soldier and wizard under Ithyka," Kronos pointed out.

"Yes, but it was simply because I got lucky, and by some twist of fate had set it all up unknowingly!" Dryn exclaimed. "It was all just the way things played out! I was destined to beat that agent!"

"What if you're destined to pass the Trials?" Theseus pointed out.

"Then I would have received letters already! Or spells that would help me! I don't know!" Dryn barked. "I don't even know what these Trials entail..."

"Either way, it might be the last thing we can do to prolong the onslaught of war. If we had a Crown Magician, we might be able to stop Odyn from the election," Theseus explained. "Kronos has failed the Trials, so we had given up on that plan..."

"Kronos failed," Dryn repeated. "How could I possibly pass? I am not as powerful as Kronos."

"I don't know how to see the Great Glyph. I could almost agree with these men in saying I can't believe it exists. However, I have faith it does," Kronos muttered. "The fact remains, Dryn; the speed with which you have become an important person.... A cycle ago no one had heard of you. A cycle from now you could be changing the realm."

Dryn slumped in his chair, and Yara could only wonder what thoughts were racing through his head. Finally, her friend spoke again. "Very well, but I want to know what these Trials involve before I agree."

"That would be perfect," Kronos said. "That would give me time to learn a bit about your... strange journey. And this Great Glyph spell..."

Within a few minutes Theseus declared the council adjourned, and planned to meet with Dryn and Kronos the next day. Yara followed Keyth to Dryn's side to discuss the events of the meeting. Dryn was obviously confused by these shocking propositions, the suggestion of him becoming the 'Crown Magician.'

Keyth was no less surprised.

45

After the council meeting, Dryn followed Kronos toward the magician's chambers. As they strode through the halls of the palace, Kronos began asking Dryn about his journey to Athyns, intent on everything Dryn said. Dryn told of the letters in Lesser Kryden, a secret he had kept to himself for so long. Now it seemed everyone knew.

"For the entire time, you had no clue it was you sending the letters?" Kronos asked.

"Not the faintest idea. There was no signature of course... And I never recognized my own writing, because an apothecary's apprentice does very little writing," Dryn explained.

"I suppose that makes sense. And so when did you find out?"

Dryn grimaced. "Not until I was nearly killed in Ithyka. I used the time teleport and awoke a day or so later in the forests near my village. There was another letter there which explained it all."

"And then you had to place the letters everywhere again, correct?" Kronos asked. "Do you still have the ones you read?"

"Yes. With my belongings. I couldn't simply use them again, because one letter explained, 'They had to be written somewhere, sometime'.... I still don't understand it all." As they walked Dryn couldn't help but admire the wealth of the palace. The corridors seemed to continue onward forever.

"It is a challenge..." Kronos commented. "And this Great Glyph?"

They at last reached Kronos' quarters, and the magician unlocked the door with a small key. Dryn opened his mouth to answer, as he stepped through the door.

Instantly he was back in the prison cell, the walls were closing around him and he couldn't breathe. Fighting to stay alert, to stay on his feet, he nearly raised a fist to defend his freedom, but some fragment of his senses realized he was still in Kronos' quarters. He forced himself to inhale, but the walls were still constricting, and his vision blurred to the point of blindness. On the edge of his panic a voice was mumbling to him, as though someone was whispering at him while he was underwater.

He fought his way forward, clawing through the narrowing space and thrashing his way through the prison cell until he reached the opening. His eyes adjusted to the light and he was staring at Athyns. The massive city stretched out toward the horizon, where two mountains met the clouds. And the open sky.

Taking deep breaths, he allowed himself to calm down before turning his gaze back. He was standing at the window of a cluttered room. On one side was a balcony and the eternity of the world. On the other was the stifling cavern.

He flinched his gaze back to the window and his mind drifted out into the open space. Freedom. Slowly his heart beat calmed.

"The prison cell?" Kronos asked, after a sigh.

He roughly nodded once without looking away from his view of safety.

"Alright. You stay there by the window. And tell me if you need to leave. We can go somewhere else..." Kronos suggested.

"No," Dryn managed. "It's alright." *Glyphs... what is happening to me?*

"Very well," Kronos said. "I was asking about the Great Glyph spell."

How to explain it? he wondered. He shook his head to clear it and remembered when Rychard had found Artemys' spell. Dryn quickly unbuttoned the flannel shirt he wore. He had taken the garment from the large wardrobe in his Palace quarters. "There it is," he declared, gesturing for Kronos to look.

The Imperial magician made his way to the window and his jaw dropped when he saw the vertical line of glyphs. "By the Maker!" Kronos gaped. "Who did this?"

"Artemys Gothikar, I believe," Dryn said. Out of habit one finger traced the characters indenting his skin. "Although, I have heard that he was still a young man."

"Just beyond his thirtieth year," Kronos said, his focus still on the ward spell.

"The man who gave me magic and then gave me this... he was a very, very old man. And he called himself Artemys Gothikar," Dryn explained. Kronos touched one the glyphs to ascertain how it was written, and Dryn jumped uncomfortably.

"There are ways," the other magician said. "Spells that change someone's age, normally used to prolong life, although there are dreadful side effects. Of course, the realm of torture recognizes the effects of inflicting old age upon a victim."

"You think Artemys was tortured?" Dryn asked.

"I certainly find it likely," Kronos said. "Great Glyph... there is a lot going on here," he commented, glancing up at Dryn's eyes but gesturing to Artemys' spell.

"He was missing limbs, so he had surely been through an ordeal," Dryn explained. "I suppose he might've been tortured or in combat. I find it hard to believe someone as powerful as he could be tortured."

"I, also. But we are dealing with powerful enemies, Dryn," Kronos murmured. "Now, if you'll be so kind, I will attempt to translate this."

"Of course," Dryn said, and turned his gaze out the window once more. A line of carriages made its way out of the nearby Palace gate. There was the echo of someone sparring below the window, but Dryn couldn't see them. A scribbling noise scratched into his ears and he watched Kronos scrawl something onto a page.

"Maker blind me..." Kronos cursed. "You're invincible!"

"Well..." Dryn muttered. "Not entirely."

"What do you mean? You can't be killed! Well, apart from magic... but I mean invincible otherwise!"

"I still feel pain," Dryn explained.

"Really?"

He nodded. "And plenty of it. Learned that the hard way. Took a crossbow bolt in my shoulder."

Kronos paled. "And you survived? Someone must have healed you?"

"I did."

Kronos shook his head and breathed, "By the Maker.... one moment a village urchin and the next a titan..."

"What?"

"Nothing," Kronos laughed. "I've never encountered this spell before. It took me a good moment to put the words together."

"The Great Glyph spell is there as well."

"Yes, I noticed it, but..." Kronos trailed off. For a moment he scribbled again and then grunted, "it doesn't make sense."

"What doesn't?"

"It has references to your True Glyph as well," Kronos said. Dryn recalled the explanation of True Glyphs or Name Glyphs from the spell book he had read. Kronos continued, "It's as though Artemys discovered that the only way to perceive the Great Glyph is to have such an ability written into your very identity."

"So you recognize the Great Glyph reference?"

"Yes, the glyph itself... It's a very practical glyph, mostly used for lesser magic. Like farming enchantments and blessings and such...." Kronos disappeared and Dryn glanced into the room long enough to see where he was going. The magician grabbed a book from one of his many shelves, but Dryn had to glance away. *It is a tiny room...* he told himself, as way of comfort. Kronos seemed to understand.

"Well... I suppose this will be no help," Kronos commented, followed by the thud of the tome back on the shelf. "Some of those glyphs... I don't even recognize them. How did this spell work again?" The magician approached the window.

"Simple," Dryn explained. "I thought it through like learning any other spell, then wrote down the Great Glyph reference symbol. I said the words... and nothing happened." He could recall frowning at the tracing in the snow, huddled there by his fire outside of Ithyka. "I realized that the glyph was already written down... on me! So I scratched out that one on the ground and just said the words."

Kronos regarded him for a moment. "That's it?"

"Yes..."

"You just said the words and then what?"

Dryn smiled patiently. "And then I could see it. See everything. All the glyphs..."

"*All* the glyphs?" Kronos repeated.

"Yes... it was quite amazing."

Kronos blinked. "I suppose it would be. And you just had to focus on what you wanted? You mentioned earlier that you concentrated on the hunter, and then you could see his glyph?"

"That's right."

Kronos shook his head. Outside, the sound of sparring had ceased and now Dryn could hear a recurring thread-like sound that reminded him of shooting targets with a bow. As a bowyer, Keyth had always been far better than he.

"Alright... so I don't think the Trials will be a problem at all..." Kronos decided. "So far, everything we've talked about is beyond my ability."

"Really?"

"I understand some of this, but I could never do some of the things you have done," Kronos explained. "There is more written there, but *that* is certainly beyond my understanding. Some seem to affect your True Name even more. Others I can't even guess at."

"So... the Trials then. What is involved? What will I need to do?" Dryn asked. *If I'm going to be their political pawn... I want to know what it requires of me!*

"There are three stages. Well, four, but only in technicality. The first is a trial of glyph knowledge. You will be shown glyphs in quick succession and must name them. The second is a test of critical reasoning. You will be placed in a number of strenuous circumstances and must come to a decision. The morality does not matter, but the skills you display at reasoning through the problem... that is the key to the second Trial. The third is the hardest. You must complete a dangerous mission, though it will be conjured by magic. If you pass out or die... you fail. If you do not complete the mission, you also fail." Kronos took a deep breath.

"And the fourth?" Dryn asked, wary of anything the magician might have left out. *By the Maker, I don't know how to complete these....*

Kronos smiled. "You must find your True Name. The Trial's master will give you a spell which will trace your glyph in the air in front of you. You must not allow anyone to see it.

Once you know it, you speak to the master once more and the Trials are complete."

"I just have to know my True Glyph?" Dryn asked.

"Yes, that's it. That's why I said it was a technicality. The only reason we include it as part of the Trials is because a Crown Magician who doesn't know his own limits is a potentially catastrophic mistake," Kronos said. "Your True Name is basically a summary of how you fit into the Great Glyph."

"Alright..." Dryn sighed. His eyes followed the path of a carriage along an Athynian avenue. "When do I attempt these Trials?"

Before Kronos could answer, commotion stirred at the gates. Someone stumbled backwards into the courtyard and fell to the cobblestones. A clatter of weapons rose into the air and then a deafening boom. Smoke and flames tore a hole in the bliss of the Palace yard, and amidst shouts of pain, someone sprinted through the gate and into the streets of Athyns.

Kronos flinched. "That was Rychard's mage!!" he gasped. "He just broke the wards I placed on him! Great Glyph, I don't know how!"

Dryn spun to face the prison of Kronos' small chamber, and lurched his way to the door. The hallway outside was open and stretched far enough that Dryn's panic subsided, and he dashed for the gates.

46

Only by preparing a counter ward in advance could a spell caster defend himself from a ward. To his enemies he would be within the clutches of their ward, unable to use magic, but when prepared, the magician could easily topple the ward when the time was right. It was like having the key before being locked in a cell.

Brother Mordyn had prepared the spell immediately before being shot by Theseus' soldiers, and activated the glyphs immediately upon waking – when the Prince's dog cast that ward onto him. It then became a game of biding his time, focusing on the enemy's ward so he could knock it away as soon as the time was right. The spell was a tingling sensation that ran cold fingers across the Brother's neck.

Andrakaz guard me, he prayed, when at last he toppled the ward and made his escape. The Prince allowed prisoners an hour outside each day, provided the guards kept them near the prison quarter itself. As his guards chatted, he dashed across the yard towards the palace's main gate.

They immediately gave chase, and he waited until they caught up before casting a fiery wind around himself. The two guards fell writhing to the dirt, still trying to cling to life, as Brother Mordyn sent a rupture in the earth towards the gate.

Amidst smoke and falling rock, the guards raised the alarm. The gates caved, buckling under a rising slab of stone like paper in a child's hands. When his spell had run its course, Brother Mordyn was one of the only men left standing in the still-settling dust.

He stumbled through the open hole in the walls and into the streets of Athyns, as a flock of soldiers pursued him. Brother Mordyn spun to face them and broke a token for his dome spell, the same one that had encircled Dryn outside the inn. Now none of them could reach him, as though there was a solid stone wall between them.

A snaking ribbon of red streamed across the ground beneath the shield and Mordyn dove headlong out of the way before the red tail exploded into a fan of livid red flames. His dome vanished and, as he climbed to his feet, he spotted Kronos Accalia and Dryn ten Rayth charging toward him.

Spinning on one heel, he sprinted into the streets.

Things had played out so perfectly until the Rayth's friends had sought aid from the Prince. Mordyn had wrapped Rychard around one finger and had begun his investigation of the villager anomaly.

A townsman waving his hands stumbled into Mordyn's path and was shoved out of the way without a second thought. Mordyn ran towards the barracks again, one thing in mind. Behind him the young magician and Kronos were desperately trying to catch up. It was too dangerous for them to use a spell on him in the crowded streets.

Dodging pedestrians, Mordyn slammed a shoulder against the wall and nearly lost his footing as he rounded the corner towards Rychard's barracks.

The Avernan soldiers were long gone and now servants of Theseus rummaged through the possessions of the stronghold. Mordyn knew exactly what he was looking for. He kicked in the door to Rychard's quarters and used air to cast away a servant who had been reading inside.

The copy of Dryn ten Rayth's glyphs was scrawled on a parchment on Rychard's desk. Mordyn had copied it from the villager's chest. He swiftly folded it and slid it inside his cloak. From the hallway he heard running footsteps, and he dashed to the window.

It was a four storey drop to the courtyard cobblestones. He reached into one of the many pouches at his belt, pulled out a token, and broke it before leaping out of the window.

He still fell, but the air spell formed a disc beneath his feet, slowing his plummet until he touched down on the ground. Above him, two heads emerged through the window, but he was already casting a blast of acid into the air. An entire section of wall exploded into a steaming hole, the brickwork melting into liquid, before the air cooled it off again. This gave Mordyn enough time to reach the stable. He took Rychard's finest horse, abandoned after the Commander's quick banishment, and galloped into the streets. More than one villager received a kick from a hoof, and one man was trampled as Mordyn spun around a corner towards the city gate.

As he escaped into the countryside, he watched the earth soar beneath him and savoured the taste of exhilaration. The Brotherhood would reward him greatly when they resurrected Andrakaz once more.

Dryn ten Rayth was following in the deity's footsteps. Andrakaz had not been awake for five centuries, not since he was bound beneath Olympus at the end of the Age of Myths. The young magician Dryn was close to becoming the ethereal god that Mordyn's leader Andrakaz had become in the end.

The spell folded in Mordyn's pocket would allow the Brotherhood to free Andrakaz, or perhaps mirror his power, creating another.

Keyth sat once more among great men. At the head of the table sat Prince Theseus, his robe worth more than Keyth's hometown. Across from him sat the Three Nobles of Athyns. Each had the power to command the huge populace of the city or tax them a fortune. Two seats away was Kronos, an Imperial magician of great power and influence.

And then there was Dryn. He sat between Keyth and Kronos, quiet as he listened to their discussion. Keyth didn't know what to think about Dryn these days. Was he another of these great men? He was arguably more powerful than Kronos in magic. He seemed the topic of the council's interests.

So what was Keyth doing here? *Watching...* he thought, unsure of any other reason for being in Athyns. *Following Dryn's footsteps?* They had been friends all their lives, and Keyth wanted to keep it that way. But so much had changed in the last month. He could remember the days when the only Imperial he knew was the man named Nalfar. Dishonest. Simply because of his origins.

"So while you were held captive... they copied this spell from you?" one of the Nobles clarified.

Dryn answered a simple, "Yes."

"And this spell..." Theseus asked, "Makes you immortal?"

"No," Dryn replied. "I still feel pain, and I can be killed by magic, and I suppose natural causes..."

The table fell silent for a moment, and Keyth tipped his head back. The ceiling was as engraved and decorated as everything else. It was all so strange to him. *What am I doing here?* he asked himself for the hundredth time. In the second largest city in the realm, in the world perhaps. That was a startling concept.

"What are the ramifications?" another Noble asked.

Keyth tipped his head back and glanced at Dryn who sullenly answered, "They could create an army of near invincible soldiers."

"Great Glyph!" the first Noble cursed. "We have to catch him!"

"Catch him?" Kronos asked. "We haven't the men to spare. And as we witnessed in our pursuit through the city... killing him will be no small task."

"We can find men to spare," Theseus spoke at last. "I must agree with the Nobles. Such a thing is a power that should not be shared. It could change the world in ways we can't imagine. We must hunt this Mordyn down."

"One question," Dryn interjected. "Why wouldn't Mordyn teleport to safety immediately after finding the spell in the barracks?"

The room became silent as the great men pondered this.

Kronos muttered, "There are many reasons.... He may not have had the time to write the spell, and had no tokens left."

"That seems unlikely, considering his resourcefulness thus far," Theseus pointed out.

"There are dozens of cults with different views on the use of magic," Kronos suggested. "He could have convictions against teleporting. Come to think of it... that's likely how he broke the ward. There are spells that the mainstream magic guilds don't use because of historical or moral reasons."

"So if he's not teleporting... we can catch him," the third Noble said.

"But who will go?" Kronos asked. "I'd be wary of entrusting such a task to a regular soldier."

Keyth's breath stopped. *Someone must hunt down Dryn's enemy. Someone trustworthy...* Tugging at Keyth's mind was a possibility. A reason for his presence. A purpose. A chance at joining these great men.

"I would agree," the first Noble decided. "It is your spell, Dryn ten Rayth... I hate to put it so, but it is because of you he captured it. I would think you should be the one to reclaim it."

Theseus shook his head. "Kronos has informed me that Dryn will be undergoing the Trials," he said sternly. "Which means he has just over a week to become the Crown Magician before we go to the Triumvirate meeting."

The nagging sensation wouldn't let go of Keyth, yet he wrestled with the courage to do such a thing. To journey into a world he knew nothing of and kill a man. *What about home? We were going to go home once we got Dryn to Athyns...* "I'll go." His voice spoke without permission, and startled even himself.

All heads at the table turned to him. Dryn's eyes were wide with surprise. "What?"

"I'll go. You need someone you can trust to be in charge of it." Suddenly slick with sweat, Keyth anxiously tried to defend his impulse and found himself believing more and more in it. "I have no place in these political schemes and matters of the realm, but I do have a part in the lives of my friends. I will go."

Kronos nodded, a look of admiration in his eyes. The second noble tugged on his pointed beard and muttered, "A common villager with no knowledge of combat or command. We can't expect him to be in charge of such an important matter..."

Theseus held up a hand. "These commoners never cease to surprise me, and so far have not disappointed me. I've respected everything you've done in Athyns, Keyth, starting with your bravery to involve me in the rescue of your friend. I respect this decision as well. If you are certain, we can arrange for you to lead the hunt for Mordyn."

"You aren't ready for this," Dryn breathed. "Think about it, Keyth! He's a powerful magician... what do you think you could do?"

"I can find him," Keyth told his friend. "I want to. I'll be alright, Dryn. I'll make you proud. He won't expect a simple villager, if he sees me. In fact, he hasn't seen me at all, apart from the raid on Rychard's barracks."

Dryn shook his head, but remained silent.

"Very well," Theseus said. "I'll have Kronos arrange a group of soldiers to accompany you. They may have some problems with a commoner having authority over them, but I'm sure you can manage with my orders. You have an Imperial Prince's support." Theseus chuckled and added, "You may also equip yourself from the Palace armoury. That is one advantage this Mordyn cannot claim."

They discussed recruitment after that, and both Dryn and Keyth remained silent. It seemed that Theseus wanted to begin drafting his citizens already, in the hopes of boosting his present fighting force before a full war broke out.

It wasn't until after those discussions that Keyth reflected once more on what he was doing. *By the Maker! I'm to command a troop of soldiers? You fool! You'll never see Kryden again! You're going to die in a foreign place! But can any villager in Kryden claim the adventure I'm choosing?* Magistrate Arbydn had been to Ithyka a few times. Most of the villagers admired him for something which seemed trivial now.

The armoury of Prince Theseus was a huge room lined with rack upon rack of weapons. The armourer tried giving him a set of plate mail, and while Keyth gaped at its beauty, he politely told the man he would not be fighting in full armour. The man forced him, at least, to take a suit of hard leather and some chainmail. Next he asked if Keyth wanted a two-handed sword, a bastard sword, or a short sword, and he answered meekly, "I prefer bows..."

The armourer smiled. "A bit of a ranger, huh? Crossbow, longbow, battle-bow...?"

"That one." Keyth gestured to the first bow he saw.

"That is far too simple. Take this one. It is the same type, yet fashioned of yew from the Valharyn Spine." The man handed him a sleek weapon, the likes of which Keyth had never seen. "And here's a quiver of arrows, fletched with the plumage of a Trident hawk."

Carrying these items, Keyth made his way back to his room, still in awe at the wealth and beauty of the weapons he held. How could such a work of art be used for killing? He once would have dreamed of firing a bow such as this, but it was even more amazing than he could have imagined. He longed to release an arrow just to feel the strength in the painted wood.

But this was not the time. Perhaps after they had set up camp on the journey.

"What is going on here?"

Keyth spun to see Yara in the doorway. He stood in his quarters with the bow and arrows set on his bed and pieces of leather armour dropped across the floor.

"Oh, hello. I'm..." Dumbfounded, Keyth tried to figure out why he hadn't thought of this earlier. He hadn't even considered how Yara figured into things. "Glyphs... I'm sorry," he breathed.

"Are we leaving again?" Yara asked.

"I am. Dryn is staying. I'm helping him. Someone has to hunt down the magician that escaped yesterday," Keyth explained quickly.

"You're hunting down a man?" she asked in confusion.

"Yes. He stole a copy of the spell that protects Dryn. If he gets away, Mordyn could create an army of invincible soldiers... I've got to hunt him down," Keyth said.

"Oh." She absorbed it for a moment. "I'll go get ready then," she decided.

"What?" he asked, confused. "No, no... you can't come."

"Pardon me?" she asked.

He stared at her for a moment. She had spun around so quickly, and the heat of her voice startled him. Her brown hair was tied behind her neck and she again wore a pair of pants instead of the dresses she had worn in Kryden. "I'm travelling with a troop of soldiers. The roads will be rough, and there will likely be fighting along the way. It is no place for a young woman," he told her.

"And you know this... from experience?"

Keyth flushed. "No, of course not. I just don't think you'll be safe..."

Her eyes softened. "Well, thank you for the concern... but I'll decide what is safe for me and what is not."

"Yara..."

"Keyth, it's alright. I've been on the 'rough roads' for a month now, and I've taken it mostly without complaint. As for those road-weary soldiers... I'll have you to protect me." She grinned and he dropped the tanned leather greave he had been holding. He crossed to her in a long stride, put his hands on her hips and gave her a quick kiss.

"No matter what."

Keyth met with his troop in the courtyard at sunrise, after rising from a night of restless sleep. He was introduced to a soldier named Greymor Finch. Captain Finch was in charge of a division of fifteen soldiers, and at first expected Keyth to inspect 'the troops.' When Keyth told him he knew nothing of such a task, the Captain did it himself.

Keyth spotted Dryn near one of the stables. Before he could speak, he noticed Dryn's finger tracing symbols only a magician could comprehend. A moment later, Dryn snapped out of the trance and blinked when he found Keyth standing right beside him.

"I thought I should give you an advantage," Dryn told him. "Mordyn is headed west. He's in fields now, and it appears he will soon reach a village."

"How do you know?" Keyth asked.

"I scried him, using the same spell used by the man who tracked us from Kryden."

From Dryn's detailed descriptions, Captain Finch knew in what direction to set out, and, within an hour, Keyth, Yara and the troop were ready. Keyth nodded to Dryn, they embraced and Dryn wished him safety as the troop departed.

48

After Keyth, Yara, and Captain Finch had set off from the city, Dryn met with Kronos and Theseus to discuss their plan. They decided the Trials would begin immediately. Theseus also surprised Dryn with the final condition in the process to appoint him the Crown Magician.

"There is one other thing," the Prince said, as they finished their meeting. "A commoner is not allowed to hold the position of Crown Magician."

"What?" Dryn questioned. *What's the point to all this then? I'm a commoner.*

"Only one of noble blood is considered. A relative of a lord or Noble, or of a Prince," Theseus said. "So there is one thing we must do before you begin the trials."

Dryn glanced between the two men in confusion. The Prince's magician responded, "The Imperial Princes hold the power to grant the status of nobility."

"Grant nobility?" Dryn asked, and then it hit him like a hammer. *By the Maker! They intend to make me a lord!* It hadn't dawned on him yet, how important this plot was to them. *It is literally the last resort for Theseus!* Dryn was still realizing the full importance of this plot to them. *He is willing to appoint me a lordship for the sake of this plan!* "Glyphs... We don't even know if this plot will work!"

Theseus laughed and ran one hand through his thick hair. Standing there in the courtyard of his palace, the Prince seemed larger than life. "Dryn, in the last few weeks, the Dominion has begun changing, and you have been playing a critical role. In the last two weeks I've rescued you, broken a law because of it, and come up with a plan to save us all. Because of you. Someone who has been so crucial... surely they are worthy of lordship."

Dryn shook his head. *It didn't happen like that... I was imprisoned and I was freed... I didn't change anything!* he thought, but he could understand the way Theseus saw things. "It seems to be a rash and speedy decision," Dryn said. "Granting me nobility. I don't know what I'd do with it. What would my responsibilities be? Or my privileges for that matter?"

"It is no more rash than our plan," Kronos commented.

"You would become a member of my court," Theseus explained. "It would entail upholding my laws, both for others and for yourself. Your responsibility: loyalty to our Dominion and to my House, which involves protecting it and respecting it. Your privileges... you will be able to command my soldiers, and in time you may command commoners as well. The latter involves their respect of you and your population. If no one knows of you, they are unlikely to embrace your orders."

"Command them?" Dryn repeated in a daze. *Great Glyph... first Keyth leaves! Now this!* Things were changing even more quickly than they had in the last month. "This is... entirely unexpected."

Kronos laughed. "You already act the part. You are speaking to one of the most powerful and renowned men in the world, and you do not even refer to him as sir!"

Dryn was taken aback, and stuttered an apology, to which Theseus raised a hand and said, "It is fine, Dryn. I enjoy the change. Kronos is the only other who doesn't refer to me with titles. All of the praise... it becomes tedious, and certainly tempts to go to my head."

Dryn bowed his head, unsure what to say now.

"Come to my throne-room after midday, and we will conduct the ceremony," Theseus decided. "After that, you may begin the first trial, if you still are committed to it. I would understand if you waited until you are more prepared. But remember: in nine days I attend a meeting of the Triumvirate, and must go with or without you."

Dryn strode briskly to his quarters and found Iris waiting in the narrow hall. "How did it go?" she asked.

"I'm still not sure," he replied, and, with closed eyes, ducked through his anteroom into the wider open space of his living chamber. He took a deep breath, glancing at the window until the paranoia dripped away. "They are going to make me a lord."

"A lord?!" she gasped. "What? Why?"

"A commoner cannot become the Crown Magician," he explained. "Glyphs, Iris... this is all happening so quickly." He poured wine into two cups and handed her one.

She sank into a chair. "I should have remembered... I'm sure I knew that. When are they going to do this?"

"At noon," Dryn answered. He sat down, and took a sip.

"And? Are you alright? This is so huge... and so abrupt."

Dryn nodded, staring at her. Her hair had grown longer since they met. She now wore it in a ponytail, and he hadn't paid any attention to it until now. He could see the nobility in her now. She had been born and raised by the upper class, yet sought an average commoner's life. With her hair a little longer and a glass of wine in one hand, she appeared to be a lady to the last detail. "I don't know about being 'alright' with it.... I'm going to go through with it either way. It's the least I can do. And besides," he said, "the more I think about it, the more I like the idea of being a lord..."

Iris snorted. "We're so opposite in some ways."

"Very few ways," he corrected.

"Agreed," she said. "I've spent ten years trying not to be Lady Lanteera. And you've spent your whole life not being a lord, and now will be."

"Ironic? Coincidence or providence?"

Iris burst into a chorus of laughter. "Why? You think the Maker himself guides our ... love?"

Dryn had opened his mouth, and now closed it. *Love.* The single word hung in front of his mind. *I'm in love.* He had been for a long time, he knew. He hadn't yet realized it to be love. He smiled, and Iris matched it. "Why not!?" he asked.

Theseus, Kronos and the Nobles had assembled after the noon meal, and they all stood in front of Theseus' throne. As Dryn approached, Theseus called, "I'm glad you came. I had worried you might not accept."

"I already respect the Dominion, uphold its laws, and serve you..."

Both Kronos and Theseus laughed, while the Nobles eyed him stoically. Iris had explained once that the Nobles were above normal lords, yet somehow felt challenged by them. While lords could not gain the status of Noble, they could affect the decisions of the Nobles, and thus influence the election of the Three Princes.

Theseus decided, "Let's start without further delay. Dryn, kneel before me."

Time slowed down as Dryn lowered himself to his knees. The three Nobles cornered themselves in the shape of a triangle around him. Each of them drew a sword; Dryn raised an eyebrow, but Kronos nodded in encouragement.

The three blades settled on his shoulders, as Theseus approached him. "Dryn ten Rayth, I, Erykus Theseus, recognize that you have served the Dominion and House Theseus, and have decided to grant you the privilege of service in my court."

The Prince drew a sword as well, a gold trimmed blade, jewelled and decorated beyond use. "This blade represents the power of the Dominion, and I gift you with its power." Theseus set the blade onto Dryn's right shoulder. "We remove our blades, but remember that you wield the power of the Dominion through their steel embrace." As one, the Nobles raised their swords away from him. The Prince sheathed his sword.

"Now rise from your knees as Lord Dryn Rayth, and may your House never again bear the symbol of the commons. Rise Lord Rayth, and take your place at my side," Theseus commanded.

As if in a dream, Dryn stood to his feet and felt both enlightened and encumbered. *What have you done now? Lord Rayth... My household and I? My father is no longer a commoner either?* Now as he stood before Theseus and the Nobles he felt more their equal. And he felt powerful, as though the ceremonial sword had imbued the power of the realm in some physical way.

One of the Nobles pronounced, "It is done," and strode away. The others soon followed.

"Will you begin the Trials now? Or tomorrow?" Kronos inquired.

"I will take the first now. I am not confident in my knowledge of glyphs," Dryn said, "but I don't think a day will make much difference. Or a week for that matter."

"Are you sure this is the time?"

"I am," Dryn decided.

Theseus nodded and said, "So be it," as Kronos led them back into the courtyard.

As they passed through the doorway, a lady appeared beside him, and he was surprised to see she was wearing an emerald green dress. "Well, Lord Rayth," she said, "may this Lady take your arm?"

"She may indeed," Dryn said, and offered it to her. He heard Theseus laugh in front of him and flushed in embarrassment. They followed Kronos to a fenced training yard. Iris was given a seat by Theseus. Dryn was permitted to sit wherever he chose, and then Kronos began writing the most elaborate spell Dryn had ever seen.

"Are there rules?" Dryn asked.

"For this Trial, you may not write glyphs," Kronos said, finishing his spell. "Remember, you are to name each glyph you are shown as quickly as possible. You are unable to re-take this trial or take further Trials if you fail this first, so you must not fail."

Dryn absorbed this with a nod, and closed his eyes for a moment, whispering a prayer to the Maker. He opened his eyes and glanced at Iris and Theseus who sat on a bench nearby. "I'm ready," he murmured, turning back at Kronos.

"I feel like I cheated."

Iris stared at Dryn as they met for breakfast at a table in the Palace great hall. She shook her head. "You didn't cheat," she told him. "You didn't write any glyphs, and you answered quickly enough. Even Kronos said you did well."

Dryn frowned. "I didn't write any glyphs, but I took advantage of the rule. I did use magic."

"What?" Iris asked, in surprise.

"I used the glyphs from the spell Artemys wrote. I used my Great Glyph spell. I simply focused on the glyph Kronos showed me, and then saw an example of it in the world. The first few I knew, but the glyph for sun... I used my Great Glyph reference and it showed me an image of the sun." Troubled, he looked away from her and glanced around the room.

He's brilliant! she thought. "I don't think there's anything wrong with that. You didn't break any rules that Kronos gave you, and he didn't accuse you for using the reference spell. You passed! You should be happy!" *He knew he could pass... he wasn't worried at all!* She knew the other Trials would be more difficult.

"I am happy, I suppose..." Dryn said, but he was still frowning.

"Hey," she said, and leaned over to give him a kiss. "You became Lord Dryn, *and* you came one step closer to being Crown Magician. I'm proud of you. You've come so far since we met in Greater Kryden."

"Thanks," he muttered. "I still can't believe some of this is happening..."

"Me neither," she said.

"I mean... I'm a lord?" he breathed.

She grinned. She knew how hard it was for him to believe. "Are you ready for today's Trial?"

He laughed dryly. "Ready? I'm not sure it's possible to prepare for something like this. There could be two today. If I pass the second Trial, I'll be taking the final one today as well."

"Really? Is there enough time?" Iris asked.

He shrugged. "The first test took an hour. Even if these are twice or three times in length.... I think I can finish today."

Iris stared at him in surprise. "So today... you could be the Crown Magician."

"Yesterday I became a lord," he laughed, "and today I become the Crown Mage." After a moment, he added, "Hopefully. A week from now, I could be face to face with Pyrsius Gothikar."

That statement turned their conversation into silence. Iris sat back and took a deep breath. Somehow she had forgotten that one of the Princes was trying to kill him. "What will happen?" she asked him. "Will he try killing you at the Council meeting?"

Dryn shook his head. "I don't know. He's never seen me in person, so I'm not sure that he'll recognize me. Besides, he was never hunting me personally, simply my kind." Dryn smiled for a moment. "Of course, seeking the Crown Magician... he may try."

Iris frowned. She didn't want him going ahead with this plan anymore. It seemed more dangerous, and she hadn't realized how much until now. "Why do you have to do this? Can't we just hide somewhere, and... and ignore all this?"

"No!" Dryn said. "If too many magicians are killed, magic itself will die. Remember? Magic is granted by a magician to those he sees fit? We cannot let the Dominion destroy a way of life, and an era of power. I will go ahead with this, and I will do all I can to help. It's who I am."

"Yes..." she murmured. "Hang on, so you can give magic to someone?"

"Yes. Kronos showed me the spell, and I recognize it from the night Artemys gave me magic," Dryn said.

"Give it to me," she said. She sat up. "That way you won't be alone anymore."

Dryn closed his eyes and his face assumed a pained expression. She was afraid she had upset him. "Don't do this, Iris. Magic has been changing my life for a month now, often for the worse. If I give you magic, you'll be hunted the same as I am."

"Yes, but I already am. I'm travelling with you! We face the same dangers!" Iris exclaimed. *What would it be like? To write a symbol on the ground and summon fire from nowhere?* "Please, Dryn? We would be a force to be reckoned with!"

"Iris, no!" he snapped, and stood up. He started walking away and returned, pacing the floor nearby.

For a moment, she just watched him, until he put his back against a wall. "Alright," she sighed. Changing the topic was easy because she had wondered about something for a while. "Dryn, have you ever been to the future? You told me all about your time traveling... Have you travelled ahead and found out how it ends?"

Dryn shook his head. "I can only travel back in time. Travelling forward in time doesn't work for some reason. The glyphs just won't activate. There is a series of symbols that represent intervals of time, which allows me to pinpoint where in time I wish to go. But I can only go into the past. And once I'm there... I have to wait it out until I reach the present again."

"What?" Iris asked, trying to wrap her head around it. "Really?"

"Yes."

"Well, what about on the rooftop? You went back in time to stop yourself from getting freed... and then you were right there again, with me," Iris explained, remembering the night clearly.

"That was only a day. I spent the day in Athyns while you and the others invaded Rychard's barracks."

Iris rubbed her eyes. "Alright..." she muttered. "I'll let that drop. I can't understand, but that's fine. You can't go forward in time. That's fair enough. Six days from now you'll be in Galinor."

"Galinor?"

"The city of the Imperial Throne. In the center of the city rises the Tower of the Throne," Iris said.

Dryn nodded. "Well, if today goes well, then you're right. Six days."

• • •

The second and third Trials took place in Theseus' audience chambers. The magician was put into a trance. Complex spells would draw his mind into a realistic realm where he would face challenges to overcome.

Despite her earlier argument, Iris did not want to be in Dryn's shoes for these trials. To go to an ethereal plane where one's mind would be put to a test as real as her own world! Despite this he went willingly, leading her through the passages of Theseus' palace until they reached the Prince's throne room. The Three Nobles had gathered as the necessary Imperial witnesses. Theseus and Kronos stood among them, and before Dryn was placed into a trance, the Prince looked at Iris and sternly requested she wait outside.

Sitting on a bench among the pillars of the courtyard, Iris shifted restlessly, and prayed for Dryn. She wasn't normally one to pray, but over the past weeks she had come to a place where prayer seemed inevitable. Her friends were divided, some pursuing enemies and the other becoming a willing pawn in a political war. All around her the Dominion seemed to be crumbling. She was unsure how she could have been so blind to it before.

"He passed the second Trial," a voice announced, what felt like moments later. One of the Nobles stood beside her, and without another word he departed. Dryn would be attempting the Third now.

Her eyes wandered across the brickwork cobbles in the middle of the yard. The tile stones were grey rock, pieced together in a pattern. Some were more chipped and weathered than others, but it wasn't until her gaze passed onto the far side that it froze.

One of the bricks was a dull red color, unlike any of its comrades. It appeared to have been placed there by accident, or perhaps the mason had run out of grey cobblestones and needed to repair this courtyard. This one red stone was not in the center of the stonework, nor on the edge.

As she sat there staring at it, she couldn't help but wonder whether the red stone, the mismatched and set apart one, was like Dryn.

50

Drifting on the waves of limbo, gasping for breath, reeling from the euphoria of nothingness, Dryn slowly became real again, his body beginning to take form as he awoke in a field he did not recognize. The ethereal mist of his previous surroundings took form as armour and settled as a solid burden upon his shoulders. His vision was narrowed to a slit-like opening in front of his eyes, heavy metal clasped to his head. In one hand the length of a spear, in the other the weight of a shield.

"SOLDIER!!!" someone bellowed. "MOVE IT!"

He turned his head until the visor showed him a man pointing and screaming at him.

"GET UP THE LADDER!" the man yelled. "RESCUE THE KING!!"

"The third is the hardest. You will be placed in a dangerous situation and must complete a mission," Kronos had said. "If you pass out or die..."

Dryn ran forward, following a line of soldiers as they charged up a hill. At the top he could see a wall and the high battlements of a castle. "Rescue the king," he repeated to himself, as he joined the charge. *I'm a soldier. I have to complete my mission. I must save the king.*

Someone screamed, "GAhhh!! Please!! Help me, help me, Maker please..." The voice trailed off into a mumble. Dryn turned his helmet to the left and choked. A crossbow bolt had blasted a hole in a man's shoulder; his armour was shredded like wood shavings, and his arm hung from his torso by threads of cloth and bloody muscle. Half of his face was slick with red from the blow, and his opposite hand clawed at the wound, trying to dam the flow of blood.

Complete your task. He forced himself away from the horrid sight and ordered one foot in front of the other. The man let out a long twisting scream, which ended abruptly, when someone put the soldier out of his misery.

The bloodstained ground quickly slanted downward and he stumbled under the unfamiliar weight of his armour. All of a sudden his feet stepped out into empty air and he plummeted down against a dirt bank. For a disconcerted moment he struggled to roll over, trying to see where he was.

Another soldier appeared in his field of vision, falling awkwardly to one side, until he vanished from Dryn's sight and grunted in pain.

Dryn sat up, clambered to his feet, and found himself standing in a ditch full of large sharpened wooden stakes. The other warrior had landed directly on one. It had broken a plate of armour, and likely done severe damage to the man's side. He grabbed hold of the man and yanked him off the trap, setting him against the dirt embankment. An arrow whistled out of nowhere and appeared quivering in the earth beside the gasping soldier.

Dryn hurriedly hauled the wounded man to the other side of the ditch and set his back against the bank for cover. "You alright?" he asked.

The man nodded roughly. "Keep going. I'll hide here..."

Dryn raised his shield and jumped back to solid ground. He was lucky to have survived the trap unscathed..

As soon as he took a step forward, a flash struck his shield and nearly knocked it out of his hand. A long iron point appeared, sticking two inches through the shield and narrowly missing his strapped arm.

Grimacing, he realized he had left his spear in the ditch. He couldn't turn back now. The archers would destroy him. He fumbled around his belt and found the hilt of a sword. Drawing the weapon, he started running uphill again.

Around him were a dozen other soldiers, some falling to the earth as arrows or bolts found their mark. He peered over the corner of his shield, staring at the castle wall as he approached. The sun was streaming over the ramparts, but he refused to be blinded.

He was nearly at the ladder when another arrow struck his shield, this time bursting through and meeting the unprotected flesh of his forearm. Blinding pain lanced through his arm and blood splattered against his helmet.

Pulling his arm close against him in agony, he forced himself to keep moving. The moment that he stopped walking, he would become an open target. He swiped his sword on the other side of his shield and cut away the other end of the shaft. Clenching his jaw and grabbing hold of the arrowhead where it protruded from his arm, he yanked with all his might and tore the remainder of the shaft out. He tasted blood in his mouth; he had bitten his tongue in the pain. He threw away the gory arrowhead and closed his eyes briefly.

He knew his mind was in a state of shock, but his limbs were laced with adrenaline. He wasn't sure of all the real-world consequences should he die in this place. Frankly, he didn't want to know. He had one task: to rescue the king inside.

He forced himself to keep going, and soon reached the corpse-littered base of the ladder. There were several soldiers already climbing it, and he set off after them. He climbed with one hand and his feet, the other hand holding his shield high to ward off any arrows. His arm throbbed dully with pain, his nerves had gone numb; thankfully the straps were designed to keep the shield manoeuvrable even should the forearm fail. Only upper arm muscles were necessary to lift it.

Halfway up, another arrow hit, but did not harm him. As he was getting closer to the top, a massive weight landed on him and nearly knocked him off into the void that surrounded him. The weight continued to push against him until he threw his body inward against the ladder and tried shrugging whatever had landed on him away.

A limp hand passed in front of his visor and then the weight was gone. He glanced down and saw a body slam against the ground far below. Whirling with vertigo, dizziness and horror, he nearly lost his footing again, but forced down his stomach and lifted one foot to the next rung of the ladder.

At the top of the ramparts he found himself standing among a sea of blood and bodies. A man was exchanging resounding blows with an opponent several feet away. Dryn glanced in the opposite direction. Much farther away was a skirmish between of a group of soldier and the archers hiding in the corner towers.

He jogged wearily towards the nearest fight and joined his comrade's assault. His companion managed to land the final blow, and Dryn glanced away as blood fanned out from the soldier's sword and splashed onto the dark stonework of the battlement.

"Thanks... Let's go," the soldier muttered, and they charged toward the archers.

The next battle was far rougher. Dryn and his companion were outnumbered two-to-one. Fortunately, most of the archers lacked shields and, even when they dropped their bows and drew short swords, they were easy kills.

Dryn nearly emptied his stomach when his sword first parted the studded leather and pale flesh of a man. His sword, dripping red, was enough to blind him. He had just killed a man.

It was different somehow. He had killed a dozen men when he rescued his father from the thieves in Kryden. But this was different. Those bandits had been more impersonal. He hadn't seen their blood. He had killed them from a further distance, and with spells, not steel.

This seemed wrong. He knew it was the same thing as using a fire ball. He knew that, morally, he was doing the very same thing. But this seemed harsher. Less merciful perhaps. The men that he cut through... they might last an hour or more with the wound, slowly dying. Most of Dryn's magical attacks killed quickly.

But it was more than that. All of this senseless killing. Rescue the King? As the last archer fell, clawing on the stones, Dryn stumbled away. No rescue was worth this. No King justified this. War. Was this war? What was the point of it?

He knew there were reasons for war. The common soldier didn't know them though! Dryn didn't know them. *By the Maker... is this worth it?* Political reasons, religious, ethical, historical reasons... there's so many that play into a war like this...

He glanced at his comrade who was gesturing to continue their wall-top raid, but Dryn shook his head. The man cursed and ran on alone.

Who is this king? Who has captured him? Dryn knew nothing of his mission. *How can I continue this without knowledge? I can't do this without... answers! If I had reason, I could continue. We need a cause, not this... senselessness...*

"I can't," he snapped. He tossed the bloody sword away and it clattered across the stones. "No. This isn't right."

And with thunder crashing through the heavens, the castle, the blood, the pain, the death, faded like a storm cloud, and Dryn floated on the waves of a void once more. Darkness began to cover his vision, until all of a sudden he was coughing, clawing the texture of rough fabric and blinded by torchlight.

He was back in Theseus' throne room, his hands clutching the collar of Kronos' robe. Recognizing his surroundings, he let go and slammed back down against the blanket on which he had been placed. He covered his face in his hands and squeezed his eyes shut. "I'm sorry," he breathed. "I'm so sorry... I tried... I just needed to know why.... Glyphs... I let you all down..."

"No, no, Dryn..." Kronos gasped. The magician had been crouching, and now dropped to both knees. "You didn't let anyone down. You passed the third Trial. You passed the Trials, Dryn.... By the Maker..."

"I passed?" Dryn hissed, sitting up. "I thought I had to complete the mission!"

"That's part of the Trial. The instructions... are part of it," Kronos replied. "The third Trial is the ultimate test of worthiness. The Crown Magician's ultimate role is to decide what issue deserves the election of a High Prince. The Crown Magician must be able to judge when a High Prince is necessary, and must understand the ramifications of such a choice. The third Trial is the realization that war is never justifiable, and yet inevitable. It is your responsibility to allow it when it becomes necessary. And you need to *know*. And those who serve you need to *know*. Without a cause, it is senselessness...

"Only those who have taken the Trial are permitted this knowledge," Kronos explained. "Whether they fail or not, they are sworn to secrecy, so that the third Trial remains the way it is."

"I passed?" Dryn repeated again. It all made sense. He already knew that was the purpose of the Crown Mage... yet he hadn't added things up. Now the puzzle pieces tumbled into place and he understood why the third Trial had played out the way it had. *Most people who tried it would keep going and rescue the 'king.'* "So my inexperience with fighting... that became an advantage in the end..."

"Either that, or your wisdom..." Theseus murmured. "Only nobility can attempt the Trials... and I imagine most nobles aren't nearly as ... compassionate as you."

The words were gracious coming from an Imperial Prince. Dryn stood up and received nods from the Three Nobles, who sat at a nearby table. "Now? I must find my Name Glyph?" he asked, glancing at Kronos.

The other magician rose from the floor and nodded. "You and you alone must know it. Anyone who learns it will have power over you, if they know how to use it. As the Trial coordinator, I will simply take your word once you know it. There are spells I could teach you that would show you the Glyph.... Although I would suggest you use your Great Glyph spell. It seems to be much simpler."

"Very well," Dryn said. "Give me a minute." Instinctually, he bent his knees to trace the glyphs for the spell, only to recall they were written in his flesh. He straightened and spoke the words of magic to activate the spell, and at once he saw the massive web of glyphs in front of him, the tapestry of the world.

He focused on himself, his appearance and his location, and this time it took a while for the spell to register what he intended. Slowly, it centered on a set of glyphs which continued to grow until they filled his vision.

He could read several element glyphs, likely the physical parts of his body. He could also see a large number of complex characters that did not translate into any glyphs he knew. If True Glyphs were truly unique to every person, it would make sense that they would not be legible.

He let the spell drop and was standing in front of Theseus and Kronos once more. "I know it," he said.

Theseus laughed, and the Nobles joined him nervously. Kronos simply stared at Dryn in unchecked awe. "I have no reason to doubt you," he replied. "So I suppose I can now pronounce you the Ninth Crown Magician. Lord Dryn Rayth, Magician of the Imperial Triumvirate."

Expecting ceremony of some kind, Dryn waited for the magician to continue, but Kronos seemed to be done. "What? There's no laying of a dozen swords upon me or anything?"

They all laughed this time, and Kronos chuckled, "Not the first fame worthy words of a Crown Mage that I would have expected...."

And that was it. Over the past week, Dryn had become a Lord and, unbelievably, the Imperial Crown Magician. Over the next week, he would attempt to save the Dominion. But right now, his 'Lady Lanteera' waited outside.

51

Defeat. Theseus knew it and feared it. All he could do was prolong its completion, and hope for the best possible outcome for the survivors. And somehow explain it to the young Crown Magician with his dreams of repairing the Dominion.

Theseus summoned Lord Rayth to his chambers and poured wine for him. They took chairs in his sitting room, and Theseus began in the only way he could. "Dryn," he said, "the Triumvirate is dead. Periander once told me that. I've wondered for years how the greatest man in our history could say that. I've only come to understand it in the weeks since my last journey to the Tower of the Throne. It's been dead for a long time."

"Don't say that," the Crown Magician replied. "I've done all I can... Surely, there is still hope."

"I know you've given your all. Every one of us has. But the system itself is flawed," Theseus explained. "It is hard to understand and far harder to come to terms with. The Triumvirate itself, as an ideal, as a government, as anything you see it as... it is something of the past. From its very inception... it was not destined to last. It has been fated to fall since the start."

"If I didn't know better," Dryn said, "that is the speech of our opposition."

"No, the sides are different here. The opposition seeks power for themselves from the fall of our government. Our position seeks to save the peace, and to save civilization from that fall," Theseus said. "But we must accept that it is an inevitable fall. You see... the Triumvirate is ultimately an aristocracy."

"Sorry, what's that?"

Theseus smiled. "Dryn, I sometimes forget that you are from a small village in the Northlands."

"I sometimes forget that I am a Lord," Dryn returned.

Theseus explained aristocracy, democracy, and monarchy to his newest Lord. And then he explained the Triumvirate. "It was designed to be a democratic system. The Nobles elect the Prince as they see fit. The Princes vote on issues, and thus each third of the realm has input on the issue at hand. That's the idea of it.

"The implementation is much different," he continued. "After a few Princes passed, the Nobles of each city had developed ties with certain families, and soon it was taken for granted: the Princes were Odyn, Gothikar, and Theseus."

"So the Nobles became corrupted?" Dryn clarified.

"No," Theseus replied, sipping from his wine glass. "They only did what could be expected. They are upper class, and therefore the lower class is excluded. That is the flaw with any aristocracy."

"So it was never democratic?" Dryn asked, quickly realizing the connections between the new words.

"There is a flaw in that system as well," Theseus said. "A flaw which sped up the corruption in the Triumvirate. A democratic system has no room for morality. Nothing is right or wrong. Everything simply is. And everyone has the right to their own existence, a right to their own truth. Nothing is absolute, and therefore nothing is governable. The democratic system is flawed, perhaps greater than aristocracy, as it drowns in an abundance of immoral rights."

"So... monarchy?" Dryn questioned.

"That is what our opposition desires. That system is the most extreme of those we discuss... It has room for the greatest success, and room for the greatest error. Should a humble monarch come to power, the good of his kingdom will flourish, and his government will be flawless. Should a power-hungry, selfish, or otherwise greedy monarch come to power... then the realm will suffer, and the government will eventually crumble. This system is just as dangerous as the others."

"So how should the government work then?" Dryn wondered, confused.

"I do not know," Theseus said. "That is a question that is far beyond me, or any individual. Perhaps a question beyond mankind itself. I only speak on these systems so that you can begin to understand. The war we are about to fight is more than we can solve in dialogue and, ultimately, impossible to resolve. There is no final outcome. There are many results, possibilities, but there is no answer."

"That sounds very..." Dryn trailed off.

"Tragic?" Theseus asked. "Defeatist?" He laughed dryly. "Yes, it is. But it is the state of things. The war we are about to fight is a war of prevention. We are trying to prolong the decay of the Triumvirate. Hence, your position as Crown Magician and our plan to stop Odyn from becoming High Prince. We are going to try to hold the Triumvirate together until we can deal with our enemies' desires for power."

"And then what?"

"I do not know," Theseus said, the second confession of its kind. "There seems to be much that I don't know. We must find another way, another path the Dominion can take. We mustn't allow it to fall into Odyn's or Pyrsius' clutches, nor any one man. Unless he be the Maker himself."

"So we're going to try to save a flawed, already dead government until we can find a different flawed government?" Dryn asked, frowning.

Theseus chuckled softly. "Yes, that's what we're trying to do." He finished his glass in one movement and set it aside.

"How do you live like that?" Dryn asked. "There is no hope, no light. What incentive is there to get up each day and fight? There *is* nothing to fight for."

Theseus sneered and shook his head. "Yes, there is," he snapped. "There are people to fight for. There is an evil to fight against – men like Pyrsius and Rychard and Odyn! There is a tradition to fight for, a way of life that should be remembered and put to rest, not torn apart like a carcass, the way those corrupt *vultures* would! There is plenty to fight for! How do I live like this? How do I find incentive to rise each day? *Someone has to,"* he declared. "I once saw the Triumvirate as a glorious triumph of mankind. I see now I was deluded, but I will fight until my dying breath to give that delusion the resting place it deserves, and to deny creatures like Odyn the depravity of taking advantage of our kind! I live like this because there has to be someone who stands up and says, 'This is wrong, and it will not end this way!'"

The young crown magician was nodding; he clenched his jaw as tears formed in his eyes.

52

Night spent beneath a tree was an experience quickly becoming normal for Keyth. Once darkness had fallen, and the moon began its rise, a camp would be made and a fire lit. After a meagre meal and the occasional campfire conversation, he would settle for the night, curled within a blanket and tucked against the trunk of a tree or a log.

It was now three days since they had left Athyns, riding out beneath the ornate pillars of the West Gate. Yara had ridden at his side, and Captain Finch directly behind them. A scout had moved ahead and then dismounted to search for tracks or signs of the magician's passage.

They camped beside the road each night, and set off as soon as the sun peaked the eastern horizon. As on the other nights, Keyth ate as soon as he dismounted. He caught one of Finch's soldiers watching him. Keyth tried to ignore him, but was nagged by the knowledge that the soldiers were keeping an eye on him.

It was because of his sudden importance. It was because he was the villager who had gone farther than any of them, right to the Prince. Given a position of power without having to earn his place there.

And it was because he knew what they didn't.

"This man we're hunting," Finch asked, just before they went to sleep, "why is he so important?"

"You don't know?" Keyth asked. He had thought that Finch at least was aware of the stakes.

"All I know is that he's the magician that was taken from Rychard's barracks, and he escaped somehow. I don't know why the Prince is so worried about a minor magician, nor am I aware of your role in all this," Finch explained. "Don't get me wrong. I respect you and I follow orders. You don't have to worry about me usurping your authority."

Authority, respect you... Keyth repeated in his mind. *By the Maker, Keyth! What are you doing?* he asked. "Come with me," he said. He led Captain Finch away from the soldiers. Yara had already gone to sleep, so Keyth didn't worry about leaving her. He'd hear if she awoke.

Once they were alone, Keyth turned to Finch and asked, "Do you know about the plans for a new Crown Magician?"

Finch nodded. "I suspect he's already passed the trials by now. It has been three days." The Captain caught one of his men staring after them, and nodded his head. It was alright.

"The Crown Magician is very powerful by way of magicians," Keyth explained.

"No doubt," Finch interjected. "Someone in his standing must be."

"Yes, well, the key to his power is a spell that was given to him by the past Crown Magician," Keyth said. "This spell was copied from him during his imprisonment."

"I see. It was copied by this magician we hunt," Finch said. He was a smart man, smarter than the other soldiers Keyth had met since leaving Kryden.

"It was," he confirmed. "Fortunately, we took him into custody. However, he escaped, and knowing the importance of Dry—the Crown Magician's spell, he stole it."

"What can he do with it?" Finch asked.

"I don't know exactly. I am no magician. As far as I know, it would allow our enemies to discover the Crown Magician's weakness," Keyth explained. "Or worse, allow them to create more magicians as powerful as he is."

"You see," Finch said. "I can understand that, but I don't understand why they don't give magic to everyone. Create an army of wizards."

Keyth nodded. "I've wondered that myself. It all goes to their leaders. The men at the top want the opposite of that. Get rid of magic once and for all. Completely level the playing field, so to speak."

"I see." After a moment of pondering: "Who are the men in charge? Who are these 'enemies'?"

Keyth glanced back at the camp, at the small group of soldiers slowly dropping onto blankets for the night. None of them knew how close their government was to destruction. "I think it's best you don't know. For now. Once... no, *if* war is to come, you'll be informed. But for now, you're better off in the dark."

"Fine," Finch said. "That's your decision. It makes me worry though. I just hope we catch this earth spawn quickly."

The following afternoon they reached the village of Ferres. Finch asked Keyth to accompany him to the village inn to ask whether a wizard had passed through, and Keyth allowed Yara to come too. Strangely, everyone they spoke to walked away. As soon as the description of Mordyn left Finch's lips, the townsfolk grew pale and excused themselves.

Keyth noticed it wasn't just Mordyn's description. The villagers ended their conversation even with the most basic details. They were scared to speak about any magician.

"Why are they so scared?" Yara asked, as she caught on.

"People have died," Finch explained. "Too many have died. Not only magicians."

"What? Why?" Yara questioned.

Keyth knew. "How do you think the enemy found all the magicians?" He could recall the terror when he had been in these villagers' shoes. The shadowy man walking down Dryn's street in Lesser Kryden. That first agent. Keyth had known he was in danger, even though he wasn't a magician.

At last they got a clue to Mordyn. A townsman gave them one word. "West." It was the direction they'd travelled for three days and it was the direction they would travel for three more.

53

With its pointed tip splitting the sky into north and south, the Tower of the Throne of Midgard rose from the center of Galinor: stones laid nearly four hundred years earlier, treasures collected by centuries of Imperial colonialism, streets fought over during the Trionus War, when the 'streets ran with the black blood of the Mountain Men.' Still the Tower stood, never wavering in the storms of time.

On a cloudless day like this, the fools wandering the streets could see how much taller Odyn was than the tower. Wearing robes that might have emptied the wealthiest treasury, Odyn rode on a purebred Olympian horse. His escort parted the crowds mercilessly, shoving men and women alike out of the path of his parade. He rode into the huge courtyards surrounding the Tower, and found a feeling of pride in the glory of the palace.

My capital... he told himself. Thus he looked up at it to admire the architectural wonder and the unfathomable wealth of his future.

It was a long climb to the top, stairwells spiralling up into the heavens. Every so often, he would pass a window and admire the view, making his two accompanying guardsmen wait. When at last he reached the Council Chambers, he humoured the petty custom and dropped to his knees in front of each statue in the entry corridor. One day there would be only one statue there, an Olympian idol.

"Who approaches the Throne of Midgard?" the ceremonial sentry asked.

"Odyn, Prince of Olympus," he replied, nearly replacing Prince with mightier title, an error which could have gotten him thrown into the streets like a common beggar.

The porter opened the thick doors, and Odyn brushed the foreign everwood as he crossed the threshold. A simple wooden chair was the first thing he saw. Looking away from the throne, he seated himself on the other side of the triangular table, facing the throne from the traditional seat of the Prince of Olympus.

Pyrsius appeared moments later, emerging from the corridor and seating himself to Odyn's left. "Odyn," he greeted, with a smile, "I trust you are doing well?"

"Never mind that, Gothikar," Odyn replied. "It is not our health I worry for."

Pyrsius nodded. "What do you think he will say?" The new Prince of Avernus gestured to Theseus' still empty chair.

"Assuming he does show up at all," Odyn commented, "he won't be pleased. But his hands are tied. He must vote, and his vote will be meaningless. We shouldn't speak more of this here."

"Of course," Pyrsius said.

The door opened again to admit an old man wearing the brown robes of a Tower servant. He bore a small chair in his hands, and crossed the room. He set the chair directly across from the door, overlooking the Triumvirate Council table.

It was the traditional seat of the Crown Magician.

Pyrsius leapt to his feet. "It cannot be!" he exclaimed. "Has my brother been found?" His sharp green eyes were suddenly blinded by rage, and Odyn could feel the young Prince's fury.

The servant bowed. "Unfortunately not, my lord. The Order of Magic has dismissed his duty because of these circumstances."

"Then what is this?" Pyrsius' snapped, pointing at the Crown Magician's seat.

Odyn heard the servant's reply in disbelief. "A new Crown Magician has been selected, my lords. It is in accordance with the laws of their Order, overseen by the Master Mage Kronos Accalia."

Odyn closed his eyes and inhaled. *A new Crown Magician? How?* With the genocide's outstanding success... how could someone be found who could pass the Trials?

The doors opened again and Theseus entered with a youth in tow. The elderly servant vanished, and the everwood doors closed. "My fellow Princes," the Prince of Athyns declared, "I present to you, Lord Rayth, Crown Magician of his Order."

The youth bowed, and Odyn was surprised by the stern control in the man's movements. The tension in the room was nearly a visible thing, yet the new Crown Magician was calm.

Then, without warning, the young man's demeanour changed completely. The Magician rose from his bow and his eyes seemed to flick about the room. Odyn watched the young man try to calm himself, heaving deep breaths, and then, after a long moment of silence, say, "I will stand by the window, if my lords permit."

Theseus nodded and seated himself in his chair.

Pyrsius remained standing, his eyes fixed on the spot where the Crown Magician had stood. Already the youth had crossed to the window, and his eyes were focused on some distant point. Pyrsius, also breathing deeply, closed his eyes and seated himself once more, so that all three Princes were at the table.

Odyn found his voice at last, and asked, "Is it true, Lord Rayth, that you have passed the Trials?"

"It is. Theseus' court magician conducted them," the Crown Magician explained. Odyn had to shift in his chair to see him, the window being directly behind Odyn's chair.

Pyrsius opened his eyes again, and they were alive once more with that sharp brilliance that could stare down the sun. "And I imagine the vote for a High Prince shall be denied?"

Lord Rayth answered maturely, "I have considered the matter and believe that a High Prince would only endanger the circumstances further." *In other words,* Odyn thought, *'We know what you're up to.'*

"You think that the master organizing this genocide can be found with our forces divided?" Pyrsius asked, glaring at the new Crown Magician. Odyn could see the knives of death in that glare.

"He can be found, rest assured," Theseus said, nodding through Pyrsius glare.

"At what cost?" Odyn asked. "We've nearly lost all of our magicians. A select few military wizards remain, seeking sanctuary in our halls. But we are talking about the survival of magic itself!"

"I know," Rayth snapped, and suddenly his force occupied his entire side of the room. One minute a weak youth seemingly claustrophobic, and the next a man to be reckoned with. "I know, because I have experienced it more than any of you. I myself was hunted across the Northlands. But my predators... they didn't know the cost of pursuing *me*."

"It was you?" Pyrsius blurted out, his features a reflection of surprise.

"Excuse me?" Theseus asked, facetiously. "How do you know?"

Odyn attempted to save Pyrsius with another lie. "I have also heard rumours of an heroic mage surviving in the Northlands. I had not realized you found him in Athyns, Theseus."

"He found me," Theseus replied. "And the Order of Magic saw fit to replace their lost Crown Magician."

Pyrsius had recovered from his surprise, but he was just beginning to witness Odyn's mounting rage. The Prince of Olympus was still realizing the ramifications of Lord Rayth's arrival. *We had hoped to force Theseus to a vote and gain the Throne smoothly. He has stopped us from a peaceful resolution,* Odyn realized. *Does he not realize we're ready for war?!*

"It doesn't matter how you came here," Pyrsius said, speaking to Rayth again. "You have denied us the hope of a united military victory over our enemy. We will have to resort to other measures."

"Other measures?" Theseus asked.

"Divided attempts."

"To stop the genocide?" Theseus asked.

"Of course," Odyn said. *We will destroy you. By the Maker, we will destroy you...*

"I suggest a recess," Pyrsius declared. "Let us resume this Council in an hour's time. I must consult with my advisors. The House of Gothikar is in chaos after my father's disappearance, and we may be unable to investigate the genocide in our lands because of the unrest."

Well said, Odyn thought. *A recess, because we must decide how to salvage this wreck.*

Rayth nodded, and glanced around the room with a pale face. He gazed out the window again.

Theseus replied, "Very well, a recess." He stood up. "Lord Rayth? I will show you to temporary quarters here in the

Tower." The two of them exited and bowed to each statue as
they passed.

54

"What do you think?" Dryn asked. He stood between Theseus and Kronos in a large room which was a few floors below the Triumvirate Council Chamber. Theseus had just informed Kronos of the Council's conversation and the now-obvious allegiance between Pyrsius and Odyn.

"I think you did well," Kronos said. "As for their alliance... we tread upon very dangerous ground. And I don't mean that rhetorically. We may even be in danger here in Galinor."

Theseus nodded. "All of their problems are standing here talking. What would you do?"

"The guards?" Dryn asked. *I've gotten out of worse situations,* he knew. But he could clearly see the threats flooding from Pyrsius Gothikar's eyes. *That's the man,* he had told himself, repeating the thought as he had stood in the Council Chamber. *That's the man who is behind it all.*

To him Odyn seemed secondary. Another man after the throne. It was Pyrsius who had orchestrated the slaughter of Dryn's Order. *Maker's Light...* he paused. That was the first time he'd thought of it as *his* Order. He was, he realized again, the master of magicians.

"The guards can only do so much. Pyrsius seems to be young and rash compared to Odyn. I'm only worried about him. Odyn is aware that such an incident here would terminate his plans," Theseus decided.

"What is that building?" Dryn asked, pointing out the window by which he was standing.

"That?" Kronos asked. It was another tower, not nearly as tall as the Tower of the Throne. The stone was different, appearing much older than the masonry of the room in which they stood. "It contains the quarters of magicians garrisoned in Galinor. Like the School at Delfie. I imagine it is mostly empty now. There hasn't been a garrison there for years, so it wasn't a target for the genocide."

"Milords?" a voice asked. A servant had appeared at the door. "Prince Gothikar has departed, and Prince Odyn wishes to speak with you briefly in the Council Chambers."

At the first comment, Theseus shook his head and Kronos stared at him concerned. The servant led the way back to the Council Chambers. Odyn was standing at the window, his back to the Throne. Far below, the Mydarius' waves lapped the shore.

"I hope you haven't ruined the Triumvirate, Theseus," Odyn snapped as soon as they had finished the bowing procession. "The High Prince serves a specific necessity in our government, and denying his installation is denying our very purpose."

"He has denied nothing," Dryn answered. Kronos heard the muffle of his voice from the hallway outside, for only the Princes and Crown Magician were allowed entrance to this sanctuary.

"Stay silent, *boy*," Odyn barked, turning on him. "Theseus, twenty years ago you, Periander and I stood in this very room and spoke of the dangers of false leadership here. Now you have fashioned yourself a puppet to stand in our way. I hope you see what you have done!"

Theseus was as livid as Odyn. "You fool! You think I don't know what is going on here? You expected me to stand aside and let you take over?"

"One of your oaths is to do the best for the people, and *prevent war*," Odyn accused.

"You are the one waging it!" Theseus shot back.

"I need not answer your accusations. You have no proof. On the other hand, I see you recklessly fighting me!" Odyn roared. "When magic has been lost, *you* will be held *solely* responsible." With that the Prince of Olympus strode toward the doors and marched past each statue without bowing.

• • •

"I fear for the future," Theseus told Dryn gravely as they stood in the courtyard below the tower.

Kronos was preparing a complex spell, and Dryn found himself compelled to watch once more. Kronos had performed the same magic to bring them here, but Dryn could not get over it. The ability to move oneself across the world with only magic. Kronos had described it as a gateway, allowing them to step from Galinor to Athyns, or vice versa.

"Can this... spell... be used anywhere? Allow a magician to cross to any destination?" Dryn asked, as they waited for Kronos to complete the gateway.

The other magician nodded. "Of course, he must know the glyphs to find it. It is said that at the beginning of the Triumvirate, the glyphs for over a dozen destinations were known. Now only a handful are. For example, this will take us to the outskirts of Athyns. Even to calculate a path to the palace courtyard... it is beyond the magicians of our day." As he spoke, they walked through his gateway and emerged in front of one of the guard towers, just inside the walls of Athyns.

Dryn stared back at the courtyard of Galinor and laughed. "I'm looking across the realm."

Kronos used a simpler spell and the gateway closed. Dryn made sure he observed all the glyphs that the other magician used. "You also walked the equivalent of a few weeks' journey... in a single step."

An escort was waiting in front of the guard tower and quickly formed around them. Horses were brought and they set off towards the palace grounds.

"Now what?" Dryn asked. "I've denied their vote and they grudgingly withdrew."

"They didn't withdraw," Theseus said. "But we took our stand. Now we wait for them. They have to choose if they accept our victory, or if they'll risk taking matters to the next level."

"We wait?" Dryn asked. "Shouldn't we prepare?"

"We are as prepared as we can be," Kronos explained.

Theseus nodded. "Our troops are ready, our armouries full. If it comes to war, there is little more we can do."

Dryn's mind wandered towards Keyth and Yara. *Perhaps I will check on them later...* he told himself. A simple glimpse at the Great Glyph would be enough. He prayed they would be free from danger, but knew it was unlikely. They were chasing a magician who had managed to escape from Athyns, a man who now had possession of the spell that provided Dryn's power.

And the world held its breath.

55

The road bent south, their footsteps headed north. Yara felt like a pack mule with two packs over her shoulders and a man she didn't know walking beside her. The soldier was grizzled after their days on the road, as was the man ahead and behind them. Several paces in front of her walked Keyth beside Captain Finch.

The people of the last village had named their shabby clump of huts Covin. The small settlement was huddled between two mountains on a small plateau. Finch assured them that these were only foothills, but Yara had never seen anything so large, and could not imagine that the mountains were larger. From where they wandered, the peaks of the Sinai Mountains were hidden by these 'foothills' and by the growing darkness.

As they trekked up another small ridge, the road curved sharply to the left and towards the Mydarius Sea, while the troop made its way deeper inland. The villagers were adamant in their story of Mordyn's journey, and told all they knew with the comment that they've got no love for wizards.

According to the people of Covin, Mordyn had arrived and left during the day, pressing northward into the mountains without heeding their warnings that the mountains were dangerous to wander at night. Yara had listened in surprise when the villagers had told of other travellers, an entire troop of soldiers who had passed through a week earlier, and other armed men who roamed the foothills. When Finch pressed them for a description, he was shocked to hear their reply.

It seemed that Rychard and his men had passed through Covin that week, instead of returning to Avernus across the Mydarius after their banishment from Athyns.

"What are they doing in the mountains?" Keyth had wanted to know.

The villagers had no reply. "What concerns me," Finch muttered, "is the size of Rychard's force. He left Athyns with twice the men of my troop."

And so, as evening cloaked the mountains and night crept upon them, Finch and Keyth led the way into the Mountains of Sinai.

"It makes no sense," Yara heard Keyth say. "According to you, and those villagers, there is nothing here for them."

Yara smiled at the grizzled warrior next to her, and stumbled ahead to her Keyth's side. "Perhaps Rychard told Mordyn to meet him here. Maybe it was their backup plan in case someone got captured. As Mordyn did."

Finch shook his head. "According to the authorities in Athyns, Rychard left by boat. He would have had to head this way intentionally and anchor offshore. There are no major ports along the northern coast until Edessa. And Rychard shouldn't have business anywhere here."

Keyth nodded. "Then I fear for what we might find."

Finch took the lead and they continued into the valley between the foothills of Covin and the next, larger mountain.

Within moments the forest cleared for the presence of old stone ruins. With a shiver, Yara recognized the architecture. It may be the stonework of the early Triumvirate, perhaps older, but she had seen it twice before, once beneath Ithyka and again where they emerged near the strange village of Scion.

"What's this now?" Finch asked, and gestured for them to pause near one of the first broken walls.

"We've seen this before," Keyth said, glancing at Yara.

"Ruins from long ago," she commented. She recalled the coin from the first days of the Triumvirate.

"Yes, but why didn't the villagers mention it?" Keyth wondered.

Finch grimaced. "They probably believe it to be haunted. Let's go in, but quietly. If Rychard did set up camp for Mordyn's arrival, they could be encamped nearby, or within."

They made their way through shadowy hallways where the roofs had caved in long ago. Upon rounding a corner, Yara could see a central building nearby. They approached it quietly, the whole troop moving slowly and stealthily. There was an old wooden door rusted open, and Finch brought them to another halt in front of it.

Torchlight flickered visibly inside. Finch put an eye to the doorframe, then turned back to them. The man's blue eyes gleamed as he held up three fingers, and then pointed to soldiers. One man pulled a bow from his shoulder and notched an arrow to it. Another, the man who had walked at Yara's side earlier, drew his sword quietly.

With a sharp gesture, Finch sprang inside, followed by those he had selected. While the rest of the troop took the rear, Keyth stuck to Yara's side. As she rounded the door, Yara heard a gasp and then a voice shout, "There's someone here!"

A sword clashed against another, and someone let out a short scream. Yara turned into the room with Keyth and saw one of the soldiers yank his sword out of a writhing man, then spin to face the third opponent. The archer, who had taken their first target by surprise, let fly another arrow, and blood blossomed from the third man's arm. With a grunt the man jumped at the bowman, but Finch's short sword soon protruded from his torso, and amidst a spray of blood, the man was dead. Yara stared at the three corpses in shock, then spun away to empty her meagre lunch.

Keyth contained himself much better, but handed Yara his canteen. She nodded and took a drink to wash her mouth. *By the Maker... I just saw men die...* "Sorry..." she muttered, apologizing for her reaction.

"No, it's fine," he said. "I'm sorry.... Let's see what they've found," he decided, as the soldiers seemed to have clustered on the other side of the room. He approached Finch first. "How do we know they deserved this?"

Finch pointed, and, as he wiped the blood from his steel onto the man's doublet, explained, "Olympian uniforms. They aren't officially trespassing, but I've paid enough attention to politics to know they're with our enemies." Turning to Yara, the Captain grimaced. "Sorry you had to see that," he muttered.

"Captain, look at this!" one of their soldiers shouted.

There was a small alcove in the wall, and within it was an arch of ancient rocks. Within them flickered a complex symbol, like the archaic language Dryn now knew. Yara stared at it in amazement. "Another Glyph Gate," she murmured.

Finch glanced at her. "A what?" he questioned.

Keyth replied, "It's called a Glyph Gate. It links two points together for faster travel. It's like a door between here and the Maker knows where."

"Like those damn gates the magician's make," Finch exclaimed, glancing at it. "Kronos Accalia once explained that armies cannot move through his gates because each man through drains more of his energy. Moving an army in such a way would kill the magician."

"Yes, but this is not sustained by a magician," Keyth said. "It... it is permanent."

"Well, where does it go?" Finch questioned, glancing back at the flickering portal.

Yara commented, "It's a fair bet to say that this is where Mordyn went. And Rychard."

Finch nodded. "We'll go through then."

Keyth held up his hand. "Let me go first. I'll check, make sure things are clear on the other side. I've been through one of these before, so I'll be able to react faster after going through."

Finch frowned. "What if there are more guards?"

Keyth pulled his own bow from behind his neck. "I'm skilled with a bow," he said. "I was a bowyer's apprentice."

"That doesn't make you a soldier," Finch said.

"Listen," Keyth argued, "the guards were on this side." He had already notched an arrow. Yara shook her head in concern, but Keyth felt this was something he had to do.

Finch nodded, and said, "We'll follow after a ten count."

Keyth locked eyes with Yara, then turned and stepped through the portal. Finch approached the gate. "Wait," he said. Then after a tense count of ten, he ordered, "Let's go."

This time Yara didn't let the soldiers go ahead of her, and plunged through the Glyph Gate immediately after Finch. Everything went black and then she stood on grass. Ten paces ahead of her, the ground seemed to fall away to void, and then water stretched halfway to the horizon where another mass of land filled the night sky.

Keyth knelt several steps away, and with a disgusting splat yanked an arrow from the corpse of another guard. He glanced sideways and saw the troop emerging one by one as he cleaned the arrowhead. "Just one guard this time," he called. "Got him without a sound, don't worry."

Finch glanced around, and then stared back at the Glyph Gate. They now stood on a small plateau with no trace of ruins. Instead of a valley, they seemed perched on the slope of a mountain. And a real mountain this time. Yara stared up behind them at the huge peak of stone. It dwarfed everything she had ever seen, even the mountains they had just left.

"Where are we?" Finch asked.

"I grew up in Edessa, sir," one of the soldiers said. "This is the Blood Strait. I'd bet a year's wage on it."

"The Blood Strait?" Finch asked, inhaling sharply. "We've travelled half the Dominion! Keyth, to get back... we need only step through this Gate again?"

"That's right. Don't worry, I wouldn't let us go through without a way back." Keyth slung the bow back over his shoulders.

"So now what?" Yara asked.

Finch grimaced. "We must continue to track that earth-spawn. After seeing this, I'm sure we must be close. The guards... that is cause for great alarm."

"There's a path over there," Keyth declared, pointing at a cluster of pine trees that clung to the edge of the cliff.

Sure enough, a narrow trail wound away from them, tracing the bend of the mountain and dropping down or sloping at different spots. Finch took the lead again and they fell into ranks of two. Any more would have been dangerous.

"The Cerden Mountains," Yara overheard a soldier mutter to his companion. "Did you know Dobler fought in the Trionus War? In these very mountains!"

It took an hour on the narrow, treacherous trail to reach the base of the mountain. Another ridge rose into the branches of the next mountain, and the trail widened and bridged it at the ridge's lowest point. They were hiking in forest once more, but as they reached the peak of the hill, they all froze in shock.

From the top of the ridge, they could see a rectangular valley open before them. It seemed like stars gleamed within its forest, but Yara realized with a shudder that they were fires. The entire valley was alight with campfires and torches.

"Maker burn me," Finch cursed. "An army."

Finch was shaking his head in disbelief. "It's an army. Maker's Light, it's a huge army. And they know about the Glyph Gate up there. Those were their sentries."

"Wait... this is an Olympian army? I thought Avernus was behind this. Pyrsius Gothikar is the only name I've heard," Keyth questioned.

Finch nodded. "Prince Theseus told all his captains that it seemed Olympus and Avernus had allied. That," he gestured, "is an army of the united south. Twice or more the size of Athyns' army. And they are going to march right into our back door."

"A back door we didn't know we had," Keyth muttered.

Finch nodded.

Once more, Yara had to ask, "Now what?"

"We must return and warn Theseus with all haste," Finch decided. "We must rally the north if we hope to survive a battle against this horde."

"No, we can't return yet," Keyth retorted. "We must catch Mordyn first!"

"Are you a fool?" Finch asked. "Look at that. There are more than five thousand men camped here. We have ten. There is no way even to search for Mordyn."

"You'd rather we let Mordyn go? And have five thousand *immortal* soldiers on Athyns' doorstep?" Keyth hissed, gesturing at the starlight valley.

Finch remained silent, staring at Keyth blankly. Yara imagined that the Captain had made the connection between immortality and the Crown Magician. After a moment, Finch turned to stare at the camp, and then finally spoke. "There is no way we can infiltrate that camp."

"Then I will go on my own," Keyth snapped, the same confidence appearing that had surfaced before stepping through the Glyph Gate. Yara immediately tried to argue with him, but he told her quietly, "I can handle myself, and one man can move freely, freely enough."

"But how will you find him?" she breathed.

"With the number of magicians left alive, there must be a separate camp for them. A walled-off area," Keyth explained. "Once the magicians serve their usefulness, the army will kill them. It will be necessary, if their plan to destroy magic is to succeed. I imagine the location of the magicians will be well known."

Finch glanced thoughtfully at Yara. "We'll wait until dawn and then return through the Glyph Gate to Athyns. The Prince must be warned, at all costs."

"Agreed. I'll meet you at the Gate, or follow you later to Athyns, if it takes too long," Keyth decided. Finch stepped aside to inform his soldiers of his plan. "Yara, go with Finch. He'll keep you safe."

"No, Keyth. I'm not letting you do this! It's madness!" she told him.

"What did you think was happening when Dryn sent me?" he asked. "He's trusting me to finish this. We can't let them get that spell!"

"Keyth..." Yara muttered, shaking her head. "You're not a soldier, mindlessly following his orders! I know Dryn is our friend, but you can't throw your life away like this!"

"What happened to the adventure?" he growled at her. "Is that all it was to you? A taste of adventure? I came along with Dryn because I am his friend. I will be there for him!"

"And you have been," Yara told him. "That's why I came too. But he's choosing his own path. He's choosing to throw in his fate with the realm. Are you as well?"

That got him. Keyth stepped back and the darkness seemed to grow across his face. "I'll take you back," he told her. "I promised we'd return and I meant it. When this is done... when Mordyn is dead... Maker burn me if I lie, Yara! I'll take you home. But I cannot do this if you are in danger! Go with Finch. Stay safe. I'll find you when it's done."

Then he was gone, his shadow merging with the darkness of the valley and the night. She stared after him for a moment, and then joined Greymor Finch on the climb back to the Glyph Gate.

56

Keyth ten Arad had lived in the Kryden District for his entire life, and had never seen so many people living so closely as he had in Athyns. He was equally as astonished at the army's camp near the Blood Strait. The camp was a small town organized like a fortress. Narrow roads separated the tents and palisades divided camp from camp.

He had been right in his idea that magicians would be set apart from the soldiers. He walked with his forest green cloak thrown over his head, but even that drew the eyes of grizzled soldiers. They were in a war against magicians and a robed man coming at night prompted suspicions. The guards had eyed him cautiously and had let him through the outer boundary with only the simplest of questions, but now Keyth was worried he might be stopped within the camp itself.

When the opportunity presented itself, he glanced around to be sure he wasn't being followed, and then shrugged out of the robe. He left the cloak beside a tent and carried on his way. He had to find out where the few magicians were situated.

After half an hour of wandering through the valley, he still had no luck in his search. Desperate to catch Mordyn, he plopped down across a campfire from two soldiers. One was cooking a skewered rabbit and the other was watching.

"I'm telling you," the second was muttering as Keyth sat, "the Northlanders are on to us. Commander Rychard was thrown out of Athyns!"

"Hey, who're you?" the first snapped, as he noticed Keyth's presence. "Not another of Gen's lads, are you?

Scrounging for a bite of food... I swear, if that Commander doesn't start feeding his men...."

"It's been a long day," Keyth muttered. "I figure he's been hoarding the food to himself!"

"No doubt," the second chuckled. "His stomach is large enough."

"That man is not a soldier," the first muttered, poking at the rabbit. "Fine, I'll give you a chop, but no more!"

"Smells wonderful," Keyth told the man, who grinned at him. Keyth frowned then, continuing his act, and said, "That reminds me: the man camped beside me... he makes the foulest concoctions. The stench is too much to bear!"

"Haha, can't be worse than Kaius' foul smell!" the chef muttered, and his companion punched him in the shoulder.

"Really, though!" Keyth exclaimed. "I wonder if this man isn't a bit of a spell caster of some kind!"

"Can't be," Kaius assured him. "They've got those earth-spawn all rounded up."

"Are you sure? I mean maybe they missed one," Keyth grumbled.

The chef shook his head and withdrew the rabbit skewer from atop their crackling fire. "Nah, the magicians are holed up on the west end, and the Commanders would burn this whole camp if they missed one."

"If you say so," Keyth said, maintaining his face of frustration, despite the relief beneath it. "Gen will have my hide if I let this slip, so maybe I'll mention the soldier."

"No, let the poor fellow be," Kaius advised.

"Rabbit?" the chef asked, and tossed a slice of meat across the fire. Keyth snatched it from the air and forced himself to bite into the hot meat. He'd been on the road with Finch for the better part of a week and was still ill-prepared for soldiers' cooking.

"Better than Gen gives us," Keyth managed.

Several moments later he took his leave of the amiable soldiers and wandered west. He glanced skyward and groaned. It was a long hike back up to the Glyph Gate and he didn't want to be caught at dawn.

Finally, he came to the palisade wall that separated the magician's camp from the rest. He passed the sleeping guard without a word. He had thought the armies of the south might abuse the power of magicians in order to fight it, enslaving many wizards to gain an advantage. However, true to the teachings of their genocide, magicians were the enemy. The five tents in their area of the valley were the smallest and were set on the lowest ground, where thick mud formed. He was sure that such men must be imprisoned. Surely they could see that they would be slain, as soon as the Princes consumed their usefulness.

He glanced at all five and saw candlelight flickering through the dark fabric of one. According to the villagers, Mordyn had been only a couple of hours ahead of Finch's troop, so Mordyn had just reached the camp.

Keyth notched an arrow to his bow and wandered to the edge of the camp circle. He took aim at the tent, right beside the candle and took a deep breath. He felt the weight of the short sword at his belt, and calmed his pulse enough to steady his aim.

When he was ready, he let the arrow fly. Without a sound, the arrow punctured the tent's fabric and struck something inside. The candlelight extinguished and Keyth heard a quiet thump.

He wandered around the circle of tents again, trying to appear casual, and then ducked into the tent he had shot. A man lay in a pool of blood, Keyth's arrow shaft protruded from the right side of his chest. He knelt to pull the shaft free, and saw that the arrowhead had gone clean through the wizard's frail form.

Without warning, the man's hand lashed towards his belt, slipping into one of his pouches. Keyth's short sword slammed into the left side of his chest, and the man died without another breath.

Trembling, Keyth moved the limp hand from the pouch and found a token clutched between two fingers. He thanked the Maker that it hadn't been broken, and drew a deep breath. Keyth pulled the hood of the thick red robe aside and was relieved to see that it was Mordyn. He shuddered and undid the belt around the magician's waist, tossing it aside on Mordyn's cot.

Keyth felt the folds of the sorcerer's cloak for the parchment of Dryn's spell, but didn't find it there. He glanced at the desk where the toppled candle had leaked wax across the wood before it cooled. There were several thick tomes and an open book full of symbols he could not understand.

Beneath the open volume was a tattered page with a string of glyphs scrawled on it and no other writing. *This must be it,* he decided. He pulled the sheet away from the desk and stared at it. *These are the letters branded upon Dryn.* He had no clue what they meant, and hopefully no one else did either.

He folded the page along its crease and started to slide it into a pocket, but a voice froze his movement.

"Mordyn?" a voice asked. "It's Nerak."

"One moment," Keyth said, with a cough. This man was standing directly outside the tent and was waiting to speak with Mordyn. *Maker's Light, Maker's Light...* he cursed. He glanced around him frantically. His eyes found Mordyn's thick red cloak. He hurriedly drew the garment off of the wizard's remains and shrugged into the large robe. Draping the cowl over his face, he stepped out of the tent and found himself beside another red-robed magician.

"Was Athyns a complete loss?" Nerak asked. "Did you get the spell?"

Praying that this Nerak didn't know Mordyn's voice well, Keyth muttered and lifted another page from Mordyn's robes. The man tried looking at it, but it was dark, and Keyth made sure the magician couldn't get a good glimpse of it.

"I hope the bandits did a good job. We weren't sure about them, Brother," Nerak said.

"The bandits?" Keyth questioned, still dimming his voice.

"We made sure they knew not to kill Rayth. And from what Rychard has mentioned, you did capture him. Everything went according to plan, yes?"

Keyth's mind froze. The brigands who attacked Yara at the inn.... Mordyn was behind that. Wait, if he knew Dryn was there before.... "Yes," he told Nerak. *What on earth is going on here?* he wondered.

The other man seemed puzzled by Keyth's responses and asked cautiously, "Are you ill, Brother?"

"Caught some Northland plague, no doubt," he said with a cough.

"Well, blessings of Andrakaz upon you. The Brotherhood wouldn't want such a prized member suffering," Nerak assured him, and Keyth was lost in the words. "With that spell, we'll be able to resurrect him from beneath Olympus."

Keyth bent over for a moment and forced himself to gag. He coughed more and more, and held up one hand. "Let me grab my water," he gasped, and made for the tent.

Nerak followed and, once inside the tent, the magician froze at the sight of Mordyn's body. Keyth was ready and spun with his short sword. The second man joined the first corpse beside the bed. Keyth wiped the blade on Nerak's robe.

Breathing heavily, he glanced around. This 'Brotherhood' had an interest in Dryn and yet spoke of things Keyth couldn't fathom. He decided to ask Theseus or Kronos about it upon his return to Athyns. He checked that he still had Dryn's spell, and then glanced at the other books on the table. One of the older tomes was named "Teachings of the Brotherhood," so Keyth took the volume with him.

He quickly made his way to the south of the camp and out onto the ridge, without stopping for the guards. Mordyn was slain and Dryn's spell was reclaimed. Keyth only had one promise left to keep.

Take Yara home.

Pyrsius Gothikar stood between pillars and, with a scowl, watched Lord Rayth and his cohorts leave the Tower of the Throne. He could hear their voices still, echoing through his mind. *The Maker burn me if I let this go...* He understood Odyn's fury for his behaviour in the Council session, but he didn't really care. The building blocks could not be taken down now; what had been done could not be undone.

"Their deaths will be a symphony," he told himself, his mind already conjuring the sound of the music he would carve into the pale flesh of their breathless bodies. "And when they are gone," he muttered, "*Magic* will be gone. *Forever.*"

Revenge, my love... another voice whispered to him. The voice settled into a steady chant calling for vengeance and glory.... The voice of his love.

She was long gone, stolen from him by his own kin.

"Artemys... your actions will be erased from the world forever..." Pyrsius breathed. "And Rayth... you will share my brother's fate. Your screams will be like... music."

He fumbled in a pouch to find his few gateway tokens. He hated to use them up. He opened a portal to Athyns, and stepped through it. The city was nothing compared to the might of Avernus. It made Pyrsius gag.

Odyn had once called him brilliant, but now, a fool. Pyrsius wished that his peer would make up his mind. That is what Pyrsius had done. He could recall his father, Periander, once saying, "You must decide what you want in life, and then pursue it. Anything can be yours, if you set your mind to it."

That is what Pyrsius had done. Now, when people like Artemys or Rayth had stepped on his road, he had made them move.

Which brought him to the task at hand. Time to move Rayth out of the way.

He strode briskly towards the Imperial Palace of Athyns. A merchant held out a colourful robe towards him and Pyrsius walked straight past. Soon the battlements of the palace wall cast a shadow across him.

He had read all of the reports thoroughly. The first agent to track Rayth had been Orion, a fighter who had survived the Edessa Arena. His reports had told of three companions, joined by a fourth. And Rayth obviously had a special interest in one of them.

Pyrsius had learned the hard way. Love is a weapon in your enemies' hands. A good reason to stop loving. Rayth hadn't learned that yet, so Pyrsius could still wield it against him.

Then there was the fool wizard who had tested Rayth for the position of Crown Magician. The man who had used Rayth to spite Pyrsius and Odyn. That man would die also. And painfully.

He approached the guards. "I have an audience with Prince Theseus."

They allowed him on Palace grounds. The guards for the Keep proper would have refused obviously. After checking Theseus' schedule, they'd have found no mention of an audience granted.

But he wasn't going into the Keep. Rayth and his companions had just arrived and would still be there. Except for Kronos Accalia. He would be on the way to his quarters, likely to rest after the long day and the use of spells such as gateways. Pyrsius could picture it now, picture the wizard's old breath slowing as he fell into the void of his mind, never to return.

Trying to focus on walking straight, Pyrsius shut his fantasies away. He could live them shortly, but he had to get to the quarters first. There was a separate wing off the Keep for housing, and he found the side door. The guard held up his hand and barked, "Business?"

Pyrsius leaned closer to him. "Just got to put a knife in there," he muttered. It took the man a second in order to realize what Pyrsius had said, but by then it was too late. Pyrsius' knife *was* in there, right between his ribs. The soldier leaned against the wall under Pyrsius' guiding hands and slid to a comfortable resting place along the ground.

The man's leather collar cleaned the knife without a sound and the blade disappeared into Pyrsius sleeve. "'Night, lad," he told the body, and then without even looking around, he opened the door and stepped inside.

The passages of the Keep were mostly abandoned, and the few pedestrians moving about ignored the wealthy young man. Pyrsius winked at a few maids, just to see their surprise. Unhindered, he wandered up and down stairs until, at last, he found the quarters of Kronos Accalia.

The wizard was standing with his back to the doorway and, when Pyrsius entered, he said, "Dryn's not here, Iris. I know I said he would be, but Theseus wanted to speak with him first."

Pyrsius wandered across the cluttered room and fingered a token he had removed from his belt outside the door. "I'm afraid I'm not looking for Dryn, yet," Pyrsius whispered behind Kronos' back.

Kronos spun, but was too late. Pyrsius jabbed his fingers forward and broke the spell token, injecting fire venom into Kronos' flesh. The wizard gasped, looked down where Pyrsius' fingers touched him, and coughed once as his paralyzed fingers released a defence token.

The spell had re-created the venom of a fire spider, one of the more dangerous inhabitants of the southern land. It caused unbearable pain, coupled with deadly paralysis. The victim couldn't even speak to shout for help.

Pyrsius shoved Kronos backward and the wizard fell flat on the floor. In five minutes the poison would collect in his heart and kill him. Until then, the magician would be unable to call for help as unimaginable agony tore through him.

"Kronos?" a female asked, the door creaking.

Pyrsius spun to see who was there, his mind realizing it was the girl named 'Iris' to whom Kronos had spoken. But then his eyes met hers and he froze. "Lanteera..." he breathed.

"Who are you?" she gasped, and he was delighted to see a dagger appear in her hand. "I've seen you. At my estate near Olympus..."

"Someone had to pay for it," he whispered, recalling his many visits. The only one left in the world to love was the child born to the woman whom Artemys had stolen from him.

But love... love was a weapon, and a dangerous one.

In that moment, as Pyrsius stared at his daughter, he realized all of the connections, and found himself caught in a web of his enemy's making. Lanteera was obviously Rayth's interest, and her purpose was clearly to spite Pyrsius and Rayth's other enemies.

There was only one thing to do. Return the spite. Break the weapon.

"He thinks he can win," Pyrsius said, and the girl turned to run.

Pyrsius grabbed her by the neck as she reached the door handle, then he threw her back into the room. She hit a table and crashed with it to the ground, spilling powders and potions onto the wood. Pyrsius opened the pouch at his belt and withdrew a handful of its contents.

Something appropriate... he told himself. His fingers found it as the thought echoed through him.

The token he chose was one that would drain the victim's years, killing them of old age within an hour's time.

"I wish it could be some other way, Lanteera," he told her. "But... victory costs much." *Let us see if he loves her when her beauty has rotted like a wilted blossom...*

The best part: this accelerated his plans.

58

Grim as ever, Dryn left Theseus' quarters and made his way through the Imperial Keep. A bird sat on the railing and fluttered away toward the rooftops of Athyns, but it only reminded Dryn of his days imprisoned in Rychard's barracks.

He and Theseus had discussed their plan, after returning from the Council session in Galinor. Theseus still thought they should await Odyn's next move. After all, they had thwarted the Olympian Prince from a political conquest, and Theseus felt they should delay any action. "We must wait to see if they accept defeat or if they are determined to take things further."

Dryn had told him, "They have slain nearly every magician they could find! Why would they possibly resign now?" but the Prince was unwilling to launch a pre-emptive attack. Dryn at last persuaded him to begin readying troops, either to defend or attack. After Odyn's furious remark in Galinor, Dryn saw little reason to hope that the Prince would back down. He was willing to see if Theseus' decision had wisdom in it or if—

The open door of Kronos' quarters ended this recollection and scattered his thoughts. He stormed inside to find Kronos stretched toward an old woman, one hand gripping her arm. "Kronos?" he gasped, "What happened!"

He dropped to his knees and grabbed Kronos' shoulders. His eyes passed across the woman's face and the room seemed to tilt upside down. "Maker's Light, Iris! Maker... please no... Iris wake up!" He slid off his knees and pulled Iris up to his chest. He listened for her breathing and was relieved at the sound of gasping in her lungs.

He rocked back against the table and pulled her against him again. "Guards!" he bellowed, his face flooding with blood. "Iris please... please..." He was incapable of worrying about the constricting walls of Kronos' small chamber. He sobbed and clutched her frail head close to his, kissing her as gently as he could.

Her eyes fluttered open and for a moment he saw Iris again. "Dryn...?" she gaped, and then she was gone, slipping into a trancelike sleep.

Guards arrived and knelt at his side. They helped him lift her on to the replaced table. "She's still alive," one told him, and sent the other for more help.

"Dryn," a parched voice barked. It was Kronos.

He dropped beside the magician and lifted the man to a sitting position. Kronos' face was pale and his features pained. His neck seemed to twitch and his pulse was visibly irregular, but he hadn't endured the aging spell which had twisted Iris.

"By the Maker... what happened, Kronos?"

"I saved her," the court magician gasped. "She'll always be old, but she'll live... She can't be brought back..."

"Who did this?" Dryn questioned, but Kronos' dim gaze seemed to pass through him.

"I will be done soon," Kronos told him. "Free from this life. Perhaps to the Maker's side..." He raised a hand weakly and whispered, "Don't try to stop it... you can't."

"Who did this?" Dryn snapped, shaking the poor man. "Tell me who!"

"It was him," Kronos coughed. "Pyrsius... it was Pyrsius Gothikar..."

Dryn closed his eyes and a rage he had never known filled his skull. It was the anger of the abyss, the wrath of the Maker himself... the only time he had felt such pain thundering his mind was when he had envisioned the entire Great Glyph, when he scried something more than he should have.

He stood up and began to mutter the words to gaze upon the Great Glyph once more, prepared to find Pyrsius and then kill him. If he had to grab hold of the Great Glyph itself and burn it down around him, if he had to spit in the face of the Maker... he would see Pyrsius dead this very day!

A hand touched his ankle, and he bent for Kronos once more. With the magician's dying breath, Dryn's friend gasped, *"Don't underestimate him!"*

Theseus appeared moments later, summoned by the shouting and commotion of his guards. When he saw Iris, he gasped, "Maker protect us..."

"It was Pyrsius," Dryn growled. "That Maker-cursed earth-spawn—"

"Pyrsius was here?" Theseus questioned, reaching for his blade.

"He was gone before I got here," Dryn gasped. He stepped to Iris' side, she was being examined by one of Theseus' best physicians. "How is she? She'll survive?"

"Yes, but the years that have been taken... it'll take great bravery to adjust."

Iris' eyes stared at the ceiling and Dryn couldn't help but glance up. The room closed its jaws on him again and he grabbed the table to steady himself.

"Sir?" the physician asked.

"Maker's Light, pay attention to her," he cursed, "Not me."

A guard stepped in and spoke quietly to Theseus, who glanced at Dryn, and said, "Keyth and Captain Finch just reached the city gates. We'd best hear the conclusion of their journey... it could require immediate attention."

"No," Dryn said. "I'm going for Pyrsius. Someone has to make him pay."

Theseus spun to him. "Are you mad? We don't know how to travel to him. His guards, his cities... you would be stopped."

"I'm not afraid, I'm angry. He came after Iris! Personally! What's to stop him from killing us one by one!" Dryn demanded, and a thought occurred to him. "By the Maker, how did he even get here? He'd have had to use a gateway to the Athyns' location, not right into these quarters! He must have followed us straight from the cursed Throne!"

"Watch your tongue!" Theseus snapped. "Come comfort your friends, and calm your fury. I'll speak to the guards about Pyrsius' arrival. He's not a magician so he must have someone making tokens for him."

It was well known that Pyrsius was not a magician, and it was hard for Dryn to picture Pyrsius allowing a magician to do even that.

He glanced at Iris' trembling form and shuddered. He took her hand. He still loved her. She was still Iris. But Pyrsius had hurt her so much.... Dryn knew she could never recover from this. Pyrsius had targeted her and Kronos, instead of facing

Dryn like a true warrior. *He's afraid of me...* he thought. *Maker's Light, he should be! I'll destroy him, un-write his True Name from history, and steal every one of his breaths back!!!* He almost raised his voice at Theseus once more, but the Prince had already turned to find Keyth and Yara.

Closing his eyes, Dryn whispered in Iris' ear that he would be back and followed. He murmured curses against Pyrsius and Odyn, as they descended the stairs, and then he approached Keyth and Yara again.

"Dryn," Keyth called, as soon as he saw him. "It's incredible! You're a Lord now, and the Crown Magician!"

Before Dryn could reply, Theseus informed them of the terror that had just befallen them. He explained that the younger Prince of Avernus followed them from the Council session in Galinor. Unaware, they had begun settling back into the palace when both Iris and Kronos fell victim to Gothikar's dark actions.

Keyth became furious, his hands clenching into fists and his jaw visibly clenching. Yara closed her eyes and couldn't stop the tremor that overcame her. The conversation that followed became a blur in Dryn's mind. There was only one face he saw and he looked on it with fury.

"The deed is done," Keyth told him. "Mordyn is dead."

"Thank you. Keyth, thank you."

Glancing at Yara, Keyth dismissed his plan. "I know it's a bad time, so I guess I'll wait a couple days."

"You're going home," Dryn said.

"We didn't know that the 'fun' adventure we started would end so quickly... and last so long," Keyth explained. "This... this..."

"Maker burn me, Keyth! I don't really care! Leave if you want to!" Dryn told him. "Maybe I'll visit some time. Maker's Light, maybe I'll go home someday. Say hello to my father for me, would you? Tell him I'm off living a dream. Great Glyph, tell him I'm the king of the world. Anything, but the truth, Keyth."

"Dryn..." Keyth interrupted, concern painted across his features. Theseus wore a frown of disapproval and was watching Dryn with the same eyes of worry.

Dryn ran his hands through his hair and shouted incoherently. After a moment, he lowered his arms and told Theseus, "Take care of Iris until it's all over." He then whispered, *"Elkobo den triios al'dei."*

The Great Glyph surged into his vision and that horrible agony speared through his chest again. He gripped the sides of his ringing head, tearing out hair, until the face of Pyrsius Gothikar entered his thoughts again and the Great Glyph found what he was looking for. He saw the glyphs of Pyrsius, striding around within a building made up of glyphs for wood and stone and the glyphs of those who served him. He saw the entire fortress and he saw the descriptions of Pyrsius' own chambers. Branding those glyphs into his head, he let the Great Glyph vanish and saw the worried faces of his friends again.

He then uttered another spell, and the air itself parted for a gateway. With a second shout of anger, Dryn jumped through and shut the portal after him.

Theseus stared in fury at the air, after Dryn vanished, and Keyth was afraid he might disappear in a similar rage. The Prince's face turned livid in a way Keyth hadn't yet seen.

"If my arrival somehow caused–" Keyth began, but Theseus interrupted.

"No, no," the Prince said, raising a hand and glancing at him. "Dryn was about to leave before he even knew you had returned. I told him not to go, and you can see how he heeded my 'advice.'"

"Apologies, my lord," Yara said, nonetheless.

"If I might ask about Iris, how is she?" Keyth questioned.

Theseus replied in a voice so quiet that Keyth could barely hear him. "My physicians inform me she will live. She will not be the girl you once knew. She is fortunate, for Kronos Accalia has already passed from this world."

Yara glanced away, and Keyth grimaced.

"What of your journey?" Theseus wondered.

"I'm sure your Captain Finch will present a report to you, but let me quickly tell you what we found," Keyth began. He recalled the fire-lit valley south of the Blood Strait and the secret Glyph Gates. "There is an army within a week's march of this city," he concluded. "The Glyph Gates will allow them to emerge from the Sinai Mountains without being detected by any of your western cities. The soldiers wear both Avernus and Olympus garb."

Theseus stepped back and shut his eyes. "They know of the Glyph Gate? You are certain?"

"Their guards stood nearby," Keyth explained. "I hope our intrusion does not alert them that we know of their presence."

"It is of no matter," Theseus decided. "I must call a meeting with my Nobles and direct the armies. Perhaps rally local militia to assist. My forces in Edessa and Trionus are of no use anymore. I trust you did slay Mordyn? We cannot allow Dryn's weakness to be exploited, wherever he has gone."

Keyth nodded. "Mordyn is dead. There is another matter, though. I'm sorry to lay another burden before you, but I discovered a group named the 'Brotherhood of Andrakaz.' They have a secret interest in Dryn and were the ones who arranged for his capture here in Athyns. It seems they have infiltrated the ranks of our enemies, but are separate from them in motive."

"The Brotherhood of Andrakaz?" Theseus questioned. "You're sure? During the Trionus War, the Disciples of Andrakaz were found to have supported both sides and were hunted to extinction. But they have somehow survived. And they have interest in Dryn?"

"From what I overheard and from a book I stole, it would seem they believe that the spell Artemys Gothikar placed on Dryn is a key to resurrecting someone known as Andrakaz." Keyth still didn't understand half of this, but he knew Theseus needed all the puzzle pieces he had found.

Theseus shook his head. "A sorcerer of legends. No more than a tale from the Age of Myths. The Disciples falsely believed in his continued survival. That is all I know of them, for even the Disciples were shrouded in secrecy, as you have now discovered this Brotherhood to be."

"I fear their obsession of Dryn," Keyth explained.

"He is beyond our help," Theseus said sternly. "He has chosen to fight our enemies on his own. I pray he hasn't chosen death."

"As do I!" Keyth said. During the journey back to Athyns, he and Yara had wrestled with the challenge of leaving Dryn, but they too had concluded that Dryn would ultimately face his problems alone. They needed to go home. "My Prince, Yara and I intend to return to support our village in these troubled times. We will go comfort Iris, but we can be of no service to Dryn and we long to return."

Theseus pondered this and nodded. "If this is your decision, then may you and your village find peace. I will not lie, though. I believe you would be more useful in my service than in your Northland village. However, I understand your choice and I wish you good fortune. Now I must call my lords into council."

"Thank you, sir," Keyth nodded. "Maker protect you."

"And you in return, Keyth. You're a good man." With that Theseus left them and disappeared into the hallway of the central Keep.

Keyth and Yara entered the side wing where Kronos' quarters were and looked for Iris. The servants in the magician's quarters explained that she had been taken to the Palace infirmary until she had recovered well enough to safely leave. After trekking a maze of hallways and staircases, they found the infirmary and were directed by a healer to Iris' bedside.

Keyth froze at the sight of her. He had prepared himself, but the shock grabbed him. Yara gasped and then tried to conceal her reaction. In a strained voice, Iris muttered, "Maker's Light, am I glad to see you two!"

It surprised Keyth just as much that she was awake. Her skin bore the wrinkles of an elder. Her short hair was withered and her eyes seemed hardly open. "Iris, we should have been here," Keyth muttered. "We might've stopped him..."

"Dryn feels the same way," Iris stuttered, "though, they tell me, he is gone again. Off to exact revenge. Every time I see him, he's dramatically different. I don't know if I can take it."

"Like Ithyka..." Yara agreed, and sank into a chair beside Iris' bed. Their friend was propped up on feather cushions, but her discomfort was impossible to miss.

Keyth pulled a chair from a nearby table and set it beside Yara's. "Are you in pain?" he worried, sitting down.

"It's hard to tell..." Iris murmured. "I can't compare it to anything I've experienced before. Probably just what old people feel like. And..." tears filled her eyes, "it's hard to describe all the changes... Even my emotions are all over the place. Maker... Dryn is off somewhere, and he'll never see my beauty again..."

"He'll love you just as much as he did before," Keyth said. "Maybe more. I've known him our entire lives, and what I just saw, his fury as he left... You are more important to Dryn than anything..."

"...yes, but I can't ask him to love me now!" Iris cried. The same light filled those eyes as it had in her youthful face. "He shouldn't... I'm old. He should have someone to share a life with. Mine's almost gone. I have a few years left at the most! It's just... so unfair..."

"I think that is what angered Dryn the most," Keyth said.

"It's the least of it. In all of this... in this devastation, I've found cruel answers. Knowledge I never thought I'd have..." Iris whispered.

"What?" Yara asked, her curiosity peaked at what Iris could possibly be speaking of.

"Pyrsius Gothikar..." Iris breathed, and trailed off. Trying again, she told them, "Pyrsius Gothikar is... my father!" Stunned, Keyth and Yara stared at her in silence. Keyth struggled to find words to reply. Iris continued, "I'd seen him before, on the estate where I was raised. I saw him several times, and when I walked into Kronos' chambers... there he was, the same man. He called me by my name. Called me Lanteera..."

"By the Maker...." Keyth sat there in shock and stammered, "Your father is the Prince of Avernus?"

Iris burst into sudden laughter, "Yes, one of the Imperial Princes! And the one trying to kill magic, at that! How's that for irony? The Maker must be splitting his sides!"

Yara bowed her head in sadness. "How could he do this to you?"

The room remained silent for a long time. Iris sighed. "You two survived your quest.... Was it a success?"

Keyth nodded. "The magician Mordyn is slain and I can no longer be of help to Dryn. I made another promise and I intend to keep it. Yara and I are leaving in the morning to return to Kryden. You're welcome to come after us when you're able."

Iris nodded. "I wondered when you'd return to your senses. I'm surprised you've stayed so long. And I don't know when I'll be able to travel, but perhaps one day before the end."

"I feel like we're abandoning you. Are you certain you don't want us to stay?" Yara inquired. "Some familiar faces around?"

"No, you should return. Your families are probably at their wits ends. Hopefully they haven't given up on you," Iris laughed. She tried to glance out the window behind her. "Is it dark?" she asked.

"Yes," Keyth answered.

"And Dryn is out there somewhere... facing my father," Iris murmured.

Pyrsius Gothikar lived in the wealth of his father. Dryn stood in a crowded room surrounded by bookshelves and chairs that could have out-bargained the monetary value of Kryden. He turned around from where he had appeared, looked across a varnished wooden table, and jumped at the sight of the Prince of Avernus himself.

Pyrsius sat with his feet set up on the table and a chalice held in one hand. He nodded to Dryn and took a sip of the dark liquid. The man's dazzling green eyes matched the grin that Pyrsius flashed, as he said, "Welcome to Avernus, Lord Rayth."

"Maker burn you, earth-spawn!" Dryn cried, and threw a bolt of lightning at Pyrsius. The man lifted a hand and a shattered token summoned a field of dust in front of him. The lightning was channelled aside and burnt holes into the tabletop. Dryn cursed incoherently and let loose a storm of fireballs, dozens of flashes spiralling through the air from his outstretched fingers.

This time the fireballs were extinguished in a wave of water, and Dryn ducked to avoid being hit as the swirl splashed toward him. He could tell it built with the heat of each fireball, and was likely boiling to the touch. Singeing holes in the hardwood floor, the water was released from its magic, and Dryn sidestepped a bolt of green energy.

"Now, now, Rayth," Pyrsius snapped. He was presenting standing, but the ornate goblet sat on the trembling tabletop. "Get your temper in check! Oh, what's wrong?" he mocked. "Your precious Lanteera lies dead?"

"AHH!" Dryn roared and rattled a string of ancient syllables. Released from some hurricane, a torrential wind surged from his two outstretched fists. Pyrsius hastily conjured energy between them in the shape of a shield. The wind grew ferociously as it encountered this force that obstructed it.

Inch by inch and then foot by foot, Pyrsius found himself pushed back across the room as his chalice splattered against his shield and papers were torn to shreds. At last Pyrsius was held against the wall, and Dryn leapt across the table toward him. Now caught in his own gale, he found himself held by the wind against Pyrsius' shield. Dryn's hand groped around its edge.

Grabbing hold of the Prince's throat, he bellowed over the still roaring wind, "YOU'LL DIE FOR WHAT YOU'VE DONE!!!"

Without warning, Pyrsius twisted his hand, and a blur of metal shot upwards under his magical shield and buried itself in Dryn's outstretched arm. Dryn buckled sideways, and with a screech of pain, was thrust against the wall by his own powerful spell. Pinned in place, he could see blood fanning out from his arm. The wind was slamming against the wall with such intensity that his blood dripped upwards and spread like a web along the wooden wall.

Pyrsius' blade had cut deep into the underside of his forearm, and the pain nearly obscured Dryn's vision. The wind spell was waning and, as it subsided, Dryn slumped down the wall. He could barely raise himself onto his knees.

"I have done nothing more than your kind has done!" Pyrsius spat, rounding on him.

Dryn found himself dragged up against the wall again, the splatter of blood squelched between his shirt and the wood. A blade appeared at his throat and he gasped as blood was drawn.

"Why did you use her?" Pyrsius screeched. "Why would you use her in such a way, just to spite *me!!*"

"Use her?" Dryn grunted, his fingers tracing glyphs against the wood. "Use her?" he repeated. Preparing to strike Pyrsius back, Dryn breathed the spell for the glyphs he had written. The spell would make liquid of any metal nearby, and Dryn was prepared to push the Prince away from him.

A metallic pendant on Pyrsius' neck slithered down his chest and dripped to the floor, but the blade at Dryn's throat remained very solid, pricking at his skin. Pyrsius smirked as he realized what Dryn had done, then threw Dryn bodily onto the nearby table. The wooden legs shattered beneath the force, leaving Dryn rolling on the floor.

Pyrsius' blade appeared at his throat again as the Prince spat out, "Foul little magician!! This blade, you see, this is enchanted... Korbios was a gift from Artemys to my father... and it cannot be undone so easily!!" The blade now punctured the outer layers of his skin.

Dryn imagined his neck was slick red, but he bit back the pain. He had felt worse. "What is Iris to you?"

Pyrsius chuckled, dragged Dryn to his feet and slammed him back against the wall, jarring his whole torso. "Don't play with *my* mind, sorcerer!! Lanteera was my daughter!"

Dryn's mind froze and the finger that was tracing another glyph paused. "Your daughter..." he trailed. "Iris is your... daughter..." Then, pressing himself forward despite the blade, he shouted, "You almost killed your own child?"

He thrust his hand forward and a pulse of opaque darkness slammed into Pyrsius' midsection. The Prince was knocked back a step, and Dryn let loose a far more powerful strike, this one mixed with fire. The Prince was blasted to the stone wall opposite Dryn. Dryn knelt and began tracing an elaborate character across the floorboards, his mind seeing an actual ink symbol.

Coughing and gasping as he came shakily to his feet, Pyrsius muttered, "So she's still alive, is she? And how is your *love* in her old age?" he sneered.

"DIE!!" Dryn screamed, releasing the spell he had prepared, a duplicate of the one Orion had used to defeat him in Ithyka. Sparkling beams of white light shot across the room and slashed through everything they touched. Planks of wood disappeared from the floor and sections fell in from the ceiling. The wall behind Pyrsius splintered and started falling in, revealing a grand hall beyond it.

Pyrsius had raised a circle of violet mist, a bizarre energy that seemed to suck in the light as it neared. By the time Dryn's light storm was done, Pyrsius had only two gashes on him, but at least Dryn had drawn blood.

Weakly grabbing his tokens, Dryn broke a spell which released a number of metal blades that shot like arrows. Pyrsius barely had time to lift his blade, Korbios. He knocked aside the first, sidestepped the next and found the third slicing the top of his shoulder. Blood sprayed into the air and the Prince stumbled a step backward.

Pyrsius started laughing. Dryn paused in his next assault to watch as the Prince ran a hand over the wound and chuckled. "Killing you... will be almost as rewarding as burning the magic school at Delfie. You see, you believe your magic to be superior... while, in fact, it is a curse. We both know that I am not a magician, but I have had this Palace protected with spells. Should you try to teleport, your destination will be changed to one I choose!"

"Yet you admit you are weak in magic..."

Pyrsius continued, "Do you feel the curse? With every assault you throw at me, you tire... and you cannot leave. I have nearly my entire reserve of energy and a sword you can't break."

Dryn's breath began heaving as his fury continued to grow. Pyrsius was insane. He had been given enough tokens to defend himself, and to target everything Dryn loved. With a scream Dryn threw everything he had at Pyrsius. Fireballs and stones the size of his head appeared from thin air and shot across the room. Shards of ice and blasts of lightning tore the room to shreds. Books ripped off the shelves, scraps of paper burned and whirled through the air.

As this storm continued, Dryn advanced toward Pyrsius. Pyrsius, blocking what he could shield off, stumbled through the rubble behind him into the abandoned great hall. *I'll burn your body before I even start on your mind,* Dryn cursed at Pyrsius. *I'll make you wish you had never been born!*

Beyond belief, Pyrsius' sword burnt through Dryn's blazing assault. Dryn found himself driven back two feet on Pyrsius' thrust. The blade had pierced his right shoulder and now protruded from his back. A shower of blood flooded into Dryn's shirt and coated the floor. He gasped in shock and then gritted his teeth as the agony hit him. His entire right arm went numb. He clawed with his left and grabbed hold of Pyrsius' throat once more. Clenching his fingers like talons, he dug pools of blood into Pyrsius' neck.

Pyrsius shrieked and planted a foot on Dryn's stomach. His boot forced Dryn backward off the blade, and he toppled into a pile on a table.

Dryn peered through red mist, and darkness tightened his vision. He gasped and tried to stand up. He knew he wouldn't black out, but he was worried one of Pyrsius' spells would kill him. He managed to tilt himself off the table until his feet touched the floor, but he couldn't hold himself up and ended up on his knees, clutching the bleeding hole in his shoulder.

"After I kill you," Pyrsius taunted, "I'll go finish the job with Lanteera, and then Theseus himself. Perhaps after I'll burn your village."

Dryn dragged himself from ground, ignoring the sheer torment of his body. Pyrsius' snapped his fingers, and shards of a stone token fell to the floor. Suddenly, Dryn was stopped by an invisible wall, and he sank down against it to the floor. When his back met another wall, he slammed his arms out to the sides, only to meet more immovable and transparent surfaces.

Like the monsters of lore, scales scraped across his scalp. His eyes shut on their own and he found himself trembling uncontrollably. He was back in the prison cell, and he was frozen in its clutches. Like the jaw he had imagined, it swallowed him in paranoia. His eyes lolled back and he felt his body fall limply against the solid prison Pyrsius had created.

"Oh my," that voice mocked, "seems we've found your flaw. Was it your capture in Athyns?"

Not again... not again... not again... he prayed. *Maker please... not again.* He lifted a hand and, as he had under Athyns, pounded against the walls. *Maker's Light, this can't be happening...*

A resounding battle cry echoed through his being, *Don't let them do it to you again. Don't let them catch you.*

"Not again!!!" he screamed, and his eyes flared open. He tore a token from his pouch. Before his weak fingers could snap it, Pyrsius' hand shot through the invisible cage and grabbed his wrist.

"There it is," the Prince whispered. He whistled as though he were impressed. "There it is." Held in Dryn's fingers was another time travel spell. Pyrsius shifted Dryn's arm in order to study both sides of the stone.

Dryn stared up at him in total fury. "You have such a narrow mind, Pyrsius. You only think of the present."

Pyrsius' eyes met his glare. "Go die in the desert, cursed mage!" he spat and thrust his blade between Dryn's ribs. The token in Dryn's fingers snapped, sending him flickering back in time.

He emerged with his knees burning in the scalding desert sands and Pyrsius' sword through his heart.

61

From the rear of the column, Theseus' army appeared as a snake weaving its way through a garden, while in fact, it stretched ahead over the hills. Hundreds upon hundreds, even thousands of soldiers, marching in ranks of ten or fifteen wide, stretched along the winding road to the horizon.

Theseus rode in his full splendour, more for morale than comfort. A packhorse followed one of his squires, his Imperial armour within its saddle bags. But today he wore a dyed fleece robe, trimmed with Imperial red and decorated with golden beads. His dark hair was combed back and hung behind his head to his neck, and his chin was freshly shaven. They had set out upon the road that morning, and already noon had strode past.

It was slow going, when every man carried his life in a pack on his back. Behind Theseus were a hundred wagonloads of food and supplies and the chefs to prepare them. Theseus knew that a direct battle would last days, and he had come prepared to hold his enemies at bay for the season, if he had to.

He hoped to reach Sinai before his enemies emerged from its Glyph Gate. That would be the easiest way to win this battle. Such a Gate could be defended indefinitely, and reaching it first would prove a complete victory. The enemy would be forced to march around the Blood Strait to Dagger's Edge, and then face the forces of Edessa, before continuing eastward to Theseus' domain.

Unfortunately, three thousand men were slow in travel and slower in camp. He feared he would have to set camp soon, and give orders to resume the march at dawn.

If asked, he would have been honest. Thoughts of Dryn
Rayth filled his mind, and he couldn't distract himself from
them. The Crown Magician had completed a great service to
Theseus and to the true Triumvirate, but now his hasty and
emotional actions may have jeopardized all they had
accomplished, and could certainly spell Dryn's own downfall.

A week's march ahead of him, the Sinai Mountains
awaited.

. . .

Odyn of Olympus sat on a warhorse, and from one of the
hills near Galinor, gazed out across the Imperial City at the
Tower of the Throne. He was dressed head-to-toe in Imperial
armor of gold and steel, and his mount wore chainmail skirts.
From his saddle he could see the city stretched out ahead of him
and his army spread out behind him in the hills.

Half of my army to be precise, he corrected himself.
Commander Rychard had charge of just over half, and remained
camping near the Blood Strait Glyph Gate until ordered to
advance onto the Northland plains.

Odyn nodded to his elite vanguard and the cavalry troop
formed up around him. "We'll ride ahead," he ordered.

He kicked his mount's sides and rode down the slope with
his troop. The guards of Galinor saw him coming, but
recognized the banner of Olympus held by one of the
cavalrymen. Together they reached the gate and rode into the
outer bailey of the Galinor walls.

"You three, with me," Odyn commanded, and, with a
gesture, led these three toward the inner gate and the city proper.

It was quick work killing the Imperial guards. The sentries
were not expecting Odyn's soldiers to turn on them, and within
moments, both gates into the city were cleared. Odyn nodded to
one of his riders and the man raised a battle horn to his lips. The
sound echoed off the walls and filled the sky, alerting both
Galinor's guards and Odyn's armies.

Before the Galinor defences could muster their soldiers to
that side of the city, Odyn's forces had reached the gates, and his
vanguard led the attack deeper into the city. They strode directly
towards the Tower of the Throne, swiftly fighting their way
through the streets. Odyn led the assault, his warhorse kicking
its way across the cobbles and his bastard sword slashing down
the few guards that found their way through the crowds.

The bulk of his army was fighting through adjoining streets and before long the entire city had fallen into a state of anarchy. Odyn, his vanguard, and several dozen infantry stormed the gates of the Tower Courtyard, but found themselves held off by the rampart archers. Odyn gestured for the horn to be blown again and a troop of siege soldiers arrived within a short time. They bore a heavy log between them and their comrades raised shields to cover the troop. Like a turtle, the battering ram fell upon the gates and, with one, two, three pounds of its head, smashed a hole in the great oaken doors. The gates teetered open, the thick bar broken by the impact, and the Imperial Guards within were set upon by the attacking troops.

Odyn bellowed, "Charge!!" and his vanguard surged forward, carving a path into the full courtyard. Odyn's warhorse took a halberd in the chest as it tried to gallop forward, and was thrown off its hooves by the impact, as much as from the wound. The halberd had barely breached the chainmail skirts, but the fall had broken ribs and perhaps a leg.

Odyn then stood amidst the carnage and, with a flash of his sword, finished off the soldier who had downed his horse.

The ensuing skirmish lasted far longer than Odyn would have wished. The Imperial Guard itself was naught but a ceremonial order, while the Galinor defences employed fierce and veteran soldiers.

Odyn fought as viciously as he ever had. As a younger man he had fought in the Trionus War and had trained avidly over the thirty years since. Blow after jarring blow knocked down his opponents, and even the Galinor soldiers couldn't withstand his assault.

His vanguard fared just as well and, though Odyn was knocked from his feet once, no major injuries were sustained. In that incident, Odyn's sword was lost in the carnage, but he grabbed the nearest weapon to defend himself. Wielding a battleaxe, Odyn cut down the last defender and kicked in the wooden door at the base of the Tower of the Throne.

His soldiers stormed up the stairs and he led the swift charge into the structure. They encountered little resistance until they reached the Great Hall beneath the Imperial Council Chamber.

Even as his men fought, Odyn pressed past them with haste and fury. His anger had been growing all day and he longed to finish the Triumvirate once and for all. He stormed up that last flight of stairs and into the corridor to the Council Chamber. First was the statue of Tiberon Odyn, and he grabbed it with rage and smashed it to the floor. The wooden head snapped and rolled away. Second was the statue of Ivos, and then the figure of Aristorn. Soon the three founding patriarchs were on their knees for him.

He kicked in the door of the Council Chamber and slammed the bloody battleaxe down in the middle of the triangular Council Table. A huge crack split into the everwood surface. He turned on the cheap wooden throne, the simplistic chair for the High Prince. He hurled it at the window, where it shattered through into the void, and smashed to splinters in the courtyard below.

For the first time in three hundred years, there was a King.

Shadows grew and shrank. When they were small, the sun burnt his skin, adding another agony to the others. When they were long again, his limbs began to freeze until they appeared blue under the night sky. He couldn't sweat and he couldn't shiver. His body was dead, his limbs pale. Every day that passed, his breath suffered because no blood could be pumped to them. Now he was suffocating as well, and had stopped breathing altogether.

With a slack jaw and wide eyes he watched his shadow grow and shrink again and again. Birds circled overhead, waiting for their feast. Even their patience ran out when the prey wouldn't submit to death.

After appearing here in the desert, his veins had run like rivers through the sand, coating the fine grains and making a delta of red lines away from his view. He could still feel the steel that transfixed him. His hands were locked upon it and without blood in his muscles he could not even remove them.

He hadn't slept in days, days that he couldn't count. He could recall two faces only... a youthful girl and her father, a middle-aged man as mad as a rabid dog. His own name drifted on the tip of his tongue and he thought he had perhaps lost the ability to pursue it, until finally he recalled that he was Dryn.

Dryn watched the days pass in the shadow of his fallen form, and even that shrank over the days as twisting winds piled sand onto him. Dirt filled his open mouth and dim thoughts of a prison cell filled his mind. He didn't know what it signified, but he felt terror inside of him, deep untameable fear.

Next, he pondered this death to which his body would never surrender. As he prepared what he could, his mind, to depart from the world entirely, he found a kind of peace he had never known. He knew his body would last sixty or seventy, years until it passed of old age, but he couldn't endure this hanging on. He couldn't last even a month in this prison, and so he decided to cease. To dismiss his mind and... leave.

Hands were touching him, moving him. The cold sensation of being pulled from his sandy grave. He saw a white sky and black sand, and then black sky and white sand. A blinding pain in his chest and a hole to his core. A buzz in his ears, and then the warmth of magic coursing through his limbs.

Dryn awoke to the sound of bubbling water and managed to open his eyes. He could feel the cold stone beneath him, and saw more stone not a foot above him. Terror driven, he rolled to his side, and threw his feet off the ledge onto the edge of a small brook. Behind him was a small cave in which he had awoken. He dropped to his knees and cupped water into his mouth, again and again and again, yet his thirst wasn't satisfied. Suddenly, he was flooded with memories of the battle against Pyrsius.

He grabbed his chest and found he was wearing a smooth red cloak. He pulled the collar down. There was no mark where Pyrsius' sword had pierced him. Only the glyphs from Artemys' Ward were visible. He searched around and found a trail of footsteps leading up a small slope out of the brook's ravine. Stumbling up to the desert surface, he found himself staring at a crouched man's back. The man rose and turned to face Dryn, revealing a fire on which he'd been focused.

Dryn stared at the man for a moment, his short brown hair, well-kept beard and sharp eyes, but couldn't recognize him. He couldn't have been older than forty. He had never seen the man's face before, but knew that the stranger must be the one who had rescued him.

"By the Maker..." Dryn muttered, "How'd you find me?"

"A lot of scrying," the man said smoothly. "Have a seat. I'm heating up some venison."

Dryn eagerly sat down. He realized abruptly he was starving. *A desert local?* he wondered. *A hermit or secluded magician? Where did he get venison?* Probing, he said, "My name is Dryn..."

"I know who you are," the man told him, sitting across the fire from him. "And we have a strong connection.... My name is Artemys Gothikar."

Dryn tried to get up but tripped and stumbled backwards. "Great Glyph!" he hissed. *By the Maker, what is going on? Who is this really?* "Artemys Gothikar is dead," he told the man. "Who are you really?"

"I am Artemys."

"He was an old man in the forest, who gave me..." Dryn trailed off. *Who is this man? Why should I trust him?* "He died. I saw him die."

"An old man?" the stranger grinned. "Perhaps that was me."

"Travelling time..." Dryn muttered, his mind whirling. It was the only explanation. *This is an Artemys Gothikar from the past...* "It never occurred to me, but it makes sense now... I should have considered that I'm not the only one who can travel through time."

Artemys remained silent and gestured for Dryn to sit again. "I have seen many things in my days, but never one like you. Tell me who left you like that, here in the desert," Artemys instructed him.

"It was... your brother, Pyrsius..." Dryn replied.

Artemys laughed. "Pyrsius defeated you? Dryn, Dryn... Pyrsius does not even have magic."

"He has tokens," Dryn blurted. "Powerful ones. And your sword!"

"The sword has a mere ward of protection from it breaking. The Order would not even be called a magic sword."

"You found me... you saw what he can do... what I've been through!"

Artemys shook his head. "So after all this, you think you can be beaten by tokens? You can best him, Dryn."

"Have you seen that? In the future?" *The advantage to do that....* he realized in awe.

Artemys' face became smug, but his words turned compassionate. "I know how much you have suffered, but there is more at stake than your life or even that of your friends. Pyrsius does not stand a chance. You need to plan though. Pyrsius' brilliance is his plotting. Take that away and you only need to wait out his tokens."

"And Odyn? His armies have rallied near the Glyph Gate to the Sinai Mountains," Dryn said. "My friends found them. Or rather will. Right now... in this time period, we just reached Ithyka. But in my *present*," Dryn explained, "war is about to break out."

"Really...?" Artemys asked, and then seemed to catch himself. "He did not become High Prince as he plotted?"

"No, I stopped him. In my time, I'm the Crown Magician, as you were in yours," Dryn said.

"I see," the great mage muttered. "So is it possible that Theseus will defend the Northlands?"

"I doubt it. The allied forces of the south would outnumber any defences of the north, especially if the enemy emerges in Sinai instead of facing Edessa," Dryn told him. "If I am able to defeat Pyrsius as you say, then I'd still have to face Odyn... and then perhaps I could save Athyns." The necessity of Artemys' challenge was still a strong conviction in Dryn, but he couldn't face the cost or the odds.

Artemys picked the lump of venison off his stake. He handed Dryn part and bit into it himself. "Defeat Pyrsius and Odyn, and I suspect the remaining enemy will yield to Theseus. The Three Nobles of each city will no doubt grant him the High Prince-hood in order to re-establish order in the realm."

"Are you sure? The Nobles of Avernus and Olympus would side with Theseus?" Dryn wondered. "Even after all this time?"

"It is law. The Nobles never fight, and they fear civil war as this realm has stood united for centuries. Their lives are full of politics and, with everyone dead, there would be no politics to play," Artemys said.

"I can't travel forward," Dryn blurted. "That is why I haven't investigated the timeline more. Any date I go back to... I'm stuck there until the time elapses."

"You are what... two or three months in your past?" Artemys asked.

Dryn nodded. "Two and a half."

"Then you have a portion of time to try to overcome your hindrances."

"And when I get back to the present?"

Artemys smiled. "Save the realm."

Dryn bobbed his head again. *Ithyka. My friends and I are just reaching Ithyka. The first time I used the time spell. And then... Scion.* "I think I know where to go..." he told Artemys. *It's far past time I spoke with the Prophet.*

"Good," Artemys said. "I have fixed your wound, and ... put you back to right."

So many thoughts flooded Dryn's mind: why he'd been chosen, what was Artemys' part in this battle, how to show his gratitude?

The magician stood up and kicked dirt onto the fire. Fumbling into a pocket in his robe, Artemys drew out a token and glanced at Dryn once more. "May the Maker protect you, Dryn Rayth. Defeat our enemies." With that, the former Crown Magician flickered away through a hole in the air and Dryn was left alone in the desert without answers.

He quickly finished the venison and stood up. The red robe in which Artemys had dressed him seemed to fit his rank much better than the tunic and breeches he'd been wearing. He looked around the small camp, and then scried the glyphs to travel to Scion.

63

Rychard of Tarroth swiftly beheaded an approaching swordsman, and ran his companion through, as the man lifted his sword. A charging cavalryman fell to the pike of one of Rychard's men, and the horse galloped away. Two more enemies approached warily and one of Rychard's rangers dropped the first with a swift bowshot. Rychard engaged the second and blocked the man's eager melee. After playing with the soldier for several blows, Rychard parried a swipe and spun around to slash the man from chest to lower back.

The plains below Covin had become the largest battlefield since the Trionus War. When Rychard's division of the Southland army had emerged from the Glyph Gate, they'd encountered a single cavalry troop riding hard to reach the gate before the horde emerged. Rychard had that troop strung up from the fiery rooftops of Covin, then set up camp for the longer battle. At dawn the following day, Theseus' army arrived.

Rychard had admired Periander's skills of strategy, but the true creator of the current war, the genius who had begun the genocide, the war and even inspired Odyn's desire for the throne, had won Rychard's respect far more. Two months ago, a week before he had captured Dryn ten Rayth, Avernus had sent him a troop of veteran soldiers. The next day a traveller arrived at Rychard's Athynian barracks and proved himself to be the true coordinator of all their plans. Rychard had once reflected that only three men might know the entire picture: Pyrsius and Odyn were the first two.

The traveller had instructed Rychard to slay Theseus. "Two and a half months from now," the man had said, "you will lead an army to a Glyph Gate near the Blood Strait. Your commanders Pyrsius and Odyn will direct you. You will emerge in Sinai and face Theseus' northern army. Whether or not you win the battle, you must ensure the demise of Prince Theseus."

To have planned and predicted the events that led to this day, such brilliance could only make Rychard marvel. *The Maker himself desires me to win this day,* he concluded. *The Maker himself guides the actions of my commander.*

And so here he stood, cutting down Northland soldiers and commanding the joint armies of Pyrsius and Odyn. Odyn would soon arrive with the other half of the army, while Pyrsius guarded the South.

Rychard's main force engaged Theseus' ranks head on, while Rychard himself led an elite troop around the edges of the enemy army, both to flank them and to accomplish his true goal. The fighting was thick as the Northland soldiers attempted to stop Rychard's diverted assault.

Rychard nearly took an arrow; the sky was full of them. One of his men toppled from the shot, and Rychard grabbed the corpse's shield. The unfortunate man had no need of it anymore, and Rychard had lost his own heater during a cavalry charge.

By the time he reached Theseus' small command camp, his elite group was weary, wounded and noticeably fewer in number than they had been when they left Covin.

Theseus' guard saw Rychard and his men approaching and charged to defend the Prince. Rychard's short sword wove its way between his enemy's blocks and levelled two men as quickly as ever. His new shield was torn away by an axe, and he was nearly knocked aside by the blow. A skilled archer let an arrow fly, saving Rychard's hide again.

The Imperial Prince himself appeared, gleaming in his royal gold-gilded armour. Rychard hated to ruin such beauty with blood, but he leapt at the chance to cross blades with Theseus. "We meet again," he called and levelled his sword toward the Prince's head.

"I told you it would be across swords," Theseus taunted.

Although Rychard had always dabbled in magic and was tempted to use it now, he decided against it. *Theseus deserves a fair fight, my strength against his.* Rychard's elite troop would make quick work of the remaining guards; he ordered them not to intervene.

It was the greatest sword fight of Rychard's life. Such finesse guided the Prince's moves, and the battle seemed to unfold like a work of art: the gold and grey of armour and sword, the white gleam of the midday sun on swords, the splash of vivid red. Rychard took his own fair share of gashes, and he nearly lost an arm, if not for a lucky dodge. The top of his armour was pierced and blood from his shoulder splattered against his cheek. Unexpectedly vulnerable because of Rychard's sidestep, Theseus' left quarter was exposed and Rychard gave the Prince a quick uppercut, nearly severing the Prince's arm above the elbow. Theseus roared in agony and stumbled back. Rychard pressed his attack, and as abruptly as the storm of colours had begun, the masterpiece was complete.

Trumpets sounded on cue at the Glyph Gate and Odyn's portion of the army arrived. By twilight the plains below Sinai were an abandoned necropolis, and the southern horde marched on Athyns.

64

Dawn was like an everyday miracle in the village of Scion. Thick fog crawled up the shore and wrapped the cozy huts in muted light and damp dew. Dryn appeared near the town square, stepping out of a hole in the air and glancing around the sleepy town. In the general direction of the horizon, a glorious painting rose into the sky, colours stretching from blue, through grey, violet, salmon, orange and back into blue.

"Welcome to Scion," a man's voice called, and Dryn was amazed to see the man who had greeted them on their first visit. The stranger smiled and said, "The Prophet has seen your arrival and–"

"And I must leave? Like you told me the last time?" Dryn interrupted.

The man frowned. "On the contrary. She will see you without delay."

Dryn raised an eyebrow. "Many days from now, you will tell me to leave as soon as I arrive with my friends," he explained.

The man laughed. "The Prophet told me you would say something to that effect. Now, if you'll accompany me..." Dryn complied and followed the man through the wide village streets. Soon they left the settlement altogether, and the stranger led Dryn along a narrow path into the adjacent woodland. A huge oak tree had fallen across the way, and they had to climb over it. Dryn's guide told him, "Happened in a recent storm. We'll have to have some villagers come up to move it."

At last they emerged from the woodland into a small clearing inhabited by a single hut. The small shack was built of rotted planks of wood and the roof of thatched straw. A small garden was its only decoration, and Dryn recognized some of the herbs growing in it from his days as an apothecary apprentice.

"The Prophet is waiting inside," his guide said, and started up the path back to the village.

Dryn knocked quietly on the door and grimaced. His skin was burnt from when he had lain wounded in the desert. He could recall Artemys' words as they ate at his fire. Dryn's stomach still grumbled with hunger, but it would have to wait.

"He said I was *waiting*," a woman's voice called out.

Dryn pushed open the door and stepped inside. A clear view of the single room was obscured by curtains of beads and blankets hanging to divide the living space. In the center of the hut a small table was set with a chair on either side. The chair opposite Dryn was occupied by a frail black-haired woman. As she gestured to the chair closest to him, she proclaimed, "At last we meet."

"At last," he repeated, staring at her blankly. In the present, *her* present, Dryn was a nameless village boy who had only recently left his home.

"Yes..." she muttered. "I have waited my whole life."

He sat down and cautiously asked, "And you knew I would come?"

"Yes."

He noticed the way her eyes stared at him, not at a young man in a red robe, but in awe at a spectre. He returned her gaze of surprise: firstly, that the Prophet of Scion was in fact a Prophetess, and secondly, that she was in such rapt focus of him. Why then would she refuse his visit in the future? Within several days, he and his companions would arrive in Scion on their way to Athyns.

"You can see the future? Scry it?" he questioned. "Can you travel to it?"

"I can scry it. I can create a gateway to it," she answered. "The Maker has blessed me with the Shadow Glyph."

"The Shadow Glyph?" he asked, confused.

"It is the events that are to come," she told him. "The Great Glyph includes everything that happens. This is why you have come to me. Artemys told you in the desert to learn."

"Yes. You've seen that?" Dryn questioned.

"I have," the Prophet replied. "And all of your lives."

"Teach me then," Dryn implored.

She laughed and said, "As you will. The Great Glyph is written in the present. Events exist in the Shadow Glyph until they reach the present, at which point they are absorbed into the Great Glyph. Travelling through gateways from one location to another is possible because both exist in the Great Glyph. Events that have been written cannot be unwritten, and so, with the same power, a magician can travel to the past as easily as travelling within the present."

He nodded. "I have traveled both."

"Travel within the present is possible for all magicians. Only those whose True Name references the Great Glyph can travel to the past," the Prophet explained. "Your True Name includes the Great Glyph because of the spell branded upon you in the forest."

"And this 'Shadow Glyph'?" Dryn questioned.

"It is the events that are to come. It is like a river with a bridge. The bridge is the present," she said, holding out a hand. "The water upstream," she gestured, "is the future, and becomes present and past as it passes the bridge."

"Are you saying that the future cannot be changed?" Dryn asked. "The events that are yet to come... they are predetermined? Prewritten?"

"When I scry the Shadow Glyph, I see events that are yet to come," she said.

"And you don't believe that such events can be changed?" Dryn inquired. "Have any of your visions ever changed or do they all come true?"

"They all come true." The Prophet stared at him stoically. "I would not be able to scry something that constantly shifted with all of our decisions. Look at your own experiences from the past. Have you ever been able to change events? No matter what your decision," she told him, "the outcome was the same. The future is similar. No matter what people choose, it is always chosen in the present, and thus the Shadow Glyph unfolds the same way."

"No," Dryn snapped. "That would mean my actions are nothing. Whether or not I face my enemies, the fate of the Dominion is set."

"It does not mean anything about your actions. You must decide to act one way or another, and doing nothing is a decision as well," she said. "Without decisions, the Shadow Glyph would not exist. Your actions and your decisions... *everyone's* actions and decisions, will be determined before the present comes to pass. The future plays out the way it must. To refuse this is to disbelieve in the existence of a future itself."

Dryn shook his head. He wrapped his mind around her words from every way he could imagine, every possibility. "That would mean that if I am going to die in my fight against Pyrsius, when I go now to face him... there is nothing I could do in any time to change that. I refuse to believe that I am only a puppet of this *Shadow Glyph*..."

"It doesn't matter if you believe in it or not," she said.

"You see, that's my point. As you've explained it, nothing matters at all. Beliefs, actions, choices... they are all purposeless."

She shook her head. "No, they are the only things that do matter. To complete the Shadow Glyph."

"But not to change it," Dryn snapped. He leaned back in the chair, and stared up at the dark ceiling. After a moment he glanced down at her again. "Fine," he said. "Show me. Show me the future, and I'll see for myself if you tell the truth."

"I can't show you. It does not work like that," she told him.

Angrily, he ordered, "Show me the spell! Show me the spell you use to scry the future."

"It won't work for you," she repeated.

"Show me!" he shouted.

She pulled a parchment from her wide sleeve and flattened it. "This," she pointed.

He whispered the words and waited, but nothing happened. "By the Maker," he growled. He sat back again, trying to wait out his anger. Leaning against the table from his chair, he pointed at the most complex glyph in the spell. "Is this it? The Shadow Glyph?"

"Yes," she nodded.

"Leave now," he commanded. "When I am done, you will know. You can return then, for I will leave by magic. I will leave by travelling *ahead* in time, to *my* present. And if you continue to try to convince me of these absurdities... If I ever see you again..."

"The Shadow Glyph will decide," she interrupted.

"Out!" he barked.

She flinched visibly and rose from her chair. She moved to the door and disappeared into the darkness. In several days,

Dryn and his friends would arrive, and she would refuse to meet them on Dryn's own orders.

To add to the glyphs on his chest, he wrote Artemys' spell on the table. His mind saw the entire string of symbols that had been burnt into him. These scribbles had begun his involvement in this entire struggle. He could see the symbols that allowed his True Name to reference the Great Glyph. He began a new line of symbols, retracing them on the tabletop, but substituting the Shadow Glyph for the Great Glyph. When he had finished, he stood back and began to whisper the words of it. *"Hayen donbreth..."* he breathed, and continued activating the glyphs for several moments. The spell would adjust his True Name itself.

He wasn't sure if such a thing had ever been done, someone rewriting their own True Name, and he wasn't sure what the long term consequences would be. He knew he needed the Shadow Glyph, and he refused to believe that the future was set in stone.

He finished, *"...elkobo draz,"* and felt a jolt jump through his muscles. A fiery mountain smashed into his mind and he could almost feel flows of scathing fire drown him like molten stone. His fists clenched until his nails drew blood and he found himself on his knees beside the table. Faintly, he recalled the same agonies slamming him when Artemys had first given him the spell in the forest, changing his True Name to reference the Great Glyph.

Then darkness came. He had lost consciousness only once before, in the forest. This second time he dreamed of the future.

Lesser Kryden was just as Keyth had left it. He walked through the village's gate around noon with Yara on one arm and his lordly chainmail still draped around his shoulders. The garment could have brought him wealth; anything in Theseus' armoury could have brought a fortune, but he would never sell it.

They drew gasps, whispers, and shocked stares. It had been months since they had left, and after the incident with bandits around that time, the villagers had believed that Keyth, Yara and Dryn were likely captured or killed.

"By the Maker!" Magistrate Arbydn exclaimed. He had been talking to Master ten Brae outside of the Grey Horse Inn. "You're alive!"

"And well," Keyth said. "And glad to be back at last."

"Run and fetch the Corins," Arbydn told a younger boy. "Keyth ten Arad.... You and your friends have been the focus of rumouring since your disappearance, and I'm certain this reappearance will secure your place in our folklore."

Keyth rolled his eyes. "I'm not sure I deserve a place in our stories, but I'm honoured that you'd say so."

"Is Dryn ten Rayth with you?" Arbydn asked, glancing through the quickly growing crowd. His eyes kept flicking back at the forest green cloak and tempered chain that Keyth wore.

"No. He lives, last I heard. He is a much different youth now. In truth, he's quite a man," he corrected himself.

"He still lives?" Telper ten Rayth gasped, stumbling through the crowd. He had only just appeared with Yara's

S H A D O W   G L Y P H

family in tow. Yara tore herself from Keyth's arm and
embraced her family in joy.

Keyth nodded to Dryn's father. "You are Master Rayth
now, not ten Rayth!"

"What?" the apothecary breathed. "He's..."

"Lord Dryn Rayth," Keyth finished, smiling. "And the
Crown Magician of the Imperial Triumvirate!"

"Great Glyphs!" Master Rayth boomed, along with nearly
everyone who had heard.

"Great Glyphs, indeed..." Keyth whispered.

"You have some stories to tell, young man," Arbydn
muttered sternly. "And I imagine she does too," he smiled.
Yara was talking excitedly with her family, in an Athynian dress
that the entire town together could hardly afford.

Master ten Lenter appeared, and Keyth excused himself to
speak with the old bowyer. He had spoken to his mother for the
first time in years as they had passed through Greater Kryden on
their way home. It had been a long journey from Athyns into the
north.

"Keyth..." the bowyer gaped. "What happened to you?
Where did you go? Look at you..."

"Athyns. The sea. Even the Blood Strait where the last
war began," Keyth told him. Seeing his old master's shock, he
added, "Yes, I've seen the world now. And I brought you
something."

He pulled an arrow from his quiver, one more exceptional
than those he'd taken on his mission to hunt Mordyn. "An
arrow from Prince Theseus' own quiver."

Master ten Lenter took the shaft between two fingers, as
though he feared to touch it. "By the Maker... How did you get
it?"

"He gave it to me when I left his company," Keyth said. "I
already have a whole outfit from his armoury, so I thought you
might treasure such an artifact of fletching."

"Of course," his master stuttered. "I'll mount it on the
wall."

"I should probably speak with the others," Keyth said,
glancing at the clustered crowd.

"Wait," ten Lenter murmured, "What are you going to do
now? I mean, in Lesser Kryden?"

"I'm thinking of building a house down on Syroh Water.
Yara and I are recently betrothed..." he grinned. Remembering

the two days they had spent in the town of Manon, a village named the 'Jewel of the North.' It's countryside was beautiful enough to draw even southland adventurers. He smiled as his eyes met Yara's, and he recalled standing on those glorious hilltops, asking for her hand, so they could always be as close as in the past three months.

A week later, he stepped out of his room in the Grey Horse and met Yara at the gate. It had been a busy week and they wanted some peace for a couple of hours, so they left at dawn and set off south along the road.

"Do you think we did the right thing?" Keyth asked.

"What do you mean?"

"Leaving Iris like that? Or Dryn?" Keyth questioned. "I keep thinking about our last conversation. He didn't seem very safe."

"It was bad timing, though I needed to come home," Yara said. "I'm glad we're here."

"Me too. And this is the life I want," he assured her, "but I'll always wonder how things might've been if I had stayed in Athyns."

"I already wonder about the war," Yara said. "Theseus marched with his army, and Dryn left to fight Pyrsius.... Will we ever know what happened?"

Keyth nodded after a moment. "I think we haven't seen the last of Dryn..."

They spent the whole day away from Lesser Kryden, and Keyth swelled with the smell of *his* forest. It had been so long since he felt the northern wind brush his skin. He welcomed those shivers.

They decided to go to Syroh Water and start looking for a place for their cabin. Keyth froze on the path when he realized they had reached the hunters' campsite where the crazed villager, Eldar, had saved him and Dryn from the bandits.

He recounted the events to Yara, and they followed his footsteps as best they could. There they had seen the firelight, here they had jumped off the trail into the ditch. And over here, the first arrow nearly struck them.

And there, the bundle of bows. Keyth stared at them in shock. They had been delivering bows to the hunters, after Keyth and Master ten Lenter had fletched them. The bows were still tied together and were lying where Keyth had dropped them.

Memories poured back. On their way toward Scion, after the battle in Ithyka, Iris had said, "Every village has a certain amount of resources or supplies that aren't used. Spoiled meat, broken things..."

"Well, Kryden doesn't..." Keyth had returned. "We don't waste stuff. If something breaks... we fix it. I never threw anything away."

Iris had smiled. "You didn't? What about the bows you and Dryn brought to the hunters? The hunters didn't use them."

"Well, someone will use them. I'm sure Master ten Lenter has already found them and brought the bundle back to the village," Keyth had muttered.

"Are you sure?" Iris had asked, smiling at him.

"Keyth?" Yara questioned, drawing him back to the present. "Are you okay?"

"Yes," he told her faintly. "I'll be fine. Yara, I think we did the wrong thing. We should have stayed." A thousand thoughts had filled his mind with the remembered conversation. It set him on edge and taunted his doubts. He picked up the bundle of bows and said, "We can't let these go to waste."

"What is it?" Yara asked.

"I really don't know," he told her. "Don't worry, I'm not going to run back to Athyns. We'll get started on our house. Maybe Dryn will turn up."

"And those bows?"

Keyth glanced at the bundle under his arm and smiled sadly. "I think these are just a reminder of how much I've learned and how much I've changed over the past two months. I think I'll enjoy going back to fletching," he decided.

66

Upon stabbing Dryn with Korbios, Pyrsius Gothikar immediately returned to his personal chambers and opened a new bottle of imported Trident wine. Shipping it across the Mydarius was expensive, and even the wealthy Imperial House could only afford enough for special occasions. Pyrsius considered this to be exactly that.

True, he hadn't destroyed magic entirely, not yet. His armies still sported a few magicians, as did Odyn's. The camps at Paxos and Calydon held a dozen valuable prisoners to be executed at the conclusion of the war. He was sure there were also village magicians and tavern tricksters to be found yet.

But magic would never recover, not without the aid of someone far greater than his brother, Artemys. And there was no one left even remotely that powerful. Pyrsius had even taken to book burnings, invading every library with magical books and burning them. Without those, lesser magicians could never grow in power, and thus Pyrsius toasted his decimation of the age of magic.

Much like the last time he had poured himself wine, he was interrupted by a gateway splitting open the air.

. . .

Travelling forward from Scion village, Dryn leapt into Pyrsius' chambers with a burst of air that smashed Pyrsius from his chair up against the wall. Dryn sent a fireball next, large enough to punch through the wall.

Pyrsius ducked under it and emerged with minor burns. "You just won't die, will you!" the Prince screamed. "I'll kill you again and again if I must!"

Dryn was ready this time. He had strategy. A new perspective. New abilities. New insight. As Pyrsius grabbed a pouch of tokens from his pocket, Dryn knelt and began writing on the floor. This new miracle was a spell too complex for a token. When he had finished the spell, he hissed the words in a quiet breath.

Pyrsius cast a bolt of lightning and it struck Dryn with full force, but instead of damaging him, Dryn's spell translated the energy into a boost of adrenaline and erased the weariness from the last few days. The unique shield could not halt physical trauma, and thus, Dryn was thrown across the room.

He could endure this physical damage for he knew it couldn't kill him.

He reclaimed his feet and faced Pyrsius' next token, a fireball. This one struck Dryn's shoulder, but left no scorch. The force of the blow flipped him on an angle and he struck the floor hard.

The Prince shouted in anger and water gushed across the floor, and, though Dryn struggled from the impact with his mouth gaping, the magically conjured liquid didn't fill it. Next Pyrsius used rays of light, the very spell which had scarred Dryn's face. The razor sharp beams of sunlight carried him back against the opposite wall, which soon split, as Pyrsius' spell slashed the room to shreds. Dryn stood shakily to his feet in the next room and clenched his fists with the excess energy the spell kept granting him.

"DIE!" Pyrsius bellowed and, with a sword he scooped up from the damage of the room, slashed at Dryn from the side. Dryn jumped back, and the blade grazed his stomach. The next blow clipped Dryn's thigh. Dryn spotted a set of blades hanging from their hilts nearby. As he stormed towards the swords, Pyrsius cast a swirl of wind and Dryn was carried along the wall. The set of swords was caught in the wind as well, and Dryn was slashed four or five times in midair as he was thrown towards the across the room.

When he hit the wall, one of the swords stabbed him, pinning his left arm. He curled around it in agony, and then yanked the steel free. Pyrsius strode towards him, and with a wrathful sneer, slashed at him.

Dryn blocked and stabbed back, and was quickly drawn into a battle of skill. Dryn had never been trained to fight with swords, while Pyrsius was obviously a blade master. Since Dryn couldn't be killed by mortal weapons, their melee progressed, and Dryn took blow after blow while his blood trailed after them.

Pyrsius threw his sword aside in fury and bellowed incoherently. The Prince crumbled a token in his fist and Dryn's next assault bounced off an invisible wall. Dryn stepped forward and placed a hand against the transparent surface.

"Ah, your weakness, still..." Pyrsius laughed hysterically. "We'll see how long you last in there!"

Dryn reached sideways and felt a corner nearby. He was back in the prison cell, unable to move. His breath shortened and he withdrew into the middle of his new confines. His shield spell did not protect him from this. From his own fears. *Please!*

He closed his eyes and took a deep breath. He was not in the prison cell; rather, he was running in the Green near Lesser Kryden. He was jumping and flying. In his mind, he brushed Iris' hair and kissed her lips, and the prison cell crumbled to dust.

Pyrsius stared at him. Dryn still stood within the confines of the imprisonment spell, but he raised his chin and levelled Pyrsius' vibrant green stare without a mite of fear.

"I'm waiting," Dryn said. "You know how this ends, and I've seen it." Dryn's collected energy pulsated about him like the sun's fire.

"Perhaps I'll leave you there," Pyrsius smiled. "I can sustain that transparent prison for a week on my own energy."

"Really?" Dryn asked. He then whispered, *"Niviso kel ovos."* A pulse of blue energy began to ebb from his hand, sparking on the invisible walls. "Now?"

Pyrsius frowned, but didn't answer.

Dryn muttered the last word of magic again and the blue energy thickened, growing until the invisible walls flamed. "And now?"

Pyrsius' brow flowed with sweat, and the frown turned into a tremble in the Prince's jaw.

Dryn repeated the word again, pouring the powerful spell out until the entire confine was like one large box of fire. Then, at last, the walls vanished and a storm of fire erupted like a potion fuelled from the apothecary's mortar. Dryn released the spell and stepped forward.

Pyrsius stood shaking, his shoulders sunken and his head at one side. He had wasted all of his energy holding Dryn inside.

Pyrsius bent and lifted the sword he had thrown down.

"I will accept your surrender," Dryn told him.

"Never," Pyrsius hissed, raising the blade toward Dryn.

Dryn next composed a spell that would alternate fire, lightning and air, blasting them in every direction around him. *"Gesiir kel'izen dev shika,"* he whispered and the room disappeared into fire. After a moment, lightning took the flame's place, and the stone walls crumbled around Dryn. Then air, and stones soared away from the growing ruins, hurled into the sky and showering the palace grounds with rubble.

Then fire again, and the citizens of Avernus could only stare in awe at the glowing sun that had come to rest on top of their palace. Lightning surged out and then torrential wind again, and at last, Dryn's energy waned.

The bottom layers of the Avernus palace remained intact, but the entire upper floor had been destroyed. Like a plateau above the city, the rubble and debris was only topped by Dryn's weary form. He stood as if frozen in place.

He had sensed Pyrsius' defence, numerous tokens being used one after another in a vain attempt to ward off the storm. The Prince had run out of tokens before the storm had ended, and now lay near the edge of the collapsing floor. Dryn knelt by the man's side. Judging by his numerous wounds and his irregular breathing, Pyrsius was near death.

"Does Lanteera still live?" he asked quietly.

"I believe so," Dryn replied.

"Tell her I love her," Pyrsius said, and there was a strange kind of reluctance in his voice. "She's the only thing left..."

"I'll tell her." Dryn sat down, exhausted. The guards would arrive soon, but he had a few moments before opening another escape gateway. "Why did you do that to her?"

Pyrsius coughed and spat out a mouthful of blood. "Love can be used as a weapon. A powerful one. Believe me, I've been cut by it, nearly killed by it.... I thought you were using her against me. I fought back."

"But did you ask her? Did you even talk to her?" Dryn demanded.

"You have to be either a god or a devil," Pyrsius breathed, his head dipping. "You will have to make that decision someday, everyone does. Most of us ignore it. I did, until they made me into a devil. When I had to choose, I accepted it.... a god or a devil." The last word was interrupted by a fit of coughing and then Pyrsius was gone.

Dryn stood up and glanced at the Valharyn Sea stretching away to the horizon. Buoys in the harbor bobbed up and down, borders of safety and danger. All of a sudden, with Pyrsius' words, pieces started to fit into place. The world seemed to simplify, and Dryn's mind found the answer for which he'd been searching. He had been like driftwood, buffeted by waves of fear, the prison cell following him for months into every closet in which Dryn glanced, and of anger, Pyrsius' invasion of Athyns, the Prophet's stubborn preaching that the future was mightier than he, and Iris.

He had to make a choice, to live by these impulses of fear and anger, or to solve life's problems with balance and wisdom. With Pyrsius Gothikar's last words, he became a buoy in that sea, and though anger might buffet him, he remained chained to solid ground. He made his decision and the world would no longer confuse him.

First, freedom.

Dryn stepped through a gateway onto an island shore. The Mydarius lapped waves against his heels, and he walked up the bank toward the 'isolation camp' of Calydon. Soon he came into range of their arrows and he raised a shield as the guards spotted him. He continued toward the camp and began releasing slashes of white light to topple the wall that faced him.

He used lightning to deal with the troop of guards, and amidst a shower of sparks and swords, the prisoners were freed.

He took the camp at Paxos in a similar manner. It was built into the side of a mountain. He defeated the guards and proceeded to burn open the cells with conjured acid. The captives, magicians and political prisoners emerged in disbelief, and eagerly abandoned their previous factions. They began their journey to Vero Port to return to their homes. The magicians who had been freed were small in number but would help re-establish their order.

A small man, bruised and battered by torture and thin from starvation, approached Dryn and beheld him with wide eyes. "You have accomplished what I attempted and my sons ruined," he told Dryn. "You've saved our realm."

"No," Dryn said, "I have given it the chance for a new beginning. You and I must learn from the flaws of the Triumvirate to establish a better realm."

Second, mercy.

Athyns had been besieged by Odyn's armies. The Three Nobles had surrendered when presented with Theseus' body. The Commanders of the Southern horde divided shares of plunder between them, and Athyns was given to them by King Odyn.

Dryn stepped through the air into the midst of one of their impotent Council sessions. They all froze when they saw him.

He surveyed the room, but there was no sign of Odyn or Rychard. One of the other Commanders questioned, "What is the meaning of this interruption?"

"You question me, while you sit in stolen authority?" Dryn raised his voice, "Get out! I will permit you to leave here with your lives, and the lives of all your soldiers. The North does not belong to you, and never will!"

With only his words, he sent the Southland army back across the Sea.

Third, love.

Iris was sitting on a balcony overlooking the cityscape of Athyns when he came to her. Her greying hair was held above her head in a knot and her wrinkled skin hid from the sun beneath the eaves. They sat beside each other in silence for a moment. Then she spoke first. "They told me you were back," she said. "That you'd banished the Commanders."

Dryn sat beside her, and nodded. "I did."

"Did you face him? My father?" she asked.

"Yes. He said he loved you," Dryn answered.

She laughed sadly. "I never knew him, so I can't speak to that." Another moment of silence lingered between them. "And Odyn? Did you defeat him?"

"No."

"You have to," she told him.

"I know," he said. "I came to see you first."

"Why? What is there to see?" she questioned bitterly.

"Your beauty," he said, and he meant it. She stared at him for a moment, and he tried to kiss her, but she turned away.

"You are a different man now, and I am a different woman," she said. "In another life, we might have been together, but that has been stolen from us."

"I can still be there for you," he told her. "We can still be happy together, if only to help one another."

"No. I can't be happy with someone else until I come to terms with what has happened to me.."

"Please," he begged her. "Maybe I can find a way to undo what he did to you."

"Dryn, you are so different. Like Ithyka. In what seems like minutes to all of us, you grow in bounds," Iris told him. "I know you still love me, but I can't... I can't love you anymore. Because of what has happened to me."

He stood up and nodded. After a moment he nodded again. He knelt back down to her and whispered, "Love ages well, Iris."

Dryn opened a gateway in an alley and stepped through it, emerging in Greater Kryden. Almost home. But he knew he wouldn't return to Lesser Kryden for a long time. He walked to the First Hearth Inn and stepped inside.

Argus Galain appeared from the back room and smiled at him. "Welcome to the First Hearth," the innkeeper called as he approached. "The common room is serviced until dinner, but I can get you a room now."

"Let me introduce myself. I am Lord Rayth from Athyns," Dryn said.

"Athyns? Dangerous lately, I hear. What, with the invasion and all."

"The enemies have left and the city is much safer," Dryn replied. "I stayed at your inn once, a long time ago. Perhaps you recall my friends Keyth, Yara, and Iris?" he asked.

"Yes, I think I remember. Only two months or so ago, right?" Argus wondered.

Dryn smiled. *Seems like so much longer...* "Yes, two months likely. I have business to discuss with you now."

"Business?"

Dryn nodded. A couple of moments later they were seated in Argus' quarters in the back room. "You want to buy the inn?" Argus repeated.

"I'm aware you haven't put it up for sale, but I will pay any price for it. A friend of mine has tried many walks of life and has met with tragedy each time. Her dream, though," Dryn said, "is to live in a tavern, perhaps to run one."

Several hours later, Dryn hired a messenger to find Iris in Athyns. "Tell her a young admirer has a gift she must come to see. Be sure she does come. And then give her these keys," he told the messenger. "The keys to the First Hearth Inn."

70

Fourth, justice.

Dryn teleported from Greater Kryden to Galinor, right into the Tower of the Throne. Of course, it was now the Throne of King Odyn, a gilded gold-plated magnificent throne.

Dryn walked unhindered through the corridors and up the stairways of the palace until he found Odyn's personal guard in one of the hallways. They stared at him in surprise and then jumped as they realized who he was. It was a quick skirmish, and soon any who had stood in his way lay dead. He strode up the stairs into the throne room.

Odyn knew he was coming, after the sounds of the battle below had stopped. Dryn found the King hiding in his bed chambers, behind locked doors. With a solid kick it fell inward and the King yelped, "I surrender! Please don't–"

"For your crimes against the people and the Triumvirate government, by the authority granted to me, the Crown Magician, I judge you guilty and sentence you to death. May the Maker have mercy on you." With that, Dryn slew him with a single blade of white light, killing him quickly and painlessly. His last objective met, Dryn surrendered to the tower guards.

As they reached the throne room, the soldiers found him on his knees with his hands held up in resignation. "I take responsibility for my actions," Dryn told the soldiers.

Dryn had ended their government, in these soldier's eyes; rumors had likely just reached them of a wizard burning the Avernan Palace. They would hold him until their superiors arrived, imprison him, perhaps torture him. But then the Nobles of each city would arrive, or Periander Gothikar, or whoever was left. If he could last until then, perhaps he would be welcomed to build the new age with them.

The corrupt leadership of Odyn had been stopped, and Pyrsius' insanity ended. Magic had been defended, and the realm had been given a fresh start as he and Theseus had once planned.

And so, Dryn surrendered to the guards, and prepared himself for the ordeal to come. He had come very close to abdicating his fate to the Shadow Glyph's determination, but now he stood at peace in his own chosen path.

Fifth, hope.

72

Rychard of Tarroth walked through the ranks of guards until he came to Lord Dryn Rayth kneeling on the ground. As he stood above his nemesis, two servants bore Odyn's body past him , out of the room and down the stairs. Rychard sighed, staring at Dryn's serene face in frustration. He glanced away at the large throne in the room and then, after a moment, back at Dryn. "We meet again," he said.

Something like surprise passed across the prisoner's face.

"You have succeeded in destroying our Princes," Rychard said. "Great Glyphs, you do know how to meddle in our affairs."

Dryn smiled.

Rychard barked a laugh, "Yes, yes, killing the Princes... it's only meddling."

Finally, a frown. Rychard smiled and pulled out a pouch. The true architect of this entire war... the genius behind it all, the man disguised as a traveller who had instructed him to kill Theseus... had given Rychard more instructions. *'Use all of these tokens on him.'*

Rychard opened the pouch. "The only thing I'm surprised about," he said, staring at Dryn, "is why you would surrender. You could have crowned yourself King, or taken the entire wealth of the realm off with you. Instead you'd rather be on your knees before me."

"I do not desire power or wealth," Dryn explained.

"Well, do you desire death? You do not think we would let you live, do you?" Rychard asked. He pulled out the first token and broke it. Blasts of ice formed around Dryn's torso and arms, and he grunted in agony. That would prevent Dryn from attempting an escape of any kind.

"I'll take responsibility for my actions," Dryn gasped, "no matter the penalty."

"Very well," Rychard said, and broke the next. A hundred shards of glass slashed across Dryn's chest and limbs, slashing skin and cloth away. One arm started to break free of the ice that encased him, but before he form a spell with his fingertips, Rychard's third token crumbled to dust as well. Black energy twirled in midair and latched onto Dryn's arm. Slowly, the limb twisted and broke and began to fade into shadows. When the spell was finished, Dryn's arm was left in a bloody stump at the elbow, and the magician had nearly lost consciousness. "I won't make the mistake this time," he told Dryn. "You'll die by magic."

The black shadows latched onto his leg next, consuming skin, flesh and bone as it leeched up to his knee and left an awful tip. Dryn was left slumped in pools of his own blood as his wounds continued to bleed.

There were two tokens left. The first would secure the mind and strengthen the nerves, allowing Dryn to feel everything that had happened to him, and feel his death in its entirety. Dryn's eyes flashed open and his mouth gasped for breath.

"Here we go, Dryn," Rychard muttered. "It's the end for you, at last."

The last token drained the life of its prey bit by bit, so that within an hour the victim died of old age. Rychard had heard that Pyrsius had used such a spell on Dryn's sweetheart, and as Rychard lifted this token between his fingers, he smiled at the beautiful irony.

He broke the token, and Dryn's features instantly began to age, his hair falling, and his skin wrinkling. As he screamed through the agonies of senescence, the magician's remaining hand finally broke through the ice around his torso and tore at a pouch in his red robe. Suddenly, the old man who had been Dryn vanished in a flickering square of air and left a string of glyphs in the blood on the floor.

Rychard glanced at the symbols and smiled. Another time spell: Dryn was a traveller to the very end. It didn't matter. There was no way for Dryn to stop the aging spell, no matter where he went. Finally, that foul Crown Magician had been dealt with.

. . .

Dryn appeared in the forests near Kryden and fell against a tree, smashing the stump at his knee against the wood. He knew he had mere moments left, and he knew no one could save him, but the forests were where he wanted his life to end. He gasped as another ten years were taken from him, and the pain caused him to cry, "Help me..." It was night time in the north, and the sky was full of stars. A shooting star tore overhead, gone as soon as it had appeared. On this lonely night, no one could find him.

Then he heard someone whistle, a quiet sound, and he redoubled his efforts at calling. If no one could help him, perhaps they would stay with him for his last minutes. "Help me! Over here!" he shouted. "Come to me!"

For what felt like forever, the night forests stared at him in silence, and then a voice called, "Hello?"

"I'm here!" Dryn shouted, "Help! Please!"

He heard foliage moving as someone fought their way through the dense forest to him. He leaned back against the tree, staring at his blood as it ran in little rivers across the woodland floor. He could only hold the tree with one hand; the other had been consumed by Rychard's torture.

Then, the bushes parted, and a young villager appeared, walking toward him in the shadows.

By the Maker... Can it be? Dryn shuddered as he watched the stranger pause with familiar movements and stare at the blood. "Come closer," he whispered, his mind repeating, *Great Glyph....* again and again. The figure stayed where he was, staring at Dryn in shock.

Feeling more years peel away from him, Dryn breathed, "Please... I am almost... finished..."

The figure stepped right up to him, and Dryn gasped in shock. Standing beside him was the young apothecary apprentice of Lesser Kryden, on his way from the delivery to the ten Brae farm. "It is beginning," he hissed. *Only beginning. This is* the *beginning.*

"What is?" the younger Dryn asked, staring at the mutilated old man in the forest.

The villager was so young and innocent, so unaware of the suffering he would endure, the love he would embrace, and the fate he entered. "This world has... spited me," he whispered, staring through his younger self at his memories. This youth would pull his friends away on a long adventure that would change them in ways they couldn't even imagine. "No one understood my intentions."

"Your intentions?" the younger Dryn questioned, and then: "What happened to you?"

As he felt death approaching, Dryn nodded as it all began to make sense. The Shadow Glyph, the Great Glyph, the puzzle of the world and the truth of time. *How do I explain it?* "You... You are the ... " *How do I not overwhelm this boy?* "...one who will understand it all... everything..."

"Understand everything?" the young apothecary questioned. "I'm sorry, I don't understand anything right now. Who are you?"

"Me?" Dryn asked. *Am I out of my mind? ... am I the man in the forest?* "I ... am..." *the man I thought was* "Artemys Gothikar.... It was..." *me in the forest!* "Never mind that... You will come to see it all... It is beginning."

"I'm sorry. Wait here, I'll get help," the youth said, and turned away.

"No!" Dryn snapped. He could feel the end beginning to crawl up his spine, and he reached out for his younger self. "Come close and be silent," he ordered. He grabbed hold of the youth's collar and pulled him close. *Time to begin. After the old man in the forest, I named this Artemys' Ward, but in fact, it is mine.* He whispered, *"Hayen donbreth shoraz elkobo'ar ath draz!"* and slammed his hand into Dryn's chest. He gave the ward of protection, the Great Glyph reference and the gift of magic.

Dryn stumbled back and grabbed his chest as that terrible pain exploded in his mind.

And then, as the youth blacked out, Dryn finally felt the peace of death, and welcomed its embrace. The future had indeed decided the past, and the Glyphs had settled one another when all became complete. The beginning of the end and the end of the beginning.

Dryn closed his eyes and released his last breath.

73

But what of the real Artemys Gothikar? He certainly did not die in a northland forest.

He stood in one of the chambers of the Palace of Galinor and wiped the blood from Korbios onto the royal tunic before sheathing his sword. He had given the sword as a gift to his father. Pyrsius had taken it when he captured Periander. Pyrsius had then sent it back in time with Dryn, and thus it came again into Artemys' hands, to be driven through this Noble's chest.

As he admired the new decoration of this particular Council room, Artemys reflected on how smoothly things had gone. He had orchestrated the entire scheme from start to finish. It had been a long campaign. Twenty years earlier he had planted the seeds of hate in Pyrsius, and begun playing on Odyn's desires for power. Of course many other details had come into play, but with the appearance of Dryn, that day in the desert.... nothing could have helped more. Artemys had never travelled in time, only disappeared after the first attack of Pyrsius' genocide. He had travelled to safety to wait it out. His plan was to wait for Pyrsius and Odyn to weaken the realm, kill Theseus, and perhaps even each other. Then afterwards, he would teleport back to the realm and finish things up: kill any remaining Princes and take the Throne. By that point, no one could have stopped him.

Of course, Dryn Rayth appeared and let him know that everything was right on track, even gave him some tips to be sure of Theseus' death. He had listened to Dryn and humoured him, and when the time was right, returned to the realm.

He found Pyrsius and Odyn dead, Dryn being held by Odyn's guards, and Odyn's golden throne waiting. Odyn had had the thing hauled all the way from Olympus. A throne fit for kings.

Artemys had given his favourite Commander, Rychard, the instructions to finish Dryn off, and then called a meeting of the Nine Nobles.

The Nobles had arrived quickly from Avernus, Athyns, and Olympus, convening immediately to decide the fate of the Dominion. As the only surviving member of royalty, Artemys was allowed to join them. The Crown Magician had other plans in mind though. He slew all nine of the Nobles, massacring them within their Council room, and there ended any hope of repairing the damaged Triumvirate.

Artemys strode from the bloody room and through the hallways of *his* Imperial Tower. He wondered if perhaps the Maker had planned this all from the start. The appearance of Rayth was unbelievable. Dryn had served Artemys better than anyone, destroying all his enemies, and even cleaning up loose ends. Artemys could only admire the impossible: a nameless villager from the northlands acquiring magic on his own, training himself in its rudiments, and then giving Artemys the benefits of his conquests.

Artemys Gothikar stepped onto the dais toward the new Throne of Midgard. Patience had paved its way to this throne and his destiny had arrived. Everything had gone according to plan.

ACKNOWLEDGMENTS

First thanks go to the first reader. Dad, I've seen you read very few books in my life, but you read mine and it meant a lot.

Next, I've got to thank those who helped get this project of mine from a massive manuscript to the book you're now holding. Mom, thank you for the long hours you spent editing. I often wondered why you couldn't just read it cover to cover without a red pen, but now I appreciate the fact that you didn't.

Dylan Tracey, one of my friends from school, made the current version of the map with what I feel must have been a lot of my complaints. He made it using a MS Paint bitmap I sent him, and changed as many things as I suggested without much comment. Thanks man, it looks great! Your editing also helped out, as well as the long hours of random plot discussion. Awesomenessdom.

Bro! You know more of the plot than anyone, I think. You know several of the many endings, <cough> ... down the road. Thanks for listening to my ideas, and thanks for someday reading this. <cough>.

To all of my friends, both when I was writing and editing this, thanks for your help! John, Dan, Aaron – you guys are great friends. Gerreke and Natalie, thanks for being there for me on previous projects. And in BC: Le, Jeff, Dylan, and the Tangents – some of the most creative and enjoyable people I've met! And in both places, Hanna, thanks for your friendship and what you once called 'trying to interpret my logic.'

Bulk Barn-ers, you guys are awesome friends even as coworkers. Paul, never stop being Paul. You're a huge inspiration and a great friend! Danielle, the air tastes like baking soda!

Lastly: Rise Against, Red and Emery play some of the best music I've ever heard. I'd never have made it through the long hours of writing, reading, and editing without you.

Oh, and thanks to my readers. If you've read up to this page, you'll have a better idea of who I am than vice versa, so I hope you've enjoyed what you experienced and tune in next time!

N. A. VREUGDENHIL grew up in Trenton, Ontario, and
attends the University of British Columbia in Kelowna.
He started writing novels at age 10, and, ten years later,
published the first of a series of five, *Shadow Glyph* (2012).

facebook.com/shadowglyph

www.ithyka.com

Made in the USA
Charleston, SC
18 September 2012